THE QUESTIONABLE BEHAVIOR OF DAHLIA MOSS

By Max Wirestone

THE QUESTIONABLE BEHAVIOR OF DAHLIA MOSS

A Dahlia Moss Mystery

MAX WIRESTONE

REDHOOK

www.redhookbooks.net

Copyright © 2018 by Max Wirestone
Excerpt from *The Rule of Luck* copyright © 2015 by Catherine Cerveny
Excerpt from *Strange Practice* copyright © 2017 by Vivian Shaw

Author photograph by Elizabeth Frantz
Cover design by Lisa Marie Pompilio
Cover art by Shutterstock
Cover copyright © 2018 by Hachette Book Group, Inc.

Redhook Books/Orbit
Hachette Book Group
1290 Avenue of the Americas
New York, NY 10104
hachettebookgroup.com

First Edition: January 2018

Redhook is an imprint of Orbit, a division of Hachette Book Group.
The Redhook name and logo are trademarks of Hachette Book Group, Inc.

The Hachette Speakers Bureau provides a wide range of authors for speaking events. To find out more, go to www.hachettespeakersbureau.com or call (866) 376-6591.

Library of Congress Cataloging-in-Publication Data:
Names: Wirestone, Max, author.
Title: The questionable behavior of Dahlia Moss / Max Wirestone.
Description: First edition. | New York : Redhook, 2018. | Series: A Dahlia
    Moss mystery ; 3
Identifiers: LCCN 2017042263| ISBN 9780316386050 (softcover) |
    ISBN 9780316386074 (ebook)
Subjects: LCSH: Women private investigators—Fiction. | BISAC: FICTION /
    Action & Adventure. | FICTION / Mystery & Detective / Women Sleuths. |
    GSAFD: Mystery fiction.
Classification: LCC PS3623.I74 Q47 2018 | DDC 813/.6—dc23
LC record available at https://lccn.loc.gov/2017042263

ISBNs: 978-0-316-38605-0 (trade paperback), 978-0-316-38607-4 (ebook)

Printed in the United States of America

LSC-C

10 9 8 7 6 5 4 3 2 1

For Tim Schafer

CHAPTER ONE

You don't want Emily Swenson, Lawyer with Money, to confront you at a breakfast bar. Honestly, you don't want her to confront you anywhere, because Emily, despite her peach silk blouses and *Vogue*-layout makeup choices, is an awfully scary lady. But a breakfast bar such as the one I was at, with its all-you-can-eat waffles and syrup packets that you had to individually unwrap, was not the natural habitat of such a person. One doesn't bump into Emily Swenson in a place that sells an omelet called "The Heart Attack." If you encounter her there, it means that she was looking for you.

I might have had a head wound, but I could at least put that together. Also, she had slid over a note that said: "Would you like to become an industrial spy?"

So there's that.

My name is Dahlia Moss. I'm twenty-six years old, burdened with college debt, and I am not a detective. Previously, I would have led off with "not a detective," and also I would have written it in all caps. Maybe underlined it.

But now I've successfully solved two cases. Yes, they were solved somewhat violently and very chaotically, but murderers were caught and deaths were avenged. Maybe I should stop saying that I'm not a detective altogether, but it still feels true.

We'll get to Emily's note in a second, but we also need to talk about my head wound, because you and I need to get on the same page.

As you may or may not know, I was a bit concussed at the end of my last adventure. It's unseemly for me to be going on about it now, a full story later, because Sam Spade gets concussed three or four times a book, and after about three paragraphs he never mentions it again. There are rules about that sort of thing, which is that detectives aren't supposed to complain about minor injuries from previous books.

Forget that, says I. And who knows, maybe Sam Spade couldn't remember the earlier concussions. Maybe he had some memory-loss issues. This can happen, or at least, that's what I've read on WebMD.

Anyway, my head smarted, and while I had felt worlds better after getting a nice night of sleep, I'm not going to pretend I wasn't thinking about my vaguely blurry vision for the sake of your narrative smoothness. The head injury was a thing, and it's going to stay a thing for the rest of this story. So get used to it.

That clear? Now let's talk about the note.

"Would you like to become an industrial spy?"

First, who walks around with notes like that? Emily Swenson, obviously. Maybe she had them for every occasion, and if she had reached in the wrong pocket I would have gotten a note that said: "Up for some arson?" or "I need a man killed."

To be fair to Emily, it wasn't like this was printed on a

custom-made card. She had jotted it down on the back of a napkin. Presumably because she didn't want everyone else at the table to hear her probably illegal, certainly unethical offer.

I had been having breakfast with Charice and Daniel, who were being more lovey in public than should be allowed before ten in the morning. I'm not entirely against public forms of affection, but in broad daylight?

Charice pretended not to notice my surprise at the note as I excused myself from the table.

"Oh, Emily," I said. "You are here to return that library book I loaned you?"

"Sure," said Emily. "That's why I'm here. You want to step out with me for a second?"

I would say that my roommate, Charice, pretended not to be interested, but I'm not sure she was pretending at all because she was basically wearing Daniel on her face. From the looks of it, Emily Swenson could have opened a suitcase full of money and said, "I need you to turn this into cocaine," and Charice still wouldn't have been interested.

We stepped out to Emily's car, which was precisely the sort of luxury car that a super-rich person who doesn't care about cars would purchase. It was simultaneously silver and nondescript and yet paradoxically made of money. It smelled like lemon verbena on the inside, and the leather seats were already warm.

"So," I said, "how have you been?"

Emily smirked, amused by my need to make small talk.

"Let's talk about the job I have in mind for you."

This was probably for the best, because I couldn't tell you the first personal detail about Emily Swenson, which made shooting the breeze somewhat challenging. Sometimes you encounter people in life who are nothing but surface. Beautiful polished people with nothing underneath. Emily Swenson wasn't that exactly—there was plenty going on in there, but hell if I had any clue what it was.

"Sure," I said. "You want me to be an industrial spy? Is this what you do, incidentally? Just go around giving people odd requests?"

"Not everyone," said Emily. "Just people with talent and no criminal records."

I preened at the talent line more than I should. But, like they say, flattery gets you everywhere. And not having a criminal record is almost always a boon.

"What are you looking for?" I asked.

"It's not what I'm looking for, Dahlia. It's never about what I'm looking for. It's about what the client is looking for."

"Who's the client?"

"Some general advice—that's rarely a question that you should ask when someone approaches you with a task they've surreptitiously written on a napkin."

"I like to know who I'm working for."

"You're working for me," said Emily simply.

"And you're working for?"

"Someone who wishes to remain nameless."

"Is it Satan?" I asked.

"Please," said Emily, "you think Satan doesn't already have people?"

"Well, what's this about, then?"

"There's a small game-development company here in St. Louis called Cahaba Apps. Ever hear of it?"

I hadn't actually, but I didn't pay much attention to local stuff, which was mostly racist and depressing in equal parts.

"Not at all," I said.

"You haven't heard of a game called *Ruby Rails*? I thought you might have played it."

I knew that Emily Swenson wasn't trying to start something, but telling someone that "you thought they might have played *Ruby Rails*" was effectively just spitting in their face and calling them a filthy casual. *Ruby Rails* was the sort of game that your grandma would play, assuming she could figure out her phone.

I had played it, actually. Honestly, everyone sort of had. It was the new *Bejeweled*. Not a match-three game, but the same kind of idea. It was only halfway a game—it was mostly kind of a Zen-like activity.

In the game, you're running a train system, and you're delivering gems—in games like these it's always either gems or candy—from mines to towns. And you're delivering people to mines. And you build houses and hotels, kind of like Monopoly. Actually describing it makes the game seem complicated—because you need more gems to build more track, that's important—but in practice it's incredibly straightforward and relaxing. It's like it had been developed by Enya.

It's the sort of game you play while waiting in line at the DMV is what I'm saying.

"Yes, Emily," I told her. "I am familiar with *Ruby Rails*."

"See," said Emily. "I knew you would be perfect for this."

"What is this?"

"The company that developed the game is based here in St. Louis, and they've been purchased by a larger developer, who had a plan for the IP. They're developing a new game together, and there appears to be some holdups."

"Holdups like?"

"The new game is significantly behind schedule, and I've heard that the company is entirely dysfunctional. I'd like you to go in there and let me know what's happening."

This didn't sound so undoable. It's not like I would be breaking into a safe and stealing company secrets. Although, the whole thing was still a lot to take before waffles.

"Okay," I said. "First of all, I don't know what you know about the gaming industry, but under what possible auspices could I possibly be there? I can't code; I'm not an artist; I can't play a musical instrument, much less compose."

"I've never understood," said Emily, addressing me with those engulfing green eyes of hers, "why you also so strongly point out all the things you cannot do. If you outlined the things you could do with half the enthusiasm of your failings, you wouldn't need my little job."

As insights went, this was both depressingly accurate and yet entirely off the mark. Accurate because Emily was certainly right—it was easy to get me going on all the things I've failed at. But off the mark because I wasn't at all disappointed about Emily's job. I was excited.

"I just want to make sure I have a good cover story," I said. "What will I be doing?"

"You'll be a secretary," said Emily. "Receptionist, actually. And just as a temp, for a few days."

Excellent. Answering phones is definitely something I was qualified for.

"And what am I looking for?"

"On day one? Just get the lay of the land."

Before I could ask any more questions, Emily Swenson gave me a check. I'm not going to put the amount here, because (1)

I'm starting to worry that the IRS might be reading these things and (2) it was not lay-of-the-land money. From the amount of money, arson was, to my mind, still on the menu.

"What do you want on day two?" I asked. "Me to kill a guy?"

"The client would like some code," said Emily. "And by some code, I mean all the code. As much code as you can get."

Okay, so maybe I would be breaking into a safe and stealing secrets.

"You want me to steal the code of an upcoming game? That's...incredibly illegal. It's probably two or three felonies."

"No one is going to use the code that's stolen," said Emily. "It's not as if the client is going to publish it or steal from it or leak it onto the Internet. They just want to take a peek, to see if they can figure out what keeps delaying the game."

Despite Emily's suggestion that I didn't need to worry about the identity of the client, I couldn't help but wonder: Who else but the parent company would care why the game was being delayed in the first place?

Emily could read my mind, as ever.

"I can't give you details," said Emily. "But our client is not so external a party as you might imagine. The developers are being very cagey about the code, and there's an idea that perhaps someone is sabotaging the game from the inside."

"You want me to become an industrial spy to catch an industrial spy?"

"You fight fire with fire," said Emily crisply.

CHAPTER TWO

You fight fire with water, incidentally. People who are fond of fighting fire with fire just like to watch things burn.

But I took the job because I wanted the money, and maybe I like watching things burn myself.

I slept the way someone recovering from a concussion slept, which is very, very deeply. I didn't do a lot of research for my role as receptionist, because this was exactly the kind of job I had been applying to for ages. I used to dream about getting a job like this. Admittedly, that was after I had given up any hope of getting a job that was actually desirable, but still. This was the part I was born to play.

I tried to do a little research into Cahaba Apps (I said, "Siri, tell me about Cahaba Apps") but I was tired and I had gotten the impression that Emily wanted me to go in blind. Cloak-and-dagger or no, Emily could have given me specific ideas about what I was trying to observe, and she didn't. Emily was no fool, and if she wanted me to go in without a lot of presupposed notions, maybe that was for the best.

The sleep was amazing. I almost recommend getting a concussion just so you can experience it. Keyword "almost."

I'd always had this dream about getting hired for this sort of job. In the dream I would always show up with a bagful of pastries. People love pastries. You can screw up a lot of things on your first day, but if you brought in a cinnamon stick and a couple of crullers you're a folk hero. Yes, it comes off as trying a little too hard, but what did I care? This receptionist thing was a ruse, and so I could try as hard as I wanted.

I stopped by La Patisserie Chouquette and picked up a grab bag of delectables that I thought would get me out of any situation. I actually wore the silver metallic houndstooth blouse that Jonah Long, Murdered Victim, had gotten me way back when. I had never really liked the blouse—it was chichi, sure, but not really my style, which is why I had to load up on things I did like. So: black khakis, silver blouse, and a gray toile scarf that I'm inclined to tell people I wear ironically, although really I have a serious thing for toile. Frankly, I thought I looked pretty good. Not Peggy Olson "Deal With It" good, but close. I was honestly thinking of taking a selfie; that's how pleased I was.

Also, I was wearing makeup.

The people at Cahaba were going to be blown the fuck away.

The people at Cahaba were not blown the fuck away. In fact, I would say that they did not even blow lightly in the breeze.

Cahaba was on the second floor of an office building tucked

off Gravois; it was a generic uninspiring space—the ground floor was a dog-grooming service—hardly the cultural hotbed of the city, but I was excited. This was a job. Yes, I had acquired it sort of unethically, but I was a working girl. I was doubly a working girl. Dahlia Moss, jobless no more!

I had gotten there a half hour early, and while I suppose I should have been nervous ascending the stairway up to Cahaba Apps, I was positively buoyant.

I really had no idea what to expect. Getting there so early, in fact, I wasn't entirely sure I could even get in. Maybe I would be the first person there? I would have to wait for another employee to show up. How impressed everyone would be! What a studious new employee we have, they would say.

But the door was open.

There was an empty Herman Miller corner cubicle that someone had sort of shoved in front of the door that, I supposed, was meant to create a reception desk, and so I went there and sat down in front of it.

And then nothing happened. I had imagined that there would be a surge of interest in my arrival, but this did not prove to be the case. Not only was there no interest, but also there was no anything. No one.

I was wearing makeup and a scarf, however, and I was not about to let this all go to waste. I ventured deeper into the offices and found, at another Herman Miller cubicle creation, a guy in a white dress shirt fast asleep.

"Hello?" I said.

"I'm awake!" said the man, his head shooting up with such a start that he could possibly get whiplash. Although, keep in mind, this is concussed Dahlia here, so head injury is on my brain.

"Hi there," I said. "I'm Dahlia Moss—the new receptionist."

He just looked me. He was black, bald—with a good head for it—and wearing round gold-rimmed Harry Potter glasses. Those, eventually, would suit him too, but at the moment they had left little marks on his skin where his face had been pressed against his desk.

"Who are you?" he asked, despite the fact we had just gone over this.

"Dahlia Moss," I told him. "I'm the new receptionist."

"What happened to Cynthia?"

"I have no idea," I said, and handed him a cinnamon stick. "Can I get you some coffee?"

To be clear, I don't think it's the receptionist's job to go around fetching people coffee, but if there ever was a guy who needed coffee, this was it.

"Oh my God, yes," said the guy. "Please."

He still hadn't introduced himself, which was fine. We'd come to it.

"Where's the coffee maker?"

"The back left corner," he said, rubbing his eyes.

I slipped back there and observed, along the way, that there was another cubicle that adjoined his, where there was another man, also sleeping. It was hard to tell much about this sleeper except that he was white, with ginger hair and either a large beard or a very disgusting pillow. I didn't wake him up and made my way to the coffee maker.

They were out of coffee, which I could see would be a problem. I searched through the shelves until I found some candy-cane-flavored coffee from Archer Farms that had probably been sitting there since last Christmas. I was betting there was a coffee mother lode somewhere, but I wasn't going to wake up anyone to find it, and so candy-cane coffee it was. I didn't know how Harry Potter took his coffee, and so I made it the way I would drink it, with lots of cream and no sugar.

"Coffee, good sir," I said. "I'm Dahlia Moss. I'm not sure you caught that the first time."

"Dahlia," he said, putting the coffee to his mouth the way a lamprey would ingest blood. "Thank you. Fuck, is there peppermint in this?"

"Flavored coffee was the best I could find. You're not allergic to peppermint, are you?"

"It just brings up bad memories," said the guy. "I'm sorry, I'm Quintrell King. Nice to meet you."

I really wanted to ask about the bad peppermint memories, which I would generally attribute to an office Christmas party gone horribly wrong, but I decided that was a little too personal. Besides which, the guy had just woken up.

"Dahlia Moss," I said, for like the fourteenth time now. "Why is everyone asleep?"

"Most people stayed here overnight," said Quintrell. "We're a little under the eight ball here. Do you have my clothes?"

"I'm sorry, what?"

"My clothes. You're filling in for Cynthia, right?"

"I guess so, yes," I said, feeling less certain than when I came in. "She's the receptionist, right?"

"Yep. So you should have my clothes. Maybe check under her desk."

This invited a number of follow-up questions, such as why would Cynthia have Black Harry Potter's clothes under her desk (was Cynthia Ginny?), but I did not feel that it was my place to ask them.

I made my way back to the Herman Miller cubicle station

that was the receptionist's desk and found an enormous clear bag filled with clothing. The bag looked like it had been professionally cleaned—everything had been carefully and fastidiously folded. It resembled my clean laundry in the same way that Metropolis resembles Gotham City. One of these things is perfect, and the other a nightmarish dystopia. At any rate, if they expected me to fold laundry this well, the folks at Cahaba were about to be grievously disappointed.

I brought the bag over to Quintrell, still not quite able to work out what was going on, precisely. There was also a teal ikat-patterned dress in the bag, and so I figured that this was probably more than just his laundry. That or Harry Potter had a kinky side.

"Mine is a gray dress shirt," said Quintrell. "Looks just like this," he said, pointing to the dress shirt he was wearing, before adding: "but gray."

Quintrell King apparently expected that I was going to go through all of this laundry to pick out his shirt.

He was wrong.

"You can find it," I said, going for a kindly, helpful tone while simultaneously dumping the bag on the table.

The ginger-bearded dude suddenly popped up. He really did have a long pointed beard and looked like a really haggard Christmas elf. He was older than Quintrell, probably in his midforties, although his lack of sleep couldn't be doing him any favors.

"How long was I out for?" said the ugliest elf.

"Two hours," said Quintrell.

Elf guy looked around wildly and seemed surprised, and maybe even a little frightened, to find me standing there.

"Who's the scarf?" he asked.

I was feeling a little overdressed now. Receptionists were supposed to look nice, I thought. I mean, that's one of the whole goals of the job, right? Best face forward and all of that. But I was starting to feel a little bit foolish compared to these guys, who were dressed like badly rumpled clowns. Well, they had dress shirts, but they were definitely clowns. No question.

The toile scarf was overselling it.

"I am Dahlia Moss," I told the elf. "Who's the rumpled pants?"

Christmas Elf seemed to recognize that I did not appreciate his attempt at metonymy, and answered: "My name's Gary. I shouldn't have called you a scarf, I'm sorry. I'm tired."

Maybe I should have been more irritated, but Gary and Quintrell really did look like they had been through a sleep-deprived hell, and so I asked:

"Did you guys both just sleep here?"

"Yes," said Gary.

"That's why we need clothes," said Quintrell.

"Are you both homeless?" I asked.

"We might as well be. No one here ever leaves."

"This is the doomed *Flying Dutchman* of software development," said Gary. Then he started singing. "Keep the boys spinning in their only little world, Whoa-oh-whoa! Whoa-oh-whoa!"

Usually when people break into song, it's out of a sort of musical optimism. But Gary managed to approach the task with equal parts of depression and delirium.

Quintrell actually looked like he was crying a little. Not sadness crying, just eye-pain crying. "I'm so tired," he said softly.

Gary continued to sing. "Tie them up, so they won't say a word. Whoa-oh-whoa. Whoa!"

Quintrell dug through the bag and found his shirt, which was indeed exactly like his other shirt. He also found a pair of khakis, a pair of orange Hawaiian-print boxers, and some brown dress socks. Then he took the pile of clothes and headed into a bathroom.

"What fresh hell awaits today?" said Quintrell.

Gary also looked like he might be close to crying and seemed to be having a lot more trouble with the bag.

"I don't even remember what clothes are mine anymore. Cynthia would label them for us."

"Well, I'm not Cynthia," I told him. This sounded a little harsher than I wanted, and so I handed him a sticky bun. "And I can't label anything because I don't even know who works here."

"Where is Cynthia?" asked Gary. "We can't go on without her, you know. She's the figurehead that holds this whole thing together."

"I don't know where Cynthia is," I told him. Although, if she had any sense, I would have guessed very, very far from here.

"Figurehead like on a pirate ship," said Gary. "Like a mermaid."

"Uh-huh," I said.

"I'm just continuing to develop my 'doomed ghost ship' metaphor."

"Well, I'm your new mermaid," I told him. "Although, I think of myself as more of a hydra."

"Cynthia was just here last night," said Gary. "It's very strange."

"I don't know," I said, and I wasn't about to dispute the strangeness with him. This place was strange. Strangeness was seeping from the walls, like blood in a haunted mansion.

Gary went through the bag and eventually came up with an ensemble of what he hoped were his clothes.

"As Quintrell is monopolizing the men's room, and I have no intention of using the ladies', I plan to change right here. I would suggest leaving my cubicle, for fear of seeing my sad, tired, sagging, and pale body."

I did not think that this plan of his was ethical (hello, Human Resources!) or for that matter, sanitary, but I don't fight every battle. At worst, these were plans to be dealt with after I had been given some sort of orientation.

I went back to my desk and searched to see if there was perhaps some sort of documentation that Cynthia, errant mermaid, had left for me. I couldn't find anything, and I even searched on the computer, like a real goddamned secretary. There was nothing, not even a welcome and good luck. And more curiously, there were signs that Cynthia hadn't planned on leaving at all. There was a half can of Diet Sprite on the desk, for example. A cartoonishly floral gauze scarf. And there was a signed picture of Mark Harmon in her work space. None of it was stuff that I would value, but they were probably all things that Cynthia would want back, give or take the Sprite.

I shouldn't go out seeking mysteries at every turn, especially since they seemed to be good at finding me regardless, but I couldn't help but wonder: Why *wasn't* Cynthia here? Had Emily bribed her into leaving to make a spot for me?

She could be on vacation, perhaps, but Gary didn't seem to expect that she was leaving.

And people didn't usually take vacations on the *Flying Dutchman.*

They walked the plank.

I hadn't worked up much more of a theory than that when a small, catlike woman came up behind me and said, "You must be Cynthia Two."

She was very small—just over five feet—and black, with an extremely short and chic Afro. She was definitely more assembled than the men had been—she was wearing a jade top with navy pants—and even had on some makeup, but she definitely still looked rumpled and tired.

"How much sleep did you get?" I asked her.

"I don't like to count," said the woman. "It just upsets me. Vanetta Jones," she said, not bothering to extend a hand to me. "I run all of this."

Vanetta made a grand gesture toward the sad nexus of cubicles, and from the back I heard Gary fall over, apparently tripping as he got into his pants. I didn't know her well enough to tell if this gesture was meant to be ironic or if she was actually proud. Or delusional, which is certainly a possibility at low levels of sleep. So I answered very cautiously:

"Software development must be very exciting."

I had described Vanettta Jones as catlike, but I want to make clear that I don't mean a little tabby with a name like "Gumpkin" or "Miss Onyx." I'm thinking of a puma, with a name like "what the fuck do you care you're about to be clawed by a puma." Because she sort of growled her answer at me.

"You have No. Idea."

And this sounded extremely ominous.

"So," I said, "what exactly should I be doing right now?"

Vanetta looked at me, and I have to stop with the cat metaphor, but I do think that she was considering eating me.

"I was told you wouldn't need any training."

"Well," I said, feeling like I was in junior high, "obviously I don't need *training*. I mean, I know how to secretary."

Vanetta narrowed her eyes at me.

"Good," she said.

"Yes, good," I told her. "Very good. Here, have a sticky bun."

I took a sticky bun out of my basket of pastries, and Vanetta looked at it. Then she looked at me. I had expected, given this reception, that she would reject my goodwill offering. She sort of did, actually, but that was only because she took the entire basket of baked goods and left me holding the bun.

She tore into an éclair.

"Right," I said, still holding the bun. "So, keeping in mind that I don't need training, what is it that you would like for me to do? Precisely. Right now."

The éclair actually seemed to do a lot of good toward Vanetta's mood, because her face relaxed. "Food is good," said Vanetta. "Food. Good."

"It's been popular in Europe for years," I told her.

"Answer the phones. Get everyone clean clothes. Food is good. Maybe some pizza. The most important thing is probably to keep up morale."

"Keep up morale," I repeated dumbly. I put down the sticky bun next to Mark Harmon. "How is morale?" I asked.

"Morale is low," said Vanetta. "Very, very low," she said, shoving more éclair into her than was probably wise. "Keeping it *up* isn't even the right word. It's not up to keep. You're trying to stop the last drops of morale from seeping away."

"I see," I said.

"You might have to actually plunge the morale up."

"You should get some more sleep," I told Vanetta.

"Can't sleep," she said. "There's too much work to be done. But thanks for the éclair. And let everyone know there's a staff meeting in a half hour. You'll probably have to rouse Archie yourself."

Vanetta then took her clothes—the ikat dress and more navy slacks—and walked, with a surprising amount of dignity for someone wearing no shoes, toward the bathroom.

And it struck me that it was not going to take a first-class industrial spy to suss out the secrets of Cahaba Apps. It was going to be hemorrhaging its secrets without me doing much at all.

CHAPTER THREE

In lieu of any proper orientation, I thought maybe I would sort through these clothes. Now that I understood that this wasn't some sort of "she has girl parts, let's make her do our laundry" situation, I figured what the heck. Besides which, I wasn't even sure how many people worked here, and sorting through the clothes would give me an idea.

There were only two things left in the bag, and it was exceptionally easy to figure out which garments matched each other.

First off, there was a floral dashiki. Everyone else's clothing had been business professional, but here we were with a floral dashiki. It was somewhat subdued, as much as a floral dashiki can be, with slate-blue flowers on indigo—and it was decidedly masculine. But certainly more outré than everyone else's clothes. Clearly, this went with the yellow, vinyl parachute pants, because once you've decided you're wearing a dashiki to work, why bother with professional pants?

The only remaining outfit was a suit with matching dress pants. Blue plaid, zingy as hell, from Burberry. The people these outfits went to were both stylish, that was clear. But one of them was also rich, and it was certainly not parachute man.

It got trickier when it came to the unmentionables, which

I will naturally mention. The socks were easy, because one pair looked very expensive, and one pair was ratty. But the underwear was tricky, because there was only one pair. I was inclined to guess that dashiki dude was the most likely to go commando, given his relative laxness in attire, but there was something about the banana-print briefs that just seemed to fit into the whole aesthetic.

I took the clothes, briefs and all, and brought them to Quintrell.

"Who wears a blue dashiki?"

"Archie Bakis," said Quintrell. "He's our art director."

"And his office is where?"

Quintrell looked frozen, as if he had been trapped in a lie.

"What's wrong?" I asked.

"Nothing's wrong," said Quintrell, sounding like something was wrong.

"So where is Archie's office again?"

"It's around the corner," said Quintrell. "Over on the south side of the building, but you probably won't find him there."

I had mountains upon mountains of sleep compared to these goons, but I still didn't have endless patience.

"Okay," I said. "So tell me where he is."

"I don't want to," said Quintrell. He sounded more frightened than belligerent, and so I said:

"You have nothing to fear from me. I just want to get these clothes taken care of."

Quintrell answered slowly and cautiously, like a gerbil surrounded by a wall of cats.

"You might check the floor in Vanetta's office."

"Why would he be on the floor in Vanetta's office?"

"I don't ask."

It was clear, however, what Archie Bakis was doing on the floor in Vanetta's office. He was sleeping, with three sofa cushions pushed against the wall, with curtains draped only somewhat over his nether regions.

He was shirtless and drooling, and this is rarely a look that I would describe as sexy—spit pooling on the pillow in front of you, but, Jesus, was Archie Bakis a fine-looking man. He looked like the sleeping, drooling star of a telenovela, his curly black hair the sort of thing that you just wanted to go over and ruffle.

"Sticky bun?" I asked him.

Sexy or not, Archie continued to sleep. He rolled over, though, and I saw the full brunt of his abs, which was something.

I jabbed his face with the sticky bun.

"Hey, buddy," I said.

He opened his eyes at me slowly, dreamily, and said, "Who is this strange woman in my bed?"

"I'm Nu-Cynthia," I told him. "Get up. There's a staff meeting."

I wasn't sure what was going on under those curtains, and it would have been very unprofessional of me to check. But the question was moot, because Archie Bakis just lay in bed and smiled at me.

"What happened to the old Cynthia? I want Cynthia Prime."

"I don't know," I told him. "People keep asking me that."

"Isn't the first question you always ask in a job interview 'what happened to the person I'm replacing?'" asked Archie, who, God help me, was stretching now, which caused his pecs to swell to the size of eggplants.

"I, uh…" I didn't know what Archie was talking about, because eggplant pecs, and so I threw the clothes at him and said, "Get dressed. Also—is this underwear yours, or?"

"It is now," said Archie.

I got out of there, because I had no business hanging about with shirtless dreamy boys, because my romantic situation is jacked up enough as it is. I'm not really involved in a love triangle so much as I'm involved in a "like triangle." Which is sort of like a love triangle, but without people being idiots. And besides which, unless someone involved here is bisexual, it's never really a triangle anyway, is it? It's a love V. It's not like I'm worried that Nathan Willing, sexy biologist, and Anson Shuler, inexplicably sort-of-alluring police detective were going to run off together.

But I digress. I had one suit left, and so I went prowling around the remaining offices looking for the dapper Dan that matched up to it.

As I combed my way through the rest of the offices, which weren't large, I kept thinking of Gary's *Flying Dutchman* metaphor. Because there were a lot of empty and abandoned workstations, and I wondered what that meant.

Quintrell had run at the sight of me this time—who knows where suit guy was sleeping—and God knows what had happened to Christmas Elf Gary—and so I just combed through the place on my own. I felt pretty sure I had found the office of suit guy—there was an honest-to-gosh gold nameplate on the door that said "Lawrence Ussary, President." And inside there was an absurdly lux-looking mahogany desk, a plush red chair with gold button ornamentation, and a very large glass statue of what was a very impressionistic take on a melting naked woman. But cool. The statue was modern and classy. This looked like the office of someone who would wear a suit from Burberry.

"Hello," I said, checking the floor behind the desk, to see if Lawrence Ussary might have been asleep behind it. Who knew how many more naked sleeping men I could rouse in a day? No dice. So I left the suit in the closet and went back to my desk.

Quintrell and Gary were waiting there for me.

"We have a staff meeting," said Gary.

"Yeah, okay," I told them, forgetting momentarily that I, too, was staff.

"You go in first," said Quintrell. "Make sure Archie is dressed."

Usually I don't go in for these sorts of "you go first" situations, but "see if Archie is dressed" is just the sort of risk I can endure. Even so, I asked:

"Why can't you check yourself?"

"We're not supposed to know that he sleeps in there," said Quintrell.

Offices were weird.

I came in to find him dressed, dashiki and parachute pants and all, and standing on a table to get the curtains hung back up.

"All clear," I said, and Gary and Quintrell filed in behind me. Vanetta, who I hadn't realized was in the room, bobbed up from her desk, apparently taking the thirty seconds of downtime as a moment to rest.

"All right, gang," said Vanetta. "Everyone sit down. We've got a lot of news to cover."

"Where's Cynthia?" asked Archie.

"Cynthia has been fired," said Vanetta.

"Oh no," said Gary. "Everybody loves Cynthia. We need Cynthia."

"It was Lawrence, wasn't it?" said Quintrell paling. "Lawrence has fired another one."

"It wasn't Lawrence," said Vanetta simply. "I fired her."

This created a lot of shock in a room so small. Gary sat down on the sofa across from Vanetta's desk—covered with the cushions that Archie had been sleeping on earlier. Quintrell pulled up a chair. Even Archie Bakis got a little upright, leaning against the wall for support.

"Why would you fire Cynthia?" he asked.

"I can't say," said Vanetta. "But I promise you that it wasn't done lightly."

"We're all going to be fired," said Quintrell. "Every last one of us. Ever since Digital Endeavors bought us out, we're just living on borrowed time."

"Oh, buck up," said Vanetta. "That's not even the bombshell. If you can't handle that, you have no hope of surviving the hard part of this."

"Hope," said Gary, "is the worst of all evils because it prolongs the torments of man."

"We haven't had the hard part yet?" asked Quintrell,

"Nietzsche," said Gary, who couldn't let a quote go unattributed.

"Thank you for sharing the useful teachings of Friedrich Nietzsche with us at this time," said Vanetta. "And nope, we haven't hit the worst of it, Quint, because I've got some more bad news."

"This game is too far behind schedule," said Gary. "We can't handle any bombshells. We're stressed out and running on fumes as it is, Vanetta."

Vanetta, who had been projecting an air of calculated serenity to this point, suddenly looked tired and exhausted herself. "You think I don't know that, Gary? You think I'm not dead inside, too? You think I'm getting more sleep than you?"

"I don't know what you do in this room when you close the doors," said Gary. "I don't know."

"We're all doomed," said Quintrell, to no one at all, really. He was just speaking quietly to himself. "*Peppermint Planes* is never going to be complete and we're all going to be fired."

"Buck up, Quintrell," said Archie this time, and I got the impression that this was something that was said a lot. "That's just your sleeplessness talking."

Everyone seemed to be getting ever more irritated, and ever more charged. I felt like I should have defused the situation, but I was out of baked goods, and I could barely follow along as it was.

"Has the meeting started yet?" I asked. "Do you guys want to wait for Lawrence Ussary? I was never able to find him."

I had inadvertently stumbled upon the right thing to say, because this provoked paroxysms of laughter from the Cahaba crowd.

"No," said Vanetta. "We're not going to wait on Lawrence." She was wiping tears from her eyes. They all were. I understood that they were all dangerously tired, but even so, I didn't get the joke.

"Why not?" I asked. "What's the matter with Lawrence? Is he...dead?"

"He's not dead," said Gary. "What the hell's the matter with you?"

What was the matter with me was that I have participated

in one murder mystery too many. When people this sleep deprived start questioning you, it's time to check yourself.

"Right, sorry," I said. "So why isn't Lawrence here?"

"Lawrence is never here," said Archie evenly. Archie definitely seemed like the most emotionally stable of this lot, and I don't think that I'm grading him on a curve because of his dreaminess. "We do the work. Lawrence just comes and goes."

"We don't have time to wait for him. I have some very alarming news," Vanetta said, passing out sheets of paper to all of us. "Over the weekend—late Saturday night, in fact—the spouse of an employee here at Digital Endeavors posted this blog post to the Internet. Read it and weep."

Digital Endeavors Is Eating Its Employees Alive

I am the spouse of an employee of Digital Endeavors— husband, wife, girlfriend, boyfriend—I'd rather not say, because I know how much blowback I should expect for whistle-blowing on the company. But I wanted to share our family's experiences with Digital Endeavors, which, even in an industry known for mistreating its employees, is shocking.

My partner was hired by Digital Endeavors some time ago, when the company he/she worked for was purchased by DE. At the time we had thought this was a godsend. The studio we had worked for before was hardscrabble— good people with great ideas—just not much in the way of resources. The insurance was garbage, the dental plan the sort of thing that would make a hygienist sigh. And while the working environment was amazing, with so few staff and games in production, everyone's job perpetually hung in the balance. If the next game, the next app failed—or even didn't meet expectations—jobs were at risk.

We didn't resent anyone for this. The software world is scary—no one promises you a rose garden when you go into it—and this was just how it was.

But then we had success after success and along came DE, who bought the company out.

And the dental plan got awesome.

After the novocaine wore off, however, we started to realize that the DE takeover was not such a great thing after all. All the people were the same, we were grateful for that, but the projects began to change. Our next app, which was supposed to be a simple and relatively straightforward update of an existing project, became ever more complicated with the company's guidance. We were told to chase trends and pursue synergies. I could give you specific examples that are so ridiculous you'd laugh—and maybe call me a liar, or both—but I won't because I want to keep my anonymity.

As our game got ever more complicated—ever more on trend—and less and less recognizable from what it was supposed to be—the time needed to complete the project ballooned and ballooned. More coding, more music, more art assets, more development. And the number of staff working on the project stayed the same. Or shrunk.

People were let go, or transferred away to work on other doomed projects by other companies DE had bought out, and our hardscrabble little company footed the bill. Forty-hour weeks became sixty-hour weeks. More people were let go, and then they became seventy-hour weeks. People complained and DE's response was to actually add more edicts into the app.

My spouse is now regularly pulling a ninety-hour work-week. We're not being compensated; we're not even being afforded comp time. We're just being told "this is how it is."

Our lives are in total disarray. I've never seen my husband/wife like this. And from what I'm hearing, the game is getting further and further behind because exhausted programmers are making mistakes, introducing more bugs into the code even as they try to solve problems.

And the worst of it is: I don't think our story is unique. From what I've heard, it's happening everywhere. Company wide. Digital Endeavors is destroying its human capital even as it brings home 3.6 billion dollars a year in profit.

$3,600,000,000. Look at all those zeroes. We're not working for a hardscrabble mom-and-pop software any-more. We're cogs in a wheel, working for an enormous corporation. And we're being treated worse than ever before.

No dental plan is worth that.

DE must be stopped. Whatever the cost.

CHAPTER FOUR

Quintrell, whom I was beginning to associate with over-reaction, punctuated my reading of this document many times with statements like: "Oh shit," and "This is not good," and even "Hell's bells," which was not a thing that I thought people actually said.

I'm a quick reader, and tried to use my free moments to study everyone's reactions. Quintrell, true to his interjections, looked alarmed, as though he expected this document to challenge the ground beneath us. Gary was serene, looking like a doomsayer whose predictions had finally been vindicated. Archie was just dreamy; that's probably bad detective work, because surely something was going on behind those brown eyes of his, but my read was mostly "dreamy."

Vanetta, on the other hand, was doing the same exercise I was. She wasn't just passing along this memo; she was checking for a reaction. Was this why Cynthia was fired? Probably not a question that a receptionist should ask.

"Has it really been this bad?" I asked.

Which was also probably a question that a receptionist shouldn't ask.

"It's not been bad here at all," said Quintrell anxiously. "It's been a privilege to work here. Every day is a joy."

"It's been hell," said Gary.

"Who posted this?" I asked. "Do we know that it came from here?"

Vanetta looked surprised by this question, and I couldn't tell if I had said something incredibly stupid or incredibly canny. But clearly I had hit one of the margins.

"That's an excellent question," mused Vanetta. "Why is it that the temp secretary is asking the most salient question here?"

"I'm in shock," said Quintrell.

"It's probably because she's slept a little," said Gary.

Vanetta ignored this crack. "We don't know where it came from, who posted it. But I'll tell you where my bosses at DE think it came from. They think it came from here."

"Why do they think that?" I asked.

"It does sound like us," said Quintrell. "Wonderful people!"

"It sounds pretty vague to me," said Archie. "It could be lots of places. Digital Endeavors does this to everybody. That's their modus operandi."

"Where'd you hear that?" asked Gary.

"Lots of people," said Archie. "Don't you ask around?"

"When," said Gary, "would I have had time to ask around?"

"When would any of us have had time to write a letter this cogent?" asked Archie.

"Not you," said Vanetta. "Spouses. Significant others. Gary, you have a wife. Archie, you have, well, various situations going."

"It's not my wife," said Gary. "Honey Badger don't care. She didn't even get angry that time Lawrence 'accidentally' drugged me."

"You call your wife Honey Badger?" I asked.

"Sometimes," said Gary a bit sheepishly. "And she calls me Cobra. It's our thing."

"I'm in the clear," said Quintrell. "No love for me. Hell, at this point, if I were to take a girl to bed, I'd dump the girl and just take the bed."

"Don't talk about beds," said Gary. "Just don't. I can't handle it."

"It could be your mom or someone," said Vanetta.

"You don't have to be insulting about it," said Quintrell. "I've had girlfriends. Lots of girlfriends. I just don't have one now because I never leave this building. I mean, going outside is a key component of meeting people."

"Not for Vanetta," said Archie.

"Listen," snapped Vanetta. "I don't want to pry into your personal lives, and I'm not going to speculate about what kinds of girlfriends or boyfriends or what you've got going on there—"

"Girlfriends," said the guys.

"Why would you even say boyfriends?" asked Archie.

"Solidly girlfriends," said Gary.

"Hey, I don't know," said Quintrell. "Describe the bed of this hypothetical dude."

"High-thread-count sheets and ergonomic pillows," said Archie.

This conversation was getting off track, I thought, although it struck me that any extended conversation with these three was eventually going to turn into a conversation about sleeping. I was about to try to refocus them, but Vanetta, who must have been used to this sort of work, had already spoken up.

"I'm sorry I need to bring it up. I get that it's intrusive. I'm just saying that DE thinks it's us. I don't know if they're right;

but they might be right. It could be us. Look into it, gentlemen. Ask your wives and girlfriends. Ask ex-girlfriends. Ask your family. Ask your pastor. Check with any stalkers you have. Just because you don't think you had anything to do with this, don't take that for granted."

"And if we do have something to do with it?" asked Quintrell. Everyone's eyes darted toward him angrily. "I mean, I'm just asking because as the lone singleton here, I thought I could pose the question."

This answer did not seem to mollify Vanetta.

"Stop it immediately. Because if the brass figures it out, heads will roll. Yours, and possibly mine as well."

I had a question, and after having fortified so many people with baked goods, I felt I had earned the goodwill to ask it.

"Even assuming that it was someone from Cahaba who posted this," I asked, "how do you know that it's not someone who left already? Somebody who got fired might be more motivated to whistle-blow."

There was no reason to take the letter at face value. Just because someone said they were a spouse, it didn't actually mean that they *were*. It could be a parent, roommate, brother, sister, anyone. "You're Working My Husband to Death" sounds much more compelling than "I Feel Bad for My Roommate."

It could also be written by the employee themselves. You write about your own conditions, and it sounds self-serving. But throw in an imaginary wife, and suddenly everyone feels sorry for you.

"You could be right," said Vanetta. "It could have been someone already dismissed. I don't know. Let's hope so."

"Or Lawrence," I said, still thinking aloud. "It could be Lawrence."

"Lawrence would not give a fuck," said Vanetta quite simply. "He's the only person around here who I can say, quite definitively, did not send this letter."

"It would also be littered with typos," said Gary.

"Does Lawrence even have a girlfriend?" asked Quintrell. "I don't know anything about him."

"Probably," said Gary. "He probably has dozens of them."

"Forget Lawrence, forget his girlfriends," said Vanetta. "Focus on your own houses, and get your work done. Digital Endeavors is breathing fire on me to get this to a playable state. Fight the good fight, gentlemen."

"Right," said the guys, and took off.

I hadn't been to a lot of staff meetings, as I've not really been employed very much, and even then, under skulduggery, but I felt it was unusual the way the meeting just sort of limply dissolved. The moment everyone walked out the door, they were all zombies with blank faces. Their energy just ran out the moment they left the room.

Welcome to corporate America, I suppose.

I followed the gang out, but my phone was ringing and so I made my way back to my desk. Receptionist, recept thyself! I lifted the phone from its cradle and said, "This is Cahaba Apps. How may I direct your call?"

Which I felt was pretty good—I had the voice down. I was channeling primo secretary—Joan Holloway / Della Street goodness. Of course, it was all an act, and a pretty badly conceived one, because no one had shown me how to use this phone system yet, and so directing their call would probably involve a lot of cursing.

"This is Ignacio Granger."

This name, which was peculiar, sounded oddly familiar to me, but I couldn't immediately place it.

"Hello, Ignacio Granger," I said. "How may I help you today?"

And no sooner had I finished saying his name aloud than it hit me. I knew this guy—he was a writer for *Stage Select*, a gaming blog. Sort of the poor man's *Destructoid*. I remembered him because he had actually written about me when I got shot by a cosplayer at a gaming convention. It was a good piece, although no primary sourcing. He hadn't interviewed me, but just repackaged the story from the *Phoenix Sun* article.

"Wait," I said. "I know you."

"Lots of people do," he said, unimpressed.

"What can I do for you, good sir?"

"I'm calling for a couple of different reasons."

"And I can help you with all of them," I said. Man, being a secretary was awesome.

"First," said Ignacio, "what's your name?"

Well, shit.

"I'm Cynthia Shaffer," I said, looking at the nameplate on my desk. I didn't want to say Dahlia Moss because this guy might— it was unlikely, I grant—just might remember me. That article he had written described me as a "geek detective" and I didn't want to do anything to imperil my industrial spy gig. "I'm just a perfectly ordinary receptionist."

"Well, we'll get along splendidly, then," said Ignacio. "I'm a perfectly ordinary journalist."

There was something about this line that seemed smarmy

and ingratiating and also a little ominous. I thought I'd take him down a notch.

"Yes," I said. "I saw that listicle of yours where you ranked all the Sonic the Hedgehog games. Groundbreaking work."

It was perhaps not the most receptionist-y thing I could have said. Della Street would have held her tongue. But this did not seem to bother Ignacio Granger.

"Hey, that Sonic thing got a lot of hits," he said. "You can't knock hits."

"That's what Matt Drudge tells himself every morning. Now, what do you want?"

Nope, still not being very reception-y. Then, remembering once more that my job was to be pleasant, I said:

"What can I do for you?"

"Well, I'm double-checking the time for my tour of the place," said Ignacio.

"Oh," I said. I had not been here very long, but it instantly seemed to me that Cahaba Apps, with its abandonment-themed decor and sleep-deprived hysterics was not a great place to allow a journalist to wander through. Still, not my call to make. "Let me see if I can put you through to Vanetta."

And I looked at the phone system, which while not overly complicated, was at least opaque. There was a button that some-one had written "Vanetta" on, and if I pressed that I'd probably have her line. But should I press Transfer first? Or maybe Hold first and then Transfer? Or did this even matter? It struck me that I should have Charice call here so I could practice transfer-ring her around.

"I'd love a quote from you too. You're at the nexus op, after all," said Ignacio, whom I suddenly suspected was trying to charm me. Why would he be trying to charm me?

"No quotes," I said, because I might not have been a great receptionist, but I was no fool. But then, because I was a detective, I asked: "Why would you want a quote from me?"

"About the DE scandal. You've seen the post, right?"

"I cannot comment on that at this time," I said. Transfer first, then Vanetta.

"Sounds like you've seen it," said Ignacio. "Listen, the word on the street is that things are falling apart over there."

"I'm transferring you now," I said. And I did just that, or, possibly, I sent him off to oblivion. Either way, problem solved.

I didn't have much time to wonder about Ignacio's fate, although I couldn't imagine it was going to go well for him, wherever he got transferred to. Given a few more moments, I might have wondered about what, exactly, he was after. Because this was Video Game Journalism, which resembles actual journalism in the way a cat resembles a zebra. He wasn't going to do an exposé on Cahaba Apps, because people in Video Games Journalism don't do exposés. On anything.

They do glowing reviews and listicles.

So what was that about?

This was an entirely reasonable question, but I did not have time to pursue it, because I was accosted by Lawrence Ussary, Man Who Did Not Give a Fuck. I wish I could say that I deduced his identity by some sort of impressive and astute observation, but he was wearing yet another Burberry suit and looked like some sort of runway model Burberry might use. It seemed plausible that he might have been playing football earlier, perhaps in the 1920s, perhaps for Harvard.

He was winning, I guess I'm saying.

"Cynthia, do you have my suit?"

It wasn't clear to me if Lawrence Ussary, Man Who Did Not Give a Fuck, was joking. As in, "Ha, ha, I see that you aren't Cynthia, but there you are sitting in front of her nameplate, and thus I will assail Humor!" Or was this "The nameplate says Cynthia so I'm going with that." But as he did not exactly stop at my desk so much as merely slow down, I tended toward the latter.

I did not have a lot of time for extended impressions of Lawrence Ussary, but suffice to say that he looked like he had been getting plenty of sleep.

"Yes, Mr. Ussary—I took the liberty of hanging it in your office."

"Thanks, Cynth, you're a doll," said Lawrence Ussary, and then he was gone.

I have not been called a doll very frequently in my life, in part because I'm really more of an Action Figure, and in part because this is not the 1940s. I felt as though I should have been properly offended, but it was such an odd exchange that I was more confused than anything.

Quintrell King showed up at my desk.

"Who was on the phone?" he asked.

"Why do you ask?"

"Well, you transferred the line, and a moment later, Vanetta threw her phone on the floor and kicked it," said Quintrell. "And I feel like that can't be a good sign."

"Lawrence Ussary called me a doll," I said, trying to change the subject.

"He spoke to you? Wow."

"And he called me Cynthia," I said.

"He usually calls me Jason," said Quintrell.

"What does he do around here?" I asked.

"I wonder that myself. I know he put up most of the money that got this place started. He and Vanetta went to college together. She was the brains, he was the money."

"So Vanetta programs?"

"She programs, yeah," said Quintrell, "but honestly, she's not that great. Don't tell her I said that. Mostly she designs. The Rails series were all her ideas. She's really good at game theory. If you ever catch her with any sleep ask her about her dinner with David Sirlin—the game designer. She'll get really excited, but also weirdly furious. It's very exciting to watch."

"And what do you do?" I asked.

"Gary and I mostly program," he said. "Although these days that means trying to repair the damage that's been done."

"And Archie does art?"

"And music, and some promotional bits, but right now mostly music."

"And that's the staff?" I asked.

"That's the local people," said Quintrell. "There used to be more of us. And, of course, there are people who work for DE out of other offices. They gave us an organizational flowchart when DE bought us, and it's honestly the most complicated thing I have ever seen in my life. And I can do the *New York Times* crossword puzzle on Fridays."

From Quintrell's bragging intonation, I suspected this meant something—do the puzzles get harder as the week goes along?—but I did not get to follow up on the point because Vanetta slammed open the door to her office and yelled, "Cynthia, my phone isn't working!"

"That's because she kicked it," whispered Quintrell.

I wasn't sure how to respond. My natural answer would be to

say "Don't kick phones," but what did I know? Maybe there was a malignant spirit on the other end of the line, like in a horror movie, and Vanetta Jones had dispelled the evil and saved us all. It was at least hypothetically possible.

But even in the universe where Vanetta was the vanquisher of phone-based evil, it wasn't like I was going to go in there and somehow reassemble her phone. There were other people for that.

I settled on: "Would you like for me to make a call for someone to come out and service it?"

Which felt like it was pitched nicely down the middle.

Vanetta did not respond, however, because Lawrence Ussary walked by and said: "Cynthia. Jason." And walked into Vanetta's office and closed the door.

There was a silence, in which Quintrell once again looked nervous and impressed. A lot of things seemed to provoke this reaction in him.

"I know you probably aren't aware of this," said Quintrell. "But Lawrence going in there is weird. It's like the south pole and the north pole just going off together."

"They're both cold," I said.

"Yes, but together they will destroy the earth," said Quintrell.

"He called you Jason again," I observed.

"Yeah," said Quintrell. "I really hate that he does that. Jason used to work here."

"Do you look like him?"

"He was three hundred and fifty pounds, so I hope not," said Quintrell. "No offense, Jason."

"Gotcha."

"Also, Jason was white. Still is, I'd assume."

"I guess Lawrence isn't really a details guy."

"You'd be surprised," said Quintrell.

CHAPTER FIVE

Quintrell, after determining that I was not going to give him any intel on the mysterious phone caller—loose lips sink ships—returned to his desk.

No one was supervising me, and before I embarked on the dark art of industrial espionage, I decided I should orient myself with the basics of the job and figure out how the phone worked. This mostly involved pressing random buttons. When that front was settled, I turned to focus on gathering intel. Apparently everyone else shared Quintrell's reaction, because the entire office had averted their gaze from the door. Which was fantastic, actually, because it provided an excellent opportunity to snoop. I walked over to the door, crouched so I was out of sight, and listened. It can't always be secret cameras and keyloggers. Sometimes the old-fashioned, low-tech ways are best.

Lawrence and Vanetta weren't yelling at each other. Quite to the contrary, there was a familiarity between them—like old friends talking.

"Vanetta," said Lawrence, sounding even smarmier than his suit. "You're looking good. Not rested, but good. The lack of sleep suits you. It's like college."

"It's nothing like college," said Vanetta.

"I don't know," said Lawrence. "Working around the clock, you sleeping with strange guys on sofas, deadlines looming. You have to admit that it rings a bell."

"Who told you about Archie?" asked Vanetta, sounding tired and resigned.

"It was Archie? I was going to place my bets on Quintrell."

I noted that Lawrence knew Quintrell's name when he wasn't around, which was interesting. His disaffection was an act, at least somewhat.

"Why are you here?" asked Vanetta. "It's obviously not to help us work."

"I've been working," said Lawrence. "I've been having meetings. I just got back from Los Angeles, and I come bearing news."

"I don't want news," said Vanetta. "I want this game done."

"I've bought us some extra time, actually."

"You're kidding."

"Well, it comes with a catch. We need to voice and animate all of the peppermints."

There was a long pause.

"This is a puzzle game. It's abstract," said Vanetta. "The candy is meaningless."

"Then you won't mind giving them voices."

"What are you talking about?"

"The main character of the game is a male peppermint. White, please. Give him a good Anglo-Saxon name, like Peppermint Tom. Or Jake. How about Jake?"

"What are you talking about?"

"And Jake has a girlfriend, maybe Sally? Is that too ethnic? She should also be white. But don't worry, I worked in some racial diversity for you."

"Stop talking and explain what you're talking about."

"There should be a wise old black peppermint," said Lawrence. "Not like a magical Negro, but, well, you know, a little like a magical Negro. He's going to help Jake learn how to manage the peppermint planes. And can maybe Sally get kidnapped? Maybe by some angry monster mint, or is that too on the nose? Maybe they could be Hispanic mints. I know how important diversity is to you."

"What the hell are you talking about?"

"I'm talking about money. DE wants to make a pilot. A little cartoon show. And cereal. They're also really keen on cereal, but that's a different discussion. Do you know how much money has been made from *Angry Birds* merchandise? That's the space we're after."

"This game is seven-eighths done, Lawrence, and there are no talking mints. We can't redo it now."

"We're not redoing it; it's still your game. It's just being reskinned a little. Now the mints will talk and have personalities."

"This is not…" started Vanetta, and I felt I could feel how tired she was just by proxy. "How much extra time would this buy the team?"

"Weeks? Months? It depends what corporate thinks of the direction. Have your new boy Archie put something together—we're thinking of a kind of fifties retro 'let's go out to the movies' look."

"I never should have taken your money," said Vanetta simply.

"Of course you should have," said Lawrence. "You're going to be rich, Vanetta. You're going to have your own stable of Quintrells when this is over."

"Archies," said Vanetta.

"Yeah," said Lawrence, "I don't know why I keep thinking Quintrell. I guess he suits you."

"We're not going to have a magical Negro peppermint."

"Corporate wants racially diverse peppermints, Vanetta."

"First of all, that doesn't mean magical Negro characters, and second of all, they're peppermints."

"Peppermints that will have voice actors."

"No old black peppermint," said Vanetta.

"You know, I've just pitched it wrong. I mean like an elder statesman who just happens to be black. That's what I mean. They're asking Morgan Freeman to do it—apparently someone at DE has an in with his people."

"I—Wait, Morgan Freeman?"

"Who wouldn't want Morgan Freeman? Get busy living or get busy dying? I love that flick."

"They're mints."

"It's not like we'd have him be in blackface or anything."

"Jesus Christ, just stop talking."

"Maybe he could be a green spearmint or something. There are other kinds of mints. Chocolate mint. No, that's not a good one. Stick with spearmint."

"I've made a deal with the devil."

"You're giving me too much credit, V. You always do. I'm just a guy that likes money. And you're going to make us so much money. A stable filled with Archies. You'll be like Calista Flockhart."

"You know, I don't even want to talk about Archie. It was just a moment of weakness."

"I don't mean Calista Flockhart. Caligula. I meant Caligula. And as to your 'moment of weakness': Don't try that with me," said Lawrence. "I've known you too long. You've had plenty of moments of weakness. You present yourself as the moral one, but you keep me around because you want the very same things I do."

"Get out, Lawrence."

"You want to tell Archie about the new direction, or should I take care of it?"

I didn't catch the answer to this question because just then a new man showed up who I did not have clothes for. He was tall and thin and had a haircut that hung down long on one side and short on the other. His hair was mostly black except for one long wisp that was, through some bit of cosmetological magic, neon green. In different clothes, he could have been taken for one of those scruffy homeless guys that you'd see on the Loop. He had the thinness of someone who wasn't a stranger to heroin.

But he was dressed as preppily as anyone here—save for Lawrence, anyway—in navy-blue chinos and a collared gingham shirt with a bow tie.

I didn't know what to make of him.

"Were you eavesdropping?" he asked.

"Welcome to Cahaba Apps," I said, stepping away from the door. "Can I help you?"

The wisp of green hair reminded me vaguely of a snake. He was a sad Medusa, this fella. And he was definitely giving me a "turn to stone" glare.

"Who the hell are you?" he said. "Why are you listening at Vanetta's door?"

"I'm the new receptionist, Dahlia," I told him. "Some call me Nu-Cynthia. Who are you?"

"I'm Tyler Banks. I work here."

Quintrell hadn't mentioned Tyler, but it wasn't as if we had gone through an employee audit. Who was this guy?

"You certainly look much better rested than your compatriots."

I thought this was a good, Human Resources–approved compliment. "You look well rested" = good. "You sure know how to fill out those pants" = bad. See, I am employable. I know things.

"Yeah, well," he said, smiling as he brushed the snake hair aside. "I'm from the main office. I'm not part of this clown car."

Tyler struck me as a little smug and a little vain, but I couldn't help but like anyone who would describe this operation as a clown car.

"I've temped lots of places," I said, exaggerating a bit, "but this has been the weirdest first hour of work ever. Did you know everyone sleeps here?"

"This place is a Dumpster fire," said Tyler. He was mixing metaphors, unless the clown car had gotten trapped inside this Dumpster and was now being consumed by flame, but it was hard to quibble with the overall picture.

"I've seen. What do you do?"

"I put out Dumpster fires," said Tyler.

I looked at Tyler differently now, because he was management. He didn't dress like management, particularly, but this was not an industry that did overly value suits. My toile scarf meant nothing here.

"I see," I said. "Do they know you're here? Vanetta and Lawrence, I mean? How long have you been around?"

"This is my second week in this office," said Tyler. "Usually I'm in Austin."

Yes, Tyler looked like someone who was usually in Austin. He looked like he should be diving from a stage at SXSW. I felt a sort of kinship with him—prickly Medusa or not—because I realized that we were on the same team. We were both here to report to Digital Endeavors. He was on the up-and-up, and

I was on the sly. Although it was weird, I suddenly thought, that DE should want this redundancy. Did they not trust Tyler? Maybe they thought he was sabotaging the project. Or maybe he was the guy who had sent the whistle-blower's letter.

Or, and this thought suddenly seemed salient—maybe I was wrong about who my client was. It struck me that it might be good to befriend Tyler Banks, to get a sense of what DE management was like. I gave it my best shot.

"You doing anything later?" I asked.

"No," said Tyler, who walked away. Befriending accomplished!

I didn't have much time to celebrate this victory, however, because Lawrence ran out of Vanetta's office, and a chair sailed through the air after him, just missing his head.

Lawrence actually made a "woo-woo-woo-woo-woo!" noise, the sound Curly from the Stooges makes when he is performing comedy high jinks. There was a spring in his step, as though he thought this was all very funny.

"Tyler, Cynthia," said Lawrence.

"Everything under control back there?" asked Tyler.

"Very much." Lawrence smiled. He honestly was insufferable. "Vanetta and I were just celebrating by throwing around some furniture."

Vanetta appeared in the doorway and looked less like a Stooge and more like an Avenging Angel. All will burn before Vanetta!

"Did you just throw a chair at Lawrence?" asked Tyler incredulously.

"Did you know about the new platform?" asked Vanetta.

"Wait, what new platform?"

"Oh," said Vanetta. "I see. Digitial Endeavors isn't keeping you in the loop either."

"What new platform?"

"When he tells you, you're going to throw that chair at him yourself."

But Lawrence was hightailing it out of this conversation, inching ever closer to the door. By the time Tyler seemed ready to approach him, he was already past me and at the doorway leading downstairs.

"Must run, everyone," Lawrence said merrily. "I've got another meeting."

"Someone tackle him," said Vanetta.

But he was gone. I'm not sure I would have been up for tackling him in any event.

CHAPTER SIX

The next hour or so was oddly productive. Programmers programmed, Tyler and Vanetta were in a meeting, Lawrence was away, which seemed to be for the best, and I further familiarized myself with the phone system. I felt 90 percent certain that I could transfer a call without sending someone into oblivion, which was good enough for temp work.

I was productive too. Given that my ultimate goal was to nick some code for Emily, I was hoping there would be a shared server that I could glean it from. There was, but I didn't have access to it. I asked a few casual, secretarily appropriate questions about the server to Quintrell, which was progress.

I also continued working on Operation Befriend Tyler Banks, which meant gathering intel. In my quiet moments of downtime I looked for Tyler on Twitter, Facebook, Instagram, even LinkedIn. I was able to get the basics of him pretty quickly. Former creative, recently involved in a breakup, terribly lonely in St. Louis—I even found his OkCupid dating profile, which was a mess.

What inspired me were the pictures of his ex—a raven-haired pseudo-Goth named Suzanne. Suzanne wasn't Asian, but something about her reminded me of my friend Masako. They

49

were broadly similar—same body type, hair color, and with a Goth-y edge.

Maybe I could set them up. That could be an entry point. Something to try later.

The phone rang again, and this time, it was for me.

"Stop what you're doing," said Charice. "And sit down."

"I'm not doing anything," I said, not bothering with "This is Cahaba Apps" because I knew the voice. "And I'm already sitting down."

"Well, pretend to sit down, because I want the moment to increase the drama," said Charice.

My roommate, Charice, who was made of Drama, who was essentially a Drama Elemental, emphatically did not need a moment to increase the drama. If anything, she could have used a moment to bring it down a notch.

"You'll manage, I'm sure. Hey, can I transfer you to a sleepy programmer?"

"Is this part of your industrial spying business?"

I had not told Charice about my industrial spying gig. I don't know how she had put that together—probably she had found the napkins. But that's Charice for you—she seems flighty but she's got the mind of a brilliant tactician. I've learned to be especially wary whenever she goes out of her way to seem disinterested.

"Ixnay on the—" I wanted to say industrial spy-nay, but there was a high chance that my coworkers spoke pig latin. "Mysterious business," I said instead, like a goon, because nothing quells suspicion like someone hastily saying "ixnay on the… mysterious business."

"Yeah, yeah," said Charice. "Fine. Are you sitting down?"

"So can I transfer you to a sleepy programmer? You can call me back after."

"No," said Charice. "I'm getting married."

She paused after this proclamation, I'm sure expecting me to be awe induced. But I wasn't. I wasn't even raised-eyebrow induced.

"Yes," I said. "You're engaged. That's what engaged people do. It's the natural evolution."

"No," said Charice. "I'm getting married today. Over lunch. Do you want to be a witness?"

Okay, now I was surprised. Perhaps not awe induced, but this wasn't how I had planned my day.

"Wait, what? I thought you wanted a wedding with doves and a tower of cheesecake."

"I've decided to scale back on the wedding and scale up on the honeymoon."

A lavish honeymoon was very Charician. If she had the money, she'd go to the moon.

"But what about the tower of cheesecake? You promised me there would be a tower of cheesecake. That's why I'm going."

"How about a tower of pancakes? We could go to IHOP after."

"What does Daniel think about this?" I asked, although I realized the stupidity of the question as soon as it escaped my lips. Daniel was in love with Charice and would have been fine with whatever she wanted, up to and including pancakes. Why wouldn't he be? Charice was, if nothing else, fun. Hell, I'd go on a honeymoon with her.

"Do you have a priest?"

"We don't need a priest," said Charice. "We're just going to city hall."

"Just hang on," I said. "Can you get married tomorrow? You can do it over lunch tomorrow."

"I want to strike while the iron is hot!"

"The iron will be hot tomorrow," I told her.

Vanetta came out of her office—Tyler was still in there—and looked at me with irritation.

"That doesn't sound business related."

It was a fair cop.

"I gotta run," I told Charice, hanging up the phone. Then, to explain to Vanetta, "I'm sorry, that was my roommate. She was calling to let me know that she's getting married. Today, over lunch."

I had described Vanetta as being somewhat catlike, but now she gave me a look that was Eeyore-esque.

"The world marches on outside these walls," said Vanetta.

I suppose it did, although marching wasn't exactly the way I'd describe it. Marching requires precision and organization. From my experience, the world tends to shamble. It's less a drum corps and more an explosion of toddlers and drunks. But I didn't address this point with Vanetta and simply said:

"What can I do for you?"

"Toner," said Vanetta. "Can you bring me some toner?"

"Sure," I said as she returned to her office. "I'd love to."

I had made an inventory of Cynthia Prime's desk and had not seen anything like toner, so I headed back to the staff room with the candy-cane coffee. I did a quick search of the place, but turned up nothing. Then, deciding that I didn't want to spend too long rummaging, lest Vanetta get rowdy, I decided to ask Quintrell for help.

"Hey, Jason," I said, "where's the supply room?"

Quintrell, who was sleeping again, popped up like some sort of Whac-A-Mole. "I'm working! I'm awake!"

"Relax. Where's the supply closet?"

"Oh," said Quintrell. "It adjoins the women's restroom. Over by Lawrence's office."

A word on the architectural choices of Cahaba Apps. It was a very odd space, and had obviously been repurposed from an apartment, which had maybe in turn been reappropriated from something else. There were odd corners and nooks, and it was probably an architect's nightmare. To be perfectly clear: There are no secret passages in this book. But it was an oddly designed space, and it seemed as though a secret passage would not be out of the question.

Regardless, I made my way over to the ladies' room, which, point in case, inexplicably had a shower in it as well as a small white wooden door. I opened the door, and, illogically, there was a supply closet. Toner, Xerox paper, office supplies galore, the mother lode of coffee and tea, all stacked up in utilitarian metal shelving.

Also next to the utilitarian shelving: a dead woman, face-down on the floor.

That was somewhat illogical too.

Here's something that did not happen: I did not panic. Corpses and I are getting to be, if not friendly, at least casual. I have Facebook friends that I'd be more upset at seeing than your average dead body. I don't know if this means I'm getting to be a better detective or if I need to purge more friends from Facebook, but both are a good bet.

Something else that did not immediately happen: I did not call the police.

Obviously, I was going to call the police. Obviously. But I took a moment to assess the situation:

First, I should make clear that what this person was not. She was not:

- stabbed to death
- bludgeoned
- burned
- shot
- killed in an imaginative way, such as left in a cage with a hungry crocodile, or something preposterous like those convoluted-ass killings in the movie *Se7en*.

She was just dead. She was cold to the touch, and rigor mortis had set in, and it seemed to me that she had just, somehow, passed away. Here's a thing that's worth remembering: People just die sometimes. Sometimes it wasn't the colonel in the library with a candlestick. Sometimes it was just Mr. Boddy alone in his study, maybe with a nice glass of gin, and his number was up.

Now, let's consider things that this person was:

- at least in her late sixties
- obese
- frumpily dressed, with a penchant for florals.

I debated including that third point here, because I don't want to imply that floral print will shorten your life span. Nor do I mean to go around commenting on the sartorial choices of the dead—although I'm sure it's a fashion blog somewhere— but I want to point out these elements because it led me to the realization as to who this was.

This was Cynthia Prime.

Right? She'd left a floral scarf on her desk, a diet beverage.

And with a name like Cynthia she was probably born in the sixties, statistically speaking. How many other frumpily dressed overweight sixty-year-old women would be in the supply closet?

Now, let's return to her weight—this lady was hefty. Again, I'm not pointing this out to be judgmental, just to say that Cynthia Shaffer was of an age and shape that if you found her dead, your first thought probably wouldn't have been: How on earth could this have happened?

That's not to say it wasn't disquieting as hell. Also, I wanted to double-check this was Cynthia. Maybe it wasn't. Maybe this was a cleaning woman, or, who knows? An assassin. Probably Cynthia, but it would be wise to double-check.

I stopped at Quintrell King's desk to ask:

"Did Cynthia like to wear floral blouses, kind of grandmotherly?"

"Sometimes," said Quintrell.

"Sixtyish, looks a bit like Conchata Ferrell?" I could have said seventyish, honestly, but I wanted to lean toward the more flattering age.

"I don't know who that is, but I guess the age is around."

"It seems that Cynthia is dead," I told him.

"Long live Cynthia!" he shouted.

"No, I mean, I think she's actually dead. Someone is, anyway, in the storeroom. I didn't search her pockets, but I'm pretty sure it was her."

Quintrell looked as though, quite suddenly, he was going to have a mental breakdown. And I realized that this was not the correct person to burden with the death of Figurehead Secretary who had kept this place afloat.

"Never mind," I said. "I'm kidding! Just get back to work."

"Wait, there's a dead person in the storeroom?"

"Well, yes. I'm calling the police. But maybe it isn't Cynthia. Maybe a homeless person wandered in there and died."

"Maybe a homeless person in a floral blouse who looks like Conchata Ferrell wandered into our office and died?!"

"You know," I said, "never mind. Just get some rest."

I needed more baked goods. That was the problem. I never should have let Vanetta sneak away with my bag of them. A whole bag! But without the curiosity-deadening power of doughnuts, there was no bringing Quintrell down.

"Cynthia's dead, everyone!" he was shouting now, and Gary came over.

"What?"

"Nu-Cynthia says that Old Cynthia is dead in the storeroom!"

"What?" said Gary. "That's ridiculous."

"She's dead! Old Cynthia is dead!"

Gary was taking this news with a healthy bit of skepticism, which, given Quintrell's bleary-eyed state, was sensible.

"I don't think we should call her Old Cynthia. It seems ageist. I liked Cynthia Prime," said Gary.

"Well, we can call her Dead Cynthia now!"

I did not want to stick around for this conversation and tried to call 911, only to realize that I needed to dial something to get to an outside line.

"Goddamn these phones," I said, altogether too loudly.

Vanetta Jones appeared at the doorway amid clouds of brimstone.

"Why are you cursing out here?" asked Vanetta. "I can hear you cursing. If anyone is going to curse around here, it's me."

"I'm trying to call the police," I told her.

"Why?" she asked.

"Cynthia Shaffer is in the storeroom," I told her, glossing

over the not-Cynthia-Shaffer possibility. "Something has happened to her. She's dead."

Vanetta Jones did not crumple into a ball, nor did she gasp or clutch at imaginary pearls. She sighed, turned around, and walked back toward her office. At the doorway she said:

"I'll call the police."

Vanetta returned into her office calmly. It wasn't that she didn't look alarmed about Cynthia's death so much as she gave the impression of having had a week in which this was not the worst part of it. *Of course Cynthia is dead; naturally that would happen this week.* I didn't know what my report to Emily was going to be, but I couldn't help but feel bad for Vanetta Jones, even if she wasn't traditionally warm.

Forgive me if this next bit makes me seem craven, but it struck me that the police, when they arrived, were not necessarily going to approve of me doing a lot of industrial spying for Emily Swenson and her mystery client, and so I took the liberty of doing what I could, while I could. I started copying files and dragging them into my private Gmail account. This was surely illegal, but if anyone was bothered by it, I could always say that I was worried that the police might confiscate Cynthia's machine, and I was trying to protect information. However, the staff was in so much disarray that it probably wasn't a worry.

Lawrence was still out at his meeting, which I suspected involved martinis. Archie had holed up in Vanetta's office, Quintrell was hyperventilating, and Gary and Tyler were trying to calm him down. Tyler, in particular, seemed ill-suited to the task of telling someone everything was going to be fine. He was someone who had developed a skill set that was focused on telling people that they were going to be downsized. There ought to be an overlap in these skills, now that I think about it, because surely someone had hyperventilated after being let go, but Tyler seemed almost as out of sorts as Quintrell. There was a wildness to him that was a little off.

"It's fine," Tyler said. "This sort of thing happens every day."

Which is not true, particularly, but this is what he said.

While everyone else was dealing with their feelings, I made a cursory look at Cynthia's calendar for the day. This was also somewhat snoopy, but the police would probably want to know where Lawrence was, and I probably had that information somewhere. I had initially taken his exit for theater, but he was in fact, marked on the calendar for a lunch meeting with "V," whoever that was. I also took note that Cynthia had a meeting on the calendar tonight, at the St. Charles First Presbyterian Knitters' Group, which seemed less immediately relevant but more poignant. Also, a little unprofessional, putting private meetings on the business calendar, although maybe this was Cynthia's fire wall against having to work late. I took a picture of this with my camera.

"Just calm down, man," said Tyler, who looked like he was considering slapping Quintrell, which is what people once did to hysterics in movies. Instead he asked Gary: "Is he always this high-strung?"

"Only when he hasn't slept for weeks," said Gary. I couldn't tell if Gary was joking or just also on the brink of collapse himself.

I made a phone call and ordered lemonade and a fruit bouquet. This seems positively ridiculous in retrospect, but this was a group that needed a break. And probably not any more caffeine. I had only just finished with the phone call when the police arrived.

CHAPTER SEVEN

It's unrealistic to pretend to work when the police are here, much less a corpse and the police, but that's what we all did.

The first to arrive were paramedics, who barely spoke to me before heading into the storeroom and trying to revive Ms. Shaffer. It wasn't long after that that a policewoman came in, who was then followed by a man I later learned was the coroner, and finally detectives. This period of time seems like it should have been more exciting than it was, but no one was very interested in me, and the primary focus was the dead body, which is perhaps as it should be.

I pretended to type for a while, and then gave it up. I made my way to the back and spoke to Tyler and Quintrell and Gary, who clearly weren't really working either.

"Why are there so many people here?" Gary asked. "Is this a normal amount of people?"

I actually wasn't sure what a normal amount of people was for a murder investigation and told this to Gary. It didn't seem out of line to me, however.

"But there's a coroner," said Gary. "Should there be a coroner?"

"I don't know," I told him. "This is not the sort of thing they teach in secretarial school." To be clear, I have never actually been to secretarial school.

"Hey," said Tyler, "I'm sorry if I was rude earlier. I'm under a lot of stress lately."

"Pssht," I said. "What? Don't worry about it. No biggie."

"I don't think it's good that there's a coroner," said Gary, who was plainly not listening to us at this point.

"Listen," I said to Tyler, "I was actually asking for a friend of mine. She's just had a breakup, and we were going out for coffee after work. You're kind of her type, and it'd be super casual, so if it doesn't work out, it'd be easy."

You didn't have to be a student of body language to tell that Tyler Banks was not interested in my offer. Every pore of his body seemed to say: "What is this secretary talking about?" Even his mouth, which at least was kind enough to translate into:

"I don't think that's going to happen."

"Sure," I said. "No big deal. She's probably not your type— black hair, short, kind of a recovering Goth. Her name's Masako."

The pores on Tyler's body now said "this is an interesting development" but his mouth wasn't along for the ride.

"I'll let you know if I change my mind," he said.

"No sweat," I said as a policeman came out of the storeroom and toward us. He looked concerned but somber, and I probably could have taken some pointers from him.

"Which of you found the body?" asked the detective.

"It was her," said the guys, in perfect unison, which felt like selling me out, although it was technically true.

"Is there an office we can use for some privacy?" he asked.

"Lawrence is still out on lunch," I told him. "I'm sure he won't mind if we used his office."

This got, I'm not kidding, an audible gasp from the guys, but the detective and I walked into Lawrence's office. Why not? It was a nice place.

Detective Tedin was white and balding and seemed to be the sort of person who, if suddenly killed in action, would be proclaimed as being a couple of weeks away from retirement. He looked weary.

He also did not look as though he were in the mood for an interrogation. Maybe it was just having spent the morning watching the Cahaba guys, who were sleep-deprived to the point of it becoming performance art, but Tedin looked like he had been awakened from a nap. He was probably in his midfifties but seemed like a much older man, with white hair and bags under his eyes. He looked like he should have been shooing college students off his lawn.

"Your name is?" asked Tedin.

"Dahlia Moss," I told him, hoping that this alone wouldn't get a reaction, given how much I had been dealing with the police as of late. It didn't so much as raise an eyebrow, which was both good and sort of disappointing. I wasn't as big a fish as I thought I was.

"And what do you do here?" asked Tedin.

"I'm the receptionist—temp receptionist," I told him. "Ms. Shaffer was dismissed recently, and I'm her replacement until they hire someone full-time."

"I see," said Tedin. "Ms. Shaffer is the body? There's no ID on her."

"I think so, yes. I'd never met her before. I've actually only been here a few hours now."

Tedin looked pleased and unsurprised by this, and it was nice, for once, to be having such a positive and chaos-free interaction with an officer. This is how police interviews were supposed to go.

"So you came in around nine this morning?"

"Eight thirty—I wanted to get here early on my first day."

"And you were the first person here?"

"No," I told him. "Everyone had spent the night. Except for Lawrence, that is. He seems to come and go as he wants." In retrospect, I had forgotten about Tyler, who had also come in late, but I didn't bother amending my statement.

Now Tedin looked surprised, his white eyebrows going up, but not necessarily irritated at me.

"Everyone slept here? Why?"

"I gather that they're behind deadline for an app the company is developing. It's crunch time now, and so everyone is working around the clock."

"Are there beds here?"

"Vanetta sleeps on her sofa—Archie too, I've gathered—but the programmers just passed out at their workstations."

"That's not good for your back," said Tedin.

"Probably not," I told him. "But you know, desperate times and desperate measures."

"If Ms. Shaffer was fired, why was she here?" asked Tedin, coming to the point I had been asking myself.

"I couldn't say," I told him. "Maybe Vanetta would have an idea—or one of the fellas. I literally just started working here hours ago."

I could tell Tedin liked this, and I could also tell why. I was a woman who had absolutely nothing to do with this. A suspect who could be cleanly wiped from his list. But if I had been a suspect, did that mean Cynthia had been murdered? Why else would my absolution move an emotional needle?

"So you get here at eight thirty," said Tedin. "What do you do?"

I walked Tedin through my morning, step-by-step. I had never imagined how easy it was to lie to the police, but there's really nothing to it. I mean, I didn't outright lie, but I glossed over the business with the whistle-blower's letter, which I felt was probably a company secret until anyone told me otherwise. I certainly glossed over my spycraft, such as it was, for Emily Swenson. And when you took out those bits, the morning wasn't that interesting.

"No one," asked Tedin, "to your knowledge, walked into that storeroom until you did at eleven?"

"No," I said. "It's built off the women's restroom, and it's not like any of the guys would get near it."

"And the only other woman working here is Vanetta Jones?" asked Tedin.

"That's right."

"Did you go in the restroom earlier and notice anything?"

"No, and when I went in, the door to the storeroom was firmly closed."

"I see. And you were watching the entrance all morning, so Ms. Shaffer couldn't have entered since you got here."

This was not wholly true.

"I tried keeping my eye on my desk during the staff meeting, but I wasn't ironclad about it. I suppose it's hypothetically possible that she entered then, although she would have had to have been sneaky, and a little lucky too."

Tedin *hmmed*. I noticed that his wedding finger had three rings on it—a black ring, a gold ring, and a silver one—all very thin bands, and I wondered what this meant. If he had three wives it would certainly explain his haggard appearance. But he was a decent detective, because he noticed my observation and tucked his hand into his pocket. He also came out with his first gotcha question.

"Detective Shuler tells me that you're studying to be a detective."

Ah. So he did know who I was. Well played, Mr. Tedin.

"I'm taking a few online classes in that direction."

"He also tells me that you have a way of putting yourself in unwise situations."

I wasn't sure where he was going with this in the slightest.

"Did he tell you that we're going skating in Forest Park together this week?"

I mentioned this to Detective Tedin not to brag about my pseudo-date but to try to get him on my side. It didn't seem to work.

"Why are you actually here?" asked Tedin.

"I'm temping," I said. "Like I told you."

"You're not here because of any kind of case?" asked Tedin.

And this was uncomfortable, because it got very close to lying.

"It can't be mysteries all the time," I said. "Besides which, I don't have a license yet."

"So you're not here for any kind of case," repeated Tedin, who was not going to let me dodge this question easily.

"No case," I said. "I'm not a detective yet."

This probably *is* a straight-up lie, but I'm choosing to interpret that detectives have cases and industrial spies have incidents. Therefore, no case. This sounded thin even in my own head, and so I tried unhinging Tedin from this line of inquiry with a question of my own.

"You seem awfully investigative. Did something untoward happen here?"

"We take every death seriously," said Tedin, looking very uncomfortable. The detective clearly didn't want me prying, which only made me want to pry that much more.

"You obviously take this one seriously, seeing as there's a coroner."

"There are a few factors that make Ms. Shaffer's death look a little more suspicious."

"Such as?"

"Well, one of them is that you're here."

Maybe I wasn't such a small fish after all. "Cynthia died before I even showed up."

"We're checking into that," said Tedin. I suppose that should have worried me, but I hadn't killed Cynthia Shaffer, quite transparently. Let him check. I had other things to think about. We spoke a bit more, and then Tedin had me send in Quintrell.

I made my way back to my desk, and Vanetta came out of her office. She was holding a drink—possibly ginger ale, but I'm going to guess that it was something alcoholic.

"Did the police finish with you?" she asked. This was an uninflected question, asked without any particular guile or even interest. Perhaps the exhaustion had pushed Vanetta over the edge into mental numbness.

"They did. They're with Quintrell now."

"That ought to be a fun interview. Buck up, Quintrell," said Vanetta, toasting her glass in the air.

"Did they talk to you?" I asked.

"Not yet. I'm supposed to stay in this room until someone comes for me."

"I see," I said. Did this mean that Vanetta was a suspect? I wasn't sure what my secretarial duties were when it came to someone being a murder suspect.

"You can go home now, if you want," said Vanetta, picking up on my uncertainty.

"Aren't we terribly behind? I want to pitch in."

"You're sweet," said Vanetta with very little emphasis behind the words. "But I think we're all going home after this. Even me. We're all rattled and there's no point in pretending otherwise. If DE doesn't understand that, they can go to hell."

Again, these words were delivered with no emotion whatsoever. It was as if I was communicating with Vanetta via semaphore, or perhaps I was a ghost. Gone was the defiant exhausted spitfire of the morning, and now there was a quiet, exhausted cipher. Exhausted was really the only point of continuity.

"Have you spoken to Lawrence?" I asked, still glimmering with secretarial energy.

"No," said Vanetta. "That's a good thing to do. I should have thought of that. Why don't you let him know what's going on before you go home."

Alerting Lawrence of anything, I found, was hard going because he wasn't answering his phone. It felt wrong to mention murder over voice mail—I felt like I was creating content for some BuzzFeed "10 Tackiest Voice Mails" listicle, but I did the best I could.

"Lawrence: This is Dahlia—Nu-Cynthia—from Cahaba Apps.

There's been a, uh, incident here and apparently Cynthia Shaffer is dead. She was found in the storeroom. The police have come and are handling it. I'm sure they'll want to speak with you, and you should get here as soon as possible. Also, the staff is going home when the police are finished with them, so don't be surprised if no one picks up when you call. You should get here as soon as possible or call the police, or both."

Looking over it now, it doesn't seem all that awful, but even as glib as Lawrence seemed to be, it didn't feel right to drop so many bombs on him in succession.

I was nowhere near as overworked as the rest of the Cahaba-ers, but I felt like I could have used a break from the chaos anyway. I drove part of the way home, stopping at La Patisserie Chouquette yet again, to hook up again with pastries and to file a report with Emily Swenson. This was going to be to a double-pastry day.

I got a bear claw, sat down, and, having found a quiet corner of the shop, called Emily.

"You're not calling me from Cahaba, are you?" said Emily. "That would be very indiscreet."

"Why, Emily," I said. "I'm the very picture of discretion."

"Naturally," said Emily. "But why aren't you at work?"

"As it happens, the secretary I was replacing was still there," I told her.

Emily was silent for a moment and said: "I apologize. That shouldn't have been possible."

"No," I said. "She wasn't working. She was dead, in the storeroom."

"What happened to her?"

"We don't know. The police are there now. But they brought in a coroner, so I think there's at least an open question as to whether it was natural."

"But it wasn't obviously unnatural."

"It wasn't obviously anything. No one even knows why she's there."

Emily was quiet, and I picked up the slack with a question of my own.

"So, I'm sure this is completely ridiculous to ask, but you didn't—by any chance—have Cynthia killed so I would have a job?"

Emily laughed. "I had no idea you were capable of such narcissism."

"I don't think you'd be doing it for me."

"As much as I enjoy the idea of you thinking of me wielding that kind of power, no. I didn't have anyone killed so you could do temp work."

"So I could spy."

"That either. It's just an unfortunate coincidence."

Although, Emily sounded uncertain on this note, and I suddenly didn't appreciate the power differential between us. Emily had the car and the map, and I was just her passenger. I couldn't even work the radio.

"How about you tell me who this client I'm working for is?"

"I appreciate your investigative powers, Dahlia, but it's really important that you're directing them in useful ways. Were you able to put your hands on the code we were after?"

"No," I said, somewhat surprised that this was even still on the table. "I got a bit waylaid with the dead woman."

"Anything else you can tell me about Cahaba?"

And so I told my findings to Emily, or at least as much as I knew. For as shocking as the conditions were, Emily didn't seem shocked by any of it. Not the sleep deprivation, not the whistle-blowing letter, not Lawrence walking out, none of it. I couldn't tell if she was already very well-informed or if this was just her professional demeanor. It would have been easier to read her if I could have seen her face—on the phone, I had no way to gauge her shock short of her audibly gasping, and Emily wasn't the gasping type.

When I finished speaking, Emily simply said:

"Not bad for four hours."

"Is there anything in particular you're looking for?"

"We want the code. Although, if you want to find out who wrote that letter," said Emily, "I certainly wouldn't interject."

"And Cynthia's death?"

"Now, that," said Emily, "is a cul-de-sac that you don't need to bother with."

I finished with Emily and ate two sugar cookies. Sugar cookies are the Aristotelian ideal of cookies, as far as I am concerned, as they do not concern themselves with unneeded frippery like chocolate or oatmeal or walnuts. Just pure cookie idealness, which was a comfort I could use.

I hated the idea of Cynthia's death being described as "a cul-de-sac." If I died, I would want my passing to be more than a dead end. I would want it to be a full-on avenue, with traffic and interesting businesses, and signs that warned to go slowly because children were playing. There are limits to this metaphor, obviously, but I just hated the idea that I was supposed to give up on Cynthia. It felt wrong.

Even worse, it felt callous. But maybe that was the gig. Hookers may have hearts of gold, but detectives not so much. And industrial spies not at all.

"Hey, Colleen," I said to a woman behind the counter.

"You again? You're becoming one of our best customers."

"I'm trying to bring up morale at work. With baked goods."

"How much do you need to bring it up?"

"Well," I said, "right now we have firings, a saboteur, and possibly a murderer."

"I'll put together the bag," said Colleen.

CHAPTER EIGHT

I had scarcely made it home when I got a text from Tyler Banks, which I was not expecting, although I should have been.

"On second thought, maybe meet for coffee after all? I'm kinda stressed out after all that."

Right. I'd forgotten about the coffee plan, given the interrogation. Now all I had to do was see if Masako was interested. Admittedly, this was doing things backward, but backward is better than nothing.

"Masako—" I said, opting for a phone call rather than a text, since this was going to be a hard sell. "What are you doing right now?"

"Who is this?"

"It's Dahlia, Nathan's...whatever I am."

"Girlfriend?"

"Sure," I said, feeling that this was dangerous water. "What are you doing?"

"Linear algebra."

"What?"

"Like with matrices."

"Do you want to have coffee with me?"

"Why?"

"Does coffee need a reason?" I asked.

"I am suspicious," said Masako.

Masako was not a detective—she was, as far as I could tell, a Goth who disguised herself in pastels and polka dots—but she certainly had the right frame of mind for the endeavor. She was right to be suspicious.

"There's a fellow I thought I might introduce you to."

"Who?" said Masako.

"He works with me."

"What is he, a bounty hunter?" asked Masako.

"Ha, ha, no. He's in middle management."

"Sounds fun," said Masako, who was a Grand Magus of Sarcasm, and was in fact capable of wielding it like an ancient tome of great power.

"I think you'll like him," I said. "And you don't want to get hooked up with bounty hunters. Those guys are the worst."

"Why are you working with a middle manager, anyway? Is this part of some kind of secret detective work?"

"No," I said. "Not at all." Jesus, Masako was good. "Although, now that you mention it, don't bring up my detective work to Tyler."

"You don't want him getting suspicious of you."

"Um."

"You're keeping secrets from this middle manager."

Masako, it dawned upon me, was entirely too clever and strong willed to be invited on a delicate operation such as this. She was not a sidekick; she was her own main character. Seriously, you should probably be looking for *The Masterful Decision Making of Masako Ueda*, in stores now.

"You know, on second thought, you don't have to come if you don't want to." Masako was going to be more trouble than she was worth.

"Maybe I do want to," said Masako.

"I can find someone else," I told her, which was almost certainly not true.

"No, I'm getting sick of this math, anyway. I'll try your middle manager. I have a middle. Maybe he can manage it."

And with that, Masako Ueda had taken over the evening.

I also called, not texted, my boyfriend/manfriend/fella-of-the-moment Nathan Willing. Nathan was a grad student in plant and microbial sciences—don't say botany, it makes him testy—and as we have determined in previous adventures, not a murderer. I thought it would be nice to have Nathan around, because he's fun, and enjoyable to look at. Also, I thought that there was an even chance that Masako and Tyler would go badly, and Nathan was good at creating the illusion of fun. There's this thing in biology where apex predators in different food chains meet, and they will have absolutely no relationship to each other. That's a little what I was worried about. I was going to have coffee with a crocodile and a vulture, and they were going to eye each other from across the table as though they belonged in different biomes. Because they sort of did.

I even told Nathan about this concern.

"I think you have the wrong animals," Nathan said. "The crocodile is just going to eat that vulture."

"The individual animals aren't the point," I told him.

"Which one is Masako, anyway?" he asked.

"She's the crocodile, obviously."

"What animal am I?" asked Nathan.

"I don't know, Tigger? I really need you to bring the fun, Nathan, if things aren't going well."

"I can bring the fun train into station," said Nathan. "But I'm picking up a prospective TA from the airport tonight, so I can't stick around."

"Cool," I said. "Awesome. This is all for a case, by the way."

"Yeah," said Nathan. "I figured that out."

The evening did not go as I planned it. Right from the start, Masako changed where we were meeting, switching from a coffeehouse to a bar, and things only got more off the rails from there.

Let's start with the bar.

The Black Fox looked as if it had been dreamed up by the people at White Wolf games, which is to say that is was the sort of Goth bar that should have stopped existing in the nineties. It was made of brick and mortar and mortality and black eyeliner. The music was loud and industrial, the waitress was pierced and sexy, and I half expected to find people playing Jihad at a table in the back.

I liked it.

Lately the Goths have added neon "industrial waste" green to their color palette, and it was on full display here. A guy near us had a green-and-black-pinstripe jacket, which was swank in a Tim Burton sort of way. A gal over at a table nearby was wearing neon-green leggings with black stripes. And over by the door a lady who was arguably too old for the club had a neon-green feather in her hair.

Someday, people will look back and be nostalgic for the days in which the Goths just wore one color.

Masako and I got there first, and she wisely had us sit outside at black metal tables, which took the edge off a lot of the Gothiness. I had taken the opportunity to change out of my toile scarf, and was wearing a peach-and-white-colored kraken-print blouse that Alden had gotten me for Christmas, in part because our mother reiterated that I should never wear peach. I feel I should wear whatever goddamned pleases me, but peach was not in style here. I also had on brown slacks, which was similarly inappropriate to the venue.

Masako, despite wearing a red-and-white-polka-dot number that frankly seemed a little Minnie Mouse, did not seem out of place at all, but she was one of those people who had the quality of always being appropriately dressed. I think this is somehow related to Masako's quality of Not Giving Fucks, which is something I envy.

Or maybe the truth is that nobody at the bar really cares.

Masako ordered a round of Midnight Kisses, which was a drink so fruity that it had to be given an intimidating name, or Goths would never order it. This is what I have learned from going out with Masako: If you order something called "Satan's Souls," you will get a drink made from sherry, peach Sparkletini, and Skittles.

"Tastes like damnation," she told me.

"I never knew that damnation tastes so much like champagne and grapefruit."

"Probably because you're so virtuous," said Masako, who again, I will point out, is a Grand Magus of Sarcasm. Young teenagers who are just starting out on their voyages of snark make shrines to her in their bedrooms. I let this remark go by.

75

"So did you really think that I would like this guy?" asked Masako. "Or am I here as a pawn in your machinations?"

"You're not a pawn in my machinations," I told Masako, which was true. She was more of a knight or a bishop.

"You say that," said Masako measuredly, "but you also haven't answered my question as to whether I would like him."

This is why I expect Masako to be anchoring her own series of detective novels at some point in the future. Not much gets by her, and that was on top of a mouthful of grapefruit and champagne.

"You could like him," I said. "There's nothing objectively wrong with him. It's not like he has a hunchback or that disease that ages you prematurely like in *The Magic Kingdom*," I said.

"So no aging disease. Well, that's high praise."

"He's cute," I said, and honestly, Tyler was, in a sideways sort of way. But I was clearly in a phase where I needed to find less boys attractive and focus on the boys at hand. I did not need to be adding new men to my repertoire as though they were new colors at a Goth club.

"Cute how?" asked Masako. "Describe this alleged cuteness—" And I was thankfully spared answering this question, as Tyler Banks entered the club. He was joined by Quintrell King, whom I was not expecting.

Neither of them had changed clothes, but Tyler's asymmetrical hair certainly anchored him into the bar. Plus, he had that bright green wisp! He was born for the place. Quintrell was out of place, but that might have been true anywhere, because he looked shell-shocked.

"Dahlia," Tyler said. "I'm glad you switched from a coffee shop to a bar. I think we could use a drink."

I shoved over the Midnight Kiss to him, which Masako had thoughtfully ordered in advance. I didn't have a drink for Quintrell, who looked like he needed it the most.

"What's in this?" asked Tyler.

"Perdition," said Masako. "Also grapefruit juice."

Tyler downed his drink, which was intended for sipping. "Wow," he said. "That's a helluva mimosa."

"I'm Masako," said Masako, not bothering to wait for me to introduce her, which was probably wise. "Do you always drink alcohol that quickly?"

"No," said Tyler. "Just after dead bodies and police interviews. Actually, we should order a second one. And something for Quint."

Quintrell, despite looking rather out of it, was shrewd enough to observe the creasing on Masako's forehead and ask: "You look surprised. Did Cynthia not tell you about the dead body she found?"

"No," said Masako, who did not throw her drink back but certainly accelerated her consumption of it. "I suppose she forgot to mention it in all the excitement. Is that it, *Cynthia*?"

"Cynthia's just my nickname," I said. "It's a little in-joke. They know my name is Dahlia."

"I didn't know that," said Quintrell. Were it not for the murder, I would have been forced to assume that Quintrell was fucking with me, because he had been told my name hundreds of times in Chapter Two. Go back and read it again. Hundreds of times.

"How did you get the nickname Cynthia?" asked Masako.

"It's the name of the dead body she found," said Quintrell. This was not an appropriate thing to say, even outside a bar having a Goth night. Maybe if we'd been inside.

"I see," said Masako.

"That's not really it," I said, but then a waiter came by, and more drinks were ordered.

At this point, I was really starting to wonder about where Nathan and his proverbial Fun Train were. Not that we needed him, but he was late, and I didn't want to be many drinks in when he arrived.

"Sorry about not ordering you something in advance, Quintrell," I said. "We didn't know that you were coming."

This sounded a little more like a complaint than I had intended, and Tyler responded:

"Quintrell was saying that he didn't feel like going home, and I thought, after what happened, I should bring him along."

That's what Tyler said, but I had an idea that Quintrell was his own Fun Train. I could respect that.

"I wanted to stay and work," said Quintrell, who didn't sound like fun regardless.

"Jesus," I said.

"Maybe we should start you with a shot. What's good?" asked Tyler.

"You should try a Sugar Sugar," said Masako. As this had a fruity name to start with, I could only assume it was made with Everclear and battery acid.

"A round of Sugar Sugars," said Tyler.

And this was how I began the road to perdition.

CHAPTER NINE

It's not possible to nurse a drink when the beverage in question is a shot. You can't sip a shot like you can a vampire-themed mimosa. If you are not doing shots with the group, you are transparently not drinking,

And I like drinking. I just didn't want to do it at this particular moment. For one, it's not a great thing to do following a concussion, and for another, I had planned to sneak away after to a Presbyterian church knitters' group and ask probing questions to old women. This was a difficult thought to articulate, though, because any thought is difficult to articulate after you've had a Sugar Sugar. Also, as these people were possibly suspects in whatever tomfoolery was surrounding Cynthia's death, it seemed unwise to bring up my sleuthing plans, however vague.

And naturally, the moment I started doing something unwise, Nathan Willing, botanist boyfriend, showed up.

Nathan entered the scene as coolly as a man wearing a messenger bag possibly can. Imagine him coming down to the table in slow motion, pastel-blue corduroy, mustard-colored messenger bag swaying back and forth, and grinning and nodding at me as he sat down. Nathan was cool. His clothes, probably not, but he was.

"Sorry I'm late," he said. "The fun train got stuck in traffic. Although, from the looks of it"—Nathan looked at the collection of burgeoning drunkards around him—"it seems like you've got plenty of fun as it is."

Nathan was looking at Tyler and Masako in particular, who couldn't be sitting any closer to each other without having sex.

"The crocodile and vulture are certainly acknowledging each other's existence."

"You know, I don't think I would do very well as a biologist."

"Tell me about your case," he said.

"Shh!" I told him, but the rest of the table didn't take much notice. They hadn't even paused their drinking and conversation. I guess he only entered in slow motion for me.

"Should you be drinking?" he asked. "It wasn't that long ago that you had a concussion."

This, to be fair to Nathan, was a very fair question, and I tried not to resent him for it.

"Certainly not," I said, taking a shot.

"I see," said Nathan.

I tried to introduce Nathan to the group, but the conversation drifted away from me, as Tyler, paying no attention to Nathan, seemed to jump in to some sort of extended *Beauty and the Beast* metaphor that I did not understand. Nathan took matters into his own hands.

"Greetings, everyone! It is I, Nathan Willing!"

"Have a drink," said Masako. "They're very alcoholic and extremely ridiculous."

This is practically Nathan's favorite combination of things, and he winced his answer. "I can't. I'm playing host to a potential grad student tonight. I have to protect the good name of Washington University."

"Its name wasn't that great to begin with," I said. "Tennessee Williams hated the place."

"Tennessee Williams was a lying whore," said Nathan, as amiably as you can imagine the line, "and, as I understand it, he had very little to do with plant and microbial sciences. Tell me about your case. You know, it really doesn't look like you're working at all."

I should have been irritated at him for bringing up detective stuff again, but it was crystal clear that the rest of the table was not listening to us. Tyler had picked up a candle from the table and was doing some sort of trick with it.

"Yes," I told him. "I'm working. I'm not always holding magnifying glasses up to windowsills and shouting out *'Zut alors!'* Sometimes I converse with loose-lipped drunkards."

Although, Tyler apparently heard this bit and said: "Aye, aye!"

"What detective is going around saying *'Zut alors'*?" asked Nathan, and this was his default state, which were happy tangents.

"Hercule Poirot, maybe?" I said, and then added in a strained voice, "Stop mentioning detective work."

"He's never said that," said Nathan. "You're thinking of the chef in *The Little Mermaid*."

"No," said Tyler. "Not *The Little Mermaid*. *Beauty and the Beast*."

"René Auberjonois isn't in *Beauty and the Beast*," said Nathan.

Tyler, however, did not debate this point, just continued on with his metaphor that I did not understand.

"In the movie they all just start out as weird objects, but in the play, it happens gradually. Like, each scene you're more like a teapot. That's what it's like while I'm there," said Tyler.

"The what now?" said Nathan.

"When you're where?" I asked.

"Tyler is explaining that working at DE is transforming him into a teapot," explained Masako.

"*Zut alors!*" said Nathan.

"How did you get into it in the first place?" Masako asked.

"I was actually a music guy," said Tyler. "Which was a great gig."

At this point, here's what I was thinking in order of relative importance:

1. It seemed to me that Masako *was* exceptionally interested in Tyler. It was certainly useful to have her here to ask him probing questions. I didn't have to do anything except observe. This is next-level detecting as far as I am concerned. Outsourcing!
2. Probably Tyler meant that DE was turning him into a mantel clock, because the teapot was actually pretty cool.
3. Quintrell had gone quiet, and I was thinking I should bring him back into the conversation. This turned out to be pretty easy because he started talking.

"I didn't know you were a music guy," said Quintrell.

This appeared to make Tyler sad.

"I was the lead composer for *Gurgle*."

"I don't know what that is," said Quintrell. This appeared to make Tyler even sadder.

"And *CoffeeQuest Two*."

"Never heard of it," said Quintrell. "What's in this drink, again?"

"*CoffeeQuest Three*?"

"I haven't even heard of *CoffeeQuest One*," said Quintrell.

"I wasn't on *CoffeeQuest One*."

"How did you get from music to management?" asked Masako.

"Oh, right, well. I acquired a reputation for getting things done on time, and eventually I started getting transferred to projects that were behind schedule, which I was really good at turning around, and then at some point, I think DE decided that I was better at turning around failing projects than I was at composition. Which is sort of depressing now that I think about it."

"At least you're good at something," I said.

"Well, it was better money. But then I took this job at DE, and that's been a nightmare. It's the worst place I've ever worked. People warned me."

"Do you think the whistle-blower's letter came from someone here at Cahaba?"

"Beats me," said Tyler. "It could be. But it could be from anywhere. I mean, it's bad at Cahaba. But it's close to as bad at a dozen other places. That's just what DE does. They buy up little mom-and-pop companies and drive them into the ground and crush everyone's souls."

"Step Three: Profit," I said, which didn't get a laugh. And then someone ordered another round of shots.

This is what the conversation was like after Sugar Sugar #2:

"I miss Cynthia," said Tyler.

"You knew her for only a week," said Quintrell, who was now slumped over a bit, like a stuffed animal. A bear, or a dog with a bow on it.

"It was a good week," said Tyler. "It was a meaningful week. She had depths. Hidden depths."

"I miss her too," said Nathan, who had never met her and was drinking only water, anyway. I'm pretty sure he was putting us on.

"But if you could see them," said Masako, who was becoming a little Sugar Sugared herself, "how were they hidden?"

"Artfully," said Tyler.

"Like with tasteful shrubbery. Proverbial shrubbery," I said. I was deeply Sugar Sugared.

"I don't think she had hidden depths at all," said Quintrell. "I think she was WYSIWYG. But a good WYSIWYG."

WYSIWYG stands for "what you see is what you get," which is an old web design term. It's also fun to say when you're drunk because you pronounce it "Wizzy-Wig." Actually, it's even fun to say sober.

"Describe the WYS for me," I said. "I never met Cynthia."

"Cynthia was just our dorm mom. She was way older than everybody there," said Quintrell.

"WAY older," said Tyler, having taken up the chorus now that Quintrell had abandoned it. "Our dorm grandmom."

"But in a good way. She didn't seem to think much of gaming as an industry—"

"She used to work for an oil company—" said Tyler.

"But that was kind of helpful. She was immune to the glamour of it."

"The relative glamour of it," said Tyler.

"And she wouldn't put up with the company's bullshit. We needed someone like her there. You are a little bit like her, actually," ventured Quintrell. "Except that you're not mothering, and you don't care about anyone."

I had had enough Sugar Sugars that I took this remark very casually.

"So," I said, not worrying much about the subtext of my investigation. "Who's single?" This was a little inartful, but I wanted to know who had a significant other who might have written the whistle-blower's letter.

"I am single," said Tyler, looking at Masako. "I am very, very single."

"I am sort of single," said Quintrell. "I'm in kind of a fourth-of-a-relationship."

"Like polyamory?" asked Masako.

"No, I mean the relationship is iffy. I'm dating this electrical engineer, who's great, but I, like, only see her every two months."

"What's her name?" asked Nathan, very sweetly.

"Gloria," said Quintrell.

"Gloria?! How old is she?" asked Nathan.

"She's a young Gloria," explained Quintrell.

"Fifty is a young Gloria," said Nathan.

"You told Vanetta you were completely single," I told Quintrell.

"I rounded down," said Quintrell.

"Well, I'm very single," said Tyler.

"I got it, cowboy," said Masako. "You're single. We'll come back to that point."

Tyler was both chastened and very happy-looking, which further underscored how very desperately single he was.

"Why do you see your electrical engineer only every two months?" asked Masako.

Quintrell blinked at her.

"I work ALL THE TIME," he said. "Haven't you been listening?"

"Off and on," said Masako.

"What's Gloria like? Does she hate corporations and have a yen for vengeance?"

"She's extremely fit. Possibly too fit. Our last date was a marathon, which I did not finish. I can't tell if she's trying to humiliate me, and I'm into it, or if she just doesn't really care whether I live or die. And I'm also into that."

"If you like women who treat you badly," said Nathan, altogether too amiably, "you should love Dahlia."

Conversation after Sugar Sugar #3:

"Quintrell King? You're under arrest for murder."

Okay, that's purposefully blindsiding you. But, hey, we didn't see it coming either.

I was blindsided. Detective Tedin should have been extremely conspicuous, although it was getting to be dusk now, and through the veil of Sugar Sugars I was not in a particularly noticing mood. Plus, things were getting emotional. Tyler and Masako were inching—inching, mind you—closer together, and I was doing everything I could to keep them from running off and abandoning us, which I felt was the inevitable coast toward which we were drifting. I had also taken Quintrell's phone, not for the purposes of investigating, but to find Gloria in his phone contacts list and send her a text.

Because I was drunk, I had texted:

"I have taken Quintrell's phone. We are at a bar, and he appears to be pining for you." I was looking for the pine tree emoji, which I thought would help things, but again, I was drunk, and I couldn't find it, and so I went for the sprout, feeling that these were perfectly interchangeable.

"What are you doing?" asked Quintrell.

"I'm sending sexy plant emojis to Gloria Peachey."

"Oh MY GOD, no!" said Quintrell.

"It will work out great," I said. "Let's get Gloria here. We can meet her."

"That's not even the right Gloria. That's a friend of my mom's," said Quintrell.

"Oh."

"Not even a friend. She's like my mom's frenemey."

"Oh," I said. "Why is she in your contacts?"

And then Detective Tedin showed up and arrested Quintrell, which happened not at all like you would expect. It wasn't that dramatic. Mostly Quintrell seemed confused by the development and was principally worried about what Gloria Peachey was going to do next.

"Quintrell King? We need to take you in," said Detective Tedin. I was trying to pull myself quickly back from drunken Dahlia mode—which is a fun mode—into detective, but there were a lot of gears that needed to shift, and you know what they say about operating heavy machinery under the influence. That said, Tedin didn't seem entirely confident as he was arresting Quintrell. He certainly didn't appear to be relishing the moment, the way I did whenever I solved a case. He looked unhappy. He looked off.

The next few minutes were a blur. Quintrell was suddenly gone, I was confused, and Masako and Tyler were utterly adrift. Also, all the people in the industrial-waste-green pinstripes were looking at us like we were the weirdos.

"So," asked Nathan, who takes the arrest of strangers almost too well, "was that what you wanted to happen?"

"No!" I said. "Of course not!"

"Sorry," said Nathan. "I should rephrase that. Was that what you expected to happen?"

"Nope," I told him. "Not even a little."

Tyler and Masako responded to the situation like normal people, which is to say that they were stunned.

"What's going on?" asked Tyler. "Like, what just happened?"

"Dahlia will fix this," said Masako. "She's an undercover detective."

"How is she undercover if you're telling me about it?" asked Tyler, who really took the words right out of my mouth.

CHAPTER TEN

Improbably, it was only six thirty at this point. Through the powerful, time-bending power of Sugar Sugars, I felt that I had lived through decades with Quintrell and Nathan and Tyler and Masako, or at least several hours, but not only was the night young, it was still day.

"What do you mean she's a private detective?" asked Tyler.

"She's a private detective," said Masako. "I think she's at Cahaba to investigate something but she won't tell me what." Basically Masako was spilling the beans on absolutely everything I had hoped to keep secret. There would be no beans left after this. I would have an empty can of beans; there wouldn't even be any beany residue.

Time to make the most of the situation.

"I am not a private detective," I said. "I'm just taking classes in that direction, on the side. And I'm not there at DE to investigate anything. I'm just temping."

"Dahlia's very good, though," said Nathan. "Show Tyler where you got shot in the arm!"

"Maybe you *should* investigate," said Tyler. "Quintrell got arrested."

"I can't imagine that's right," said Masako. "He seemed very unconcerned about it. He was mostly going on about Gloria."

"There's no way he's murdered anyone," said Tyler. "It's completely impossible."

This was probably true. What possible reason would Quintrell have had for bumping Cynthia off? He had described her as being a pleasant WYSIWYG. That's just not murder talk.

Earlier, I had planned to attend Cynthia's old knitting circle incognito and learn what I could about her. That plan was jettisoned when it seemed like it would be more fun to drink. However, now that Quintrell King, Obvious Victim of Fate, had been arrested, it seemed like I should reconstitute it, except that I was:

1. Drunk.
2. In a party of three.
3. Drunk.

I put drunk twice, as it was the principal problem with this plan, and also because I got confused while making this list.

"You guys should go home," I said. "I've got some work to do."

"I think we should get a cab," said Tyler. "I'm not really up for driving."

"I have to leave," said Nathan. "As plant and microbial sciences goes, so goes my country."

"What kind of work?" asked Masako.

"Well," I said. "I suppose you might be inclined to call it detective work. And it's fine, Nathan. I got this."

"I don't know," said Nathan. "You've been attacked in some pretty unusual places. You got concussed in a family restroom."

"Family restrooms are hotbeds of sin," I said.

"We're coming with you," said Masako.

"What?" said Tyler.

"We'll help," said Masako. "We'll keep guard."

"What are you going to do?" asked Tyler. "Specifically."

I relayed my plan to the gang, who each took it differently. Tyler, although impressed that I had sussed out this bit of Cynthia's schedule, seemed to regard my sleuthing as a profound waste of time. (I guess his hidden depths speech was just drunk talk.) Masako, on the other hand, regarded my little plan as a work of Holmesian genius, and instantly confirmed they would come along. I am not sure which of these reactions surprised or concerned me more.

Nathan admitted: "It does seem like you'd be pretty safe at a knitting group at a church."

"I think so," I said.

"Vampires can't even get in," said Nathan.

"How long are you going to be playing host to your grad student?" I asked.

"Three days," groaned Nathan. But then he smiled his own apex predator smile at me. "Although I get time off for good behavior."

As a rule, I don't go to church a lot. I don't have a particularly antagonistic relationship with churches, as my friend Steven does, who thinks he will burst into flames the moment he walks through the door. I just don't get around to it very much. Church is something my parents do, and even then not very well. We Mosses are not a naturally religious people.

But I like the idea, at least in the abstract. Nothing wrong with church; it's just that most Sunday mornings I tend to be hungover.

Now, however, as I stumbled into the First Presbyterian Church of St. Charles, Steven's church/flame scenario seemed not entirely out of the question. Walking into the basement of a church while somewhat drunk, it was hard not to feel a little bit pagan. And not in a charming roguish way. In a sad drunk way.

On the plus side, I was at least walking into the basement, which was carpeted in this horrible orange stuff that really looked like it belonged in a dorm room and not the actual chapel. This was essentially a rumpus room, a natural place to be a little tipsy. The problem was that it was God's rumpus room. Sorry about that, God. The evening had taken a few hard turns.

Hopefully God would understand this particular transgression, because I really was aiming to do good, and he had god-sight, after all. The bigger issue I faced was with the knitting ladies, who did not have god-sight and were likely inclined toward Old Testament justice.

I had gotten there a hair on the early side, and there were three ladies so far. Their total ages probably summed up to be more than two hundred. The first of them, Linda, had improbably long stringy hair. She was tall and thin and wispy and seemed a bit like a flower child that had been left out in the sun too long. Next to her was Margery, the very picture of venereal brawn. She was stout and had short, wiry black-to-gray hair. In between the two of them was Joanne, who was exceptionally well dressed, with a fancy ruby brooch and gold-rimmed glasses. Joanne was obviously the ringleader of this operation.

"Are you in the right place, dear?" said Joanne.

Joanne had a faint Southern accent—but an aristocratic one. She looked like old money and new clothes, which was not a bad combination.

"I'm here for Presbyterian knitting," I said. I had bummed a breath mint off the Uber I had taken on the way over here, and I felt that this was pretty helpful for covering the smell of Sugar Sugar on my breath. I mean, nobody would hand me the keys to their car if they got close enough, but I didn't think I was wafting off an aura of drunken woman.

"Can I get you some water?" asked Joanne, who was glaring at me. She gave good glare. Professional-level glare.

"Are you, by any chance, a retired teacher?" I asked her.

Margery, of the wire hair, slapped her knee with delight.

"I'm not a retired teacher," said Joanne. "I was an organizer for the teachers union."

"Don't be pedantic," said Margery. "You taught for many years before that. Now, how could you tell?"

Some quick judgments about Joanne: She *was* pedantic, and was not about to make any admissions that were going to give me a gold star. She probably didn't realize this, but she would have fit in great on Reddit.

"It was just a lucky guess," I said. "Although, I'm a private detective. Lucky guesses are sort of my thing."

I had planned on arriving here under a cover story of some

kind, but suddenly playing a couple of my cards here seemed like a good idea. It gave me a good pretext for asking questions. And an element of danger. And it also explained why I might smell like booze and breath mints.

"I'm impressed," said Linda, also delighted.

"Where are your knitting needles?" asked Joanne, who was just as clearly not impressed.

"Do you need needles?" I asked, posing perhaps the dumbest question that had ever formed on my lips, which, if you've read my previous adventures, was saying something.

"Yes," said Joanne. "You need needles."

"I've got some extra," said Margery.

"Did you bring any yarn?" asked Joanne, who had a face that was capable of sending you to the principal's office without a word.

"I left my yarn at home," I said.

"Then maybe you should go back and get it," said Joanne.

I sat down, which was pushy, arguably, but I could use the rest. The gals were seated around a dinged-up wooden folding table, which looked to be part and parcel with the basement, although the chairs were nice.

"I suppose," I said, "to be perfectly honest, I mostly came to ask you a few questions."

"Knitting questions?" asked Linda, her voice flooding with optimism.

"Questions about a fellow knitter of yours—Cynthia Shaffer?"

"You're here to ask us about Cynthia?" asked Joanne, who was in more disbelief at that revelation than at my forgotten yarn.

"Yes, actually."

"How do we know you're really a detective?" asked Joanne.

"She could be one of those Internet identity thieves," said Linda.

"I suppose you'll just have to take it on faith," I said. "I'm a private detective. I'm not with the police. But I'm definitely not going to ask identity-thieving questions."

"What would be an identity-thieving question?" asked Margery, quite contemplatively, as though she were taking up the idea herself.

"Social security number, birthday, all those things they ask you when you want to reset a password."

"Where did you go to elementary school?" said Linda.

"Right."

"What's the name of the first boy you ever kissed?" said Linda.

"Yup," I said. "And it was Leland."

"What possible reason could you be investigating Cynthia for?" asked Joanne. "She hasn't done anything."

In the moment, I observed that the topic of Cynthia Shaffer had affected the three ladies in markedly different ways. Linda had brightened, and I got the impression she'd have been perfectly happy to talk about Cynthia ad infinitum. Joanne had darkened, which was impressive given the skeptical point she had started from, and Margery just seemed like she was along for the ride.

"I didn't say I was investigating Cynthia," I said. And suddenly I was at a crux point. For once, I hadn't hit upon it blindly; I had known this moment would come. I had even made a little mental flowchart about it on the ride over here.

I didn't love this flowchart. It wasn't my best work, as I'm sure there should be other options, nor was I fond of its moral implications. But, it was decision time. I did not want to deal

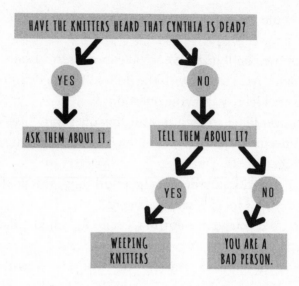

with weeping knitters, and so I decided not to bring up Cynthia's passing.

"I'm not investigating Cynthia," I said. "I'm investigating the company that she worked for."

"Worked for?" said Joanne. "She doesn't work there anymore?"

"She was fired."

Joanne looked floored by this somehow, although the other ladies didn't even miss a purl.

"I don't think it's appropriate," said Joanne, "for us to be talking about her behind her back."

"She could walk in on us," said Linda. "What would we say?"

"I would love if she walked in on us," I told Linda, in what was certainly an epic lie. "My questions aren't anything secret. I'd like to talk to her too. I haven't been able to reach her."

"Me neither," said Margery. "But I'm sure she'll be here. She's often a little late."

"I don't like this," said Joanne.

"Anyway," said Linda. "She hated that place she worked for. What was it called? Caldera?"

"Cahaba," said Joanne. "It's named for a river in Alabama."

"It sounded like a nightmare. Cynthia would tell us all about it every week. I always figured she was making some of it up, you know, for the sake of a good story, but, goodness, now there's a detective here," said Linda.

Joanne, for her part, was shooting off daggers and also knitting in a loud and dangerous-sounding manner, as though she intended her needles to be a sort of threat. But Linda was one of those people who possessed powerful rockets of optimism, such that things like threatening scowls and needles were rendered powerless.

"What kinds of things went on?" I asked. "I'd heard the work schedule was crushing."

"For everyone else," said Linda. "Cynthia didn't stay any longer than her eight hours."

"She'd stay nine hours some days," Joanne said. "And she'd bake for the kids that worked there. She just felt terrible for them. Being run ragged by some corporate monster."

"Did you know," asked Linda, "they had a special room for crying? Isn't that amazing? It was called 'The Crying Room.' People would just go in there and cry, you know, privately."

"They had to add a second room," said Margery. "There was 'Crying Room A' and 'Crying Room B.'"

"Did she mention anyone who particularly hated the company?" I asked. "Did Cynthia hate the company?"

"These are questions for Cynthia," said Joanne.

"I wouldn't say Cynthia hates the company," said Linda. "She just thought it was very badly run. The only thing I've ever heard of Cynthia hating is Kanye West."

"Who's that?" asked Margery.

"Some rap man," said Linda.

"Why is she even familiar with him?" asked Margery, and I was grateful to Kanye for taking some of the heat off me.

"Her granddaughter is a big fan," said Joanne. "She keeps making Cynthia listen to his songs so she will appreciate his genius."

"Oh," said Linda, "that sounds terrible," and I was a little with her on this point, although I did not have time to interrogate these ladies over Kanye's career.

"I thought Cynthia was single," I asked. "She has a granddaughter?"

"She has three," said Margery.

"Her husband died ages ago," said Linda. "In the eighties. Drunk driver."

"I just don't think we should be spilling Cynthia's personal details like this," said Joanne.

I asked another question to head this off.

"Did Cynthia mention anyone else from Cahaba who hated the company—maybe about not being able to spend enough time with their spouse?"

"Maybe Joanne is right, Linda," said Margery. "This is getting a little personal. We should wait for Cynthia to show up."

But there was no stopping Linda.

"Everyone there hated it," said Linda. "The boss lady, the artist, black guy, beard guy. Everyone hated it, except for the rich one—what was his name? Lawrence?"

"That's the guy."

"He was happy. What are you looking for, exactly?"

"Linda," said Joanne. "Let's not answer all of these questions."

"Did you know that the boss lady and the artist were having an affair?"

"Linda," said Joanne again.

"How about that the boss lady was pregnant—or that's what Cynthia said—"

"What?"

"Linda," said Joanne. "Let's wait for Cynthia."

"She found a used pregnancy kit in the trash. Two blue stripes."

"Linda," said Joanne, with remarkable patience at this point.

"I assume it was the artist. Oh, did anyone tell you about his violent drawings?"

"Linda," came a voice, which I initially assumed was from Joanne again, even though it had come from behind me. I suppose I had assumed that Joanne was employing ventriloquism to make her case, since normal speech wasn't working. But I turned, and found, quite to my shock, that it wasn't Joanne.

"Hey look," said Linda. "Cynthia's here! Margery was just talking about you."

I'll be damned.

CHAPTER ELEVEN

Cynthia Shaffer, dead woman, walking into the room and giving me guff was not a scenario that I had included in my flowcharts. If I had, it would look like this:

This was roughly my mental state. I stood up and was rapidly moving into a sprinting stance. Dead women don't show up while you are investigating them. I was not ready to cross the line into urban fantasy, and if I was, I wanted to do it with a shirtless guy who could turn into a hawk, not a dead old woman with a calico knitting bag.

Anyway, I was a freaked-out mess, which was a marked contrast to everyone else there, who were saying things like:

"Hi, Cynthia!" and "Sit yourself down."

"Why are you standing?" asked Linda.

The answer to this question was that I was giving even odds that Cynthia Shaffer was a dead apparition who meant me harm. But I did not want to state that aloud because it (1) sounds crazy and (2) might give the apparition some ideas. But I sat down.

"This detective," said Joanne, who was still gruff, but less so, "has been asking questions about Cahaba."

"A detective," said Cynthia. "That's exciting. Of course, a detective's not going to help that place. They should send an exorcist."

Then Cynthia laughed. It wasn't a booming, see-the-face-behind-the-skull laugh, although I may have processed it that way at the time. With the power of retrospect, it was just a plain old guffaw.

I was beginning to pull my wits about me. I've discovered enough corpses now that I just don't get as upset as I once did. I'm not a superstitious person, but when you encounter a dead woman at a knitting group—a live dead woman—it tends to pull at your rationalism.

"You're"—I was going to say alive, but I decided that this was the wrong word choice—"looking well." Which meant the same thing but was less suspicious.

And the thing was, Cynthia was looking well. She exuded

energy and relaxation. She also smelled like lemongrass and lavender. And her hair was exceptionally coifed. She did not look at all like a dead woman. She looked like she could be above an infographic in *AARP* magazine about living your best life. She seemed exceptionally alive. "Jonathan Strange back from the dead" alive. She looked like she could go jogging.

"Why thanks," said Cynthia. "I knew I liked you when I walked in."

"What's that smell?" said Margery.

"Some fancy shampoo," said Cynthia. "After they fired me, I took a spa day."

"Well, that seems decadent," said Joanne.

"I had a coupon," said Cynthia. "Valerie got it for me for my birthday."

"Was it the place out on Hamilton?" asked Linda. "That place is the best."

"No," said Cynthia. "I don't know that one. What's it called?"

"Something about Wax. WaxWorks? House of Wax?"

"*House of Wax* is a horror movie," said Cynthia.

"Excuse me," I said. "I need to run to the bathroom."

"Don't you have questions for Cynthia?" asked Linda.

I had plenty of questions for Cynthia. Some of which now included: How are you alive? Can you tell me what the afterlife is like? But I did not venture into these philosophical waters with the knitters. I found the women's bathroom and I hid there.

As I calmed down, I put together some salient points. I had not closely studied the corpse on the ground. Corpse woman was facedown, and I only got her in profile. While this person certainly looked like Cynthia Shaffer—the same age, the same body type—maybe this was my mind playing tricks on me. Surely they were different people. They had to be.

I decided to call Detective Anson Shuler, which I felt was entirely reasonable given the circumstances.

"Dahlia?" he said. "Are we still on for roller-skating tomorrow evening?"

I had unwisely agreed to—nay, suggested this plan—a few days ago after being hit on the head. But there was no backing out of it now.

"I found a body," I said.

"What?" said Shuler. "Another dead body? What are you, Harper Connelly?"

"No," I said. "This is a living person. She's just walking around, talking about spa days."

"You found a living person," said Shuler.

"Talking about spa days," I added. "Like it's no big deal."

"Are spa days a big deal?" asked Shuler. "I've never been to one. I was reading this article in the *New York Times* about how men are starting to use them, but I'd feel weird about it. Why, did you want to go?"

Taking a spa day with Shuler would be more fun than roller-skating, I imagined, but this was not the point.

"She is supposed to be dead," I said. "I found a woman who is supposed to be dead."

"What do you mean?"

"She is supposed to be dead."

"And she's—"

"Talking about her spa day."

"Hmm," said Shuler. It was a noncommittal hmm. It was a hmm that possibly meant: I think Dahlia is out of her mind. And so I updated Shuler on my adventure thus far, carefully leaving out that I entered into this shitshow because I was doing work for Emily Swenson. When I finished, Shuler asked me where I was, and then told me that he would be there in a half hour.

My next task was to leave the restroom and interrogate the obviously not-dead dead woman. I had come to my senses now and regarded Cynthia Shaffer as I would any living woman who had somehow elaborately faked her death. Which is to say: wtf. But I wasn't worried about her killing me with her wraith touch, so that was good.

Mostly because I wanted to forestall this interview, I called Emily, who also needed some updating.

"Dahlia," said Emily. "Two phone calls in one day. Any progress on that stolen code?"

"No," I said. "None whatsoever. But I thought I'd keep you posted on the lay of the land."

"I like knowing the lay of the land," said Emily.

"Quintrell King, a programmer for Cahaba, was arrested about an hour ago for Cynthia Shaffer's murder."

"Yes," said Emily. "I'd heard that. Why, do you know anything about it?"

"I know that he didn't do it," I said.

"How do you know that?" asked Emily.

"Because Cynthia Shaffer is in the next room, talking about shampoo."

Emily, for once, was quiet.

"Cynthia Shaffer is alive?"

"Not only is she alive," I said, "she's knitting."

"And that's the lay of the land," said Emily.

"Yes," I told her. "The lay of the land is a Boschian hellscape."

"Thanks for letting me know," said Emily. "But don't get tangled up in this. Just focus on the whistle-blower letter and the code. We need that code."

I did have to admire Emily's single-mindedness. A woman getting murdered, a man getting arrested, and the murdered woman apparently returning from the underworld to cash in a coupon at the House of Wax was not enough to bend her from her task. I did not possess this level of focus, but I told her I'd try.

I then got off the phone and returned to the room.

Even coming to my senses, as I now was, I found that it wasn't any easier being in the room a second time. The banality of the knitters' discussions mixed with the improbable element of a dead woman sitting around, talking about missed purls, proved to be a bizarre and distracting cocktail. What was happening?

"It's very strange," said Joanne, "that you came here on this big cloud of puffery about needing to ask questions to Cynthia, and then when she arrives, you disappear."

Had I arrived on a cloud of puffery? I felt cloudy, but I was pretty sure I had kept the puffery to a minimum.

"I had some intestinal experiences in the bathroom, Joanne. It's not like I ran for the border."

Joanne looked exceptionally irked by my tart response, but it buoyed Linda, who slid over some yarn to me. Still no needles, but there was a pile of yarn. I had no idea what to do with it. Literally everything I know about knitting is from *Yoshi's Woolly*

World, a game in which a dinosaur eats yarn and spits out sweaters. It was not a great point of reference.

"It's fine," said Cynthia. "It's not like I'm leaving anytime soon."

I picked up the yarn, which was tangled, and tried to fix it, both because this looked like a productive thing to do and because it was a metaphor. As I wound up the yarn, I put together what I knew.

1. I had found someone in that storeroom.

Right? Somebody was dead. I didn't hallucinate it.

2. The dead person was not Cynthia.

Because she was here, obviously.

3. The dead person was Cynthia shaped.

Everyone thought it was Cynthia. Yeah, I didn't really roll over the corpse and take photos of her, but the impression was that this was Cynthia Shaffer. So why was there a dead person shaped like the secretary in the storeroom?

"So anyway," said Cynthia. "Did you see *CSI* last Thursday? It was a good one."

"No," said Joanne, "we all hate that show. You're the only person here who likes to discuss it."

"I like the show," said Margery.

And they carried on, apparently untroubled by my rattled yarn skeining. The fact that they were so untroubled by my presence—Joanne was irritated, but no more—led me to another point.

4. Cynthia Shaffer had no idea about the Cynthia Shaffer-shaped dead woman, or else she wouldn't be so blasé.

"So," I said. "Do you have time to answer a few questions about Cahaba?"

"Oh look," said Margery, "she's come back to us."

"Are you on drugs?" asked Linda. "I'm asking without judgment. It's just—you were miles away for a moment there."

"It's just been a long day," I said.

"You're really a detective?" asked Cynthia.

"I'm really more of a junior detective," I said, regretting my choice of words, because it made me sound like I should be operating out of a wooden tree house. "I'm still taking coursework. I guess you could call me sort of a working intern. Although I'm getting paid."

While this was arguably oversharing, I had found that the more honest I was about being legit but inexperienced, the more people tended to open up to me.

"Why are you looking into Cahaba?" asked Cynthia.

"That's an interesting question itself," I told her. "But my client really wouldn't want me to say."

"What do you want to know from me?" asked Cynthia.

"Do you want to go somewhere private?" I asked.

"No, I want to knit," said Cynthia. "These gals know everything about me anyway."

I found myself thinking of Sydelle Pulaski, a character in *The Westing Game* who, in working out the mystery of that book, incorrectly thinks the solution involves someone having a twin. As such, she spends much of the book trying to work twins into conversation, such as the Bobbsey Twins or the Minnesota Twins or Twin Jets. I thought of her then, because I suddenly identified with Sydelle's plight. I certainly wanted to know if, by any chance, Cynthia had an identical twin, but this was a weird question to come out and pose. At least initially, anyway.

I started with:

"Why did Vanetta Jones fire you?"

"It was more of a mutual parting," said Cynthia.

Anytime anyone tells you that it was a "mutual parting," you should be skeptical. The term gets thrown around very loosely. ("I didn't burn down my house; we mutually parted.") But I decided not to grill Cynthia on this probably precarious point. Flattery would get me farther.

"That's surprising," I said. "From what I hear of it, everyone around there loved you to pieces."

"Oh, not everyone," said Cynthia.

"Quintrell King adores you, Gary spoke well of you, Tyler thought you were interesting and complicated."

"Well, well, well," said Margery, dispelling the fleeting dream that this interview wasn't going to be interrupted, "interesting *and* complicated."

"I'm with you on complicated," said Linda jovially, "but interesting?"

"That doesn't sound like something Tyler would say. And he barely knows me."

"That's probably why he thought you were interesting," said Linda.

"Hush, you. No, Vanetta fired me because I was trying to mother her, and she didn't want a mother. I"—Cynthia was quiet for a moment—"I crossed a line with her that I shouldn't have crossed. That place was so screwed up, you start to treat the people there like broken dolls—you just want to fix everyone—and I shouldn't have tried to do that with her."

"Is this about the pregnancy test?" I asked.

"What?" said Cynthia, quite shocked. "How did you hear about that?"

"I told her," said Linda.

"What?"

"I tried to stop her," said Joanne.

"I like having dirt," said Linda. "Sue me."

"We both tried to stop her," said Margery.

"It's fine," said Linda.

Cynthia looked rattled for a moment, but then quickly composed herself. "You're right, it's probably fine. I just—well—yes, Vanetta was pregnant, is pregnant, I suppose, and I involved myself a little more than I should have."

"Did Vanetta tell you this?" I asked. "After you found the pregnancy test in her trash?"

"What?" said Cynthia. "I didn't go through her trash. Who told you that?"

"I told her that," said Linda.

"That's not what happened!"

"Maybe not," said Linda. "But my version of the story is more colorful."

"So what really happened?" I asked.

"Vanetta took the pregnancy test there at work—"

"Why would you take a pregnancy test at work?" asked Joanne.

"Well, this is Cahaba. No one goes home. They all just live there, and Vanetta especially."

"Right," said Margery.

"Yes, and so she apparently took the test in the bathroom, and when she came out she started crying. Now, I wasn't born yesterday, and when a woman goes into the bathroom and then comes out crying, I can put two and two together."

"I cry in the bathroom all the time," said Linda.

"And you are an exceptional person," said Cynthia. "I had just gotten that vibe from her before. I could tell that she was worried about something, anyway—personal, because I had learned how Vanetta compartmentalizes her emotions."

"Which is how?"

"Carefully."

"And this wasn't that?"

"No," said Cynthia. "She was mopey and strange. I asked her if she was pregnant, and then she ran into her office, crying harder."

"That's very impertinent of you," said Joanne disapprovingly.

"Yes, I know," said Cynthia. "I'm not proud. So then, of course, I couldn't leave well enough alone, so at lunch I went out and got her a cake, and then I came and asked her all about it."

"The father is Archie?" I asked.

"I believe so."

"And she fired you because you found this out?"

"She fired me because I told Archie about it."

"Oh, Cynthia," said Joanne, her voice dripping with disappointment.

"I know," said Cynthia. "Don't give me that look. You see why I needed this spa day."

"You didn't tell us this part," said Linda.

"That's because it makes me look bad," Cynthia said.

"Vanetta didn't want to tell Archie about it until the project was done."

"Wait, is she keeping the baby?" asked Margery.

"She hadn't gotten to that. She was going to wait another month and see if it 'sticks,' and then maybe tell Archie about it. But that didn't sit right with me."

"Archie's the roguish one, right?" asked Linda.

"I think Archie would be a splendid boyfriend, and an excellent father," said Cynthia, quite approvingly. But then a cloud of doubt formed on her face. "Although I'm not sure that he'd work out as a husband."

"Let's set up him up with Dorothy's daughter," said Linda, then added, to me, "We hate Dorothy."

Everyone else ignored this remark, although Joanne's knitting needles were doing Wolverine SNIKTs.

"Anyway," said Cynthia. "I told him, and it was sort of awful, and then he told her, and then Vanetta brought me into her office and told me that I should probably be fired for this. And I agreed with her, and so I quit. I made a huge mess of things. I don't even think they're talking to each other now."

"Oh, they're talking," I said, remembering Archie shirtless in her office.

"Are they? That's good," said Cynthia.

"All this meddling reminds me of the movie *The Parent Trap*. Wasn't that a great flick? Hey, speaking of *The Parent Trap*, does anyone have a twin?"

CHAPTER TWELVE

I did not get an answer to my twin question because Masako and Tyler came down the stairwell. The first question, if the least salient at this point, was: Had I seemed as drunk as these two? Because they looked drunk. Masako, in fairness, might have passed for sober were it not for the presence of Tyler, who scaled the basement stairwell with the grace and focus of a gelatinous ooze. That is to say, he was not using the steps as such, but was making more of a full body experience out of them with the handrails and walls.

Drunk.

"Masako," I said. "Why are you here? I thought you said you were going to stay outside."

"There are police sirens outside," said Masako.

"We thought we would take sanctuary in here," said Tyler, drunk, who then slowly appeared to notice Cynthia grinning at him.

"It's a ghost!" said Tyler.

"It's Tyler," said Cynthia. "I heard you thought I was complicated and interesting."

"Is this the dead woman?" asked Masako, who truly took everything in stride.

"No," I said.

"It's the dead woman," said Tyler. "This woman is dead."

"Fascinating," said Masako.

"What's this about a dead woman?" asked Margery.

I felt, in that moment, as though I had gone down an unwise path that I was now powerless to leave. It was like being on a roller coaster as you come close to cresting the hill. You were moving slowly, it was quiet but for the *clunk-a-clunk-a* of gears slowly moving you forward—but you could tell, quite perfectly, that in about three seconds you were going to be in free fall. And there was nothing to be done about it.

"Cynthia is dead," said Tyler. "You're dead! This woman is dead!"

"I'm not dead," said Cynthia. "What an idea. Did Vanetta tell everyone I was dead?"

"It's a ghost!" said Tyler. "Ghost Cynthia!"

"I don't think it's a ghost," said Masako. To the knitters, she asked: "What are you guys making?"

"I'm making gloves," said Linda. "Although something has gone very wrong with them."

"I can't believe Vanetta told you I was dead," said Cynthia. "What a coward. You know, she fired me!"

So much for mutual parting.

"You're dead," said Tyler.

"Have you been drinking?" asked Joanne.

"Yes!" said Tyler. "We were mourning Cynthia!"

"Oh, that's very sweet," said Cynthia. "Wrong, but sweet."

"It's terribly irresponsible," said Joanne. "I hope you didn't drive here."

"But I'm quite alive, as you can see," said Cynthia.

I don't know if Masako actually delights in conveying

information I wish to keep secret, but she can give that impression. She said, very unhelpfully, "Dahlia found your corpse this morning."

"It's been an incredibly stressful day," said Tyler. "I can drink if I want. I worked eight hours today with police just lingering outside my office. Also we took an Uber."

"It wasn't my corpse," said Cynthia. "Must have been someone else's."

"I don't mean to change the subject," said Linda, "but what is an Uber? I hear people talk about them, but I can't figure it out. Is it another rap thing?"

"Yes," said Margery, winking at me so I didn't give away the game. "Uber is a rapper. There's two of them, Uber and Ice Uber. And they don't get along."

"They found a corpse, and they didn't send you home early," asked Joanne, mostly rhetorically. "That's monstrous."

"Or maybe there never was a corpse. I'm not dead," said Cynthia. "I'm not a ghost. Look," she said, holding up a hideous green-and-orange knitted sweater. "Could a ghost make this?"

The sweater stopped Tyler from talking, although whether it was due to its unfortunate styling or to its irrefutable proof that Cynthia walked the earth with us was not clear. No one spoke for a moment, and Masako decided to sit down.

"Dahlia found your corpse in our supply closet," said Tyler. "The police came and took it away. Did you come back to life?"

"How much have you had to drink?" asked Cynthia amiably.

"Why were you in the supply closet at Cahaba?" asked Joanne.

And then the police came downstairs.

Detective Tedin was remarkably calm about the incongruous elements presented before him in this church basement, which included:

1. a dead woman, knitting
2. a woman who claimed to not be a detective, clearly detectiving with said dead woman
3. a suspect, drunk
4. a non-suspect, also drunk
5. scowling knitters, sober
6. Linda, who, as far as I could tell, was giving Tedin what I would describe as "hubba hubba" eyes.

When you put it together, it seems like a lot, and that's not even considering Cynthia's sweater. But Detective Tedin seemed unsurprised by these elements, as though they were things that he encountered regularly. Why wouldn't he? This was a man with three rings on his finger and multiple wives.

"Detective Tedin," I said. "I didn't know you knitted."

"Who is this strapping gentleman?" asked Linda.

"Dahlia Moss," said Tedin. "What a remarkable coincidence to find you here."

"You'll never guess who I ran into," I said. "Guess who this is?" This question was meant to be posed to Detective Tedin, and the answer was meant to be Cynthia Shaffer. However, it was intercepted.

"Is this the sex cop?" asked Tyler, in what I suppose he

imagined was a whisper but was quite audible to everyone. "Masako said that you were seeing a sex cop on the side. But why is he so old?"

"This is not the sex cop," I said. "There is no sex cop. There never was a sex cop."

"He looks very youthful to me," said Linda. "What can we do for you?"

I was grateful for Linda in that moment, who was definitely throwing Tedin off his game.

"Are you investigating this case?" asked Tedin.

"Who, me?"

"How did you find yourself here?" asked Tedin.

This was a difficult question to answer honestly without also implicating myself, but I tried it.

"Well, I saw a notice for a knitting group at Cynthia's desk while I was at work this morning, and I've always wanted to learn to knit. I've been saying that for ages, haven't I, Masako?"

I could tell from Masako's face that she planned on saying something like: "Dahlia hates knitting and came here for illegal purposes," but Tyler, whom I like more each successive chapter, stepped in and said:

"She was just saying that. We were talking this morning about how trendy knitting was getting these days."

"Right!" I said. "And he should know, because he lived in Austin!"

Tedin was only barely listening to us. "Cynthia Shaffer?"

Cynthia seemed less charmed by the introduction of police into the situation. She seemed downright thorny about it.

"Why is it that you're here?" she asked.

"Cynthia has done nothing wrong," said Joanne, touching Cynthia's hand in a rather protective way. I had the feeling that

Joanne would have gone to blows for any of her fellow knitters. Even Linda.

"I got a phone call saying that you were here," said Tedin.

Damn Anson Shuler! He sold me out.

"Ms. Shaffer," said Tedin gently. "Can you come downtown with me?"

"What's this about?"

"I'm afraid I'm going to need you to identify a body. I'm afraid something has happened to your sister."

A lot of yarn was spilled at that point, but I'm going to spare you the bitter aftermath. Cynthia, for her part, was somber, if strangely unsurprised. Joanne was apoplectic; Margery was concerned; Linda was entertained. And I didn't know what to make of Tyler and Masako, whose faces were completely unreadable. Mostly they looked tired and drunk.

Tedin did not lay into me any further, but perhaps it was simply that he was occupied and he was saving further interrogation for later. He took Cynthia away in his cop car. Masako and Tyler and I piled into another Uber and headed home.

When I got back to our apartment, my roommate, Charice, and her fiancé, Daniel, were building houses out of cards. Literal card houses. I did not make any inquiries into this action, nor did I ask why they were so improbably and nicely dressed. Charice was wearing a little black dress with her hair slicked back, and Daniel was in a full suit and tie. But not every mystery is worth solving, and so I just ignored the fancy dress, ignored the cards, and collapsed on the sofa.

"Careful, Dahlia," said Charice. "We've been building now for almost ten minutes."

I had been reasonably careful, I thought, although perhaps this is the kind of sentence that a drunk person is inclined to believe. It also struck me that ten minutes was not a lot of work to lose, but I kept these thoughts to myself.

"How was your first day of work?" Daniel asked.

"Oh, that's right," said Charice. "You're a temp and an industrial spy."

"Let's see. I found a dead body," I told her.

"Classic Dahlia," she said.

"It didn't seem like a murder, initially, just an old dead person."

"Less classic, more sad," observed Charice.

"On the plus side, it turned into a half day, because everyone was sent home early on account of the corpse."

"If it was a half day, why are you only coming home now?"

"I went out drinking with some coworkers, and while we were out, one of my drinking buddies got arrested for murder."

"That sounds about right," said Charice.

"Then I went to a knitting circle."

"Are you just making things up?" asked Daniel.

"The dead woman had an appointment for knitting in her desk calendar, and so I thought I would show up."

"Did you learn anything?"

"Not about knitting, but I did run into the murdered woman there."

"I want this story to end," said Daniel.

"That's what I said. So, yes, I called Anson Shuler, and then the police showed up and took away the not-dead dead lady. Then I came here. How was your evening?"

"I got a job recording an audiobook," said Daniel. This was said in a tone that meant we were done discussing my murder problems and were now moving on to the far more salient and exciting discussion of audiobook narration.

"Is that good?" I asked.

"Yes," said Daniel. "It's very good."

"He's reading a book called *The Tomes of Magic*."

"Epic fantasy?" I asked.

"Not in the slightest," said Daniel. "It's a history of stage magicians."

Hence the cards, I assumed. And the clothes—they were out celebrating. "Congratulations," I said. Daniel then reached into my ear and pulled out a quarter.

"Look what we have here," he said, quite pleased with himself.

"Please don't do that," I said.

He did it again and pulled out a half-dollar.

"Maybe this is a clue," he said.

"Daniel, don't pull any more coins out of my ear," I told him.

"What's that?" he said. "I can't hear you," he added, reaching into his own ear. "My hearing is a bit stopped up because of this SOUTH AFRICAN KRUGERAND!"

"He's pretty good, right?" said Charice.

He was. Despite the coin-in-the-ear shtick being one of the lamest tricks in the world, I couldn't precisely work out how he was doing it. Although, everything is magic when you're drunk. How did I get up the stairs? Where are my pants? When did the carpet in front of the toilet become so luxurious?

"You're a regular Houdini," I told him. "Although I don't

think that this prestidigitation will show up especially well on audio."

"This?" said Daniel. "This is just fun. I suppose I could claim it was for the sense memory, but who are we kidding? So were you telling the truth about all the stuff in your evening?"

"I'm telling you everything I know to be the truth," I said. "Which I have found, in my limited experience as a detective, is an important and often relevant distinction."

"So maybe this woman really is dead," said Daniel.

"Maybe so. So did you two get married today?" I asked.

"We decided not to rush into things," said Daniel.

"Oh good," I said.

"We're doing it the day after tomorrow," said Charice.

CHAPTER THIRTEEN

The next morning I was back at Cahaba Apps. I had once again stopped by the bakery on my way in and came prepared with delectables, which I felt were a necessary implement against reality. Gone was the naive ingenue of yesterday, who imagined that an office would not be filled with insane, possibly sleeping people and disguised corpses. This time I was prepared for insanity; I had brought sprinkles.

And yet, even with all of that, I managed to be weirded out, first thing, right as I walked in. I headed to the coffee machine in the back offices, having also brought coffee grounds, because I was in no mood for candy-cane-flavored nonsense. Instead I opted for hot buttered rum. As a coffee flavor—not with actual rum, although now that you mention it, it's not a bad idea. As I made my way back there, Quintrell King darted upward from his desk as though he had been hit with electroshock.

"I'm awake!" he said.

Frankly, it scared the bejesus out of me, and I dropped my bag of coffee, which was thankfully not opened.

"What the hell are you doing here?" I asked.

That morning I had been mentally going over ways to break it to Vanetta that Quintrell had been arrested for murder. She had thrown a chair the day before, and so I had been contemplating the softest way to deliver this news. Perhaps a poem?

"I have arrested / your employee / that was in his cubicle / and that you probably needed / for programming / or something like that. Forgive me / he was delicious / and sweet / and yet guilty."

But these plans were thrown right out the door. I had composed a poem for nothing.

"Why are you here?"

"I thought I would work," said Quintrell, suddenly conscious of the fact that he hadn't been working at all but sleeping. "I mean, I started out working, but I nodded off for a moment."

"How did you get out of jail?" I asked, although in retrospect I could have focused more on the "why are you here?" bit, because what kind of employee gets out of jail and then just goes in to work? I mean, that's dedication. If you're arrested for murder, you're entitled to a mental health day, regardless of the circumstances.

"I made bail," said Quintrell. "Why do you look so surprised?"

"I just," I started. "I don't know why. I suppose I thought you'd stay in the slammer a little longer. I imagined that jail would be a little less Monopoly-like."

"My parents are both lawyers," said Quintrell, with a combination of pride and embarrassment, which is the proper reaction to having lawyers for parents. "And they're pretty good at what they do. I don't think the police knew who my parents were when they arrested me. Probably they wouldn't have."

This made it seem like Quintrell's parents were important people, although I was not familiar enough with the world of St. Louis criminal law to have any perspective on this point. A question for Emily later.

"Also," said Quintrell, not waiting for me to work through the maze of my thoughts regarding his parents, "the woman I was arrested for murdering is apparently not dead. This is the kind of detail that really takes the wind out of a murder case."

"Yes," I said. "I met with Cynthia last night. I went to her knitting group, and she was there."

"Wait, after we were drinking?"

"It's a long story," I told him. "So do the police think that you killed her—what, twin? Have we established that?"

"No twin. It's just her sister," said Quintrell, "and who knows what the police think? They didn't seem to want to overshare with me as I was checking out."

There was a certain blasé delivery to this statement that ran fundamentally counter to my experiences with Quintrell thus far. He was almost calm, which was odd given that he had been a bundle of nervous energy this time yesterday.

I asked him about it.

"Yeah," he said. "I was nervous for a while, but then, honestly, it just hit me that it was nicer in jail than in my real life. I mean, there was a bed, Dahlia, and I just lay on it, and I fell so asleep. I think it was probably the most comfortable bed in the world."

"Probably it wasn't," I ventured.

"Probably not," said Quintrell. "I felt bad about falling asleep. There's that line in *The Usual Suspects* about how you can recognize a guilty man in prison because he sleeps like a baby?"

"Don't know that one," I said.

"Really?" said Quintrell, who seemed surprised by this. "Well, I hope the police don't know it either, because I slept like I was in a coma. It wasn't even really a bed. Just a bed-shaped thing. But when you've been chained to your workstation for a week, bed-shaped goes a long way. And then when I slept,

I don't know, I started feeling really good again. Feeling like myself. They woke me up and told me I was free to go, and my first thought was: What's the rush? I could sleep a little longer."

Quintrell still seemed a little delirious, now that I was listening to him, given his propensity to string sentences and thoughts together, but he was a genial delirious now, not manic. The rest had changed him.

"Wait, so you're on bail," I asked, "or is it that they dropped the charge?"

"Bail, right now," said Quintrell. "I don't know, I don't think they had much of a case when they thought it was Cynthia. It seemed to me that the plan was arrest the black guy and see what they could make happen."

"You seem to be taking that awfully well," I said.

"It's amazing what six hours of rest will do," said Quintrell. "Probably I will be upset or angry later. But I'm not at that stage yet. Plus: you know, freedom and sleep? What more do you want?"

I could think of many more things I would want, such as:

- not being arrested for murder
- job security
- not returning to work immediately after being released from jail

But what do I know?

"You hear back from Gloria?" I asked, feeling guilty about that pine emoji text.

"She came to the police station. She's a lawyer too. Criminal," said Quintrell. "That's fremeny Gloria, not electrical engineer Gloria. She's actually weirdly excited about the development.

Me getting arrested, not your weird text. She didn't ask me about that. I guess it got overshadowed."

"That must have been quite a party," I said.

"And all it took was a murder charge," said Quintrell.

"You seem to know a lot of lawyers," I observed.

"They run in packs, and it was lucky to have Gloria around. My parents are mostly torts."

"Why didn't you become a lawyer?" I asked.

"If you met my parents, you'd understand."

The next person to come in was Vanetta Jones, who also appeared to be benefiting from a night away from the office. It struck me, suddenly, that my impressions of everyone except perhaps Lawrence, were probably pretty jaundiced. I would hate for someone to meet me after a few weeks of sleep deprivation and try to form opinions based upon that. Sleep-deprived Dahlia does not resemble actual Dahlia very much. I'm not wacky at all—I just sort of become depressed and self-loathing, which accounts for much of my college experience, now that I think about it.

Rested Vanetta looked very different. For one, she was dressed very casually, in a gold "Afrofuturist Affair" T-shirt, white jeans, and blazer. Also, no makeup. A low-key Vanetta, although it suited her. It also made me wonder if nice clothes and makeup were her armor. Now that she was rested, she didn't need the crutch.

"Dahlia," she said, seeing me. "I owe you some baked goods."

She sounded nice, and friendly, and seemed unlikely to throw a chair in any immediate circumstances. She was also holding a cake pan.

"What did you bring?" I asked.

Vanetta placed the cake pan on my desk and opened it to reveal this yellowish cheesecake-y thing that was molded into a Bundt shape. "Orange Bavarian cream," said Vanetta. "I know what you're thinking. You're thinking it's cheesecake."

I was actually thinking: Put it in me, but Vanetta's guess was reasonable. In terms of cake, I'm perfectly willing to eat first and ask questions later.

"Did you bake this?" I asked.

Vanetta made a horse noise with her mouth, which I took to mean: "To hell with that."

It clearly wasn't store-bought, or if it had been, Vanetta had taken great pains to disguise it. However, this is me focusing on the wrong mystery. It's a weakness of mine—focusing on whatever puzzle is in front of me as opposed to my long-term goal. Sometimes it even works out in my favor. But today I was keeping my eyes on the prize.

"I'll be sure to share this with everyone as they come in," I said.

"No, we'll have it at the staff meeting," Vanetta said. "Let everyone know."

"Are you abreast of the news of the evening?"

"Are you?" asked Vanetta, delivering the line in such a way as to suggest that she had a secret.

"Let's compare notes, then. Let's see, Quintrell got arrested for Cynthia's murder," I said.

"They think it's Quintrell?" said Vanetta. "Quintrell King?"

"I was there when they cuffed him," I said.

Vanetta couldn't believe it. "Quintrell-cries-in-the-bathroom-King? That's the guy they think killed Cynthia."

Poor Vanetta, she was behind. She had probably spent her evening sleeping somewhere, and disguising store-bought cake.

"Oh yes," I said. "Well, no. I mean, yes to Quintrell, no to Cynthia. Apparently the body is not Cynthia."

"That's monstrous. We have to do something to help Quintrell!" said Vanetta.

Vanetta didn't seem to entertain the idea that Quintrell was guilty for even a millisecond. Good for her. "We don't need to do that; he's made bail."

"Is he okay?"

"I think so. You can talk to him yourself. He's just over there."

We both looked over at Quintrell's cubicle, and he waved at us.

"What's this about me crying in the bathroom?" he asked.

"On second thought," considered Vanetta. "Perhaps I will have some of that cake now."

"I'm sorry, I could have broken it to you more gently. I guess I thought you were in the know. What's your news?"

"We don't have a deadline anymore," said Vanetta.

"What do you mean?" I asked.

"No deadline. DE says to take the time we need."

"Wow," I said. No wonder she looked rested. "Behold the power of whistle-blowing." This invited a number of questions, all of which I had the good grace to not ask aloud. *Was* DE being benevolent all of a sudden because of the whistle-blowing? Or was it because of the murder? Or, heck, was this all to do with Lawrence's efforts to tie the game to a TV pilot and a cereal? I'd ask about it later.

"Yes," said Vanetta.

"It's nice to be surprised by something that's not awful," said Quintrell. "It will be great to have a chance to breathe."

"Breathing is good," I said.

"Let everyone know what's up when they come in. I'll be in my office. Meeting at ten."

I spent the next few minutes answering emails and phone calls about Cynthia's death, although I should say Joyce's death, as Joyce was the name of the dead woman in question. There was a little journalistic interest in the story, which I fended off by saying that we could not comment at this time.

I also got an email from Cynthia herself, which was weird in this context.

```
Dahlia:
I'd like to come by today to pick up my things. Is
there a time of day that would be the least disrup-
tive? I really don't want to see Vanetta or Archie,
and I don't want people making a scene over me.
    Cynthia
```

I responded by letting her know about the staff meeting, which was probably her best bet, and by telling her that I was willing to stay late, although I couldn't guarantee she'd miss the rest of the staff this way. She'd have to come in very, very late if she wanted to do that. Then, it struck me, suddenly, that perhaps this is how her sister had gotten in. I didn't get much further down that line of thought when I looked up to see that Gary had come in.

Of all the Cahaba-ers, it seemed to me that Gary was the least transformed by sleep. He looked as rough as ever.

"Didn't get quality shut-eye, Gary?" I asked.

"No," said Gary. He sounded not exactly angry, but certainly very peeved.

"Too upset about the murder to sleep?" I asked.

"Up all night with an eight-month-old," said Gary.

"You have an eight-month-old?" I asked.

"Apparently," said Gary. "I really should get home more.

I'm like Odysseus. Although, since I had been sleeping here so much, my wife decided that I should be 'on-duty' last night. Which apparently means not sleeping. Babies are tiny harbingers of disease and evil."

"At least you're acclimated to it. You want a pastry?" I was happy that I had a good target for my pastries, since my baked goods had been shown up by Vanetta's fancier dessert.

"Yes," said Gary, taking a strawberry twist out of the bag. "God bless you."

"Staff meeting at ten!"

Tyler and Lawrence entered together, which I thought was a bit curious, although it could have been that they just happened upon the stairs at the same time.

"Good morning, Cynthia," said Lawrence, who must have been putting me on at this point.

"Did you get my voice mail yesterday?" I asked, because I really didn't want to go over the murder situation a third time.

"I did," said Lawrence. "Thanks for the heads-up. Yes, I had a very productive conversation with the police yesterday afternoon. And, since I was the ranking person around here, they had me identify her body."

"I see," I said.

"They think she was poisoned, you know."

"No one would poison Cynthia," said Tyler. "Everyone loves Cynthia."

"Hidden depths," I said.

"Oh, I don't know," said Lawrence. "Quintrell hated her, didn't he? He was always going on about how pushy she was."

"Quintrell said that?" I asked.

"Yes, didn't he? Or maybe it was Jason, now that I think about it. I always confuse those two. Which one did we fire?"

"I've never met Jason," I said.

"Yes, I guess I mean Jason. Oh well, I told the police Quintrell. *Que será, será.*"

"How do you confuse those people? One of them is black and thin, and the other is white and large," I said. I felt a bit like I was arguing with Charice, which was never a good idea. Lawrence, like my roommate, had a performative quality to him. I couldn't quite tell when he was being genuine and when he was putting me on, and I suspected that he didn't always quite know the difference himself.

"Well, you see, Cynthia," said Lawrence loftily, "unlike you, I don't see color. I just see people."

Incidentally: "I don't see color, I just see people" is a line that is exclusively spoken by rich white guys. I believe it's the motto of at least three secret societies at Harvard. In Latin.

"Right," I told him.

"You ratted out Quintrell?" said Tyler, shocked.

"I didn't rat him out," said Lawrence. "I'm just providing the police with valuable information."

"Which was wrong," said Tyler.

"Well, possibly," said Lawrence.

"He got arrested because of you," said Tyler.

"That seems like a stretch. If he were arrested, I'm sure the police had lots of reasons."

Lawrence was a jackass, but this was a good point. Even allowing for a little racism within the St. Louis police department, which, if you follow current events, has not proved itself to be a bastion of nondiscrimination, surely the police had more evidence pointing them to Quintrell than him allegedly calling her "pushy."

"You smug self-righteous bastard," said Tyler. "This is someone's life you're playing with."

To judge from Lawrence's face, he liked being called a bastard, but the bit about playing with someone's life was a little too on the nose for him, and he darkened.

"Careful, Tyler," said Lawrence. "You should stay in my good graces."

"Quintrell is out on bail," I told Lawrence. "I don't think the case is going anywhere."

"See," said Lawrence, summoning his grinning Buddha. "It's all working out. I didn't sell anyone down the river."

"It's very callous of you," said Tyler.

"That's my brand," said Lawrence.

"How did Quintrell get out so quickly?" asked Tyler, and it pleased me to see that other people also thought this strange.

"I guess Cynthia being alive sort of deep-sixed the case."

"Cynthia's alive?" spat Lawrence. "But she was dead for, like, six hours!"

"Cynthia's fine."

"The hell she is," said Lawrence. "Is she some kind of zombie? Do I need to start coming in here with brains to feed her?"

"The body wasn't Cynthia. It was her sister."

Lawrence, for once, was silent. He said, after a moment: "I'm going to be in my office."

"Staff meeting at ten," I told him.

"I'm not staff," he snapped at me.

"There's going to be Bavarian cream," I told him, but he slammed the door.

CHAPTER FOURTEEN

Archie Bakis didn't show up. I spent the next few minutes pretending to work, but mostly I was anticipating his arrival, because I thought I might try asking him a little bit about Vanetta's alleged pregnancy. Maybe he was the person who had written the widow's letter, concerned about Vanetta overworking herself while being the mother of his child? I wouldn't have thought this yesterday, but seeing the difference between rested Vanetta and yesterday's counterpart made the idea of whistle-blowing on her behalf seem more reasonable.

But Archie didn't show up, which was a fact that went noticed by everyone, not just me. As people filed past my desk toward Vanetta's office, it became a point of discussion.

"You don't think Archie was fired, do you?" asked Quintrell, whose first assumption for everything is termination. I would be judgmental about this except that my first assumption for everything now is murder. When I'm in a line at Target that takes too long, I periodically look up to make sure that the cashier has not been murdered whilst I was not looking. So I can't be too proud.

"No," I said. "I think that sounds crazy."

"Maybe he's taking a half day. He could be upset about the

murder," said Quintrell, a man who had been accused of murder, made bail, and come to work anyway. Early.

"I guess we'll have to ask Vanetta."

We all piled into the room, this time with the benefit of Tyler, who had skipped yesterday's meeting, and waited to hear the news of the day, which was bound to be plentiful.

"Am I taking notes for this?" I asked.

"No," said Vanetta. "Please stop asking. But where's Archie?"

Murdered, I thought, very unhelpfully. You're probably thinking it, too, because let's be honest, that's what happens to people who don't show up to meetings in stories like this.

"I'm not sure," I said. "We were going to ask you."

"Why would I know where he was?" asked Vanetta.

Maybe you killed him, I was thinking. Then I decided that this was maybe a little over the top, and so I geared down to a less accusatory question.

"Maybe he spent the night with you?"

Delicacy is not my best quality. Anyway, the question did not seem to rattle Vanetta in any particular way. She was neither embarrassed nor angry.

"Nope," she said. "I haven't seen him since yesterday afternoon."

"It's not like Archie to be late," said Gary.

"Well," said Vanetta, "less cake for him."

Then the Bavarian cream was dispensed, and the meeting began.

The first bit of news, which Vanetta had already leaked to me, was that the project was now without a deadline. It was instructive to watch everyone's reaction to this, especially since I wasn't digesting it myself. I saw something akin to tears. Not actual tears, but very close in that male, I'm not going to cry, but just let the water pool in my eye way, as if that were somehow less emotional. There was a lot of that.

"It's a miracle," said Gary. "A Christmas miracle." It was September, by the way. "A goddamned Christmas miracle."

"It's fantastic," said Vanetta. "Now we have time, which was what this project really needed. I believe that *Peppermint Planes* can be a fantastic fucking game. All we needed, really, was the time to develop it."

"This is unbelievable," said Quintrell. "This is the best day ever." Again, lines spoken by someone who started their day in jail. For murder.

"We can do this," said Vanetta. "We're going to do this!"

"Also: This cake is amazing," said Gary.

Perhaps it was natural that Tyler, who had been among the least sleep-deprived of them in the first place, would also be the least swept away now. "So," said Tyler. "Are you still adding voice work and this fifties-art style to the game? Or has that been tossed to the curb as well?"

"We still have to do the proposal," said Vanetta. "Archie will need to put together a sort of lookbook and some dialogue for this thing. But for now we're going to forge onward—our focus should be gameplay and working out bugs, anyway."

"Maybe we could accomplish most of what they want with interstitial videos," said Quintrell.

"Ooh, that's a good thought," said Vanetta. "I'll have Archie mention that in the proposal."

"The whole proposal business is very strange," said Tyler.

"It's been strange days over here," said Vanetta.

"Yes," said Tyler. "It's also very strange that there's not any kind of deadline. Like, that's not good, in my experience."

"Not good how?" asked Quintrell.

"DE likes deadlines."

"I don't want to be indelicate," said Vanetta. "But I think that the combination of the whistle-blower and the murder has meant that the ordinary rules don't apply here. DE probably wants us to lie very low for a while. As it happens, this works to our advantage."

"I get their motivation," said Tyler. "But I'd be wary of the complete lack of a deadline. I hate being the voice of doom here, but they could be preparing to end the project."

"That's crazy," said Gary. "After all this work has been put into it, that would be insanely myopic. There are bugs, but we'll work them out."

"Try to get a deadline on a calendar somewhere. A publicly posted one."

Vanetta appeared more rattled by this than the Archie business, but even then she wasn't shaken.

"I appreciate your honesty, Tyler. But I will see this project to completion if I have to do the damned artwork myself."

"I hear you," said Tyler, who was now toying, a little nervously, with his wisp of green hair. Had he heard something? He gave the impression of someone sitting on more bad news than he could dispense.

"So that was the good news," said Vanetta.

"Oh lord," said nearly everyone at once, and Vanetta smiled.

"Have any of you fellas seen the front page of Reddit?" asked Vanetta.

"Cat memes?" asked Quintrell.

"No," said Vanetta. "Well, probably yes, but also us. We are on the front page of Reddit."

"The whistle-blowing?" asked Gary. "Or the murder?"

"Yes," said Vanetta. "We have two spots."

"There's no such thing as Bad Publicity," said Gary, shifting into song.

"Do not speak to anyone in the press about this," said Vanetta.

"About what?" asked Quintrell.

"About anything. If you see a member of the press, I want you to close up your face as if you are trying to swallow it."

"And they know just what we do," sang Gary. "That we toss and turn at night. They're waiting to make their moves."

"Please don't sing so ominously," said Vanetta.

"At least he's off Nickelback," said Tyler.

"And here's an ironic segue for you," said Vanetta. "Given that we were just discussing that DE probably would like us to lay very low over the next few weeks, allow me to remind you that we are giving a tour of the place tomorrow."

"What do you mean, a tour?" Gary asked.

"I mean a tour. Ignacio Granger will be doing a profile of me that should come out next week sometime, and DE still wants this to happen."

"That seems very inappropriate right after a murder," said Quintrell.

"Isn't he going to ask about the murder?" asked Gary, alarmed enough from this that he didn't allow himself to finish the song.

"I am assured by his bosses that he will not," said Vanetta. "The interview was arranged ages ago, and apparently the powers that be trust him. Besides, DE wants this place to look as normal and as unchanged as possible."

"That's...good?" asked Quintrell.

"I don't even know anymore," said Vanetta. "But we need

something to show him that doesn't fall apart. Do we have a working build of the game? Any kind of demo?"

"The most stable one is from last week," said Quintrell. "It's pretty solid if you don't let him get to the rock candy stage."

"Then spend the day buffing that up as much as you can," said Vanetta. "I know it's backtracking, but we want this place to seem stable. Now one final thing—now that we're all rested and happy—did anyone make any discoveries regarding the whistle-blower's letter?"

The group was completely silent.

"Regarding their families?" continued Vanetta.

More silence. The vast empty reaches of space were louder than these guys.

"Gary?" asked Vanetta.

"Why do you always pick on me about this?"

"Because you're the only person here who has anyone who cares about them," said Vanetta, which was putting a fine enough point on it that it actually made Quintrell squirm.

"My wife doesn't care. And she couldn't have done it, anyway."

"If you say so," said Vanetta suspiciously. "Although I wonder—"

I really have no idea how Vanetta might have finished this sentence, but for the sake of poetry, let us say that she was going for "where the hell Archie is" because it is the most interesting. And ironic, assuming we use the word in an Alanis Morrissette-y way.

Because it became very clear where Archie Bakis was. All too clear. There was music—loud music, coming from outside.

For music to be so loud that it bothers people on the second floor of an office building, it must be very loud indeed. And it was. It seemed possible that we were under attack. Possibly by '80s pop stars. Because the music that was coming at us was the 1986 Chris de Burgh hit "The Lady in Red."

"Oh gods," said Vanetta, who put together what was happening before the rest of us, not even needing to make it to the window.

I, however, did need to go to the window, because I enjoy watching train wrecks. Down below us, in the parking lot, was Archie Bakis, dressed rather snazzily in a suit and tie, although it was a bolo tie, and the suit was velour. Still, he looked sharp. He was kneeling, on one knee, between two large speakers, beneath a banner that read: WILL YOU MARRY ME VANETTA?

It was, I observed, maybe for the best that the journalist was coming tomorrow and not today.

"Does he have a banner?" asked Vanetta, who refused to even go near the window, as if we were playing *Resident Evil*, and the window was just a trap for zombie dogs to jump through.

"He does have a banner, yes," I answered, although only after all the men refused to speak at all.

"Does it say: 'Take Me Back, Vanetta' on it?" asked Vanetta, which, again, seemed reasonable.

"It does not," I told her.

"Oh no," said Vanetta.

"Oh yes," I told her.

"Tell me it's not a wedding proposal," she said.

"I guess I better get to work on that build," said Quintrell, speaking loudly to make sure he was heard over the music.

"I'm afraid it's a marriage proposal," I told her.

"Dahlia," said Vanetta. "Go down there and deal with that."

"Isn't that kind of a personal matter between the two of you?"

"I order you to deal with him," said Vanetta, closing the

curtains. The same curtains that had been draped over Archie's nether regions just this time yesterday. "I command it," said Vanetta. This sounded as ridiculous as you're probably imagining it.

"Wait, is this meeting over?" asked Tyler. "Shouldn't we be talking about the murder? Or you know, Quintrell being out on bail."

"I cannot deal with anyone while that music is playing," said Vanetta. "And believe me, you don't want to hear the next track."

The meeting dispersed, although Tyler was right. We needed to discuss the murder. But this was how Cahaba Apps worked; something was always on fire, and you had to ignore some of the problems just to stay alive.

I went downstairs to deal with Archie.

As I mentioned before, below us was a dog-washing business. I can't imagine what they must have thought about us as neighbors. Murder, police, thrown chairs, and now this. A woman with hair that was not quite a beehive but was significantly more than a bun leaned against the front doors of the dog-washing shop, smoking a cigarette. Her orange T-shirt indicated that she was involved with the business.

"Are you Vanetta?" she asked me, glancing toward the banner.

"No," I said.

"Vanetta wasn't the name of the murdered lady, was it? That'd be an ugly scene."

"No," I said. "It wasn't."

The woman took a long drag off her cigarette and said: "Where's Vanetta, then? She just gonna leave this guy down here to rot?"

"Vanetta is staying upstairs."

"It's like that, is it? Well, you're gonna have to get him to turn off that music, then. We got two Pomeranians in there, and they don't like it."

Vanetta doesn't like it either, I thought, and walked over to the banner.

"Archie," I said. "How's it going?"

I nearly said how's it hanging, but I decided that this was too informal. There's really no road map for a conversation like this.

"Where is Vanetta?" asked Archie. "Why are you down here and not her?"

Archie, for his own part, was no dummy, which made this simultaneously easier and more difficult.

"I think that Vanetta, you know with the murder and Quintrell being arrested and all"—a detail I threw in solely to throw Archie off his track—"that she's just not ready to discuss marriage right now."

"So is that a no?"

Jesus Christ if I knew.

"I think it's more of an ask again later?"

"I don't think that's what it is," said Archie, who didn't exactly sound deflated. Although, he turned off the music, so thank God. He sounded a little relieved. "I suppose this is what I should have expected."

I suppose I was a little relieved as well, come to think of it. This was the second marriage proposal I'd experienced (secondhand) in a week. I didn't really care for them—and it was more than just worry that everyone I knew was going to start families and I would die alone. There's something embarrassing about them, even without a dopey sound track.

"I didn't even realize you guys were dating," I said.

"We weren't dating," said Archie. "Anyway, I tried. You wanna help put these things in my trunk?" he said, indicating his speakers and banner. The banner I could manage, but the speakers would require a dolly.

"I can try," I said. "You really went all out here," I said.

"Someone loaned me the speakers, and I got the banner from a buddy who works at Office Depot. So, free banners. I guess I just thought I should make a go of it."

I decided to play dumb here, which is something that I'm embarrassingly natural at.

"So if you guys weren't dating," I said, "why the wedding proposal?"

"Well," said Archie, "we weren't in a romantic relationship, like, you know, with fancy dinners. But you saw me yesterday on the floor in her office."

"So what was your relationship?" I asked. I told you I was playing dumb.

"I am her stress ball."

"Just hers? I got the impression you played around a bit," I said.

"I do play around a bit." Archie grinned. "Vanetta's not my only pastime. But—well—I shouldn't be telling you this, but she's pregnant."

"No!" I said, perhaps laying it on too thickly.

"Yeah," said Archie. "I guess we got a little careless. It scares the shit out of me, really."

"Is Vanetta keeping the baby?" I asked.

"The fuck if I know," said Archie. "She won't even talk to me about it. She didn't want to mention being pregnant to me. I heard through the grapevine. The fucking grapevine."

The Cynthia Shaffer Grapevine. I trod delicately, pouring on an extra helping of airhead.

"Maybe she just wanted to make sure the pregnancy stuck, you know? My friend Charlene got pregnant and was super excited about it, and then like three days later, she wasn't. I mean, how early in the process are we talking?"

I don't even know anyone named Charlene, by the way. It just felt like the right touch.

"She didn't want to talk about it with me until the game was finished."

"That was supposed to be in a week or two?"

"Yeah, except that deadline has been blown hundreds of times at this point. Hundreds of thousands of times. This baby's gonna graduate college before the game is finished."

Archie stopped moving speakers and sat down suddenly. He wasn't crying, or even letting manly bits of water pool in his eye, but he looked emotionally exhausted. Like he had been attacked by several emotions at once, and they were getting a flanking bonus on him.

"It just makes me feel like such a jerk, you know? Just even getting someone pregnant. It's like: I'm the dick. I'm the bad guy. I literally have fucked things up. Literally, Dahlia."

"Yeah, I got it."

Clearly, my role in this conversation was to tell Archie that he wasn't being a dick—I mean, that's how Fate had apparently cast the roles, but I was dubious. I mean, certainly, Vanetta wasn't clothing herself in glory, but I didn't really know the details of what his behavior had been. Admittedly, that's true a lot of the time when you're cast into this role, but it wasn't like Archie was an old friend I was going to defend at all costs. I barely knew the guy, eggplant pecs or not.

"Yeah," I repeated. Which committed to nothing and yet was enough to launch Archie forward.

"And I'm angry that she didn't tell me. I mean, why not tell me? And I'm embarrassed that I'm angry about it, because I feel like that makes me even more of a dick. I actually googled 'men's rights' last night. That's fucked up, right?"

"Well," I said. I was hoping I could just stop there, but Archie seemed unduly focused on me finishing the sentence. Frankly, it did seem a little fucked up, but then the whole situation could be broadly described as jacked. I was trying to find an honest and yet noncommittal answer to further the conversation, and I settled on: "It's natural that you'd be experiencing a lot of conflicting emotions right now."

"I just want to do the right thing, but I don't know what that actually is."

"It probably doesn't involve a marriage proposal."

"Yeah," said Archie. "I don't want to marry Vanetta, anyway. I just wanted her to know that I'd take the bullet."

"Okay," I said, "if you have this conversation with her, definitely avoid the phrase 'take the bullet' to describe your hypothetical wedding."

Throughout this conversation, Archie had been so emotionally fraught that I had basically forgotten about the pretense of investigating Cahaba for Emily. I had guessed earlier that maybe Archie had written the whistle-blower's letter on Vanetta's behalf, and I tried testing those waters.

"Do you want her to keep the baby?" I asked, instantly, belatedly realizing that this was preposterously inappropriate to ask. But Archie wasn't bothered.

"I don't know," he said. "What's the non-dick answer?"

"Here's some advice that I will probably never give anyone again, but just this once: Forget about whether you're being a dick. What do you want?"

"I don't know," said Archie, sounding totally lost. "I'm off the map."

"It's not rocket science, Archie," I said.

"I suppose," he said, thinking, "I just want to keep having lots of sex with different women."

This answer, if you will, sort of blew me away, because it sounded as though Archie had been headed for some sort of emotional epiphany. The signs were there: searching eyes, contemplative tone, vulnerability. And instead we got this. I could see why he was worried about being a dick.

I tried steering this conversation back toward my investigation, such as it was.

"Are you worried about the baby? I mean, do you think Vanetta is overstressing herself?"

"No," said Archie. "Why, is that something I should be worried about? Does stress harm unborn children?"

There are women, many of whom were in the knitting circle I attended last night, who could undoubtedly answer this question in a reasonable and marginally informed way. I am emphatically not one of these women.

"I don't know," I said. "Let's see what BuzzFeed has to say about it."

But then Archie was suddenly resolute.

"I don't think it's reasonable to ask Vanetta to work less. I mean, that's what she loves, and she's more invested in this game than anyone. I mean, I'm less invested than the rest of the team, and even I don't want to work less. Asking for her to take it easy is a nonstarter."

"That's...a pretty non-dickish answer," I said. Which was true. And useful too. Archie wasn't acting. I mean, hell, maybe he had written the whistle-blower's letter, but he certainly didn't do it for Vanetta.

"I guess so," said Archie. "And if she wants to de-stress, I have other ways to help her out with that."

Ugh.

"Right," I said. "You two should probably talk. You know, directly, to each other. Not using me as a conduit."

"No, I'm going to give her some space. But let her know I'd take the bullet for her."

"I really think you want to find a different euphemism."

"Maybe," said Archie. "But this way sounds more honest."

Our conversation wasn't terrible, but I think I liked Archie better when he was shirtless and sleeping. Maybe Vanetta and I had this in common. It wasn't that he was a bad guy, really, it was just that he was not quite what his image conveyed. Then again, maybe no one is. And I had to remind myself that I definitely was not getting him in his best light. Given a week of normal sleep, he was probably a better guy.

I tried to imagine what I would do if Nathan were having my baby somehow, which I grant would involve some kind of weird magic. Suppose he picked up the phone now and said: "Dahlia, I'm pregnant." Obviously, I would not take the news well, although again, I think the weird magic would be my primary line of inquiry.

Archie dragged his speakers away, and the dog-washing lady yelled at me, which I wasn't expecting.

"Hey, Upstairs Woman!"

That's what she called me. Upstairs Woman. I've been called much worse. I walked over to her mainly because I didn't want her yelling Upstairs Woman at me again.

"Yeah?" I said.

"You got a second?" she asked. She was still smoking a cigarette, so she was somehow making it really last or had moved on to cigarette #2. I couldn't tell you which, but she had a voice that suggested the latter. Actually, her voice suggested that this was cigarette #6 or #7.

"I suppose," I said, bracing myself for a hard sell about the benefits of professionally done dog washing.

"There's a woman inside who wants to see you," she said.

"At Cahaba?" I asked.

Smoking lady, who had on no name tag whatsoever, and whose name remains a mystery, gave me a look that suggested I was an idiot.

"Not upstairs," she said. Barb said. I'm going to call her Barb, just because it suits her. "At my shop. She's hiding in the back. Wants to be sub rosa."

Well, Barb knew a little Latin. The benefits of a liberal arts education.

"There's a woman waiting for me in your shop?" I repeated dumbly. I guess the airhead act takes a little while to wear off.

"That's what I said. You got a weird organization upstairs; you realize that, right?" Although Barb seemed to feel that this was admirable, based upon her facial expression, which I would describe as "shooting off waves of warm light," although I might be thinking of the cigarette smoke.

"It's a kick," I said, which it was.

I went into the dog-grooming shop, which smelled remarkably like a dog-grooming shop. I suppose I sort of expected that there would be an effort to cover up the scents of shampoo and wet dog with patchouli or something, but no: it was eau de dog-grooming shop in full effect.

"Hello?" I said. Barb hadn't even come in with me and just stayed out here smoking.

"Dahlia, it's me. I'm in the back."

It was a relief to hear Cynthia Shaffer's voice. It could have hypothetically been Emily Swenson, which would have been unlikely but also a terrible portent. If Emily Swenson is waiting for you "sub rosa" in a dog-grooming shop, she probably has come to have you erased. So hooray, it was Cynthia.

"Hang on, I'm coming back there," I said, marveling at the strange directions this case seemed to be taking me. The dog smell only got stronger, which was curious because there were two, completely tiny Pomeranians back here, only one of which was even wet. But it had the smell of a much larger dog.

Cynthia was leaning against the wall, quite far away from the dogs, and there was a black woman with dreads that she had tied up in a bun in the middle of the room. That's two for two for buns at the dog shop.

"I can't believe they let you back here," I said.

"Oh, I'm a regular here," said Cynthia. "And I'm old pals with Deb."

Deb. Barb was agonizingly close.

"Anyway," Cynthia continued, "I wasn't planning on coming in here, but as soon as I got out of the car, Archie was out setting up sound kind of sound system."

"He proposed," I said. "To the hip tune of 'The Lady in Red.' "

"Yes," said Cynthia. "I was peering through a curtain."

"We were all peering through the curtain," said the woman washing the dog, who, unlike Deb, was wearing her name tag. It read: "Drea."

"I felt like a spy," said Cynthia. "A very terrible spy."

"Terrible like inefficient, or terrible like you've ruined people's lives."

"Both," said Cynthia.

"I guess you came back for your things?"

"Yeah," said Cynthia. "You think maybe you could just go upstairs and grab them for me?"

I considered this. Hypothetically yes, although it would look a little weird to throw all of Cynthia's things in a garbage bag and then scamper downstairs. If anyone were paying attention at all, I would come off as the secretarial version of the Hamburglar.

"You're sure you don't want to just go up there with me?"

"I'm absolutely sure," said Cynthia. "I didn't want to go back there when I had just been fired. Now that my sister was killed there, it's just absolutely somewhere I don't want to be."

Right. Murdered sister. I could see where that might be uncomfortable. I didn't naturally consider it, because I am a terrible empath, but now that it had been pointed out to me, it seemed like a normal human reaction.

"I'm so sorry about your sister," I said. Because this was a thing you said, and I was sorry, at least in the very superficial sense of having never met her.

"It's such a shock," said Cynthia. "It's so funny, because she'd been having all these problems with her pancreas, and I had been bracing myself for that. And then this happened. Murdered. She was murdered."

Here's a question that's fun to ask anyone: "Do you think that maybe the murderer meant to kill you?" Like, honestly, try in your head to find a way to pose that question now without coming off like a psychopath. If you've got anything, you've lapped me, because I went into a holding pattern.

"Why was she there, anyway?"

"It's my fault," said Cynthia. "It's all my fault. It's the same reason I'm hiding downstairs here. I didn't want to have to deal with everyone. It's humiliating having been fired. I was so flustered when I walked out of there that I left almost every-thing behind. I didn't want to make the walk of shame back there."

My guess had been right.

"So you asked your sister. Did she know anyone at Cahaba?"

"Not at all!" said Cynthia, on the verge of crying. "It's so bizarre. We weren't even that close. It was just weird chance that she called me when I was looking for someone to go pick up my stuff, and Joyce lives in the neighborhood."

"Did you ask her to come at night?" I asked.

"No," said Cynthia thoughtfully. "Although come to think of it, she asked me when it would be the quietest. I told her that people were always there, but around dawn most everyone was asleep. Did she come at night?"

"We think so," I told her, although I don't know who the "we" were in the situation. The police weren't informing me of their thinking. "You don't think anyone would have wanted Joyce dead, do you?"

"No," said Cynthia. "I can't imagine why they would. Maybe they were trying to kill me."

"I guess that's another good reason not to go upstairs," I said. I meant this as a joke to lighten the mood, but Cynthia took me quite seriously.

"Exactly," she said.

"Wait," said Drea, stepping away from the Pomeranians, "it was your sister that got killed upstairs?"

"My older sister," said Cynthia. "And I think they maybe meant to kill me."

God bless Drea, because she actually asked the question I wanted to know the answer to. "Who would want you dead?" Although she posed it in a perhaps overly skeptical way, more "Who would want YOU dead?" But even so, it was a fair sentiment.

"Who knows?" said Cynthia. "That place is a smoldering hellhole."

"Did you send the whistle-blower's letter?"

"What whistle-blower's letter?"

"On Reddit?"

"What's Reddit?"

"There was a whistle-blower. Online. Someone posted about it and exposed a lot of DE's wrongdoings."

"No," said Cynthia. "I wouldn't do that."

"Well, you told everyone at your knitting circle."

"That's what knitting circles are for. It's like therapy, but you end up with a pot holder at the end."

"I'm guess I'm saying it wouldn't be out of character for you to have posted about it."

Cynthia was getting annoyed with me.

"Maybe it's not out of character, but you asked me if I did it, and I told you I didn't."

I don't know why I was pushing her so hard on that point. I suppose I just hadn't gotten anywhere with the whistle-blower's letter, and it was the one thing that Emily had consistently been pushing me to investigate. I wasn't any closer now than when I began.

"All right," I said. "Forget I brought it up. I'm just trying to imagine a reason someone might want you dead. You didn't run across any terrible secrets up there. No one embezzling, or..." I felt I should say something else, but I wasn't sure what my other options were. Embezzling is the only illegal thing I could think to do at a company, which means that although I might be okay as a detective, as a corporate criminal I would be pretty lousy. Or at least unimaginative. "Nothing? No smoking gun."

"I'm pretty sure that the acupuncturist that Lawrence claims to go to every Wednesday is actually a personal trainer."

"How is that a smoking gun?"

"I didn't say it was. But he does lie about it."

"Why?"

"Knowing Lawrence, he probably just thinks it sounds cooler to have an acupuncturist."

This was not anywhere close to a smoking gun. It was not smoking; it was absorbing smoke from the air and cleansing it, like a high-end dehumidifier.

"Any other dirt?"

"Quintrell goes into the bathroom to cry sometimes. We call it the Crying Room."

"Also not that damning. Or even really surprising."

"Tyler looks at pornography on his iPhone."

"I'm not exactly bowled over. Although: How did you figure that out?"

"He left out his phone one day, and I started going through it."

"Anything weird?" I asked. By this, I meant dark or terrible, something that could plausibly be a motive for murder, but Cynthia simply said: "Foot stuff."

And I felt very badly in the moment, because I now had a mental image of Tyler that I emphatically Did Not Want, and also, this was really none of my business anyway.

"So your theory is that Tyler tried poisoning your sister to keep his iPhone foot fetish a secret? That's it?"

"No," said Cynthia. "I don't even have a theory. I just want my stuff from upstairs back. Especially my collection of holiday teas."

CHAPTER FIFTEEN

Let's take a moment, shall we, to consider who might have written the whistle-blower's letter, which I put here to show that I am, in fact, investigating and not merely putting out fires. This was one of the proverbial diamonds that Emily was after, and even if I didn't have an answer, I still wanted to be able to show my work.

So, if you're reading, Emily:

Cynthia—Knew everything; had reason to be grumpy after having been let go. CONS: Says she didn't do it. Seems like she didn't do it. Probably didn't do it.

Cynthia's Spouse—Dead.

Cynthia's Sister—Also dead, and didn't communicate much with Cynthia. Although—maybe?

Quintrell King—Seems too wishy-washy and weirdly loyal. Why whistle-blow on a company you continue to work for so slavishly?

Gloria the Electrical Engineer of Booty—Implausible, possibly not even a real person.

Gary—Could be. People who broke into song that much were probably dangerous. Look at Sweeney Todd.

Gary's wife, whom he called "Honey Badger"—Ditto.

Tyler—Enormously single, save for the recent developments with Masako. Probably too shrewd to mess with DE in this way. Still a possibility.

Archie—Says he didn't do it; seems like he wouldn't although, as his Office Depot banner would attest, is capable of big, ill-thought-through gestures.

Archie's ladyfriends—Possibly?

Vanetta—Unlikely? But not impossible. Maybe it was all a weird, black-market way of advocating for her employees? Investigate.

Lawrence—Fat chance.

Admittedly that's not much, but still—there were leads, of a kind. When you're investigating, you shouldn't let dead ends get you down, because even though they're depressing, they gradually lead you to the truth, just by cutting off possibilities.

When I got back upstairs, I could see that Vanetta was watching my desk, waiting for me. She was pretending not to be concerned, although not very effectively. I liked having this piece of information as well—Vanetta, for all her many skills and virtues, was not a good actor.

"Oh, you're back," she said when I came to the door, actually feigning surprise at me.

"Yes," I said. "Sorry I was gone for so long."

"How did he take it?"

"He seemed relieved, honestly."

"Relieved?" said Vanetta, who did not sound relieved herself but put out. "He sounded relieved?"

"A bit, yes. I think he was just trying to do the right thing. Or at least, show you that he was willing to do the right thing, if you think that the right thing is getting married."

"What did he tell you?" said Vanetta suspiciously.

"He mentioned the pregnancy to me," I said, making Vanetta suddenly look less rested again. "Although frankly, I already knew about that."

"What? How?"

"Cynthia told me about it."

Vanetta was reasonably self-absorbed with her pregnancy problem, I thought, because she did not have follow-up questions about how I had been consorting with Cynthia. Instead she said:

"My God, why is she telling people? Cynthia's the worst! She's just this awful, awful woman."

I nearly asked, God help me, "So would you kill her?" but something held me back.

"Yeah," I said. "I guess Cynthia likes spreading gossip around."

"She does. Always going on about dumb shit like Lawrence's acupuncturist being a therapist, or some such garbage. Who cares? If Lawrence needs a psychiatrist, more power to him."

I was pretty sure that Cynthia had described him as a personal trainer, but no matter. This was the first negative description of Cynthia anyone had given, and it was actually a little helpful. Cynthia liked to gossip—and if she had found the wrong piece of information, even unknowingly—well, that could have caused some problems.

And it also struck me, quite suddenly, that people might be much more willing to say negative things about Cynthia now that she wasn't actually dead. When you're dead, it's impolite to speak ill of people—even awful people, right? And so it would be definitely unseemly to go in on a dead woman for what were only mild character flaws. I would need to repoll everyone as to their thoughts on Cynthia, now that she was among the living. Food for later.

"So how are you doing?" I asked Vanetta, trying to sound empathetic.

"I'm fine. The project was extended, and so everything is great. Also, DE really does have a connection with Morgan Freeman, and so there's that. We could have a talking spearmint voiced by Morgan Freeman."

"I mean about the pregnancy." Although, as an aside: Wow, Morgan Freeman.

"I'm not talking about the pregnancy."

"Are you keeping the baby?" I asked, the question being arguably even less appropriate here than the last time I asked.

"Perhaps you didn't hear me say earlier, to your face, loudly and clearly, that I was not discussing this pregnancy."

"Well, it's just, you know, if you're going to have the baby, you should probably take it a little easy."

Was this true? I had no idea. I actually wasn't sure how many months pregnant Vanetta was—she certainly wasn't showing—and I had no idea at what point a gal should start resting. My knowledge of pregnancy mostly stems from a video in my tenth-grade health class, which I pretended to watch while actually reading *Love and Rockets*, which was way better, if less immediately useful now. Still, I have no regrets.

"What are you, Cynthia's homunculus? This isn't your business. Just back off about it."

The problem about being a detective, however, is that you are necessarily up in things that aren't your business. That's the job, really. Still, I couldn't argue with Vanetta on this point. After all, where was the lie?

"You should talk to someone about it," I said. "Have you told anyone about it?"

Vanetta's body tensed up like she was ready to sock me, but her face looked like it was going to disembark from the rest of her and run.

"I just need some time to process it," said Vanetta. "I'm not saying that I'm going to ignore it forever like I'm an idiot. I only just found out about it, and my game is in terrible trouble and a woman was murdered, and I just want a couple of nights' sleep before I make any decisions. Is that really so fucking unreasonable?"

Put this way, it was not unreasonable. I hated being such an ass, but my job was to try to figure out who the father was and not be pleasant, and so I just kept hitting the beehive with a stick.

"Do you know who the father is?"

Vanetta's face—I swear to God—did a black hole thing where part of it drew in on itself. It was not a natural face, and I was frightened.

"Of course I know who the father is," she said, her face puckering so much that I was being drawn toward her against my will. "What kind of a question is that?"

"I don't know, why did you try to keep it a secret from Archie?"

Vanetta grabbed me, physically grabbed me, and pulled me into her office. Then she closed the door. I half expected that she was going to open the window and throw me through it, and honestly, I'm not sure that I could blame her, but instead she said:

"I'm ninety percent sure who the father is."

"Ninety percent?!?" I said, with way more punctuation than was necessary.

"Maybe eighty percent."

"Oh my God. Who's the other candidate?" I asked, but I knew. I already knew.

"Lawrence and I have known each other for a very long time," said Vanetta.

"Lawrence is an ass," I said.

"Yes," said Vanetta, irritated and embarrassed in equal parts. "Of course he's an ass. But he's an ass I've known for a very long time. He probably knows me better than anyone, which is dumb, I grant, that the person who knows me best is Lawrence Ussary, but that's just how Fate worked it out."

I was momentarily past investigating anything and was just processing the sheer horror of Lawrence Ussary possibly being the father of Vanetta's child. It was like Rosemary's baby, except instead of Satan it was a really douchey guy. "But Lawrence is such an ass," I said, unnecessarily, for the second time.

"He is," said Vanetta. "Hell, Archie's kind of an ass. Neither of these people are life partners."

"I guess I can identify with that," I said, thinking of the weird middle place I'd found myself with Nathan and Shuler.

"No. You can't with this. None of this is any of your business," said Vanetta, finding herself. "And if you tell anyone, I will break your neck."

"Of course," I said.

Although, Vanetta looked a little happier now and said: "Maybe you're right, though. It maybe was a good idea to tell someone about it. I've just been sitting on that news for days."

"You should find out who the father is. I mean, there are tests for that."

"First of all, it makes me feel like some sort of goddamn Maury Povich guest. Do you have any idea how disappointed my parents would be if I had to take a paternity test?"

"I'm not suggesting that you bring them with you to the clinic. You don't need to involve them at all."

"Well, I can't."

"You really need to buck up about this, Vanetta."

"No, I actually can't. The test doesn't work until I'm eight weeks pregnant."

"How many weeks are you?"

"Not eight."

The mental ramifications of this gradually began to seep into my head. Waiting long enough to be able to test for the father also meant that that the baby...well, I had stopped investigating and suddenly started commiserating with Vanetta.

"So what are you going to do?"

"I'm going to make this game fucking awesome. It's going to be so awesome that nothing else in my life will exist or even matter."

I finished with the conversation and then proceeded to Hamburglar up all of Cynthia's possessions. I tried doing this quietly and slowly, but Cynthia actually had a lot of stuff here, and I had to fill up multiple white kitchen bags from the workroom with her things. Gary, in particular, noticed me doing this and after several moments of watching and saying nothing, finally decided to come over.

"You realize that Cynthia's alive, right?" he said, a little too conspiratorially.

"I do," I said.

"So..." said Gary. "It's not like you're robbing the dead."

"It's more that I thought people would be happier if her possessions were out of sight."

"Why would we be happier?" asked Gary.

"We could all move on from this terrible tragedy," I said.

"I suppose," said Gary. "But Cynthia's not dead. So why hide her stuff?"

"Right," I said. And he had me there. "I guess I hadn't thought about that."

Gary took a moment to survey the contents of one of the white bags, which suggested a storied life, even if the stories weren't very interesting. There were Mardi Gras beads, a rock that said "Branson Missouri" on it, pictures of a presumed grandchild—a nine-year-old with red-rimmed glasses.

"There used to be a picture of her sister around here," said Gary. "That's what you should take down."

I hadn't seen a picture of Joyce, but I hadn't exactly been looking for it either. I asked Gary about it.

"Yeah, it was one of those pictures that's taken when you go down a roller coaster. They're both screaming. It's probably not the way you'd want to remember her, regardless."

Cynthia had an entire drawer filled with knickknacks like this, and it wasn't as if I had made a catalog of them, given that (1) they weren't especially interesting and (2) Cynthia was waiting for me, still, downstairs. But I started going through the bags now, trying to find the picture that Gary had been referring to.

"That's it," said Gary, finding an unframed photograph of the two of them, just as he had said, plummeting down a coaster called the Death Drop. He was right; it wasn't how I would want to be remembered, because Joyce (and Cynthia too) looked like they were screaming their heads off.

But it was nice to have a picture of the two of them together, however unconventional. They weren't twins, it was clear now, but they were similar-looking people in the broad strokes. Cynthia's hair was resolutely brown, whereas Joyce had let her hair go gray. Cynthia also looked younger, although not necessarily better—and appeared to be a woman who believed very strongly in suntan lotion and skin moisturizer. Joyce's face was a little more rugged, showed a little more mileage.

Joyce also looked like she was having the time of her life on that coaster, while Cynthia just looked scared. Actually, the more I looked at the picture, the more I thought that perhaps it wasn't such a bad way to be remembered after all.

I packed up the stuff as discreetly as I could, although I'm pretty sure that Gary was watching me, and headed back downstairs.

I never did find the holiday tea.

Shocking developments in murder mysteries typically involve massive amounts of blood, killers with guns in closets, and police flooding the scene at a pivotal moment. I don't want to take away from those things, because they are shocking—but in life, honest, day-to-day life, it's often the smaller things that really gobsmack you. And we come to one of these moments now, because I came downstairs, back to the dog-washing shop, and discovered that Cynthia was now wearing an orange T-shirt and was blow-drying a peekapoo.

"Oh, just put my stuff down in the corner," said Cynthia.

In retrospect, I'm not quite sure why I was so surprised by this turn of events because:

1. I didn't know Cynthia very well.
2. I had, admittedly, left her down here for a very long time, having had a heart-to-heart with Vanetta and a mini-investigation with Gary.
3. She did need a job.

But I didn't expect to her to be blow-drying a dog. It just wasn't how I imagined the scene going down.

"Do you work here now?" I asked.

"It's a funny story," said Cynthia. "While I was waiting downstairs, I was complaining to Deb about how hard it is to find work once you get to be a certain age, and then she said she was shorthanded around here ever since Evan fell in love with that baker and moved to Chicago, and then one thing led to another."

"And now you work here," I said.

"Just for now," she said.

"Aren't you concerned about running into Vanetta and company?"

Cynthia looked contemplative. "Well," she said. "I guess not. For one, I don't think they come down here very much. But for another, I've got a job now. Like within two days. Maybe they'll see me and think: Wow, we shouldn't have let Cynthia get away. She's been scooped right up."

I didn't think that Vanetta would be particularly displaced by the burgeoning career of a woman wearing a button that said "ask me about free bows," but I understood the sentiment. When you're unemployed, you feel gross, and you want to stay out of sight. When you've got a gig, other people's opinions of you seem not to matter so very much.

"So I saw a picture of Joyce up there. I put it on top, in case, I don't know, you wanted to do something with it."

"Oh, on the Death Drop? I don't know what I'll do with it. We were out with my granddaughter, who was celebrating her sixteenth birthday. But Paisley didn't want to do the roller coaster, and Joyce insisted that we go. Paisley is such a cautious child, not at all like most kids these days."

Cynthia seemed to be revving up into a story about her granddaughter of all things—but I was trying to stay on track.

"Joyce was a fan of roller coasters?"

"Oh," said Cynthia, still looking for a way to turn the topic back to her granddaughter. "She just liked getting her picture taken, really. Not like Paisley. Paisley doesn't use Twitter or MySpace because she doesn't approve of social media."

"You and Joyce look a lot alike," I said.

"Everyone says that," said Cynthia. "People say I look ten years younger than her."

Who were these people, I wondered, and why would they lie to Cynthia in this way? Five years, tops.

"You don't really think of people Joyce's age being a fan of roller coasters, you know? I always thought of it as a teenager's game."

"Oh, well, Joyce sort of took a professional interest in being scared. She used to manage the House of Hell."

"I'm sorry, what?"

"The House of Hell?" said Cynthia. "It's this big haunted house that's built into a cave. A fake cave. It was a huge deal in the nineties; I don't know if it's still around."

"She managed a haunted house?"

"I mean, it's not actually haunted. She had that job for years, until corporate decided she started looking too much like Mrs. Claus, and then she moved over to Santa's Village."

It struck me, suddenly, that Joyce was, by far, the more interesting of the two sisters.

"Did anyone at Cahaba ever meet Joyce?"

CHAPTER SIXTEEN

I didn't push very much at Cynthia's theory about being a murder target, mostly because I didn't think that she believed it very much herself. She was taking a job immediately below where this alleged attempt on her life went down, which is not the behavior of someone who was in fear of being murdered. But I would have been deeply skeptical even before that point, simply from her tone and body language.

Cynthia liked the idea that she was important. She was flattered by the notion—I could tell because she talked about the murder in a vaguely bragging manner. Frankly, I didn't think she thought the attempt on her life was real at all. I wish I had more specifics about how Joyce had actually been killed, but even I couldn't find a way to casually ask:

"What kind of poison killed your sister?"

I came back upstairs half expecting Gary to give me the third degree, but I instead ran into Tyler, and by ran into I mean that he was waiting for me at my desk.

"There's a rumor going around that you just stole all of Cynthia's possessions," he said.

"My God, when did all of you become so detail oriented?"

"I credit the healing power of sleep," said Tyler.

I lowered my voice down to a whisper and said, "I'm trying to keep this on the down low, but Cynthia was downstairs. She didn't want to come up here and have everyone make a fuss over her."

"I wouldn't have made a fuss over her."

"Well, she also was wary about coming back to the place where her sister was killed." Although not wary about hanging out downstairs.

"Are you investigating this case?" asked Tyler, too loudly for my tastes.

"Ix-nay on the vestigation-nay."

"Well, that answers my question," said Tyler.

"I'm mostly focused on this whistle-blower's letter," I said. Also, code theft, which I kept forgetting about.

"Not on the murder," said Tyler.

"Apparently not," I told him, thinking of Emily's weird insistence that I give the Cynthia business the brush-off.

"I can give you details about how Joyce got killed," said Tyler.

"How did you learn that?" I asked.

"I just got off the phone with Detective Tedin, who asked me some very revealing questions. Also, I'm a murder suspect, so there's that."

"What did you learn?"

"But wait, I thought you weren't interested in this murder?"

"I'm taking an academic interest in it."

"Well, I'm not giving this information away for free," said Tyler. He toyed with his wisp of green hair again. If we were playing poker, that would have certainly been his tell. Here it was just telling me what I already knew: Tyler was a bastard.

"Are you trying to shake me down?" I asked.

"I'm not trying to shake you down," said Tyler. "I am shaking you down."

"If you want money, you came to the wrong gal."

"Tell me about Masako."

"Oh lord," I said. "Do your own detective work."

"She's friends with you. She likes you. Just give me some tips."

"Just ask her your own questions. Masako is very direct."

"We had a really good time last night," Tyler said, and that mixed with the foot business was giving me entirely too much information.

"I don't want to hear about it," I said, assuming that there had to be some kind of funny business, because hanging drunkenly around a church until the police showed up was surely not the good time he was referring to.

"Well I'm not giving you a play-by-play," said Tyler. "I just want an excuse to text her. Help me come up with some sort of pretext."

"It's Masako. You don't need a pretext. She lives in a world without pretexts."

"We all live in a world with pretexts."

"Okay, but Masako is better at ignoring them than most people I know."

"How about a dinner?" asked Tyler. "Is there a restaurant she likes?"

Again, this was more madness. Low-key madness, like Cynthia in an orange dog-washing shirt, and not Grand Guignol madness, but even so. Bonkersville.

"Just to be clear, you are ransoming information about a murder to learn the name of a restaurant a girl likes."

"I don't like your tone," said Tyler.

I told him the name of a place—the King & I, which despite its somewhat dopey name was actually pretty swank. This whole conversation was incredibly dumb, although I did think that Masako would be flattered by it, somehow. If I was feeling charitable to Tyler at the end of this conversation, perhaps I would tell her about it.

"Joyce died of drug poisoning—and I'm thinking methadone because they asked me a lot about it."

"Methadone? Like crystal meth, methadone?"

"That's methamphetamine. Methadone is a painkiller that's used for heroin addicts."

"Yikes," I said. Joyce did not seem like the sort of person that would be partaking of heroin, roller coaster lover or not.

"So the police don't think this was a suicide or an accident or anything?"

"What do I know?" said Tyler. "But I didn't get the impression that was the angle they were pursuing."

"Why were they asking questions of you?" I asked.

"See," said Tyler. "I think you're the person who lives in a world without pretext. Not Masako. I think you're just projecting that."

"What did the police want from you, Tyler?" I asked again, not particularly wanting to engage in a lot of self-analysis. And by this I mean *any* self-analysis.

"Well, as it happens, I had a prescription for methadone from a few years ago."

"That explains why you know so much about it."

"It's a painkiller. I was in a car accident. I nearly died. I still have scars," he said, pausing. "Ask Masako."

"So the police want to know if you methadoned Joyce into oblivion." That would make anyone anxious.

"Apparently," he said.

"You don't seem too worried about their investigation."

"That's because the idea is dumb. I didn't know Joyce, I barely knew Cynthia, and they only gave me that stuff while I was in the hospital. It's not like I would smuggle it out of there, save it up, and then use the stash to kill an old woman I didn't know."

This was true, but it was an addictive drug. "Maybe they think you took up a meth habit?"

"Please," said Tyler. "And risk my beautiful teeth?"

Tyler flashed his pearly whites at me, which I would have called a little snaggly, frankly, not his best feature, but were nonetheless all there.

It is at this point that I committed a little industrial espionage, which is a fancier way of saying I stole stuff. Stealing data is not an exciting process. You can tell this because films in which it happens invariably involve an insane amount of props. In *Rogue One*, people climb up a tower and use some machine that looks like R.O.B. the Robot. In *Disclosure*, Michael Douglas enters some kind of virtual reality filing cabinet, like *Tron* if *Tron* had been really boring.

Anyway, I didn't have any props, at least none that were related to the theft. It went down like this:

"Hey, Gary," I said. "Vanetta needs a current copy of the code on a USB drive or something."

This was a very brazen approach, in that it could have come back to haunt me if Gary had asked Vanetta about it, but I was willing to bet things were chaotic enough that this would never happen. And even if it did, I figured I could lie my way around it. Maybe I wanted to play-test a copy of the game at home to help find bugs. That sounded dumbly plausible.

"I don't know why she wants it," I said. "I think it was something that Lawrence was asking about?"

I probably shouldn't have said that, because it was working against my play-test at home lie. But Gary just said, "Ugh, I'll get it."

Then Gary and I got into our laser motorcycles and drove into the Vault of Data. No, just kidding, although if this is somehow ever made into a movie, there will totally be laser cycles. Actually, Gary just copied it onto a USB and handed it to me.

I felt like I should talk to Gary a little bit more, just to wash the taste of this particular illegal activity out of his memories.

"So," I said, "how about them Blues?" referring to our city's venerable ice hockey team. This gambit was not so much dumbly plausible as simply dumb, because what the hell do I know about the Blues? I had a roommate in college who was obsessed with them, and from a year of living with her, I had learned nothing except that I wanted a new roommate.

Gary, however, took this more literally, and began to sing, as he had now done several times in our interactions. Gregorian chanting, this time, which I guess were the original Blues.

"*Vidi aquam egredientem,*" sang Gary.

It's hard to know how to respond to this, a grown man randomly chanting at you, although I could get behind the sentiment, and it was preferable to discussing ice hockey regardless.

"What's with you and singing, anyway?" I asked.

Gary regarded this question academically.

"My wife doesn't much like it when I sing," said Gary. "So I suppose I try to get it out of my system here."

"But what if we don't like it?" I asked.

"I suppose you could complain to Human Resources," said Gary, who also turned this into something of a song.

"Is there Human Resources?" I asked.

"Not since the drugging incident," said Gary, who I assumed, erroneously, was making a joke.

CHAPTER SEVENTEEN

The longer I worked at Cahaba, the less certain I became that they actually needed a secretary. Certainly, they did not need a receptionist, because no one visited, and there was no one to receive. A UPS guy named Frank came by and dropped off a few packages, but that was it. Of course, this could be one of those jobs that had a high tide and a low tide, and I just happened to be catching it at low tide. Or, maybe it was like my brother, Alden, was fond of saying: that most jobs are two hours of work spread out over an eight-hour period, although this is typically spoken by someone who has not done a lot in the service industry.

Productive things I did in the next hour:

- responded to email, which seemed to be the bulk of my job
- made coffee
- signed for some packages from Frank the UPS guy
- spoke to several reporters for various local news outlets, whereupon I found many delightful and interesting ways of saying "no comment at this time"

- ordered sandwiches for lunch for the staff, as per Vanetta's orders
- spoke with Ignacio Granger on the phone
- sent Emily the stolen code, only when things were very quiet

Of these, the only points of detective-y interest were the latter two, although I really liked Frank.

Let's start with the stolen code. I emailed to it Emily—or at least an email account that was distantly connected to her, and a few minutes later she had texted me an emoji of a martini glass.

Industrial espionage is nothing like I imagined it.

A few minutes after that I got a phone call on the Cahaba main line.

"Dahlia?"

It was Emily's voice, which surprised me. It wasn't a flunky or an underling, but her. I was especially surprised because she had warned me not to call her from work, but I supposed she could speak freely, even if I couldn't.

"Hello, madam," I said, indicating that I wasn't going to say her name. "What can I do for you?"

"Did you get my martini?" Emily asked. "I thought you would like it."

"Yes," I said. "I would love to hear about your deal on toner and other useful office supplies."

"And you're being secretive," said Emily. "You don't need to worry about me. I'm calling from a burner phone."

I cut straight to the chase.

"So am I done here?" I asked. "I mean, with this discussion of discounts on office supplies."

"The client will need to review the code, which could take an uncertain period of time, depending on what's happening with it. No more than a couple of days. We think it makes sense to leave you where you are for now."

This was about what I had expected, which was why I hadn't been exactly racing to get the code out to her. If I thought it was going to magically transport me out of here, I think I would have kicked it up a notch. But even spies can't escape bureaucracy.

"Sounds great," I said. "If you want to send a free toner sample, we'd be happy to try it."

The conversation with Ignacio went like this:

"Is this the secretary I spoke with yesterday?"

"I am, I think," I said, wondering if anyone else had picked up the phone after I had left. "Did you call in the morning, yesterday? Who is this?"

"This is Ignacio Granger. You spoke very highly of my Sonic the Hedgehog listicle."

Right. You could tell that Ignacio was a writer, because he held on to his slights.

"You can't argue with hits," I parroted back at him. "Should I put you through to Vanetta again?"

"Actually I wanted to speak with you," said Ignacio.

This could not possibly be a good thing.

"Why would you want that?" I said. God, I hoped that Ignacio hadn't found out who I was, because I did not want to explain why an amateur geek detective was working at a dying development company in the midst of a corruption scandal and murder. I knew I hadn't given him my real name—what did I call myself when I spoke to him yesterday?

"Well," said Ignacio. "For one, I think it's very surprising that you're still answering the phone, since you were murdered yesterday. That's a level of dedication you don't see a lot of in this industry."

Right. Cynthia Shaffer. I had told Ignacio that I was Cynthia Shaffer.

"Yeah," I said. "Well, maybe this is a Five People You Meet in Heaven Situation?"

"You're confusing your Mitch Albom," said Ignacio. "I think you mean the First Phone Call from Heaven."

I did not, as a point of order, want to discuss the literature of Mitch Albom with Ignacio, which was an oeuvre for which I had gleaned details from the back covers of books that I had picked up, read, and put back down. However, this was preferable to discussing my identity, and so I went on.

"Yes," I said. "I love Albom. His sentences are like lush grapes, ripe with meaning."

"How are you alive?" asked Ignacio, coming straight to the point. I originally wouldn't have been revealing Cahaba's private business (and the police's business) to inquiring journalists, but my first priority was covering my ass.

"It wasn't me that was killed. It was Cynthia's sister, Joyce. There was a bit of confusion about that."

"I thought you were Cynthia. Why are you talking about yourself in the third person?"

I was not willing to pretend to be Cynthia Shaffer on the phone. This was the sort of lie that led you into a terrible elaborate web of deceit. And while men of God might suggest that any lie necessarily led into a terrible web of deceit, I am firmly of the opinion that the well-placed lie can maneuver away from these webs and get you out of parking tickets to boot.

"Me?" I said. "No! I'm not Cynthia Shaffer."

"I'm quite sure that was the name you told me yesterday," said Ignacio.

I briefly considered the virtues of pretending to have not been the person on the phone yesterday, which were pretty bleak given my Sonic the Hedgehog blathering. Clearly that wasn't going to work.

"No, no, I'm not Cynthia Shaffer," I said. "She doesn't work here anymore. I'm Cynthia Shaver."

"I'm sorry?" said Ignacio, who sounded about as believing of this statement as you're imagining.

"Shaver. With a 'V.' It's a remarkable coincidence."

"I should think so," said Ignacio.

"Yes," I said. "Everyone commented on it relentlessly."

"I've never met a Shaver before," said Ignacio, with a journalist's instinct for bullshit. "What's the origin of that name?"

God bless Washington University, and the benefits of a broad education.

"Germanic. Comes from *schaffaere*—means like a steward. A manager. Which is ironic, I guess, given that I'm a secretary."

This momentarily silenced Ignacio Granger, because I lied like a pro. I wasn't even one hundred percent sure I was right about that, but I did know a little German and it was confidently delivered.

"That's interesting," he finally said. "We can discuss it when I'm there tomorrow."

I wasn't sure if I was moving inexorably into a web of lies, but certainly I wasn't moving away from them. At best, I was traveling parallel to the web of lies.

"Sure," I said. "I'd love that." Let's see, all I would need to do was convince everyone else in the office to back up my story, and also, probably, have Charice make me a fake ID with the name Cynthia Shaver on it. This would be a great project, since I had nothing else to do. "Should I put you through to Vanetta now?"

"Not just yet," said Ignacio. "I wanted to ask you what you thought about the new whistle-blower's letter."

"As I told you, I can't comment on that."

"That was for the previous letter," said Ignacio. "This is for the new letter. The one about the murder?"

It was my turn to be silent now, and Ignacio relished it.

"What second letter?"

"Not aware of it yet, are you?"

"I'm not," I said. "Do you have a link?"

"Sure," said Ignacio. "I can email it to you. It can be my little present to you, so you can seem like a good secretary for Vanetta. And then you can pay me back with information later."

"Just send me the link," I told him, and the conversation was done.

"That's cshaver@cahaba.com?" asked Ignacio, who was bound and determined to call my bluff.

"Never mind," I said. "I'll look it up myself."

It was not hard to find.

DE Employee Murdered—Nothing Changes

In my previous post, I had said that DE was eating its employees alive. It's hard to imagine that we could end up in a worse position, but here we are.

Two days ago, a woman thought to be a DE employee was murdered—straight up murdered—on-site at their offices. Police came, coroners arrived, autopsies were apparently done. While this poor woman's body was rotting away in the break room, staff were expected to stay and program. Even as the police arrived, even as the situation became increasingly and apparently wrong—stay and work, because the company demanded it.

But I am writing you, not because of the company's tremendous indifference to the death of one of its employees. I'm not writing you because of the murder investigation, about which I frankly do not know a whit.

I'm writing because, we are not one day later, and everyone is all back at work.

I know there are deadlines. This is a deadline-driven industry. But one of our colleagues was murdered, and the police investigation is still ongoing, and no one is in the right frame of mind to work.

It is beyond madness that we are back in the office. It is corporate irresponsibility. Yet, we are all afraid for our jobs, and so here we are.

These are not acceptable work conditions. Something must be done.

DE must be stopped.

A concerned spouse

I'm not actually sure how Ignacio Granger would ever come up with the idea that Vanetta would be pleased with me for bringing her this letter. As if I were a cat presenting its kill to its adoring owner. To imagine that Vanetta would regard this letter with anything other than a combination of abject horror and thrown chairs would be a fundamental misread of the situation.

Emily Swenson, on the other hand. She would be delighted.

Being the servant of two masters, I decided to first focus on the one who wouldn't throw furniture at me. I copied the link and pasted the contents of the letter into an email—a private email—to Emily. It was tempting to analyze the letter or provide commentary—because there were certainly peculiar things about it (most notably the letter writer's insistence on referring to Joyce as "the employee," which was obfuscating and untrue), but I figured I'd have time for that later.

I just wrote:

```
Emily:
Look what just showed up on the Internet. Looks
like the DE writer is definitely from Cahaba. More to
come later.
    Dahlia
```

I then walked into Vanetta's office, who visibly braced herself as though she were expecting bad news. Probably she was just getting used to it.

"What's wrong?" said Vanetta. "Something terrible has happened, hasn't it? It's all over your face."

As a side note, I can't tell you how much I wish I had a face that didn't naturally broadcast things like: "Something Terrible Has Happened" or "I Just Had Sex." It seems so fundamentally unfair that every thought in my head has to be visible to onlookers. This is a serious disadvantage as a detective, although it would serve me well if I ever were on reality TV.

"Not the best," I said, trying to break it to her gently.

"It's Morgan Freeman, isn't it? Did he turn us down?"

I was stunned by this question, mostly because I had momentarily forgotten about Morgan Freeman, and my mind was trying to piece together his connection to the business at hand.

"He's dead," said Vanetta, filling in the silence. "My God, Morgan Freeman is dead."

That this would be Vanetta's first guess as to "what terrible thing has happened" is perhaps indicative of how deeply she was entrenched in her own drama.

"Morgan Freeman is not dead," I said, which was true as far as I knew. "This has nothing to do with Morgan Freeman."

I handed Vanetta a printout of the second whistle-blower's letter, which she read. I could tell she was reading it because her face fell off her head and landed on the floor.

"Dear God," said Vanetta's face from the floor. "If only we could have had Ignacio in here last week."

"He called earlier," I said. "He's very excited about coming in."

"I'll bet he is."

Vanetta scooped up her face, which was clearly very agitated, and smooshed it back on her skull. All things considered, it could have been worse.

"Who did this?" she asked.

This question, I'm slightly embarrassed to admit, made me happy. Because my two masters were in a weird and probably elusive alignment. Vanetta and Emily wanted exactly the same thing, at least in this limited moment, and I was savvy enough to recognize that this was the industrial espionage equivalent of a solar eclipse. Planets had aligned, and it was magical, and it would probably not last very long.

"I'm not sure," I said. "Someone who works here, obviously. I mean, assuming no one else was murdered at another DE subsidiary."

"I don't know why they don't just come out and say Cahaba," said Vanetta, shaking her head at the letter. "The last one was at least circumspect; this one just comes and tells you exactly where it's from."

"Maybe they wrote it in a hurry," I said.

Vanetta was quiet for a moment and appeared to consider this.

"When, exactly, was this sent?" Vanetta asked.

I could see her thinking, which was perhaps easy because I was thinking too. Plus, she didn't have one of those faces that was well suited to hiding her thoughts either. We could be on reality TV together.

"It was posted at 10:43," I said, and I was surely making the mental calculations she was. What were we all doing at 10:43?

"When did the staff meeting finish?" she asked.

"Well before that—maybe around 10:30?"

"Does the rest of the staff know about this yet?"

Again, a well-placed question. Vanetta was not playing around.

"Certainly no one has mentioned it to me," I told her. "And I haven't told anyone but you."

"Go around, and find out what everyone has been working on this morning. I want you to literally see the work that they've created."

"Should we have a staff meeting, and everyone can do a show-and-tell of their work?"

Vanetta looked impressed by this idea, and I could see her mulling it over.

"No," she said. "Why don't you just go around and make discreet inquiries? You seem good at reading people. No one should be concerned unless they've done something wrong."

While I'd like to pretend that I didn't preen at Vanetta's compliment of my people-reading skills, especially since it meant, in one sense, that she was on to me, I positively did a shoulder shimmy at the approbation.

"On it, boss," I said. "I'll see what I can learn. Although," I added, just thinking of it, "this almost certainly means that Archie wasn't involved."

"Hooray," said Vanetta with no enthusiasm.

CHAPTER EIGHTEEN

Of course, as soon as I left her office, deductions started kicking in. First of all:

- Vanetta was awfully confident that I didn't do it. So much so, in fact, that it was vaguely suspicious. I couldn't have written the first letter, logically, but there was no reason, from her perspective, that I couldn't have written this one.
- Just because the post was made at 10:43 didn't necessarily mean that it was written in the preceding hour. It could have been drafted even earlier and posted later.
- In fact, the whole posting could have been automated. Someone could have written it last night and just scheduled the post to go live at a predetermined time. This is exactly what I would have done. I would have set it up to post and then made sure I was conspicuously not using a computer at the allotted time.
- A bit like Archie was, come to think of it.
- Although: 10:43? Who schedules a post at 10:43?

That's the problem with real-life logic. If Sherlock were working on this, all of his ruminations would have led in one direction, in a beautiful and unerring line. When I worked out thoughts—even logical thoughts—they spread out in all directions, like a fractal. It was still beautiful, in its own way, but not practical and certainly not unerring. The only thing I had really worked out was that it probably wasn't Archie, unless it was.

This actually gave me an odd sense of optimism, because I figured that it meant checking with staff was the most important way to tackle this problem. It meant that reactions were more important than ever.

There was probably a best order to do this in, which involved talking to Quintrell last. Yesterday he had blabbed the news about Cynthia to the whole office, and I was not about to make that mistake again. Even though he had gotten some sleep, Quintrell could get excited, and he was in a central location to boot.

I started with Tyler, who had his own office, or at least a cubicle in a room with a door.

Tyler was sitting at a computer and appeared to be doing nothing, or at least nothing involving work. He had an open web browser and was looking at an Amazon page of Ziggy Stardust T-shirts. I think it's Ziggy Stardust—you know, David Bowie with the red lightning bolt over his right eye—whichever character that was.

"Working hard or hardly working?" I asked.

"Honestly, you'd think the Internet would be more helpful," said Tyler, gesturing to the grid of Bowies before him on the monitor.

"These are not the Bowies you're looking for?" I asked.

"I was, well, going through Masako's old Facebook profile—and do you know what her favorite movie is?"

Without intending to, I made a face expressing displeasure

at this sort of reconnaissance, although it's exactly the sort of thing I would do. "The Life of Ziggy Stardust?" I guessed.

"*Stardust Memories*," sighed Tyler.

This bit of information perched at Morgan Freeman levels of relevance.

"I see," I said, although I didn't completely. "That's great, but I'm trying to find out: What actual work have you done this morning?"

"They don't make *Stardust Memories* T-shirts, apparently," said Tyler. "Apparently that's too weird."

"What kind of work have you done this morning? Vanetta wants to know."

"Vanetta doesn't really have purview over me," said Tyler, unthreatened. "Just so you know. But maybe this is just as well. About the T-shirt I mean. Maybe wearing a *Stardust Memories* T-shirt is trying too hard."

Was I like this when I first met Nathan? Or Erik? (Or, hell, Shuler?) I tended to think not, and maybe that meant I had never truly been in love with someone. Or, alternatively, it meant that I wasn't an idiot. I was inclined toward the latter, and Tyler's goo-goo-eyed intractability made me take more direct measures than I had been planning.

"Did you know that there was a new whistle-blower's letter posted?"

"That's my problem," said Tyler, which I thought was an interesting response until I realized that he was quite plainly not listening to me. "I always try too hard. But I actually do like *Stardust Memories*. I mean, I wouldn't say it's my favorite movie, but I like it. And it's a mysterious and inviting choice for some- one to say it's their favorite movie. It's not like, I don't know, *Flash Gordon*."

There's a Tumblr post I saw where a YA character says to a mysterious cool girl: "You're not like the other girls," and is responded to with a heartening: "What the fuck is wrong with the other girls?" I was inclined to say this now, except with *Flash Gordon*. What the fuck is wrong with *Flash Gordon*? But all of this is a gigantic digression.

"Tyler," I said. "Snap out of this," I said. "And you are definitely trying too hard. Masako will not want you to wear a novelty T-shirt to impress her."

"What about a tie?" asked Tyler. "Redbubble does ties now."

I had no choice but to step out of detective mode, just to bring Tyler back into reality.

"Dude: Nothing says I am desperately trying too hard like a *Stardust Memories* tie."

"Maybe you're right," Tyler said, then added, "Why are you in here again?"

"There's a new whistle-blower's letter."

"Oh, fuck me."

"Did you write it?"

"Psssh," said Tyler. "As far as I'm concerned, this place can burn."

"If it burns completely," I said, "you won't be working here in St. Louis, and you won't see Masako again."

"I can make long distance work," said Tyler. "I'm getting ready for a change from DE anyway. I actually spent the morning doing a little job hunting. Did you know that the St. Louis arts center is looking for a composition instructor?"

No, I had clearly never fallen for anyone as quickly or as hard as Tyler had for Masako. I couldn't tell you in the moment whether Tyler was just powerfully lovestruck or out of his damned mind, and the answer would have a lot to do with what Masako thought of the situation. I suppose it was possible that Masako was off somewhere Internet-stalking him, and job hunting in Austin, but this seemed supremely unlikely. Then again, she had been known to make rash romantic decisions too.

At least I had worked out what Tyler had been up to this morning. Job hunting, T-shirt shopping, and stupidity. I decided to put Tyler in the "obviously innocent" category.

Interviewing the rest of the office went more easily than my conversation with dream-bound Tyler. Lawrence went easiest of all, given that I had no idea where he was. Quintrell and Gary were the trickiest because I had hoped to talk to them separately, but they suddenly were tied together at the waist.

The two of them were at a third cubicle that was neither Quintrell's nor Gary's. I had initially pegged this as the old cubical of an ex-employee who had been fired, although it was littered with inexplicable objets d'art, such as a miniature snow globe with the Tower of Pisa in it, and a tiny papier-mâché tiger.

More to the point, there was an enormous monitor, which was filled with error messages, and Gary and Quintrell looked as though they planned to solve this problem by pushing their heads through the monitor and looking around inside. I suddenly felt like a mother compelled to yell at children to not sit so close to the television.

"Why is this crashing?" said Quintrell.

"This is the wrong question to ask," said Gary. "You should just begin with the presupposition that life equals suffering. Of course it is crashing. Life is torment. Torment is life. The more salient question is: Why did this once ever not crash?"

"Gary, Quintrell," I said, interrupting Gary's Zen and the Art of Coding Maintenance lecture, "how are you?"

"We are fucked," said Quintrell. "If you can pardon my French."

"*Zut alors*," I said. "You holding up, Gary? Worldview shattered yet?"

"My worldview consists of nothing but a universe destroying–blackness," said Gary.

I had grown, inexplicably, to like these buffoons, and I asked if I could get them anything, like a coffee. I generally don't go around offering to bring drinks to people, but I thought I would this time, on account of them being doomed.

"I'll have a Fresca," said Gary.

"We don't have a Fresca," I told him. I really didn't know this precisely, but I didn't feel like hammering around in the refrigerator.

"I probably shouldn't have any more coffee," said Quintrell. "I feel like I can hear my heart. In my face."

"How much have you had?" I asked.

"Simultaneously too much and not enough," said Quintrell.

"What have you guys been doing this morning?"

"Making gears spin, to no greater purpose," said Gary, who really was growing into a philosopher, aside from the Fresca thing. Fresca is the beverage choice of no philosopher. Not even Ayn Rand would drink a Fresca.

"Specifically, what have you been working on?" I asked, then feeling that I owed them an explanation, added, "Vanetta wants to know."

"We've been doing what she asked," said Quintrell. "We've been trying to get a version of this game going for the journalist. But it keeps crashing."

"It crashes on start-up now," said Gary. "So far all we've done is make it worse."

"Maybe just a little more coffee would help me," said Quintrell.

"Do you think you guys are maybe making it worse because you're still overtired? It's going to take at least a week of sleep before you get right again."

"I feel great!" said Quintrell a little maniacally. "I've never felt better than this!"

"You woke up in jail," I observed.

"Better. Worse," said Gary. "These are just arbitrary states. This code will someday die, just like all of us."

As ridiculous as this line was, it somehow seemed meaningful at the time, and then all of us got suddenly quiet and somber.

"We'll never make this work," said Quintrell. "I'm starting to think now that it never did work. That was just a mirage."

"The past is the past," said Gary. "You can't go home again."

Dumping the whistle-blower's letter on these two was just going to make them even sadder, and I didn't really want to do that.

So I didn't. They could find out later.

CHAPTER NINETEEN

I still couldn't find Lawrence anywhere, which was probably the least surprising thing that has happened in this, or perhaps any, book. Lawrence, I was quickly realizing, made it his business to not be found. Because being found meant that possibly, just possibly, someone might make you do something that vaguely resembled work.

Even with that, I wasn't exactly sure how or when he had left. Presumably he must have ducked out while I was in Tyler's office, or Vanetta's. I sat down at my workstation and decided to call his cell number, which had been helpfully printed and tacked to the corkboard next to my computer. I did this almost idly, because I did not expect him to pick up. This would defeat the entire purpose of ducking out.

But lo and behold, he did. I was a little speechless, actually.

"Cynthia?" he said. "Are we calling you Cynthia now? I can't remember. Maybe that's disrespectful to the dead."

"Cynthia is not dead," I said. "Remember? That was Joyce, and it is disrespectful to the living, to me, for you to not call me by my actual name."

"What was your name again? Maude? Shirley? Agnes?"

"Dahlia," I said, grumbling despite my best intentions not to.

"I don't know why you're persisting in saddling me with an old woman name."

"I guess it just suits you," said Lawrence. "Anyway, what kind of crisis is going on there now? Let me guess: I can't come back to the office because Vanetta has been run through with an awl?"

"No," I said.

"Quintrell has been consumed by a fire?"

"No," I said.

"Jason has been devoured by mice?"

"There is no Jason, and I'm not aware of any mice."

"Twenty-four hours without a murder," said Lawrence. "You should type that up and put that on a sign. Maybe it would raise morale."

Having lived with Charice and dated Nathan, I was used to people who enjoyed the sound of their own voice. I knew how to speak their language, which generally means letting them make whatever jokes they want, and then cut in with relevant questions and information. It does no good to try and prevent whatever ridiculous jokes they have in mind, because it only makes them cranky. And, like trying to stop a leaky faucet with your finger, only makes the tomfoolery come out elsewhere.

So I let Lawrence have his moment, as I suspect everyone did.

"I'll take it under advisement," I said, not bothering to express the opinion that an "X Days Since Last Murder" sign was probably not likely to raise morale, nor would it make a good talking point when Ignacio Granger came through. I was expecting to have to reorient Lawrence to the topic at hand, as I might with Charice, when he surprised me by taking up the subject himself.

"So, what's the crisis? I assume there's a crisis. I assume that you wouldn't just call me to see how I'm doing."

"It's not how you're doing," I asked. "It's what you're doing. Vanetta wants to know what you've been working on this morning, and where you went."

"I hope this doesn't sound callous," said Lawrence, in a voice that sounded completely callous, "but I'm being wherever the fuck I want to be and doing whatever the fuck I want to do. As per usual."

"Can you be less broad?" I asked.

"I don't answer to Vanetta," said Lawrence, who was suddenly surprisingly peevish about this. I had expected him to be a little breezier. "Or to you."

What was the likelihood that this clown was the father of Vanetta's proto-baby?

"You ought to treat Vanetta with more respect," I said, which wasn't at all what I had planned or intended to say. Maybe having been surrounded by all the talismanic belongings of Cynthia had summoned up the old woman inside me. "She works so hard trying to keep this place together. She's not asking for you to give up your personal secrets—as if she doesn't already know them—she just wants to know where you are and what you've been up to."

Lawrence, to my even greater shock, sounded sad. Reproached, even.

"I know she does. Believe me, I know how much Vanetta wants this. Anyway, I'm at the Beechwood."

"That's a restaurant?"

"At the moment, I prefer to think of it as a bar."

"You're day-drinking now? You're gonna have to pull your shit together before this journalist comes here tomorrow."

"I am a big believer in tradition," said Lawrence. "I'm practically superstitious about it."

"You have a drinking tradition?" I asked.

"I have lots of drinking traditions. I have a tall glass of kefir before an important negotiation, and then if it goes well, I follow it up with a shot of Jägermeister."

"That's a disgusting combination of beverages," I said.

"Tradition is frequently disgusting," said Lawrence, which was a fair observation.

"So you're out because your negotiation went well," I said.

"I haven't finished telling you about the tradition," said Lawrence. "If it goes very badly, I have bourbon on the rocks. And if it goes very, very well, I open a bottle of champagne."

"The details of this are unnecessary to me."

"If it goes very, very badly, I drink ouzo. Into oblivion."

"So what are you drinking?" I asked.

"Bourbon on the rocks," said Lawrence. "Did Vanetta get the bad news yet?"

"That Quintrell and Gary can't make last week's build work?"

"No," said Lawrence. And now that I had been clued into it, I noticed music in the background—Steve Winwood, from the sounds of it.

"You mean about the second whistle-blower's letter?" I ventured.

"Jesus, no. There's a second whistle-blower's letter? Garçon! Get me some ouzo."

"Apparently so," I said. "That's partially why I'm checking on your whereabouts this morning."

"What, Vanetta thinks I did it?"

"I doubt it. But it's like Ronald Reagan said: 'Trust, but verify.'"

"It's like Winston Churchill said: Fuck you, Vanetta."

I did not like being told off by Lawrence in this way, but neither did I feel that it was out of character for him. I suppose this could have made me suspicious—what was he trying to hide?— but mostly I thought that this was his general response to being called out on anything.

Also, I doubted that Winston Churchill had a lot of opinions about Vanetta one way or the other.

"So," I said. "Like I was getting at—what were you doing earlier this morning?"

"I was on the phone with DE, actually. Getting the bad news that led me to this bar."

I was getting off topic, but I was curious.

"Okay, fine, what's your bad news?"

"Morgan Freeman is out."

"He's alive, right?" I asked, because at this point you never know.

"Of course he's alive," said Lawrence. "But his people say that he's turned down the project. Apparently, he doesn't do video games."

This did not seem like the most terrible news I had heard in the past week, or frankly even the past hour, and I told this to Lawrence.

"Oh yeah? Wait until Vanetta finds out."

I got off the phone with Lawrence and checked Archie's office, which was empty. It was possible that he was still putting away sound equipment downstairs, although this would have required moving at a glacial pace. It seemed somehow more likely that he was at the Beechwood himself. I should have asked Lawrence to keep a lookout for him.

As it happens, I did not have Archie's cell number helpfully printed out at my desk, probably because he was less inclined to disappearances than Lawrence was. So, I gave up on Archie for now, and headed back to Vanetta's office to report.

Vanetta was clearly on the phone with DE, and from appearances, was having one of those conversations that a Bond villain henchman has with his boss shortly before getting bumped off. I could only hear one half of the conversation, but this is how I imagined it going:

Vanetta, actual dialogue: "It came as a shock to me as well, Frank."

Man on phone, imagined dialogue: "AT OUR ORGANIZATION, WE DON'T CARE FOR SHOCKS, VANETTA. WE RELY UPON YOU TO BE OUR EYES AND EARS. PRAY THAT YOU DO NOT DISAPPOINT ME A SECOND TIME."

Vanetta, actual dialogue: "We're doing everything we can to solve this problem."

Man on phone, imagined, cracking knuckles. "SEE THAT YOU DO. I'D HATE TO SEE SOMETHING…HAPPEN TO YOU."

"We're working on it right now. I can promise you that there won't be another letter."

"EXCELLENT. YOU'VE ALWAYS BEEN MY FAVORITE, VANETTA. I'D HATE TO…STOP DOING BUSINESS WITH YOU."

"Of course, sir. I'll keep you abreast of the situation."

White cat, in man's lap: HISS.

Vanetta put down the phone and stared at me, although her face was, for once, completely unreadable. She was looking at me, but in a dreamy and oddly assessing way, as though my head were a Bob Ross painting. I didn't much care for it, actually.

"You all right, boss?"

I actually called her boss, and this came out in a goon-like manner, as if I were suddenly from New Jersey and the next phrase out of me would have been "you want I should whack this guy?" I guess my James Bond fantasia had put me in a mood.

"I'm fine," said Vanetta, sounding Not Fine. "DE is not happy about the leak, but I had expected them to be not happy about the leak. Why should they be?"

"They want someone's head, I take it?"

"You take it right," said Vanetta. "No one fessed up to it, did they?"

"No," I said. And thinking over it, I was doubtful that anyone had actually done it. Tyler had the means, I suppose, but no particular motivation, and I didn't think that he was that great an actor. Gary and Quintrell certainly had the impression of people who had been working all morning, and besides which, Quintrell HAD WILLINGLY COME HERE FROM JAIL, and thus did not seem like the sort of person inclined to complain about working. Quintrell could be fired, and he would probably still be working. Lawrence could have done it but seemed genuinely surprised by the news and had no motivation besides.

That just left Archie, which was possible, hypothetically, but also felt like the sort of theory that a cop would use on some awful Netflix documentary about a wrongfully imprisoned man. You could technically line up the facts so that it worked, but if you spent much time thinking about it at all, it was bound to fall apart. Even more so if you played dramatic music behind it.

I told all this to Vanetta, even the Netflix part.

"We know it's someone from here, though," she said. "It must be a spouse."

"There aren't a lot of spouses," I said. "Quintrell's got some sort of proto-girlfriend that he sees on a semimonthly basis. Tyler is imminently single. Archie's ladyfriend is you—"

"Among others—" said Vanetta.

"I don't know what Lawrence's situation is, but he doesn't seem like someone you'd fight to spend more time with."

"Ha!" said Vanetta. "And also, true."

"That just leaves Gary's wife."

"Call her," said Vanetta.

"That seems really invasive," I said. "And would that even be legal? Like, from a Human Resources standpoint?"

"CALL HER," said Vanetta again. "I'll email you her phone number. Her name is Maura, I think. Or Laura. Maura or Laura."

This conversation sounded like a nightmare, but I was getting reasonably good at nightmares these days.

"You realize that whoever wrote the whistle-blower's letter could be someone who already left," I said. "Cynthia, or Jason, or whoever used to work here before me."

Vanetta sighed. "Of course I realize that. But this isn't even really about figuring out who the writer is. It's about assuring DE that we're doing everything we can to figure out who the letter writer is. I'm not ready to start harassing old employees."

"Gary's wife it is, then," I said. At least I had legit work to do.

"Actually," said Vanetta. "I just remembered. It's Cora."

"Great," I said. "Although I've got some bad news from Lawrence. Morgan Freeman does not do video games."

Vanetta said nothing and sat down. I had expected fireworks from her, at least a raised voice, but she was completely quiet for a long moment, whereupon she slowly got into her chair, and said, very quietly:

"I want to be alone."

CHAPTER TWENTY

Gary's wife was named Adalbjorg, which emphatically does not rhyme with or even resemble Laura, Cora, or Maura. This is the quality of information I'm working with. I learned this by asking Gary before I made the call, which perhaps wasn't terribly artful, but there's nothing wrong with the occasional direct approach.

I was not keen on this conversation, even before I knew about the wrong name, because it felt like a shakedown, and while I was getting shakedown money from Emily, I was not getting it from Vanetta. Also, I find that I like a little more time to gear up for a shakedown. It's the sort of thing that you want to mentally prep for. You can't just show up and threaten someone. You've got to psych yourself up, maybe listen to an appropriately violent playlist.

I just went and called Gary's wife.

"Hello," I said. "Is this Ms. Bright?"

"Yes," said a voice, which I will note was youthful and unaccented, because these might not be the associations you form for the name Adalbjorg. "Who is this?"

"This is Dahlia—I'm the new receptionist over at Cahaba Apps."

"Oh," said Adalbjorg, concerned, "everything okay over there? Lawrence hasn't drugged my husband again, has he?"

"Wait, what?"

"If he has, just let him sleep it off like last time."

"No one has drugged your husband."

"Oh, well, good. Everything else fine?"

"Yes," I said. "Twenty-four hours without a murder. Longer probably."

Adalbjorg laughed at my joke—not uproariously—but a light chuckle of the perfect length. "You can only go up from there."

This was not wholly true. I'd already been worried at various points that Archie, Lawrence, and improbably, Morgan Freeman had somehow gotten murdered this morning, and so I certainly did not think that upward progress was an inevitability. Although I went along with the idea.

"Why did Lawrence drug your husband?" I asked.

"Oh, it was just some mix-up. You know Lawrence."

I did not know Lawrence, apparently. I would want to follow up on this.

"So," said Adalbjorg, "What's going on?"

I wasn't sure exactly how I wanted to play this conversation. I'd had some ideas, but it had depended upon what kind of Adalbjorg had picked up the receiver:

- Nervous, anxious Adalbjorg, at which point I would assume her guilt and press hard.
- Indignant, irritated Adalbjorg, at which point I would tread softly.
- Swedish Chef Adalbjorg, who would speak with an indecipherably thick Icelandic accent and periodically say things like "bjork, bjork, bjork." At which point I would question mark, question mark, question mark.

But I had gotten a friendly "Is my husband drugged again Adalbjorg," which certainly wasn't one of my initial sketches. So I settled on a new angle.

"Listen," I said, using my most earnest voice while also lying through my teeth. "I'm not supposed to be calling you, but I wanted to give you a heads-up."

"A heads-up about what?"

"There was a new whistle-blower's letter this morning. It just came out. And apparently, the top brass think that it's you."

"Why would they think that?" Adalbjorg sounded more bewildered than indignant or suspicious.

"This new letter definitely came from our office. And it's from a spouse," I said—which wasn't exactly true—"and you're the only spouse. Everyone else is single."

"What about Jason's wife, Carla?"

"Jason got fired," I said.

"What about that accounts guy—what was his name—Derek? Didn't he have a live-in boyfriend?"

I had never even heard of Derek, or his alleged live-in boyfriend. "He doesn't work here anymore either."

"Jesus, they cut Derek?" said Adalbjorg. "I didn't realize how cleared out that place had gotten."

"So, did you send it?" I asked.

"No," said Adalbjorg. "I try to make nice with everyone. At the Christmas party I spent the whole time talking to Derek. He's really gone?"

Fuck Derek. He was a dead end.

"I guess so," I said, trying to figure out a way to get this conversation back on track.

"I liked him," said Adalbjorg. "But he didn't get along with Lawrence, I suppose."

"You didn't write the whistle-blower's letter?" I asked again. I had expected more of a vociferous denial, but I got the impression that Adalbjorg regarded Cahaba as a place that was only mostly real. Maybe that sounds silly, typed out, but it's a thing that happens. Occasionally, my brother, Alden, will try telling me about TA'ing at the University of Maine, and while I'm willing to listen, the stories come infrequently enough that they feel vaguely fable-like. It's hard to take them seriously, and I love my brother, obviously.

"Of course not," said Adalbjorg. "If Gary lost that job, it'd be a real inconvenience."

"A real inconvenience" was her word choice. She did not sound like someone on the brink of financial ruin.

"You're not upset about him working so much?" I asked.

"He's more upset about it than I am," said Adalbjorg. "I mean, I love my husband, of course, but since Pieter was born everything's been kind of surreal anyway. My mother says I'm nesting. It's almost sort of nice to have the time alone with the baby. I think he's more upset about it than I am, always going on about 'Cat's in the Cradle.' The song. Not the string. Gary sings a lot, you know."

This did not need to be said.

"What were you doing at 10:43 this morning?" I asked.

"Eating a mango-lassi parfait. Why, what happened at 10:43?"

I thought this question would have been self-evident, but I wasn't sure if Adalbjorg was playing dumb or just genuinely didn't understand what I was getting at.

"I'm checking to see if you had the opportunity," I said honestly.

"Oh!" said Adalbjorg. "Like an alibi! Aren't you industrious? Well, I would think so. I mean, it's just yogurt with oats on it, really. And mango. And some cardamom. You make it the night before and leave it in fridge."

While this sounded delicious, it was once again not what I wanted to pursue.

"So you can't prove you didn't send it?"

"I guess the biggest obstacle is that there's no Internet here."

"You mean it's down?"

"No, I mean we don't have Internet."

. . .

"You mean it's down?"

"No," said Adalbjorg, now moving slowly as if I were the stupid one, "I mean we don't have Internet access here."

"But like on a cell phone," I said.

"I don't have a cell phone. We have no Internet."

I'd been shot at by trees, knocked off a steamboat, and been hired as industrial spy, and yet this was the least believable thing I had ever heard.

"How old are you?" I asked.

"Thirty-six," said Adalbjorg. "Gary's got a few years on me."

"How do you live?" I asked. "And wait—your husband develops games. He's a programmer!"

"We started doing it during the election—I just got so tense, I didn't want to follow it anymore. So we started cutting cords. We said we were going to go back after November, but then you get used to it. Then I got pregnant, and I'm kind of a hypochondriac anyway; it just seemed that my life was easier without WebMD in it."

"How does Gary work from home?"

"He doesn't," said Adalbjorg. "And why should he?"

"Right," I said, a bit shaken. "Well, I just wanted to give you the heads-up."

"Thanks, I suppose," said Adalbjorg. "But I'm not too worried. I'm sure they'll figure out who the culprit really is. And if you could send Derek's contact information home with Gary, I'd love to catch up with him."

If I had determined anything from talking to Adalbjorg, it was that this was a wild-goose chase. No one had reacted in a suspicious way, and there was no smoking gun. Moreover, it was entirely possible that the letter writer was a former employee that I had never met—or worse, the spouse of a former employee I had never met—who was just trolling the company because they were pissed off about being fired. This seemed entirely reasonable. And I didn't have the time, or frankly interest, to hunt down and interview Derek's live-in boyfriend, whether Adalbjorg liked him or not.

So, I decided, in lieu of any other productive course of action, to go back to the source.

I read the letter again, this time with the benefit of not being shocked, to try to suss out some sort of clue that would indict someone. Turns out, clues abounded.

Two days ago, a DE employee was murdered—straight-up murdered—on-site at their offices. Police came, coroners arrived, autopsies apparently done. While this poor woman's body was rotting away in the storeroom, staff were expected to stay and program. Even as the police arrived, even as the situation became increasingly and apparently wrong—stay and code, because the company demands.

There were a few things wrong to wonder about here. First of all, it was awfully definitive about there being a murder. It was a drug overdose, which was *probably* a murder as far as the police thought. But it could have been a suicide, potentially. The lead suspect had been released, after all. "Straight-up murdered" felt curiously confident and made me wonder, briefly, if the letter writer was the person who killed Joyce. How else could they be so sure about it?

Second, it alluded to the fact that Joyce wasn't an employee of Cahaba, which was not a piece of information everyone had. It made it much more likely that the writer was still working here, or was at least keeping very well-informed.

Lastly, and most oddly, the staff didn't stay in all day. Vanetta had let people go home. Some people had chosen to stay, but it wasn't mandatory, and she didn't stay herself. That was the oddest and strangest bit about this bit of whistle-blowing. It was whistle-blowing on a thing that didn't exactly happen.

Of course, this last bit could have been written just to make DE look bad, and it was certainly arguable that any time spent in an office with a corpse is too much time. But it was an awful lot of wrong data.

It definitely started to lend credence to the idea that the whistle-blower was someone who wasn't directly in contact with the company—perhaps an old employee. But of course, even an old employee had to have a source on the inside for all this stuff. Someone had to be spilling out information.

Everyone was working so hard at this point that it felt challenging to interrupt anyone for the purposes of my investigation, but I managed to catch Gary as he was exiting the men's restroom and thus completely not working.

"Did Lawrence drug you?" I asked.

"Where'd you hear that?" he asked.

"Your wife," I said.

"Honey Badger don't care," he said, not to me so much as to the air around me.

"What happened?" I asked.

Gary looked embarrassed by the question. "It's really not a big deal, and you don't need to worry about it. It's not like he's going to drug you," Gary said. "It was just a prank that got out of hand."

"Your wife said it was a mix-up," I said.

"Yes," said Gary. "The mix-up was that I started ever working here."

The rest of the day went on in a relatively ordered way, if that phrase has any more meaning at this point. Archie came in and finally started working. Gary and Quintrell seemed to get something up and going, although I didn't know what. Vanetta appeared to be hard at work in her office—certainly she was typing prodigiously, but I wasn't exactly sure as to the nature of her work either. Despite the alleged lack of general deadlines, when five o'clock hit, and the day was ostensibly over, no one seemed to head for the doors. Not even Tyler, who had spent the morning shopping for David Bowie paraphernalia.

I had still hoped to ask Quintrell a few questions, but it seemed wrong to bother him, since he and Gary appeared to be on the edge of a breakthrough. "It's finally working!" I could hear them saying—then backtracking, "It's finally mostly working."

And besides which, I had made arrangements for the evening. Unwise arrangements.

I had been struck in the head and was obviously not in my right mind when I had suggested meeting Detective Anson Shuler in Forest Park for a roller-skating excursion. I specifically use the word "excursion" here, because I did not and do not want to use the word "date," although that is probably a fair approximation of the event.

It was a stupid thing to do, given that I had a boyfriend, of sorts, and that I wasn't even really sure I wanted to be in a relationship with Anson Shuler. But when you get hit in the head, you make rash decisions. Perhaps those decisions are more indicative of your true nature than the one your non-concussed self would make, but who knows. I was going skating.

I needed to get out of Cahaba quickly, because the sun wasn't going to stay up forever, and I wasn't that keen on hanging around Forest Park in the dark; although, if you had to do it, a police officer is your best possible choice of companion. As I drove there I naturally got a phone call from Nathan.

The whole situation made me feel like I was a suspect in the sort of ridiculous case that I would ordinarily be employed to investigate. Dahlia has a boyfriend, yes, but is off having secret meetings with another fellow! What does this mean? (Actually this is a fair question. I ought to hire myself to find out.)

But I was feeling duplicitous and guilty, and even though I hadn't, technically, done anything terribly wrong yet, it all made me feel sort of awful.

I had to answer the phone, even though it was terrible, because the prospect of not answering the phone was even more terrible.

"Hey, Dahlia," said Nathan. "You have a sec?"

"Well," I told Nathan, "I'm driving right now. What's up?"

"I just wanted to touch base with you before you met up with Shuler," said Nathan. He said this casually, very casually, and I nearly ran off the road.

"How did you hear about that?" I asked.

"Shuler mentioned it to me," said Nathan. "It was really awkward because he seemed to think that I already knew about it, except that I didn't know about it. You forgot to mention it to me, I guess," said Nathan.

"Well, we're just skating," I said. "And I was going to talk with him about the case."

"Masako seems to think that you have a crush on Shuler," said Nathan.

I will crush Masako with my bare hands.

"I wouldn't say that necessarily," I said. And I wouldn't necessarily.

"I feel like we need to have a relationship conversation," said Nathan.

I really do like Nathan, but when I die and go to hell, Satan will greet me at the fiery gates with the phrase "we need to have a relationship conversation." I'm not good at relationships or conversations, and when you put them together, I do even worse.

"Yes," I said. "A relationship conversation. You start."

"I just don't want to be weird about this," said Nathan. "Is this weird?"

"Yes," I said honestly. "It's a little weird."

"Well, we never said that we were exclusive," said Nathan. "I guess I just sort of took that as written. So: Are we exclusive?"

"Maybe?"

"I don't want to be someone in a love triangle," said Nathan. This could very reasonably have been a prelude for the next sentence of: "And so I'm breaking up with you," but it wasn't. It was its own declarative sentence, to which I had to respond.

"Listen," I said. "I don't know what this thing with Shuler is tonight. I agreed to it when I had a head wound."

"Well, it would appear to be a date, Dahlia."

"Yes," I said.

"No polyamory. I'm just not into that."

"What?"

"I mean, not with another guy," Nathan said, then paused, as if contemplating other possible permutations. "Nah, no polyamory—it's just not my scene."

"What made you think this was an option on the table in the first place?"

"I didn't say that it was," said Nathan. "I just wanted to make clear that it wasn't."

"Well, we're on the same page. So this is not a 'you're dead to me' phone call?" I asked.

"No," said Nathan. "But just so you know, I'm also going out with a beautiful model this evening."

"Seriously?"

"Well," said Nathan. "She's a hand model. It's not like you said we couldn't see other people."

"I guess," I said. "That seems fair."

Although, it didn't seem fair. It seemed like a massive misstep.

"Don't do anything I wouldn't do," said Nathan.

CHAPTER TWENTY-ONE

I met Anson Shuler at the parking lot. This was, any way you put it, madness, because I had brought roller skates with me. It was hard to imagine how this was going to go. But there was an upside to all of it, which was that I could maybe learn a little bit about what the police knew regarding Cahaba. It's a rare disadvantage to not be a murder suspect, but I hated not knowing what the police were thinking. All of my information was second- or thirdhand, and getting just a few choice bits of their reasoning would have been tremendously helpful.

Shuler met me at my car, and I immediately noticed that he hadn't brought his skateboard, which was the ostensible, if insane, plan for outing. I asked him about it.

"Yeah, well," said Shuler. "I changed my mind. The universe does not want to see me skateboarding."

"I was thinking we could listen to Blink-182, and I could use nineties slang, like: What's the dealio?"

Shuler did not seem persuaded by this, and instead pointed out that I had recently suffered a head wound.

"Should you really be on roller skates after a concussion?" asked Shuler. "Upon reflection, it seems like a terrible idea."

"So what should we do instead?" I asked.

"Zoo or art museum?" asked Shuler—and thanks to the magic of Forest Park, each of these was just a short walk away. "But I think we should go somewhere, because I've got kind of a proposition for you."

We settled on the art museum, and can I just take a moment to praise the Saint Louis Art Museum, which I think is one of the best museums in the world. Okay, yes, I've been to fancier, better endowed places—the MoMA and the Guggenheim—but here's the kicker about the Saint Louis Art Museum. It's free.

Typing that out makes me sound like a cheapskate, but once you've got an awesome free art museum in your neighborhood, you suddenly realize that visiting every other museum is like going on Supermarket Sweep. You've got to stuff as much art into your eyeballs as you can to get your money's worth. "Dahlia's going straight for the Lichtensteins—those are worth about two million apiece—and, look, she's found the bonus prize—a giant inflatable banana!"

The Saint Louis Art Museum is the only place where you could go in, casually walk around for a half hour, look at your favorite painting, leave, and not feel cheated.

But I digress.

It took us a minute to decide what to go look at. They've got a Seurat that I generally like, even if it isn't the absolute showiest of his work, but Shuler was making a case for early American furniture. I had never known anyone who went out of their way to look at Early American Furniture, and I had always sort of assumed that the category was only included for some mandatory purpose I didn't understand. The results of the powerful American desk lobby, I assumed.

Anyway, we were looking at a red mahogany desk hutch when Shuler dropped his proposition at me.

"So, Dahlia," said Shuler. "You asked me when we first went out if I liked being a cop. You remember that?"

I did remember that. We had gone out for frozen custard, and I had mostly asked him just to have something to talk about. I also remember that the question had struck him oddly, as if it wasn't the sort of thing he was used to being asked.

"Yeah," I said. "What did you tell me—that you were still deciding?"

"Well," said Shuler. "I think I've decided."

I felt that this would naturally lead to further conversation, as it sounds uncannily like the prelude to the rest of a sentence, but Shuler just continued to look at the desk. Honestly, it was a tiny little desk. People were smaller then.

Finally, after I realized that Shuler wasn't going to voluntarily continue his thought, I bit:

"So, what's the verdict?"

"I think I'm out," said Shuler.

This seemed to me to be a major life revelation—certainly Shuler's brows suggested so—because they sighed up and down along with the rest of him as he spoke.

"Wow," I said.

I was feeling better about this outing now, because it was feeling less and less like flirty fun and more like staring into the abyss. Where here, the part of the abyss is played by a tiny desk. Questions began to bubble up, of course, not the least of which was: "Why are you telling me?" but there is a time for questions and a time for silence, and this was the latter.

And he answered one of my questions anyway without it needing to be asked.

"I'm just so tired of it," he said. "I got into this because I wanted to be one of the good guys. And, also, maybe because I thought it would irritate my parents."

"Always a good reasoning for major life decisions," I said.

"I know, right? At the time, it seemed almost noble," he chuckled. "Now, not so much. I just can't deal with it anymore."

What "it" was here, precisely, was something of a mini-mystery, but I'd read enough stories about policing lately that I didn't want to push too hard. Instead I asked:

"So what are you going to do instead?" I started to add "build desks?" as a snarky rider, to lighten the mood a little, but then thought the better of it. Besides which, maybe that was his plan. Maybe we were here gathering blueprints.

"That's what I wanted to talk to you about," said Shuler. "You're getting certified as a private detective, right? That's what Maddocks tells me."

"Slowly," I said. Although, in truth, it wasn't a huge amount of coursework. In some states, Mississippi, for example, anyone can be a private detective, if you've got the nerve to call yourself one. Missouri was a little harder than that, but not overly so.

"Well, how soon before you're done?" asked Shuler.

I was suddenly feeling cornered. Although, I don't know why I should have been anxious. I suppose I just don't like having my plans pinned down.

"Maybe six months," I said.

"I was thinking about becoming a private detective myself," said Shuler.

And it hit me. This was the statement that had augured this meeting, not a romantic interest in me. I could tell that Shuler was anxious about telling me this because of the carefully rehearsed and overly casual way he said it. I appreciated the theater.

"Right," I said. "So you're becoming a private detective, and I'm becoming a private detective. And you came here to tell me—"

"This town's not big enough for the two of us," said Shuler. And I laughed. Too loudly, because a security guard glared at me.

"Scram, Shuler, University City's my territory," I told him, approximating a 1930s gangster voice very badly.

"What I was thinking," said Shuler, "is that we could maybe go into business together?"

"Moss and Shuler Investigations," I said. "It'd look good on a door."

I had fully expected Shuler to say "Shuler and Moss Investigations," because that is how this patter always goes, but instead he upped the ante:

"I was thinking Shuler and Co."

"Well," I said. "Two's company."

"What do you think?" asked Shuler.

I thought that I wasn't ready for discussions for names on the door.

"I'll take it under advisement."

I did not, as it happened, ask Anson Shuler any actual useful questions about the case. I had figured I'd get into it with him later, but the business about "Shuler & Moss Investigations" had kind of knocked me out of orbit. All of my follow-up questions were about that. How much money would we need to start such an endeavor? Answer: a fair amount, but we could get a bank loan. Where could we find office space to rent? Would we need office space? And Shuler had answers for all of these. He had me at a disadvantage, because he'd clearly been thinking about this for a very long time. And, I have a business degree, after all. This was a thing that was doable.

The question I didn't ask, maybe because I didn't want to know the answer myself, is what he actually gained by teaming up with me. Was this a weird way for him to just spend time with me? No, probably not, because that's already clearly doable without involving bank loans. But I could easily see the advantage of working with him—ex-cop, with lots of police connections? Who wouldn't hire him?

But here I am going down the wrong path again.

When I arrived back at my house, I was only somewhat surprised to see Tyler on the floor, eating ramen noodles with Charice.

Let's start with the ramen. First of all, this was not Maruchan, store-bought 99 cent stuff. This was a dish, made by Charice, that had grilled mushrooms and tofu and actual chopped vegetables. I point this out purely out of bitterness, because there was none left for me.

Next there was Tyler, who had changed into a T-shirt and sweatpants and looked possibly as though he had jogged over here. His green wisp of hair was limp and looked like it had been brutally mauled by the St. Louis humidity.

Finally, there was Charice, who was wearing a lavender vest with white trim that made her look vaguely like an extra on *Battlestar Galactica*. She was casually futuristic, which is not a bad way to think about Charice in general, honestly.

"Dahlia," said Charice. "You have a visitor. You know, I remember when weeks would go by without anyone visiting you."

"Yes," I said, "those were good times." Although, they weren't, truthfully. There was just no reason to tell Tyler that.

"Tyler," I said, "you come by to dig up more intel on Masako?"

Tyler spat out his soup. "Wait—does your roommate know Masako?"

"I know everybody," said Charice in what was probably only a partial exaggeration of the truth.

"I didn't," said Tyler. "Maybe I should..."

"I'm sorry I brought it up," I told him. "Why are you here, then?"

"I came to see you," said Tyler. "I got some big news about Cahaba."

"What kind of big news?" I asked.

I hadn't been in communication with Emily yet today, and it would be great if I had something impressive to tell her.

"Let's just say the lack of a deadline is not a good sign," said Tyler.

"No," I told him. "Let's not 'just say' that. Let's say everything, including the subtext."

Tyler lowered his voice, although I couldn't have told you why. "So, I heard that DE is selling the studio."

"Is that bad? I mean, no one is overly fond of DE, anyway, right? It could be good for the game."

"DE is keeping *Peppermint Planes*. They're keeping all the intellectual property—it's just the people they're getting rid of."

I took a moment to process this.

"So the code that these people have been working on day and night, month in, month out—it's all just going to be handed over to someone else to finish?"

"It's probably going to be tossed altogether," said Tyler.

"But I don't understand—there was that proposal for a new art style, and the bit with voice acting?"

"That proposal is probably all that's going to survive. DE loves Archie, so they're going to keep him. DE does shit like this all the time—look at what happened at Wayward Studios in Austin."

I hate when knowledgeable people throw out references like that, as though you are also an expert in the field and can reasonably follow along. "Why, look at what happened to William McKinley's vice president, Garret Hobart! The parallels are countless!" I mean, honestly.

I had never heard of Wayward Studios in Austin, and I did not know what had happened there, though I could at least gather that it was Not Good. But I was still processing DE's motivations, because I was not used to dealing with a corporate mind, which despite what the Supreme Court tells us, is not like the human mind at all.

"Hang on a sec—we have a visitor tomorrow—why did DE instruct us to impress this goon if we're about to be sold off?"

"It's a secret, Dahlia. That's the reason."

"Then how did you hear about it?"

"I know a guy who works in their Contract Department—I like to know which way the wind is blowing."

I was still putting this together.

"So do you think that the murder scared DE off, and now they want to unload the company because of the bad publicity?"

"Dahlia, this has been in the works for weeks," said Tyler. "I'm just hearing about it now, but it's been brewing for ages."

"So why is this relevant?"

"Find out who knew about this, and I'll bet you find your whistle-blower."

CHAPTER TWENTY-TWO

I spent the night dreaming about "Moss & Shuler Investigations" or at least about how good it would look on a door—painted in black, maybe Arial small caps, maybe Helvetica, but something with dignity. It'd be the kind of pane of glass that you'd want to throw a guy through. I don't want to make too much more of this, because I also had a less relevant dream in which Marilyn Quayle had inexplicably been elected president, except that we were also on a boat somehow, and the boat was also America. So it's not like the dream was a prophecy, is what I am saying. (Although, if by the time you are reading this Marilyn Quayle has become president, perhaps it was.)

This was my third, count them, third day at Cahaba, and I already felt like I had worked there for thousands of years. I did not particularly want to go in, which is usually the sign that you are now a veteran.

Of course, also weighing on that decision was the fact that I was going to have to deal with Ignacio Granger, Irritating Journalist, and also the fact that apparently the company had been sold down the river. Probably that was going to come out into the open soon, if not from Cahaba, at least from Tyler, who did not strike me as the sort of person who could sit on secrets for a long period of time.

My bag of pastries trick had done the job earlier, and so I decided to redouble my efforts now, swinging by La Patisserie Chouquette for what was undoubtedly an epic haul of baked goods. I wanted a bag of pastries that would cover financial ruin, betrayal, and another murder, should they come up.

And as it turns out, I would need it.

Unsurprisingly, I was not the first person in the office, despite getting in twenty-five minutes early. Gary and Quintrell had both spent the night, again, and it's hard to get there earlier than people who never leave. I was somewhat, if not terrifically, more surprised to find that Vanetta was there, having also spent the night, and that even Tyler had come in a bit early.

I walked over to Quintrell's and Gary's desks, which had at this point merged into a single station of exhaustion and half-eaten pizza, and asked:

"What gives, you guys?" I asked. "The deadline is over. It's like you have Stockholm syndrome."

"We have to make this work," said Quintrell. "It has to be perfect."

"It has to be functional," said Gary.

"Is it perfect?" I asked.

"It's functional," said Gary. "But yeah, we should have gone home."

I was feeling a knot in my stomach just looking at these two. They had been working so hard—so very hard—at code that was going to be taken away from them. Or just thrown out. All this time they believed that what they were making would outlast them, and it's just ephemeral performance art. But they didn't notice my concern. Why would they? They hadn't slept.

"Old habits are hard to break," said Quintrell. "And I think I was beginning to freak out about getting arrested."

"Just now?" I asked.

"Yes," said Quintrell. "It sort of hits you slowly."

Freaking out over getting arrested was not the sort of thing that would hit me slowly. It would hit me suddenly, like a shovel to the face. But Quintrell and I were obviously very different people.

"I'll tell you when it hit you," said Gary. "At 2:34 last night. You just started shaking."

"That was the caffeine," said Quintrell.

"It was also the caffeine. But it was the arrest, too, because you kept talking about it," said Gary. "You wouldn't shut up about it. I mean, I didn't mind except that you weren't making a lot of sense."

"I wish I'd been there," I said, in a mercenary combination of empathy and a desire for clues. "Why did the police arrest you?"

"They found some pills in my desk and they thought it was methadone."

"It wasn't methadone?" I asked.

"Of course it wasn't methadone," said Quintrell. "Why would I have methadone?"

"I don't know," I said. "What was it, then?"

In retrospect, this is an impossibly personal question, but at the time I threw it out there with no regrets.

"Not methadone," said Quintrell.

"He's shy," said Gary. "It must be something embarrassing. What is it, Viagra?"

"No, it's not Viagra," said Quintrell, for once actually irritated.

"Propecia?" I guessed.

Quintrell just looked at me. "I'm already bald. Why would I be taking Propecia?"

"What's the mystery pill that the police thought was methadone?"

"Dulcolax," said Quintrell.

"What's that?" I asked, although after I posed the question, I realized that any drug with the word "lax" in it is probably none of my business.

"If you must know, it is a stool softener. I keep them unlabeled in my desk, because I don't like everyone knowing that I need a stool softener."

"Is that why you cry in the bathroom?" asked Gary.

"Damn your eyes," said Quintrell.

Despite having initiated this conversation, I felt it was very important to end it now, before it got any more terrible. Thankfully, I had presents for Gary and Quintrell.

"Coffee," I said, presenting a gallon's worth of coffee in a cardboard box, courtesy of La Patisserie Chouquette.

"We have coffee here," said Quintrell.

"Arguably too much of it," said Gary.

"But this coffee comes in a box," I told them. "Which makes it better."

"I do like the way you bring us things," said Gary.

"Also, I have doughnuts," I said. At which point I was

literally attacked by Gary and Quintrell. Okay, fine, figuratively attacked. But it was like feeding chum to sharks. The ideal feeding situation would have involved handing them doughnuts through a protective cage.

The frenzy was interrupted by Lawrence Ussary—Lawrence—who was also, apparently, in early.

"Why is everyone here early?" I asked. "Was there a time change I didn't know about?"

"We are dedicated to our work," said Lawrence, at which point Gary fake-coughed while simultaneously saying something like "doughnut thief."

"Why are you back here, Lawrence?" asked Quintrell. "It makes me anxious. You don't come back here to where normal people work."

"He's here for the doughnuts," said Gary. "He's here to steal the doughnuts of the proletariat."

"Not just that," said Lawrence. "But to partake of some of this cardboard-shaped coffee." He shook his empty coffee cup in the air.

"Vanetta's called for a staff meeting at nine," said Quintrell.

"How fun for you," said Lawrence.

Lawrence looked as though he had something else to say, or at least, as though he expected one of us to ask him something, but he didn't say anything, and no one asked. He just kept looking at Quintrell and awkwardly moving his coffee cup. He looked a bit like a beggar. I mean, a really rich and well-dressed beggar, but with the shaky mug he definitely had an "alms for the poor" vibe.

"Well," he said, when he was done with that bit of acting, "I'm off."

This whole interaction was weird, but it was early, and so

I poured some coffee myself, figuring that with caffeine the world might make more sense. It worked, sort of.

"Quintrell, I think that was your apology from Lawrence," Gary explained.

"What, that stagecraft?" asked Quintrell.

"I think it was," said Gary. "Lawrence is a man of great subtlety."

CHAPTER TWENTY-THREE

Today's staff meeting was the most orderly that I'd ever seen it, although admittedly I didn't have a large sample size. Vanetta looked cheerful and optimistic and was wearing a sort of bronze power suit that said "don't fuck with me." Tyler was looking preppy in a Calcutta collar and brown blazer, and even Gary was less schlubby. I think there had been a general effort to dress up for Mr. Granger, and I hoped he appreciated it. This was what it felt like to not be on a sinking ship. It seemed like yesterday's good news, such as it was, had finally percolated through. The poor saps.

Not present, once again, was Archie. This time his absence went entirely without comment, almost without observation. So much so, in fact, that I took it that there was a natural and mundane reason that he wasn't around. This turned out to not be the case, but I get ahead of myself.

"Good morning, everyone," said Vanetta. "I didn't ask you, but I can see we all dressed up a little. We're looking good, fellas."

"I always look good," said Gary, who, in point of order, did not look good on this or any other occasion I had seen him.

"Mr. Granger should be here in an hour or so, and DE would like for this event to go as smoothly as possible. He's going to do what is called in the business a puff piece, and while I usually hate this kind of thing, I think it's the least we can do for our corporate overlords."

"All praise the Dark Ones," said Gary, who had clearly already had too much caffeine.

"Dahlia," said Vanetta. "You're going to get to play hostess here. Lead Mr. Granger around the office, and make nice."

"I am the physical embodiment of niceness," I said, which didn't even prompt a snarky remark.

"Start at Lawrence's office," said Vanetta, "and after a half hour pick him up and escort him to Archie."

"Does Lawrence know about this?" I asked.

"This was all Lawrence's idea," said Vanetta. "He's awful, but this kind of business-media relationship thing is his bread and butter."

"It's good to know you have a reason for keeping him around," said Gary.

Vanetta did not respond to this remark either. Like I said, it was early.

"Gary and Quintrell, that means you get our visitor at eleven, and then I'll have him from eleven thirty until whenever he leaves. When you're not with him, look busy and productive, and when you are with him, seem engaging and act like you are not busy and have all the time in the world."

"Those are opposite things," said Gary.

"Ours is a house of lies," said Vanetta.

"When do I see him?" asked Tyler.

"Let me check my schedule. Ah, yes, that would be never," said Vanetta.

This irritated Tyler more than I thought it should, because he became positively peevish.

"I'm interesting. I could be profiled."

"I'm not suggesting that you aren't interesting," said Vanetta. "But he didn't mention wanting to meet with middle management."

"I used to be a musician, you know," said Tyler. "PocketApp called my score to *CoffeeQuest Two* 'bracing.'"

"Please don't do *CoffeeQuest* stories again," said Gary. "We cannot endure them."

I was keeping an eye, as best I could, on the desk in case of the—what I perceived to be unlikely—circumstance that someone would show up there. This was fortunate, because someone did show up there, just now, in a green paisley shirt.

"Hang on," I said to the group, and left to greet the visitor, closing the door behind me, because I am a model of discretion.

"Cynthia Shaver?" said the man in front of me.

"Oh my God," I told him.

This is probably the wrong response to any journalist visiting you, puff piece or no, but as I was not expecting Ignacio Granger to arrive for another fifty-five minutes, I was somewhat taken aback. I assumed it was Ignacio Granger, because who else would call me Cynthia Shaver, with an odd and distinctly menacing emphasis on the "v," but I did double-check.

"Are you Mr. Granger? We weren't expecting you to be here for another hour."

"At last we meet. And please, call me Ignacio."

Okay: a lot of simultaneous thoughts here, but I'll try to turn through them in an orderly way. First and foremost: Did I screw up? I had been so occupied by the mysteries here, with the murders and the corporate espionage, had I actually just screwed up on secretarial stuff? Was he really supposed to be here at nine all along? Or was this jackass just early?

Secondly: I had sort of assumed that with the first name Ignacio, our touring journalist would be Hispanic, but in fact, Mr. Granger looked to be exceedingly Irish. He had short, wavy red hair and peach skin with freckles and was even wearing green. He looked like the leprechaun on a box of Lucky Charms.

Thirdly, I still had to deal with my ridiculous explanation that my name was Cynthia, which was now coming back to haunt me like we were in the final act of a Greek play.

Of these, I asked about question two, because it was the safest territory.

"You don't look like an Ignacio," I told him.

Ignacio responded to this in a way that suggested that he had been subjected to this observation hundreds of thousands of times. He wasn't irritated or bored, but somehow both together in a DQ Blizzard of petulant emotions. I shall call him boritated. He looked so wearied by the inquiry, that detective or not, I felt guilty for pointing it out.

"I was named for the cabbie that delivered my mother to the hospital," he said. "There was a whole thing, family lore, big story, blah, blah, blah."

"It sounds fascinating," I said, despite the fact I could clearly tell that Ignacio did not want to discuss his name. It couldn't have been clearer if he had been wearing a T-shirt that said: DON'T ASK ME ABOUT MY NAME. But there I was.

"It's really not," said Ignacio.

"I find names fascinating," I said, which was also not true, but I felt like I needed to stall this goon for forty-five minutes, and we had to talk about something.

"The full version of the story isn't that great. Plus," said Ignacio, displaying a reporter's instincts for separating fact from fiction, "I think my family has exaggerated it."

"Parents lie about names," I told him. I wanted to tell him the origin of my name, which my mom said came from a dream, where she was walking in a field of dahlias, and which I later learned was bullshit, because she just ripped the name from *Knots Landing.* I couldn't tell that story, however, so I made up one for Cynthia.

"My parents claimed that they named me for Cynthia Ozick, the poet," I told them. "But it turned out that I was named after my grandmother's dog."

This appeared to be the right thing to say to Ignacio Granger, because he smiled and seemed less odious.

"Could be worse," he said. "You could be named Fido."

I feel as though there is undoubtedly some hipster named Fido reading this passage now, and to him, I apologize. These are Ignacio's words, not mine. Feel free to cross out the phrase "less odious" in the preceding paragraph, and replace it with "more odious" or even "a real jerkface." Or just improvise, Fido! You are the captain of your own ship.

"Things could always be worse," I said, probably hollowly, because at the time I was thinking: "This is rock bottom."

"So your name is really Cynthia Shaver?"

"Yes," I said, quickly and confidently, because stalling on an easy question like "what is your name?" is not the way to inspire trust.

"You wanna show me an ID that says that?" asked Ignacio.

"No," I said. "I'm not doing that."

Then I stood up, confidently strode to Vanetta's office, and said: "Give me just a second to let everyone know you're here." Ignacio wanted to follow behind me, because he is an ass, but I told him to sit down and to wait a damned moment, and that we would be with him in a second. Only I didn't say "damned." At least not with my lips. I said it with looks and with gestures.

I reentered the office to find that Tyler was still whining about not getting a special visit from this idiot journalist. It was hard to diagnose the origin of this obsession, given that he alone knew that the company was doomed, but we all have our private quirks. I interrupted his whining, which brought me goodwill from everyone, even Tyler.

"Ignacio Granger is here early," I said. "Surprise!"

Thankfully the gang wasn't hit as hard by this news as I had feared might be the case.

"Nothing ever goes as planned," said Vanetta. "We'll just have to move up our schedule. Does that work for everyone?"

"Stall him fifteen minutes," said Gary.

"Got it," I said.

Everyone did not leave the office at once—I suppose because Vanetta had a few more things to say, and so I returned to the room to talk to Ignacio Granger a little more.

"There's a funny story about my brother's name, actually," I said, stalling.

"Oh?"

"It was supposed to be Alder, like the tree, but it was typed incorrectly on his birth certificate. And my parents just went with it."

"What his name?" asked Ignacio.

"Alden."

"It's hard to fact check stories like that."

People began quietly filing out of Vanetta's office, but slowly and gracefully, and not desperately running toward their cubicles.

"Do you have any questions for me about how Cahaba works?" I asked, which was stupid, really, because I didn't fully understand how Cahaba worked.

"I really want to speak mostly to Vanetta," said Ignacio. "This is mostly about her, actually. There are so few female designers, much less black designers, she's sort of like a unicorn."

This question made me a little wary of Ignacio, because I was guessing that this was not how Vanetta wanted to brand herself. But, of course, I couldn't speak for her. Maybe she knew about this angle all along and was delighted by it.

"I don't know that I'd call her a unicorn," I said. "She's more of a dragon, or perhaps a sphinx."

"What's it like having a lady as a boss?" asked Ignacio, blithely, as if this were the sort of question a human could ask in 2017.

"You know," I said, "let me check on Lawrence, very quickly, because he's going to be the first person to meet with you."

Ignacio smiled at me and reached over my desk and took an éclair. I didn't offer him the éclair, and this irritated me. As I left, I told Ignacio:

"It'll be just a second—and trust me, you'll love Lawrence."

CHAPTER TWENTY-FOUR

I came into Lawrence's office, closing the door carefully behind me, and found that he was slumped over at his desk. My instant assumption was that he was dead, because this is the sort of thing that happens around me. He looked dead. He was leaning forward and sprawled out in a very unnatural-looking way, the way one might if you were to die suddenly. There was a pool of drool on the desk around his mouth, which was open.

Being, at this point, a Corpse Pro, I took this in stride. I'm honestly just a few dead bodies away from giving a TED Talk on the topic. I did not want to touch Lawrence, so as not to contaminate anything, so I gently struck him in the head with a pencil. This caused two reactions:

1. The eraser nub broke off and landed in his hair, and
2. Lawrence said, "Mmmmmrrrggggh."

Did I say Corpse Pro? Maybe I was not yet up to Corpse Pro. Maybe this was the 30-day trial version, Corpse Lite. Because "mmmmmrrrggggh" is not usually the sort of thing that corpses say outside of *The Walking Dead*, and even then, rarely following a pencil striking.

"Hey, buddy," I said.

"Mmmmmrrrgggh," said Lawrence.

I hit Lawrence in the head again, and I admit that this time it was not strictly necessary. Was Lawrence drunk? I assumed yes, following the same flawed logic that had initially led me to think that he was dead. I deal with a lot of drunk people. Even more than corpses. Occasionally, I am a drunk person myself.

"You okay?" I asked.

"Drrrrink," said Lawrence.

"I think you've had enough."

I pushed Lawrence backward into his chair, which was one of those fancy leather swivel chairs that an important business executive would dramatically turn around in and say something like: "Mr. Peterson, I expected you were coming." It did that now, in fact, when I pushed Lawrence back into it, except that it turned backward toward the window, and instead of saying, "Mr. Peterson, I expected you were coming," Lawrence said: "Mmmmmrrrrgggh," again. Which was dramatic, too, even if it did not inspire confidence.

An aside: Is it wrong to admit that I like "mmmrrrgggh" Lawrence better than any Lawrence to date? He was a good drunk, or was at least a good drunk when he was not able to speak full sentences.

And another aside: One that you are probably having now. Was Lawrence _really_ drunk? Here are observations and questions I would pose later:

- He was awfully sober earlier this morning.
- How quickly can a man reliably get this drunk, especially after stealing doughnuts?

- He did not smell like alcohol.
- Why would you drink right before you were having a journalist over?

I include these postmortem observations here so that you can feel superior to me, which is fun, I am told. That's the entire reason anyone watches *Wheel of Fortune*. But at the time I wasn't really giving them a lot of thought. Mostly I was thinking about Ignacio Granger, asshole, who was sitting at my desk and stealing éclairs. Obviously, I could not bring Ignacio Granger into this room, because it seemed at the moment that Lawrence was drunk off his ass, and this was not the impression of Cahaba that our all-powerful Corporate Overlords wanted to form.

I did not move, because I did not have a plan.

"I'm going to get you some water," I told Lawrence, for all the good that was going to do.

"Waaarrggh," said Lawrence, which I will not interpret on your behalf.

I gingerly closed the door and immediately saw Ignacio looking at me. Not merely looking, but fixatedly gazing, the way a hawk might be watching a field mouse.

"Everything okay in there?" he asked.

"Things are splendid," I said. "Just a few minutes more and we'll be right ready for you—I apologize—your getting here early has thrown us off the tracks just the teensiest bit."

Vanetta. I should go to Vanetta.

"Please stay where you are," I said, and strode confidently and calmly into Vanetta's office. I closed the door behind me, gingerly again, although this time the ginger was a lot spicier, and probably served alongside some wasabi.

"Lawrence is drunk," I said. "Completely drunk."

Vanetta stared at me blankly, as one would, and the next question just fell out of me.

"Did he find out that he was the father of your child? Did you tell him?"

Vanetta's blank stare quickly filled up with fire.

"No," said Vanetta. "I did not tell him. As I don't know for sure, as we went over yesterday. Do you not understand how medical science works?"

Broadly speaking, I do not understand how medical science works. I took Organic Chemistry once and lasted in there for about two weeks before I realized that I have no business in chemistry. I did not wade into this point with Vanetta.

"Well, he's drunk," I told her. "And he was sober earlier. Something persuaded him to get very drunk, very quickly."

The sale, I realized. He must have found out about the sale.

"Fucking Lawrence Ussary," said Vanetta. "Well, we'll have to just go with plan B."

What plan B was going to be never materialized because we were interrupted by the song "The Lady in Red," which, once again, blared its way from the parking lot below.

"I do not understand why he feels that this should be my signature song," said Vanetta, who was suddenly standing with impeccable posture, like a mannequin. "I don't even particularly like the color red."

"It's Archie," I said unnecessarily.

"Of course it's Archie," said Vanetta. "How many men would be down there playing Chris de Burgh hits as though they were some sort of romantic salve?"

"Ordinarily," I said, "the answer would be zero."

"I don't even think I own any red clothes. I have one dress

that's sort of burgundy colored. And it has snakes on it. That's the memorable thing about the dress. Snakes!"

"This is not going to set a good mood for this interview," I told her.

"No," said Vanetta, bringing herself to peer out the window at Archie.

"You going to deal with Archie?" I asked.

"Absolutely not," said Vanetta, which I somehow expected was going to be her answer.

"Okay, then," I said, and gave her my éclair. "You are obviously the Lawrence whisperer. Why don't you deal with him, and I'll deal with Archie. And also Ignacio."

"How are you going to deal with both of them?" asked Vanetta, and the hell if I knew.

I left the office first, and Ignacio Granger, while still sharp-eyed, was thankfully looking a little more sated now that he had eaten a powdered doughnut.

"What's that music?" asked Ignacio.

This, naturally, was a good question, although I don't know that we need to credit Ignacio with any excellence in journalism for coming up with it, because the sound was coming through the walls and floor.

"The dog-washing place downstairs is doing a thing with a local radio station," I said, stringing together what I thought was a pretty good lie. "I'm going down there to get it straightened out."

I was watching the door because it felt very likely, and even logical, that Vanetta would come through it to deal with

Lawrence, but it remained firmly shut. Possibly, Vanetta wanted Ignacio out of sight before she made her egress.

"Does this happen very often?" asked Ignacio. "The music, I mean?"

"Only once before," I answered, honestly, even. "But don't worry. I'm going down there now and shutting the music down," I said.

Then I had a revelation.

Usually when a detective has a realization that is sparked by a word or sentence, it means that the case is solved. "Jessica, this soup is delicious—what's in it, mushrooms?"

Jessica Fletcher: "Why, that's it! Mushrooms!"

And the mystery is over in five minutes, plus commercial breaks.

If I knew Jessica Fletcher, I would go around making odd and peculiar observations all the time, on the off chance they would be useful to her. "This velvet clown painting is curiously askew." "Those horses are getting perilously close to the promontory." "Ever since I twisted my ankle last summer, I prefer the elevator to stairs." And so on. I think I would make an excellent sidekick.

But I digress. I had such a realization now, but it did not solve the case. It solved the question of where to put Ignacio while I dealt with Archie, which was frankly more pressing.

"Speaking of music," I said, "let me introduce you to Tyler Banks. Fascinating guy. I don't suppose you've heard of *Coffee-Quest Two* and *CoffeeQuest Three*?"

"I'm actually mostly just here to see Vanetta," said Ignacio.

"And see her you will," I said, physically pulling Ignacio down past my workstation and into Tyler's office. "But I just insist that you meet Tyler—his music does for coffee what Tchaikovsky did for sugar plums."

We entered Tyler's office without knocking and despite the door being fully closed. He jumped up with such a start that I was a little alarmed as to what he might be looking at on his computer. But then I saw that he was designing a *Stardust Memories* wallpaper on Spoonflower. Because that's what a girl wants to be wooed with. Wallpaper.

"Dahl—" started Tyler.

"Don't call me doll," I said. "My name is Cynthia. Human Resources has reminded you about this."

Tyler looked chastened and also confused, which was about right.

"Right," said Tyler. "Why are you here, Cynthia?"

"I'm showing Ignacio around, and I thought you might like to meet him."

Tyler brightened instantly.

"Oh, well then, sit down, Ignacio. Great to meet you! It's nice for us creatives to have a little time together, don't you think?"

Ignacio sat down, and although he said yes with his mouth, the rest of his face was saying no, or even hell no and possibly even don't you leave me in here with him, Cynthia.

"Excellent," I said. "I'll be back for you in a few minutes," or possibly hours, "and bring you to your next guest."

I closed the door, firmly, and wondered if I could possibly lock it from the outside. The mechanism for this did not appear to work, and so my next thought was to push furniture in front of the door so that it could not be opened. However, I was worried that this might appear suspicious. Also I didn't feel like pushing furniture.

I needed to let Tyler know that I didn't want to have Ignacio wandering around unsupervised. I could call or text him, which would probably be the most effective way of letting him know. But there was a fair chance that he would ignore me. I picked up my cell phone and made another intuitive leap as I headed downstairs to deal with Archie.

"Masako?" I said.

"Yes," said Masako. "Is this Dahlia? You never call me."

"That's not true," I said. Although it was certainly mostly true. Masako was one of those people I never needed to seek out, because she always seemed to be around.

"You only call me when you want something," said Masako.

"Ha, ha, ha, ha," I said. Not laughed, but said. "That's not true one bit. Although, now that you mention it, I don't suppose you could do a favor for me?"

"What kind of favor?" asked Masako.

I liked Masako's wise and slow way of entering into agreements. A less shrewd person, me probably, would have just said yes. Masako, not in the slightest.

"Well," I said. "This doesn't impact the favor, particularly, it's more of an aside, but how do you feel about Tyler? He seems to have fallen for you in a serious way."

"Against all good reason," said Masako. "I like him."

"He's sort of goofy," I observed.

"Yes," said Masako.

There was silence, and I kind of expected Masako to offer up some counterpoint as to Tyler's attractive qualities. She did not. That's not necessarily to say that Tyler did not have good qualities, just that she was not a sharer.

"So," I said. "The favor."

"Yes," said Masako patiently.

"Can you call Tyler and tell him to keep Ignacio Granger in his office until I come back. At all costs, Masako. AT ALL COSTS."

Masako was silent.

"What kind of tomfoolery is this?" asked Masako.

It struck me suddenly that it would be nice to have a well-laminated graphics poster illustrating the various nomenclatures of tomfoolery that I get involved in. There would be high jinks (kooky and zany), hubbub, hullaballo, foolery, and buffoonery, maybe even mischief.

"I would describe this incident as shenanigans on the precipice of danger."

"Why can't you call him?" she asked. "You can call me."

"If you call," I said, "he'll get excited and pick up. If I call, he'll sigh and look at the phone while he turns off the ringer."

"Fine," said Masako, which here also meant good-bye.

Downstairs, Deb from the dog shop was once again outside, smoking. Also she was singing along to the words of "The Lady in Red," which was now just apparently on loop.

"If at first you don't succeed," said Deb, "try, try again."

Whoever had coined that phrase was surely not thinking of wedding proposals.

"Dear God," I told her.

The banner was back up, although it had somehow gotten very dirty, and now Archie was just lying on the ground, making an X with his body. He looked like he planned for someone to do a chalk outline of him.

"How long has he been on the ground?" I asked.

"Since about the fifth loop," said Deb, taking a drag of her cigarette. "First he just sat down. Then he collapsed around the second chorus. Beautiful lyrics, though," said Deb. "Great choice for a thing like this."

We listened to the lyrics:

"I've never seen you looking so gorgeous as you did tonight / I've never seen you shine so bright / You were amazing."

"I'm joking," said Deb after a beat. "In case you didn't catch that. I don't want you to think I'm a no-class lady."

This was beside the point, although I certainly think that Deb was a no-class lady.

"You want I should bring the dog hose out here?" asked Deb. "We could hose him down, snap him out of whatever spell he's under."

This is not, precisely, a high-class thing to say.

"I'll keep it in mind."

I walked over to Archie, and before I did anything else, I turned off the music. Honestly, I was surprised the police hadn't shown up. Then I sat down next to Archie, who was surprisingly not drunk.

"Archie," I said.

"She closed the window," said Archie. "Just closed the window and walked away."

"Archie," I said. "Didn't we just go over this yesterday? Didn't we just do this? Is it *Groundhog Day*?"

"Well," said Archie, "but Vanetta and I went out together last night, and things seemed to go very well. I thought I would try again."

"Why would you think that the same fool approach was going to work?" I asked, genuinely confused.

"Should I have tried a different song?" asked Archie. "I had thought about going with 'Glory of Love.'"

"From *The Karate Kid*?" I asked. I was trying not to become incredulous, but it was happening anyway.

"From *Karate Kid II*," said Archie.

"I don't think that your song choice is the problem," I said. Although, it wasn't helping.

"I just thought things had changed," said Archie. "I thought it would work. And besides, I wanted Lawrence to know that I wasn't giving up."

This seemed like a very strange thing to say. My reflex would have been to say: "How did you hear about Lawrence?" but I held back and decided to play dumb.

"How does this involve Lawrence?" I asked—which was a similar question, but more naive.

"Never mind," said Archie. "It doesn't matter anyway."

Detectives, as a rule, don't like it when people tell them "never mind," and I did not like it now. I minded. I also wanted to tell Archie that his plan did not make a whit of an impression on Lawrence, as he was drunk off his ass. Unless, wait—the wedding proposal was the reason Lawrence was drunk. But the timing on that didn't work out. Or did it?

Instead, I said:

"You realize that there's a reporter up there who's supposed to meet with you."

Archie sat up suddenly and said: "Good grief, is that today?"

"Yes, it's today."

"They didn't cancel that, after the murder and everything?"

"No," I told him. I began the "n" of that word feeling exasperated and not a little irritated by this clown, but by the time I hit the "o" I was thinking about covering my ass. Technically, it was probably a secretarial duty of mine to have mentioned this to Archie. He wasn't at yesterday's staff meeting. He wasn't at today's. Probably I should have brought this up.

"I'll go up there," he said. "First help me move the speakers."

CHAPTER TWENTY-FIVE

I went back upstairs—so much stair climbing at this job—and found that Charice had somehow gotten into the building and was now sitting at my workstation. She was wearing a wedding dress, an improbably lacey one, with sort of a '70s flower-child vibe, although maybe I was just saying that because there were also wildflowers in her hair. Also, she had white doughnut powder on her hands and face.

I stared at her, agog, and then the phone rang, which she picked up and answered.

"Cahaba Apps, this is Charice, how may I direct your call?"

I could not hear the other end of the line, but after a beat Charice said:

"One moment, please," and confidently pressed a series of buttons on the phone system before putting the receiver down.

"Am I dreaming this?" I asked. "Is this some sort of nightmare I'm living?"

"Dahlia," said Charice. "It's nice to see you too. I love your office. It's so...dilapidated."

"I take it that you're getting married," I said.

"You really are a pretty good detective," said Charice, which ought to have been patronizing, given that she was wearing a full goddamn wedding dress and had flowers in her hair, but it somehow wasn't.

"Why are you in my chair?" I asked.

"We've decided to strike now, while the iron is hot."

"You can't wait until the weekend?"

"Then the iron would be cold."

"End of the workday?"

"Are you familiar with irons?" asked Charice.

"I just always assumed that you would have a big wedding."

"That's a very reasonable guess," said Charice. "But I was thinking we could have a tiny impromptu wedding, and then blow all that money on the honeymoon. It feels like that would be more gratifying."

It was hard to argue with that. It's always hard to argue with Charice, but especially hard now. For one, I agreed with her, and for another, it's rarely wise to argue with a woman in a wedding dress. I don't know that I would call Charice a Bridezilla, but she was at least a Bride-Mothra.

"I can't leave right now, Charice," I said.

"We can wait for your lunch," said Charice. "I want you to be my maid of honor."

This, despite everything else, made me very happy, and if I had time to think about it, which I didn't, I probably would have gotten a bit weepy.

"That's really sweet," I said.

"And you're actually my only maid, so it doesn't really matter how much honor you have."

"Convenient," I observed. "I'll try to get away at lunch," I said. "But I can't really promise it."

"I'll wait for you. You won't know I'm here," said Charice, a woman in a wedding dress.

"On an unrelated note, have you seen a tiny black woman dragging a drunken blond guy?"

"They went in the bathroom."

I returned to the same bathroom that I had found Joyce in earlier to see Lawrence leaning over the toilet. He wasn't puking, just leaning over it.

"The lambs have stopped screaming," said Vanetta, and it took me several seconds to realize that this was a *Silence of the Lambs* reference and not a screaming lamb problem that I would have to deal with in another room.

"Ha, ha," I said, going for my second spoken laugh of the day. "I talked Archie down from the brink. He's going to his office to entertain Ignacio."

"Where did you get that woman at the desk from?"

What woman? Oh—Charice! "The one in the wedding dress?"

"Was that a wedding dress? I just thought she was wearing a lot of white." Vanetta looked a bit embarrassed to have missed that particular beat. "I was a little distracted with Lawrence here."

Lawrence, as if on cue, collapsed a little lower over the toilet.

"But she's a good secretary," said Vanetta. "That's how you should act all the time."

I was not in the mood to take secretarial pointers from a woman who had made me break up with her boyfriend, and was about to tell her so when Lawrence dry-heaved.

"Unnnngggh," said Lawrence.

"Apparently you went out with Archie last night," I said.

Vanetta shot daggers at me, but then relented and said: "I owed him an explanation."

"Did you tell him everything?"

"You know what," said Vanetta, standing up suddenly. "Never mind. I'm not discussing this right now. We have too many other problems for me to be worried about this small personal matter. There is a journalist waiting in someone's office to do a puff piece—where is Ignacio, anyway?"

"I gave him to Tyler," I said.

"Oh, that's good. That's very good. Although, he could probably hear Lawrence yelling from there."

"Lawrence was yelling?"

"Sort of grunting. Sort of yelling," said Vanetta. "So, plan B."

"There's a plan B?"

"We do Lawrence last now, and you get him sobered up. I'll check in with Quintrell and Gary to see if they're ready to meet with Ignacio yet. Also, and I don't want to be alarmist about this, but I don't think that Lawrence is drunk. I think that he has been drugged. Possibly by whoever killed Cynthia."

"Joyce," I corrected her. You mean whoever killed Joyce."

"This is not the time to get fussy about names," said Vanetta.

It struck me that Vanetta was taking the idea of a poisoner running unchecked through Cahaba rather lightly, and I asked her about it. "No," said Vanetta. "It's very concerning; it's just that in this particular moment, it still ranks about third or fourth."

"Shouldn't we call the police, then?" I said.

"Nope!" said Vanetta in a tone of voice that was definitely unhinged. "We can solve this ourselves. We're going to induce vomiting, and Lawrence is going to be absolutely fine, and this interview is going to be great, and the game is going to work perfectly when we show it to Ignacio, and Archie is going to give the appearance of a normal emotionally stable non-man-child, and everything is going to be wrapped up in a perfect beautiful bow BECAUSE I WILL IT INTO EXISTENCE."

"We don't know what he's had," I said. "We should call poison control."

"And tell them what? We don't know what he's had. Look, induce vomiting. He's not dying. If he starts dying, call the police, fine. But I know Lawrence. It's probably just too much of some crazy good-times drug of his. I know him. I know his mother. I know his older sister, who is actually a really lovely person. If he dies, the blood is on my hands, but I'm telling you, Cynthia, that he is not going to die. Not today. Maybe tomorrow, and possibly because I will kill him myself, but not today."

This was the sort of speech that could either be played behind patriotic music, or alternatively, be spliced up into a dystopian David Lynch film. It could go either way.

I grant you that this is questionable behavior (see what I did there?) but I went along with this plan, in part because I didn't have a better one of my own.

"How are you going to induce vomiting?" I asked.

"I've been sticking my finger down his throat," said Vanetta.

That was Vanetta's exit line, incidentally. She took off, and I looked at the sad and supine form of Lawrence Ussary and mused that I clearly did not have the same level of intimacy that he and Vanetta did, because I was not very keen on sticking my fingers in his throat.

But God, in his infinite wisdom, heard my prayers on this one small and single note, and lo and behold, a miracle was upon us.

Lawrence threw up doughnuts everywhere.

By "everywhere" I mean: the toilet, the floor, and my pants. I should state right up front, that in contrast to my last adventure, I will not be taking off my pants at all but will in fact leave them on me, despite their having vomit stains.

Also, Lawrence was suddenly much more talkative now, which I initially chalked up to the vomiting, but I realized later was because Vanetta was out of the room.

"Not poisoned," said Lawrence. "M'okay."

Then Lawrence threw up again. He was actually sticking his own fingers down his throat now, so I guess you could call him a self-starter. He threw up some more, this time getting almost everything in the toilet, although his shirt had looked a lot better this morning.

I had questions, but I wasn't sure what level of conversation Lawrence was able to maintain. If I had to guess, I would have said "very low," and so I asked my next question very slowly and very loudly, as though I were dealing with an elderly deaf man. Typing that out, I immediately realize the illogic of it, but let's face it: When faced with adversity, many of us default to "elderly deaf man."

"HOW DO YOU KNOW YOU WEREN'T POISONED?" I asked.

"Uunnggh," said Lawrence. Then he took his finger—still covered in mouthy vomitus—and held it in front of his closed lips, in a librarian's "shh" gesture.

"ARE YOU SHHING ME?" I asked. "ARE YOU FUCKING SHHING ME?"

"Roofied," said Lawrence, sounding like death if death were also trying to keep his voice down. "Someone gave me a roofie."

This was an encouraging response in that (1) I could understand what Lawrence was saying and that (2) it meant that

Vanetta was correct and that he wasn't dying, but it also led to other questions. Most principally, how would Lawrence know he had been roofied?

A note on Lawrence's speech here—it's super slurred. I'm not going to type it out that way, but if you like, here are some extra "S"s you can add to the document yourself:

SSSSSSSSSSSSSSSSSSSSSSSSSSSSSSSSSSSSSSSSS

Go crazy.

Lawrence answered the question. "Because," said Lawrence slowly and with more stuff coming out of his mouth. "I had some roofies in my desk. I got roofied with my own roofie."

Aside from the fact that the sentence is ridiculous-looking on the page and almost Smurf-like in its construction, I was shocked and furious. I stood up, left the room, went to my desk, asked Charice for an éclair, took a bite out of it, then went back into the bathroom and hit Lawrence Ussary in the head with the éclair. Hard, although this did more damage to the pastry than his head.

"What the fuck is WRONG WITH YOU? Why would you have roofies? What kind of weird, creepy psychopath are you?"

"I don't know," said Lawrence. "A friend of mine asked if I wanted some and I said sure, why not? I didn't drug a girl or anything."

Another éclair smack.

"What the fuck kind of answer is that?"

"It just seemed like a fun thing to have," said Lawrence.

Éclair smack again. They make great weapons, actually. "The hell kind of person does that? I mean, pull yourself together! Do you realize that you could be a father? What kind of father goes around with roofies in his desk because he has a friend?"

Éclair smack.

"What kind of guy even has a roofie-friend? That's not the kind of friend you should have!"

Lawrence, for his part in this, was taking the pastry beating with relatively good graces, or at least he was until I got to the bit about him being a dad.

"Wait," he said, suddenly pulling together a lot more clarity than I was comfortable with. "What did you say about me being a dad?"

Oh, bloody hell.

"Nothing," I said. "I didn't say 'dad.' I said 'cad.' Rhymes with 'dad.'"

"You said 'father,'" said Lawrence, who sounded awfully clearheaded now, although his speech was still slurred, so keep coming with those "S"s.

"Did I?" I said.

Lawrence looked at me, and then he looked at the éclair. Looking at the éclair seemed to focus him somewhat. "Is Vanetta pregnant?" he asked.

"Nope," I said, "absolutely not." And I thought I was lying pretty well.

"Oh my God," said Lawrence. "Vanetta is pregnant. Of course she is. That..." He paused for a very long time. "That explains everything. She's been so weird lately."

Then Lawrence started crying. What was it lately with me and crying men? "Oh my God, Vanetta is pregnant with my child, and I've screwed her. I've totally screwed her."

"I did not say Vanetta was pregnant," I said. "I said no such thing."

But of course I had. I had given away the game. I screwed it up, the same way Cynthia had with Archie.

"Oh no," I said. "I'm Cynthia. I'm just like Cynthia."

"Are you just like Cynthia," asked Lawrence, "or are you Cynthia? I never really quite got your name."

"Oh, fuck you," I told him.

"I have to call my sister," said Lawrence, in what was perhaps the most human sentence I had ever heard him say. But then he stood up, and it was like a Jenga tower was trying to walk out of the room. He was back on the floor very soon, landing unceremoniously in his own puke.

Were this a movie of some kind, and Lawrence unequivocally the villain (although roofie-friend, Jesus Christ!), this is the sort of moment that would be the end of the story. Look, the villain has pathetically fallen in his own vomit, and there's a *wah-wah-wah* of horns, and now we check in with the hero and heroine for the denouement and a closing montage of '80s tunes. But it wasn't that. Nobody's story was ending, and Lawrence wasn't a completely evil villain, just a self-righteous prick who needed to be a lot better than he was. (This is taking him at his word about the roofie. If that turns out to not be true, fuck this whole paragraph. Just get red Magic Marker and write over it with the word "EVIL.")

Regardless, I didn't have any time to deal with any of this, because I was having a breakdown of my own. Also, Charice was calling me.

CHAPTER TWENTY-SIX

Dahlia," said Charice.

"I'm Cynthia," I yelled through the closed door, although who knows why at this point. Charice opened the door, and, my God, she was looking resplendent. I don't know why it didn't hit me earlier, maybe because she was sitting down. But she was beautiful—utterly beautiful. Speaking of hokey '80s movies, there's often this moment where the dad sees the daughter in the wedding dress and suddenly gets choked up. Or sometimes it's the husband. I can't recall the maid of honor ever doing it, but it happened now.

"My God," I said. "You're getting married."

And Charice knew what I meant. I felt like it was a nice little moment until Charice said:

"You're covered in vomit."

She said it in an amused way, but it still broke the moment, which was probably just as well, because I did not have time for this.

"There are some things happening in there," I said.

"Bring me a cell phone," said Lawrence. "Call my sister!"

"Bring him nothing, and call no one," I said.

"Okay," said Charice, cheerfully ambivalent. "I hate to bother you, but you've got a visitor at the desk."

There were few phrases that I wanted to hear less than "you've got a visitor at the desk" at this moment. Even Frank the UPS guy was not someone I wanted to spend a moment with, and he had adorable grandchildren photos. I'm not being ironic there. I walked back to the desk to find Cynthia Shaffer staring at me.

Cynthia, I noted, was not dressed for work—by which I mean dog washing. She looked more the part of the secretary than me, with a mauve top and even a red-ruby brooch that looked oddly familiar.

As I saw her, I felt my face collapse like a soufflé, or a meringue pie that you didn't do a good job of sealing the edges of. God had brought this woman to me to punish me. This is what I got for going to that church-knitting thing drunk.

"Dahlia," she said. "I wanted to talk to you."

"Oh," I said. "Why?"

"Masako was telling me that you're some kind of secret detective."

I just looked at her.

"Masako told you this?"

"Yes," said Cynthia.

"Masako Ueda?"

"I don't know her last name. Tyler's girlfriend."

"She told you I was a secret detective."

"She said you do odd jobs on the side."

"Yeah," I said, confused. "That's true."

"There's something I want to hire you for," said Cynthia. "I'm still trying to find my old Christmas tea."

What? I didn't say that, but it hung over the situation.

"Christmas tea," said Cynthia. "You know, like Celestial Seasonings. I think Lawrence might have stolen it."

"You want me to find Christmas tea," I asked. "You can't just buy more tea."

"It's limited edition," said Cynthia. "Is this enough?"

And then Cynthia put five dollars on my desk. What the holy fuck. Five dollars. Am I Encyclopedia Brown now? But I took the five bucks, because why not? And hell, we'd practically given Lawrence truth serum, so it would be an easy job.

"As a personal favor," I said, "I will do this for you."

"Dahlia," yelled Quintrell. "Can you come back here?"

"Should I wait downstairs?" asked Cynthia.

I headed back to Quintrell, who was horrified, next to Gary, who looked smug and yet also sort of in shock. Lawrence was sort of draped over the two of them.

"Something has happened to your lovely suit," said Gary, who appeared happy to see Lawrence taken down a peg, although unhappy that he should be touching him.

"Yes," said Lawrence. "It's covered in vomit."

"You don't have to sit on us," said Quintrell.

"I want to apologize to the two of you," said Lawrence. "I am sorry. I am so very, very sorry."

"It's fine," said Quintrell.

"What did you do?" asked Gary.

"*Mea culpa, mea culpa, mea maxima culpa.*"

"Are you just saying sorry in Latin now?"

"*Es tut mir leid,*" said Lawrence.

"What did you do?" said Gary.

"Let's just say that you don't need to be so worried about the details of this game you're making."

251

"What does that mean?" said Gary.

"We aren't worried about the details of the game," said Quintrell. "We are the living embodiments of its hopes and fears."

"Yes, well," said Lawrence. "The company is being sold, and DE is keeping *Peppermint Planes*."

"What?" said Gary.

"Someone else is going to finish *Peppermint Planes*?"

"Possibly," said Lawrence. "It might just be a cartoon and cereal."

"What cartoon? What cereal?"

"There's a lot of money in cereal."

"What happens to us?" asked Gary, who was pushing Lawrence off him.

"Dixon is buying us up," said Lawrence. "It's a great deal."

"For you," said Quintrell. "What does Dixon make?"

"Hidden object games, I think," said Lawrence.

And Quintrell and Gary, who had now fused into a single super being based upon sheer oneness of thought, finally pushed Lawrence off the two of them, where he rolled along the floor.

"I say we kill him," said Gary.

"I knew this was coming," said Quintrell, eating doughnuts. "I knew this was coming. I've known it since I started here. This game has been doomed. DOOMED!"

Quintrell collapsed on his desk. He wasn't crying, but it was hitting him hard, and this was a man who had been pretty upbeat, all things considered, about getting arrested for murder.

"Our lives are over," said Quintrell. "Everything I've ever worked for is a sham."

Gary looked at Quintrell, and he looked at me. Gary seemed on the verge of saying something meaningful, and I sort of hoped that he was going to talk Quintrell down, but instead of saying anything, he picked up his computer monitor and threw it on the floor.

Lawrence asked me: "Are they grateful I told them? They don't sound grateful."

I did not remark on this, as I was distracted by the monitor, which was connected via cable to what was apparently a very heavy desktop unit, and so it just hung there over the edge of the table. It looked, in a word, sad.

"Do you know what the worst of this is?" said Gary.

"That you're too weak to properly throw a monitor?" I asked.

"No," said Gary. "The worst of this is that I've suspected this was coming for a week now. I overheard Lawrence talking about it."

"Here?" asked Quintrell.

"Of course here," said Gary. "I never leave. I don't have a home—I just wander through the earth like some poor ghost seeking vengeance on a man who's been dead for thousands of years. Of course here."

"What did you hear?"

"He was all excited to meet with some representative from Dixon."

"Maybe it'll be good for the game," said Quintrell.

"Dixon is going to have us make hidden object games. Where is the trident? Where is the coin?"

"Where is the Christmas tea?" I added.

"Where is the Christmas tea?" continued Gary.

"No," said Quintrell.

"Yes," said Gary. "Hidden. Fucking. Objects. They're not even really games; they're just activities for old people while they stave off death."

I actually like hidden object games, which I feel should be said to someone. They're a lot of fun. Plus, some of them include mahjongg. But I did not interrupt Gary with my mahjongg counterpoint, because it was not the time.

Quintrell calmly and decisively began unscrewing the monitor cable so that it could be thrown more thoroughly:

"Guys—stop."

"We are men and we want to destroy things."

"Why don't you go downstairs for a bit," I said. "Take a walk, get some fresh air, maybe offer to help wash a dog."

"Fucking DE," said Quintrell.

"Fucking Lawrence," said Gary.

"Now let's go see Tyler," said Lawrence. "I must repent to him."

"Does Vanetta know yet?" asked Quintrell. I initially assumed he was asking Lawrence but then realized: Oh no, he's asking me.

"I doubt it. Vanetta's been a little busy with a situation," I said. "Actually, I thought she was back here with you."

"Vanetta knows nothing," said Lawrence.

"Oh God," said Gary. "Is the journalist coming back here, because I'd like to hit him in the face."

"What did he do to you?" I asked.

"Nothing," said Gary. "I just feel I should hit someone."

Just then, Charice poked her head in, looking even more resplendent than before, and it was at this point that I began to appreciate her train.

"This place is getting fucking weird," said Gary as Charice, Radiant Bride of Womanhood, headed toward us. He did not ask who Charice was or why she was here, but just accepted it, as if this were a thing that happened regularly.

"Dahlia, it's the phone again. A very strange message. Mysterious, you might even say."

Quintrell squinted at Charice. I assume he was wondering if she were some sort of panic-induced apparition.

"Well, okay. Excuse me, boys," I said. "Grab Lawrence's arm," I told Charice. "We need to get this guy back in the bathroom and out of sight."

"I am on a tour of repentance!" he exclaimed.

"I've got him," said Charice, although I could tell from her face that she quite liked the idea of Lawrence's repentance tour.

"So we really have a mysterious phone caller?" I asked, mostly to keep her from thinking about the tour too deeply.

"Check for yourself."

Charice dropped Lawrence on the floor when we got back to my station, and handed me the phone. Over the receiver was an irritating *BEEEP-BEEEP-BEEEP BEEP BEEP BEEP BEEEP-BEEEP-BEEEEP*. Repeated over and over again.

"It's an SOS," I said. This was technically not true, as it was, strictly speaking, an OSO, which is an SOS delivered by someone who had not looked at their Morse code guidebook since elementary school and had confused their "s"s with their "o"s. But the end result was the same.

"I figured it was an SOS," said Charice. "But from whom?"

"I don't know, maybe Vanetta?" I ventured, thinking that she would be due for a breakdown at some point soon. "Have you seen her?"

"No," said Charice.

"Perhaps some terrible fate has befallen her," I said. And it astonished me how naturally I was able to deliver this line, which is, to be clear, a batshit crazy thing to say. Someone is out of my sight for three minutes and I assume that something terrible has happened to them. This is what they call in the detective biz an occupational hazard.

"Maybe we should go looking for her," said Charice. "Daniel is going to be here soon. He's renting a tux. When he gets here, I can go looking for her."

This was a ridiculous thing to say, for any number of reasons, not the least of which was that the Cahaba offices weren't that big. For another, I had just realized who was sending the SOS, and it wasn't Vanetta.

"Get Lawrence out of sight," I said. "I'll deal with our caller."

I opened the door to Tyler's office, and sure enough, Ignacio Granger was discreetly pressing buttons on his phone. Also, Tyler was playing some sort of Native American music on his computer's speakers.

"We're listening to the *CoffeeQuest Two* soundtrack," said Tyler.

Please. Kill. Me, mouthed Igncacio to me.

"I see," I said.

I don't want to comment on the quality of Tyler's soundtrack work, other than to say it was more atmospheric than something you would actively listen to and also that it was being played on his computer's tinny internal speakers, and not any fancy sound system, which was not doing any favors to the music.

"Cynthia," said Tyler. "Is Lawrence ready to meet with Mr. Granger now? I think we've just about run out of things to talk about."

"Sure," I said, sensing the desperation in both men's voices. "Just hold on one second."

"I'll come with you," said Ignacio, grabbing my arm, which wasn't cool, but sort of understandable in the circumstances.

"Okay," I said, walking out of the room with Ignacio literally in tow and no idea where I was going to take him.

I closed the door behind me and began walking very slowly—exceptionally slowly—toward Lawrence's office. I could hear vomiting again from the bathroom. This would have worried me greatly except for the fact that the sound was largely covered by the noise of a computer monitor being thrown at a wall.

"What the hell?" said Ignacio.

From our vantage point, we saw the computer monitor sail through the air and hit the wall, but we could not see its hurler.

I wasn't sure what sort of comment I could or should provide to Ignacio Granger regarding the thrown monitor, but I considered the following avenues:

- I didn't see any thrown monitor. What thrown monitor? You're imagining things.
- It's part of an art installation, very modern you know, and it's also some kind of metaphor.
- The really genius programmers are all a little eccentric, don't you think?

But instead I just embraced the gallows humor and simply said:

"And you'll be meeting with those men later."

I suppose I was walking Ignacio down to the bathroom to meet with vomiting Lawrence. But as we headed toward my station, I saw that Daniel was there, also looking resplendent, and was in a tuxedo. Charice, mysteriously, was missing, but perhaps Daniel's presence meant that she had gone out on that Vanetta search party after all.

I was feeling foolish and insane, and so I said to Daniel:

"Lawrence, how are you? I, of course, am Cynthia Shaver, the receptionist here."

"This is Lawrence Ussary?" asked Ignacio. To be fair, in his tux, Daniel was not someone who looked like Lawrence, really, but was at least vaguely Lawrence shaped.

"Sure," I said. "Sure it is. Lawrence, why don't you go into your office and meet with Ignacio, who is a reporter here to interview you."

Daniel managed to take this particular bit of insanity with the delightful nutso spirit it was given.

"Why, of course, Cynthia Shaver," said Daniel. "Of course, I will."

Daniel, for reasons that remain unclear to me—although at this point, who am I to throw stones?—opted to speak in a ridiculous American accent. It was the American accent that British people used when making fun of American accents, as heard on Monty Python, or "Temporary Secretary."

"Why, yessir, I'm always happy to talk to a member of the press. Sure I am! Why don't you walk me to my office, Cynthia Shaver, since I always like being escorted places, and it's not unnatural at all for a man to be taken places by his secretary."

Right. Daniel had no idea where Lawrence's office was. I walked him to his office, suddenly feeling giddy and insane, and also having a terrible idea as to where Vanetta had gone. She was probably having the same thought I was having right now. She had probably made a run for it.

"Why are you wearing a tuxedo?" asked Ignacio.

"Always wear them," said Daniel, who was yes-anding his way into a very peculiar character. "Can never be too over-dressed. Makes you stand out in a crowd."

"I suppose they would," said Ignacio.

I opened the door, and Daniel looked in at the glass naked woman statue and the fancy desk and chair and said: "Well, what a beautiful office I have. That's a rhetorical question, of course—what's your name, son?"

"Ignacio," said Ignacio. "And I think I'm older than you."

"Yes, well, it's a rhetorical question, because I clearly do have a beautiful office. It's self-evident. Cost a pretty penny too. Now, you'll have to tell me the story of that name of yours in a second, but I do have a little bit of business here with Cynthia, first. Just sit down anywhere, and make yourself comfortable."

Daniel walked to the door and said to me, quietly, "What the hell is this about?"

I said: "The real Lawrence Ussary has been roofied. Also Vanetta is missing, the computer programmers are throwing actual computers, and Archie is also missing—" As I thought of this, I considered that possibly he and Vanetta were missing together, and also that Daniel didn't know who any of these people were regardless. "And I assume that the entire building will be on fire soon."

I didn't even mention the financial ruin of the company or that the sister of the murdered woman I had discovered was lurking around the offices in the dog-grooming studio down-stairs. Why should I? This was a man who was about to be mar-ried and should march into matrimonial life untroubled and happy.

"So," said Daniel. "Are you still going to be able to slip away for lunch? We'd really like you there."

He was talking about the wedding, I realized, and I was astonished that he was still that focused.

"At this rate, I assume I'll be dead by lunch."

"Well, how about eleven forty-five?"

I understood that this was a joke, or at least what Daniel believed was a joke, and I closed the door.

Honestly, it was going better than I expected.

CHAPTER TWENTY-SEVEN

I had become unhinged, it seemed to me, but for once I didn't think that it was entirely my fault. It seemed that everyone had become unhinged, and that suddenly all of us were coming apart like an old hardcover with too many pages and not enough glue. Who could blame these guys? There had been too much madness here and not enough sleep. The day's reprieve had given us all the illusion of hope and restedness, but it was clear that it was nothing but a cruel, cruel mirage.

That's what I was thinking, anyway.

I had mostly, and somewhat intentionally screwed the pooch by giving Ignacio to Daniel, given that he was impersonating a man he knew nothing about. I suppose it wasn't clear to me anymore if I was trying to keep the cart on the track or if I was simply driving into oblivion and laughing as I fell into the abyss. Maybe fifty-fifty.

I should look for Vanetta and Charice and also Archie. Just to keep tabs on them. I should try to calm down Quintrell and Gary. And most immediately, I thought, I should check back in on Lawrence, who was still making loud retching noises from the bathroom.

I walked in on him. He had gotten a phone, somehow, which I found worrying.

"I can't press the buttons," he said, pawing at his iPhone screen ineffectually.

Lawrence looked incredibly tired. As tired, perhaps, as I've ever seen anyone. His eyelids were not fluttering so much as being pulled down by wet bags of sand. Also, when he moved his hands at me, they zipped about in a bizarre and muppet-like way, like there was a rod attached to them.

He looked drugged.

I googled the symptoms of roofie-dum, and rattled them off to Lawrence, just to make sure that he was right and that he wasn't dying.

"Dizziness?"

"Yes," said Lawrence.

"Moments of clarity?" I asked.

"What?" said Lawrence, but he had exhibited clarity earlier.

"Blackouts?" I said.

"Not yet," said Lawrence. "Is that coming?"

Possibly it was. At least if he blacked out I wasn't going to have to worry about him running away later.

"And amnesia," I said. "You're probably not going to remember any of this later."

Putting that aloud, it made me think that this was a blessing. I wouldn't have minded being able to forget this day entirely. I wasn't planning on roofie-ing myself, but the notion of total amnesia was not unappealing.

"I won't know tomorrow that Vanetta is pregnant," said Lawrence. "Oh no."

"I never said she was pregnant. No one has said that."

"I have to write it down. Cynthia, write that down. Vanetta pregnant."

"No."

"Are you the ghost of Christmas Past or of Christmas Present?" asked Lawrence.

I did not know if this was a joke or if Lawrence was just this far gone now, and I never found out which.

"I am the ghost of Christmas never. Although, come to think of it, did you steal any tea?"

"Help me take a shower," said Lawrence.

"No," I told him. "Answer my tea question."

"Fine," he said. "I'll do it myself. I'm taking off this jacket."

Lawrence then fell over. It was a strange fall, as he was already on the ground, but he had moved from vaguely sitting up to total Oneness with the Floor.

"It's still on me, isn't it?"

"Is what still on you?"

"The jacket," said Lawrence.

"Hello?" a male voice called. "Is anyone here?"

I realized that with Charice wherever she was, there was no one to actually receive visitors at the desk. And a visitor was out there now.

"Stay on the ground," I told him. "And be quiet."

"You never did bring me water," said Lawrence. "I was promised water."

I closed the door to the bathroom and headed hastily back to my receptionist's desk. I had had virtually no visitors in the previous days I had been here, and of course, naturally today there was a small army of people passing through. Point in case: Detective Tedin was here. Waving at me with his inexplicable three rings.

I tried to smile, although I don't know how well it turned out. Probably not well.

"Detective," I said. "Good to see you. So very good. Indescribably good. My God, I'm just on fire with how completely and totally good it is that you're here. Now, please sit down and wait and don't move or touch anything, especially doors."

"I haven't said why I'm here."

"Whatever it is, we're not ready for it. It's a very big day here, and we're all a bit stressed."

"Why?" said Detective Tedin.

"There's a journalist here doing a story on the company. It's going superbly well."

Tedin's face, however, gave up all of its skepticism at the mention of the word "journalist." I was guessing he had done his share of pole dances for reporters as well.

"I won't bother your journalist. I'm here to see Vanetta Jones," he said.

"You're not here to arrest her, are you?"

This was my attempt at a joke, and I certainly said it in a cheerful and lighthearted way. Sure, it was absolutely the wrong thing to say, but the delivery was fine.

"No," said Tedin, humorlessly. "What, do you think we just go around arresting everyone who's black?"

I was not prepared for the rather sudden injection of race into the conversation, although now that he said it, it was a bit what I thought, yes. I didn't say that, however, because I am a receptionist/detective, not an interrogator of police. Although I did say:

"Why did you arrest Quintrell, anyway? Something about confusing stool softener with methadone?"

"We're not sharing that information," said Tedin. "May I see Ms. Jones now?"

"I'm afraid I wasn't aware that you would be coming by—did you have an appointment?"

I felt a weird surge of power when I said "did you have an appointment?" I almost wanted to fly off into a little reception-ism fantasia and say: "Let's check the book, shall we? Hmm... I don't see your name in the book." But I figured that Tedin was not particularly in the mood for my brand of nonsense in this moment.

"No," said Tedin. "One of the great things about being with the police is that you can just show up," he said. He sounded, well, I wanted to type "menacing," but that's entirely too strong. "Grouchy" is closer.

"I see," I said. "Well, the problem with just showing up is that the person you're looking for won't necessarily be around."

"She's not here?"

"I haven't been able to find her, although she was around, like, ten minutes ago. I think she might have stepped out for coffee."

This was a pure lie, as there was an abundance of coffee here, there were entire oceans of coffee, and I hadn't the slightest idea where she was.

"You think that," said Tedin, putting emphasis on "think."

"I'm not entirely sure," I told him.

"Does Ms. Jones frequently disappear during the day?" asked Tedin, and for the life of me, I couldn't understand why he was going to litigate this point.

"Usually when she goes out, she tells me," I said, practically marinating myself in the lie, "but I was very preoccupied with playing hostess to our journalist friend here, and so I haven't been available all morning. However," I said, "I'm sure that wherever she is, she's going to be back very soon."

This was quite possibly true given that I wasn't completely sure that she had left. However, I certainly didn't want Tedin poking around here with Lawrence drugged on the floor.

"I suppose I'll just wait here, then," said Tedin.

This was not my favorite option either.

"I'm sure she wouldn't mind you waiting in her office."

And this seemed to please Tedin. "All right, then," he said. "You mind getting me a coffee while I wait?"

"We don't have any coffee, but just because I'm so incredibly nice, I can give you a doughnut instead."

This worked just fine, and Tedin shuffled away into Vanetta's office, where I'm sure she would be delighted to find him, assuming she ever showed up again.

Right, the next thing to do was to check in with Quintrell and Gary, who were throwing things now. Obviously, it would be great to find Vanetta and also, one hoped, Charice, and maybe even Archie, but monitors were being thrown, and that shit had to get dealt with, stat.

"The police are here," I told them.

"Oh no," said Quintrell. "They're not here to arrest me again, are they?"

"They're here to see Vanetta," I said. "But this is not the moment to throw monitors. Or to punch anyone in the face. This is the moment to appear calm and rational, and to look like you know what you're doing."

"We do know what we're doing," said Gary.

"We've decided to create a virus," said Quintrell. "We are going to destroy DE from within."

"Okay," I said, "but if you do that, do it quietly and don't contaminate me."

"Well, it would be a computer virus," said Gary. "It's not like we'd be back here doing germ warfare."

"Can we borrow your monitor?" asked Quintrell. "Ours got smashed."

Before I had a chance to grapple with this question, Daniel Simone showed up, approaching our workstations in a very Lawrencian manner, with a little kick in his step.

"Hello there, Cynthia," said Daniel. "It is I, Lawrence. Might you have a moment to meet with me?"

"You can drop the act. These people know who Lawrence is," I said.

Quintrell and Gary, once again, continued to be surprisingly sanguine about a stranger showing up at their workstation and claiming to be their boss. It honestly didn't bother them at this point, although Quintrell asked:

"Is there some kind of wedding going on? I saw someone dressed as a bride earlier."

"It's like there's a production of *Rocky Horror* that's happening around the edge of our lives," said Gary.

This was a very poetic analogy, I thought, and on some level, Gary was right. And not just now. There is always a production of *Rocky Horror* occurring, somewhere, at the edges of your life.

"I'm getting married later," said Daniel. "You're all invited!"

"I'm in," said Gary, despite not having a clue who this person was.

"Dahlia," said Daniel. "I don't want to alarm you, but I think that you might want to step into Lawrence's office."

It suddenly occurred to me that no one was watching Ignacio, which was surely a very bad thing, and also that there was decidedly an undercurrent of concern in Daniel's voice. Daniel was a professional actor, or at least a semiprofessional one, and if an emotion had cracked through his patina of calmness, this was not a good sign.

"Sure," I said. "Destroy the world quietly, you two."

We headed back to Lawrence's office and found that Ignacio was now passed out on Lawrence's desk, just like Lawrence had been earlier, only Ignacio was on the other side of the desk.

"What happened?" I asked.

"We were just talking and then he started to get sleepy. At first I thought maybe I was boring him, but then it started to seem weird."

"What...have...you done to me?" said Ignacio.

"We didn't do anything to you, Ignacio," I said. "We love you, don't we, Daniel?"

"My name is Lawrence," said Daniel.

"Yes, of course." Although, I didn't think that this was really the sticking point now that the reporter we were trying to fool was roofied and sprawled out across the CEO's desk.

"You're both liars," said Ignacio. "You're all liars. Death to the infidels! Death to the enemies of France!"

I have no idea what that last bit was about, and frankly I didn't think that Ignacio much did either. I did observe, however, that there was some sort of creamy-coffee-colored drink on Lawrence's side of the table.

"Why did you give him a drink?" I said. "I told you that the real Lawrence was drugged!"

"You didn't say with a drink!" said Daniel. "I just assumed that someone had hit him with a blowgun or a hypodermic needle or something."

I very nearly yelled at Daniel for saying something so basically crazy, but I didn't because I quickly realized that:

1. none of this was any of his fault
2. he was, at the moment, the sanest, most sober ally I had, and I shouldn't take him for granted
3. assuming, very optimistically, that there was going to be a wedding, this sort of infighting would put a damper on it, and
4. "Who the hell gets hit by a blow dart?" while rarely spoken aloud, is precisely the sort of question that is asked by someone right before they get hit by a blow dart. Why tempt fate?

So I didn't say any of these things, but apparently my silence was indictment enough to Daniel, who continued to defend himself, even though I had already given up the ghost.

"I just like props!" he said. "I didn't think the interview was going very well, and I thought a good prop would be helpful."

I looked at the drink, which looked disgusting, whatever it was.

"What did you give him?" I asked.

"Kefir," said Daniel. "It's kind of this milk drink that's made from...well, I don't really know what it's made from."

"I know what kefir is," I said. Although, my knowledge of it apparently extended about as far as Daniel's did. I knew that it didn't generally contain roofies, at least.

Daniel could tell that I wasn't mad at him anymore, though, because my next question was:

"You didn't take any of it, did you?"

"No," said Daniel. "Is he going to die?"

"Die?!" said Ignacio, who was apparently listening to us in spurts.

"No, he's not going to die," I said. "Where did you get that from?" I asked.

"Lawrence has a little minibar under his desk. There's four bottles of kefir and some champagne."

God, Lawrence was such an ass. "You never know when you want impromptu champagne."

"I know when I want impromptu champagne," said Daniel. "After I get married."

This was Daniel's way of asking if he could possibly steal this bottle of champagne, and so I said, "I see," which was apparently my way of saying "yes, go ahead and take it." Because he picked it up.

"So are you still going to make the wedding or not?" asked Daniel, in an admirable, if mad, showing of single-mindedness.

"I don't know," I said. "Although, I wouldn't be so sure about drinking that champagne. Someone's already put Lawrence's private stash of roofies into his private stash of kefir."

Daniel shrugged. "I don't know," he said. "You can always tell if a champagne bottle has been opened."

Ignacio tried to stand and fell on the floor, hitting his chin on the chair, which was thankfully padded.

Daniel said, very reasonably: "Maybe we should call the police."

This could certainly be done easily, at this point by simply yelling: "Hey, police!" but now that Tedin was skulking among us, it felt like the wrong time to bring him in, because he would want to know why I had waited this long.

"Take Ignacio into the bathroom," I said. "See if you can't get him to throw up."

"Where's the bathroom?" Daniel asked.

"Oh, come on," I said, although I did take the time to walk Daniel and Ignacio there, feeling quite certain that Tedin was going to open the door, because that was how these things worked.

Tedin didn't open the door, however. Instead I was faced with a new problem, one that we only discovered after we made it safely inside.

Lawrence wasn't in the bathroom.

This, in itself, was concerning. But the capper, the bit that foretold that things were certainly going to go very downhill, very soon was this:

His clothes were there, on the floor.

Oh joy.

CHAPTER TWENTY-EIGHT

Just a brief recap, in case you've lost track, we have the following elements running around the offices at Cahaba. They are:

- A poisoner
- A whistle-blower
- A saboteur, possibly?
- Vanetta, missing
- Archie, missing
- My roommate in full bridal garb, missing
- A police detective
- A drugged journalist
- A drugged and presumably naked CEO, also missing.

At that point, I was thinking that having a hit of that kefir maybe wasn't such a bad idea. Having put all of these things together, I tried to manage triage. Naturally my phone rang, and naturally it was Emily, which was probably the worst possible option, although I don't think I would have relished my mother calling either. I decided, however unwisely, that I would decline this call from Emily. This was a risk, of course, as she was my employer, and I did not want to tick her off. But she should have known better than to call me while I was at work.

"I'm going to check on the detective," I said, and left Daniel in the room with Ignacio.

"Detective Tedin," I said. "Everything okay?"

"Haven't found Vanetta anywhere?" he asked.

"No," I said. "But I was just dealing with a different problem," I said. "I'm going to call her cell now."

"I don't have all day," said Tedin, and I tried to look appropriately apologetic and secretarial.

"Of course you don't," I said. "I'll make sure she comes in here first thing. And if I can't reach her, I'll let you know."

I had mostly poked my head in on Tedin to make sure that naked Lawrence was not in the room with him, although in retrospect this seems like the sort of thing that Tedin would not silently endure. But I also wanted to check in just to make sure that Vanetta hadn't slipped in there during the chaos, because I frequently find that when I lose things, such as keys or corpses, they are usually in the most obvious place.

Unsurprisingly, Vanetta did not pick up her cell phone when I called. I then tried to make a mental list of the places she could be, but this was not helpful, because the list was predominated by things like "in a cab driving quickly away" or "aboard a plane to Mexico." I checked Tyler's office, which was absurdly calm, given the circumstances. Lawrence's office was empty. And Quintrell's workstation was as chaotic as you would expect.

The break room contained Cynthia Shaffer, of all people, who was standing precariously on a chair, pulling something out of the top shelf of the cabinet. This would look suspicious, on some level, were it not for the friendly way that she greeted my arrival.

"Oh, hello there, dear," said Cynthia. "You didn't reorganize the cabinets, did you? I decided I'd look for the tea myself."

"No," I said.

"Well," said Cynthia. "Now that you're here I can describe them to you. Of course, they are all Christmas teas. Sugar Plum Fairy and Gingerbread Cookie, and I think there's one called Sleigh Ride, although I might be confusing that with a candle. I'm sure Lawrence took them. Who else would want tea that tastes like a gingerbread cookie?"

This was a reasonable question, albeit posed in unusual circumstances. Cynthia had told me that she didn't want to be seen by anyone, and raiding the office for Christmas teas seemed to go against this idea. Also, she answered the question herself, because she apparently wanted a Gingerbread Cookie tea, as she was here. Stupidly, I pressed on the latter point.

"Says the lady standing on the chair," I said. "Do you want me to spot you?"

The last thing we needed was a Cynthia with a snapped neck in the break room. This would have really ruined the day, which was saying something, as the day was already a Dumpster fire.

"No, no, I'm fine," said Cynthia, and I immediately put her in the category of old people who never wanted to admit to any infirmity. I went over to hold the chair steady anyway.

"You must want the Gingerbread Cookie tea pretty badly," I said. "I thought you said that you didn't want to be seen by anyone."

"Oh well," said Cynthia. "I want the Sugar Plum Fairy. The Gingerbread I would give away. Terrible tea. Even at Christmas, where I feel that drinking ridiculous teas is a sort of time-honored tradition. Joyce would get them for me, you know. She once got me this Candy Apple tea that was so positively awful that it took us six years to get through."

Cynthia got off the chair and suddenly looked sad.

"It's not up there," she said.

"I'm sorry about your sister," I said, and I was suddenly alarmed that I hadn't said it earlier. I even tried going in for a hug with Cynthia, but she—elegantly—pushed me off.

"Is it weird to say that I think she would have liked it better this way? Going out like this? She'd been diagnosed with pancreatic cancer, and her number was up. It's not a pretty death, pancreatic cancer. It's a lousy cancer."

It struck me that poisoning wasn't a pretty death either, but maybe death is one of those things like dancing. Everyone worries so about it, but ultimately the details aren't important. I didn't share this thought with Cynthia.

"I thought you were in hiding."

Cynthia was still on tea, however. I suppose she must have wanted it because it was something of her sister's.

"Of course, I haven't seen my holiday tea stash in nine months. Other people could have drank it, or thrown it out. Maybe I should ask Vanetta if she remembers seeing it. She's the only other person who drinks tea."

"If Lawrence doesn't drink tea, why would he steal it?" I asked.

"Spitefulness."

"You know, I thought you wanted to stay out of sight," I said. If I kept repeating this, Cynthia would eventually respond.

"I did," said Cynthia. "I came up the fire escape and thought I would just slip in. I appreciate you smuggling out my things the other day, but I'm afraid you just didn't do as good a job at it as I would have liked." Then Cynthia's face reddened, as if she had made an inconsiderate remark. Although, I didn't take it that way at all.

"It was my fault to try to farm it out to you, of course. I should have come back in here myself. I was just afraid it would be strange. Although, now that I'm here, it doesn't seem strange at all. It frankly doesn't even feel like I was fired. It feels like I never left."

"This place is on fire without you," I said honestly.

"It was on fire with me," said Cynthia. "That's the danger of naming a company after a doomed flower."

"It thought it was a river," I said, remembering that I heard that somewhere.

"It's a flower on a river. The Cahaba lily is only found there. I've been there actually—canoeing with a friend. The blooms only last a single day before they wilt. Central Alabama—it's beautiful country."

"You went there with Joyce?" I asked, and Cynthia, I noted, ducked the question.

"It's just like this place," she said. "Beautiful while it lasted. Now it's all wilting."

"So it is," I said, privately wondering if she knew about the sale.

"Let me know if you run across my tea."

"Stay out of sight," I told her.

I found Vanetta and Charice hiding in Archie's office, of all places. I probably would not have noticed either of them, save for the train on Charice's wedding dress, which lingered out from behind Archie's desk like toilet paper trailing from a leg. With metaphors like that, I should write for *Brides* magazine, I know.

"Are you actually crouched and hiding behind a desk?" I asked. "Has it come to this?" This question was posed to Charice, who I did not need to create extra problems in this moment. However, the voice that came from behind the desk was actually Vanetta's.

"She's not hiding. I'm hiding."

Charice chimed in. "I wouldn't say that I wasn't also hiding. I'm somewhat hiding. But I could have made a better go of it if I really put my heart into it."

This was undoubtedly true.

I walked around to the other side of the desk, and sure enough there were Vanetta and Charice sitting cross-legged on the floor. It was so casual, and so friendly-looking that I half expected there to be a bong involved. Or at least some kind of incense.

"Sit down," said Charice.

"There's kind of a crisis out there," I told them.

"Sit down."

I sat down because Charice, when she really puts her heart into something, is hard to stop. Also, despite the impression she gives off, she's also whip smart, so when she wants something, it's also worth considering that maybe you should want it too.

"What are you guys doing down here?"

"I was having a brief mental breakdown," said Vanetta. "But I think I've recovered."

"You shouldn't let things build up so much," said Charice.

"The trick is that I don't have time for a proper mental breakdown," said Vanetta. "I have to focus it; like a power nap."

"Do you know the police are here?" I asked. This is certainly the sort of question that would help someone on the cusp of a mental breakdown.

"No," said Vanetta. "I did not. Are they just running around out there?"

"They're in your office," I said. "They want to speak to you."

I don't know why I was pluralizing Detective Tedin here. It was, after all, just him. Not that this made a lick of difference to Vanetta.

"Well, we can just line them up after Ignacio."

"Ignacio has been roofied," I said. I wasn't even trying to be helpful at this point, and I could see how this would not make me a very good secretary.

Vanetta took this, of all news, pretty well, and was merely tsking about it. "It's Lawrence's damned roofie supply, isn't it? Of course it is. Why wouldn't it be? Another way Lawrence is ruining my life."

I did not think this was a tsking matter, but given her attitude, I suppose Vanetta had come to terms with Lawrence's drug collection. I don't suppose this meant that she did it?

"You didn't drug Lawrence?" I asked.

"No," said Vanetta.

"Hmm," I said.

"Dahlia," said Charice, who was surprisingly scolding. "You're coming in here and interrupting with your detective stuff when Vanetta and I were having a real human-to-human moment."

It seemed bizarre to me, even amid the usually bizarre life of Charice Baumgarten, that she would be having a human-to-human moment on the floor with Vanetta Jones.

"What are you having a moment about?" I asked.

"She was telling me about her problems," said Charice. "And I was telling her about my problems, and as it happened, they sort of overlap."

"You don't have problems," I told Charice.

"Of course I have problems," said Charice. "Being alive means having problems."

Yes, but Charice's problems were, I imagined, things like "How do I keep this ice sculpture from melting before the party ends?" and "Why is it so hard to find really good weed?" The places that this would overlap with Vanetta's problems, which involved financial ruin, a mystery father, and angry police—it seemed hard to imagine.

"I don't have time for this," I said.

"You think I do?" asked Vanetta.

"I'm getting married in an hour," said Charice.

"Who else knew about Lawrence's roofie collection?" I asked.

"Who knows," said Vanetta. "Archie, I assume. I mean, Archie is the person from whom he got them, I'd imagine. Oh, and Gary."

"He got them from Archie and Gary?"

"No, Gary also knew about them."

Either way, this statement seemed baffling to me, because Gary was not the sort of person you would share drug stories and adventures with. He was a grown-ass man, with a baby and a wife. Also, I didn't think Lawrence had acknowledged him directly in all the time I had been there.

"Why Gary?"

"He roofied Gary one day," said Vanetta. "As a joke. That was the day our last Human Resources person left. Just walked up and left, laughing as she went out the door."

This was a lot of information to digest. I could envision Gary, sprawled out at his desk, and I could envision Lawrence, laughing at it.

"Are you going to deal with the police?" I asked.

"Yes," said Vanetta. "Give me five minutes to make my peace with God. I just never expected everything would go up in flames like this."

"That's what you get for naming your company after an ephemeral flower," I said.

"That damned flower metaphor. Where did that even come from? It's named for the shower in the bathroom."

"What?"

"There's a shower here. But no bath. And when we started the company together, Lawrence and I were sharing an apartment at this place that only had a shower too. So we named it Can't Have Baths Apps."

"And you decided it was too long and you shortened it to Ca Ha Ba," I said.

"No," said Vanetta. "We never thought it was too long. It was just that the name was already taken. Can you believe that? There's a Can't Have Baths film development company in Burbank. So we shortened it."

I sort of assume that Vanetta was joking about the name being taken, but she did not look or sound like someone who was joking, so who knows? Life is strange sometimes, and never in the ways you expect.

"It was Cynthia who told me about that," I said.

"Figures," said Vanetta. "That woman is wrong about everything."

"Are you done badgering this poor woman with questions?" asked Charice.

"Just one last one," I said. "Have you seen Archie?"

And then, as if on cue, "The Lady in Red" began to play again.

I don't mean to pick on Chris de Burgh, composer and performer of the venerable '80s hit "The Lady in Red." But I was at this moment harboring a strong theory that he was somehow an agent of Satan, or perhaps even Satan himself. Even now, it seems not entirely unreasonable to think that after I die, if I've lived a bad life, I will hear the dulcet tones of "The Lady in Red" greeting me as I enter the gates of hell.

"I'll talk to Archie," I said.

"I'll go see the police."

When I got out into the main room, I saw that Quintrell and Gary were taking apart the walls of the Herman Miller cubicle system and were now re-forming it into something else.

"We're building a Lemarchand's box," said Quintrell. "Out of Herman Miller pieces."

Reader, I will freely admit that I did not know what a Lemarchand's box was. I assumed it was some sort of fancy math thing, but after asking, I learned that it is, in fact, the evil puzzle box from the *Hellraiser* movies. Clive Barker, your legacy lives on, albeit in temporary office furniture form.

"You do that," I said. "I'm going to deal with the music."

Vanetta ran to her office—literally she was running, just as Ignacio and Daniel sputtered out of the bathroom, whereupon Ignacio collapsed on the floor.

"I'm doing the best I can, Dahlia," said Daniel. "But he's slippery!"

"I've figured out who you really are, Dahlia Moss!" said Ignacio, who was just sort of hemorrhaging for the door.

"Grab his legs!" I said, and ran down the stairs to stop the music.

Deb was outside, smoking. I'm not even sure if she worked at the dog-grooming place at all, now—she might just have been some sort of smoldering gargoyle.

"What happened?" I asked Deb.

The question was salient because there was no banner. And no Archie. Just a speaker.

"What happened with what?" asked Deb, exhaling one gloriously long stream at me.

She was putting me on.

"With the music?" I submitted.

"Oh, that," she said. "I only caught the end of it, when the girl ran off."

"What girl?" I asked.

"Some skinny white girl in a teal dress. I only caught the back of her. Real cute, though."

Who the hell was she talking about?

"There was a girl?" I asked.

"That's what I said," said Deb.

"It wasn't Cynthia Shaffer."

"I'd call her a woman," considered Deb.

"She wasn't black?" I asked.

"Nope," said Deb.

"Was her name Adalbjorg?" I asked, stabbing about as blindly as a person can.

"Dunno," said Deb.

"If you see her again," I said, "stop her."

"I'm not gonna do that," said Deb.

And then I turned off the music and took the boom box. Whoever this girl was, she was going to have to see me in order to get her radio back.

CHAPTER TWENTY-NINE

As I was walking back upstairs, I ran into Masako Ueda. I was, at this point, basically insane and careening out of control, and Masako was exactly as calm as she is in every circumstance. This was both a comfort and a consternation. Mostly the latter, but I do take pleasure in the unchanging.

"Dahlia," said Masako flatly.

"Masako," I said not at all flatly. "Don't go upstairs. Everything is horrible up there. There are two drugged men, one of whom who is naked and missing, a journalist, a police detective asking questions, and two insane and vengeful engineers who are doing unspeakable things with the furniture."

Masako simply continued walking up the stairs at the same pace as before and said: "I'm having lunch with Tyler."

"Yes, but," I said, "maybe you don't want to go up there."

"I don't want to wait downstairs," said Masako. "It smells like dog."

"Okay. But it could be crazy in there if the police get free. Also—you didn't by any chance play the eighties hit 'The Lady in Red' on a speaker system downstairs?"

"No," said Masako.

Masako opened the door.

And just like that, the situation went from being metaphorically on fire to literally on fire. A pyre of cubicles was in the middle of the room and there were literal—not metaphorical—flames coming from it.

"We didn't mean to!" said Quintrell.

"We didn't start the fire," started Gary, normally, and then gradually turning into, if not song, at least spoken poetry. "It was always burning, since the world was turning!"

"No," said Quintrell. "You did. You literally started the fire when you threw those Christmas candles at it."

"It was for luck!" said Gary.

I was going to ask—against all logic—if there was tea near the Christmas candles—but was interrupted by Tyler, leaping from his office with a fire extinguisher and spraying the burning box of office furniture.

Vanetta and Detective Tedin also ran from their office.

"What the HELL is happening here?" Vanetta screamed. "I leave you alone for two minutes and this is the shit you pull—"

"They're going to sell Cahaba, Vanetta," said Quintrell.

"What?"

"DE is selling the company. They're taking the *Peppermint Planes* IP and they're going to make us do hidden puzzle games!"

"What?!"

Vanetta was, as they say on the Internet, SHOOK.

"Did you know about this, Tyler?" asked Vanetta, and the question was sharp enough to cut the air. Honestly, the flames subsided on their own, out of concern for Tyler's well-being.

"I can't hear you over this fire extinguisher!" said Tyler.

"Let's just everyone calm down now," said Tedin, apparently the voice of reason now that he wasn't arresting people willy-nilly.

Ignacio Granger escaped from the bathroom yet again, probably to yell out something incriminating to the police, like "I've been drugged!" or "That woman is a liar!" but he didn't get very far because Daniel was pulling him back into the bathroom. The best he managed was an "Aaarrggh!"

"What is going on here, precisely?" asked Detective Tedin, which would have been scary except he was tackled to the ground by Lawrence Ussary.

I will now describe this for you in slow motion, which is how I remember it in my nightmares.

Tedin, who had crossed the room, presumably to get farther away from the flames, was standing in front of the door to the break room, which was closed.

The door opened, silently, or at least silently in comparison to everything else.

Lawrence was not naked, in fact, but was wearing Vanetta's teal ikat dress from a few days ago, which was just as alarming as you are imagining.

Lawrence knocked down Tedin. Tackled him. I told you earlier that I thought he looked like a 1920s football player for Harvard. He tackled like one too.

Tedin, for his own part, seem astonished that a drugged man in a dress had sneaked behind him and taken him down so easily.

"Stay away from Vanetta!" yelled Lawrence as he was rolling around on the floor with Detective Tedin, who, if he will forgive the phrase, was too old for this shit. "Stay away from Vanetta!"

Cynthia opened the door to Lawrence's office—having apparently been inside—and said: "I found the tea! It was in his desk drawer the whole time!"

Archie entered, naturally, because why wouldn't he, with

flowers. He did not have a bouquet, but a preposterously large terra-cotta-colored pot, which was filled with marigolds. He saw Vanetta first and said, "Vanetta, these flowers aren't part of a proposal or anything, but I just wanted to say—"

And then he noticed the smoldering fire, and the CEO in Vanetta's dress rolling around on the floor with a policeman, and Cynthia, and also Ignacio, who was trying to get out again. He seemed not to know how to take all of this. "What the hell is happening in here?"

The phone was ringing, and I was still the secretary, and so I picked it up. While this was happening, Vanetta walked over and took the flowerpot, then walked back to where Tedin and Lawrence were wrestling on the floor and smashed the pot over Lawrence's head. However, being cheap plastic, this did nothing except get dirt on the floor.

"I spent eight dollars on that!" said Archie.

"That's a good price," said Cynthia. "Where did you get them?"

"Cahaba Apps," I said into the phone. "Cynthia speaking."

"How much longer are you going to be in there?" a voice with a Southern accent said. "You're taking forever."

"I think I quit," said Quintrell.

"No quitting," said Vanetta. "No one can quit! We can still save this!"

"Seriously," said Gary. "Don't quit. Make sure you get your benefits. Do you have any idea what it's like to live without health insurance?"

Lawrence, on the floor, gradually seemed to realize that he had not tackled Archie, but in fact, someone else. "Wait a second," he said. "You're not Archie."

"The hell I'm not," said Tedin.

"Now that I've found that tea," asked Cynthia, "any chance I could get my five dollars back?"

And then the Herman Miller hellbox collapsed. Perhaps the flames had destroyed its structural integrity; perhaps it had decided that it did not want to live in a world such as this. It was like the lily of the Cahaba River. Beautiful for a moment, and then gone in an instant.

I just sat there for a moment and let all of this chaos wash over me. It was madness—almost Lovecraftian madness—where normal people had too many nights of not sleeping bring them over into a place where it seemed like a good idea to set office furniture on fire.

These people were nuts, but I was no better than any of them. I had blabbed like Cynthia. My love life was as messy as Vanetta's. I had made unwise romantic gestures just as Archie had done. I had even had my own flirtations with not-as-yet-legal drugs like Lawrence had, which are not detailed here.

"Are you okay, Cynthia?" asked the voice on the phone. "Or has the lily finally wilted?"

But somehow, amid all the chaos, it came to me. I could see the answer swirling through the hell farce. I knew who was on the phone.

"Joanne," I said in a poor but apparently serviceable re-creation of Cynthia's voice. "I'll be down in a minute."

"Don't let them rope you back into that horrible place," said Joanne. "There's no saving it. It's quixotic to even try."

"Hang on," I told Joanne. "I'm going to have to call you back."

CHAPTER THIRTY

Everyone sit down," I said, although no one was listening to me.

Tedin was pulling himself together. "You're under arrest for assaulting an officer."

"I'm sorry," said Lawrence with a surprising politeness. "I thought you were Archie." He then attempted to dive at Archie, but I stood on top of my workstation and said, louder, "I have solved the case."

"What case?" asked Vanetta.

Charice and Daniel entered the room with Ignacio, who had seen better days.

"Everyone sit down and shut the fuck up," I said. "I know how Joyce died."

"Who is Joyce?" asked Lawrence.

I am not, as a rule, very good at commanding a room. But somehow, this worked. It helped that Detective Tedin was already on the floor and, from the looks of it, was going to have a hard time getting up. It also probably helped that Charice and Daniel sat on the floor themselves, thus prompting everyone else to follow along. Those two are, by contrast, extremely good at commanding a room.

"First off," I said, "a confession. I am a private detective, and I was hired to keep tabs on Cahaba and to learn, if I could, the identity of the whistle-blower."

"I knew there was something like that going on," said Tedin.

"Well," I said. "You were right."

"Wait," said Tedin. "Are you seriously doing that thing where you gather all the suspects together and say: 'The murderer is among you'?"

"I suppose I am," I said. I had expected Tedin to arrest me for this or at least look consternated, but he simply sighed and said, "I've always wanted to do that."

"The murderer is among us?" asked Quintrell, looking appropriately cowed by this thought.

"I'm just here for lunch," said Masako.

"She's the murderer, get her!" said Gary.

"Silence!" I said, and this was suddenly fun again. "I have gathered you all here to explain what happened. Let's start with the whistle-blower."

"It's Quintrell, isn't it?" said Vanetta. "I have no evidence, but I just think it's Quintrell."

"It's Tyler," said Cynthia. "I know it's Tyler."

"Why would you think that?" said Tyler.

"It's that lunch woman," said Gary. "Let's get her!"

"I shall put the whistle-blower on speakerphone!" I said, and pressed a button on the phone. Only I think I pressed the wrong button, and I caused the phone to hang up. A loud dial tone played to the room.

"I'm confused," said Ignacio.

"Okay," I said. "So I fucked up the phone. But I still have the answer. You see, in the second letter, the whistle-blower referred to Cahaba being named for a river, but that's not true. It's actually named for—"

"No one cares how you figured it out," said Vanetta. "Just tell us."

"Well, I thought it was named for a river," said Cynthia, "and I didn't do it."

"Of course she doesn't think it was you," said Tedin helpfully. "Obviously you are not on the other end of the phone."

"Fine, Jesus. It has to be Joanne," I said.

"Who the fuck is Joanne?" asked Archie.

"Joanne—and this part is just a guess—is Cynthia's significant other," I said.

"That is my private business," said Cynthia.

"Oh well, private business," said Vanetta, still sore about being ratted out.

"How did you make the connection?" asked Cynthia.

"You're wearing her brooch," I said.

"Bah," said Cynthia. "She was wearing my brooch. She's always borrowing my things."

"Also, Joanne is from the South," I said. "I'm guessing somewhere near the Cahaba River, since the two of you are the only folks who think the company is named for an obscure Alabama waterway. Joanne's the person you went on your canoeing trip with, right?"

"Hidden depths!" said Tyler. "I was right!"

"But Joanne wouldn't make angry posts on the Internet," said Cynthia. "Would she?"

"The poster did think that DE had made everyone work even after the corpse was found. And Tyler had told her that he worked all day."

"That's not even true," said Vanetta.

Tyler shrank a foot or two and said quietly, "I was trying to impress Masako."

"See," said Gary, "she is responsible! Let's get her."

"Joanne always hated DE," said Cynthia. "She prizes respect and efficiency, and that's not something we have a lot of here. But I didn't realize she had done that."

Cynthia grew quiet, and thoughtful.

"The next question we have is who killed Joyce," I said, and suddenly the room was very quiet. "This took me a long time, because I couldn't figure out who was the person that the overdose was originally intended for. No one, as I see it, wanted to kill Joyce. No one knew her, and certainly no one had any beef with her. Most of us didn't even know she existed. Besides that, she was dying of pancreatic cancer and wasn't that long for the world anyway. Who kills a person who is already dying?"

I had expected a snarky remark from someone in this group, but apparently pancreatic cancer is a bridge too far.

"I kept thinking that the target was Cynthia," I said. "But it wasn't. It was Lawrence."

"Wrong!" said Lawrence. "Everyone loves me. I am beloved."

"Why," asked Archie, "are you wearing Vanetta's clothes?"

"My own clothes were covered in regurgitated pastry, and there were people in my office, so I sneaked into the break room and put on what was in there."

"It's very disturbing," said Vanetta.

"I think I pull it off," said Lawrence.

"There are lots of reasons for people to want Lawrence dead," I said.

"What?" said Lawrence. "There are no reasons."

"He sold the company down the river, shepherding the sale

of Vanetta's IP to DE, while the rest of the staff gets consigned to work on hidden object games."

"What? You bastard," said Vanetta.

"Let's get him," said Gary.

"What's wrong with hidden object games?" asked Tedin. "I think they're fun."

"Well," considered Lawrence, "I suppose I did do that."

"He also is potentially the father of Vanetta's child."

"Oh my God, Dahlia. Seriously?" said Vanetta. "What the hell is wrong with you?"

"Vanetta has a child?" asked Gary.

"I'm pregnant, okay, everyone? I am pregnant. Not even very pregnant. Just a few weeks. But there, now, everyone in the world can know my private business, because I am apparently not allowed even an inkling of privacy. I can just go walking around the office with a scarlet 'P' for 'pregnancy,' like the god-damned Lady in Red I keep hearing so much about."

"At least you didn't have to talk to the police about your stool softener," said Quintrell.

"Wow," said Masako.

"Also," I said, "he drugged Gary, once, just for fun."

"Oh," said Lawrence, "that was months ago. And it was for science."

"And he stole my Christmas tea!" said Cynthia.

"Right," I said. "I wouldn't necessarily call that a motive for murder, but he did also do that."

"Do you have anything to say for yourself, Lawrence?" asked Quintrell.

"It was June," said Lawrence. "I didn't think anyone else was going to drink it."

"Is there anything else I failed to mention?" I asked Lawrence.

"Quintrell, that dent in your car came from me. I hit it one day when I was on my bike. It was an accident, not on purpose."

"Well, thank you for telling me," said Quintrell.

"Now," I said, "as long as we're all sharing, does anyone else want to share any reasons they might have wanted to kill Lawrence?"

"Is this related to the case?" asked Tedin.

"It's more therapeutic at this point," I said.

"Huzzah!" said Charice.

"I think that Lawrence is an absolutely terrible person," said Vanetta, "and I worry that I am exactly like him, except that I'm just better at hiding it."

"Is that really a motive for murder, though?" asked Quintrell.

"I think that's the sweetest thing anyone's ever said to me," said Lawrence.

"You should call your sister," said Vanetta.

"I've been trying!" said Lawrence.

"Anyone else?" I asked.

"I worry that he's closer to Vanetta than me," said Archie. "And I worry about the fact that this is even a thing that I would care about," said Archie.

"Aww," said Lawrence.

"And he stole my Christmas tea!" said Cynthia.

"Seriously," said Vanetta. "Fuck all of you. When this game is over, I am going to change my name and move to New Zealand and I will never see any of you again."

"Who killed Joyce?" said Masako, who was good at cutting to the point.

This would have been dramatic, except the phone rang, and Charice picked it up.

"Welcome to Cahaba Apps," said Charice. "Where Games Go Down the River. What can I do for you?"

"That's a good slogan," said Lawrence.

"Ignore the phone. Tell us who killed Joyce," said Masako.

"The person on the phone says it's Morgan Freeman."

"WHAT?" said Vanetta.

"Tell him to call back," said Detective Tedin.

"Does it sound like Morgan Freeman?" asked Ignacio, wandering into consciousness.

"It sounds like Morgan Freeman," said Charice.

"No," said Vanetta. "Emphatically no. What does he want?"

Charice relayed this question, and the answer. "He wants to speak with the person who wrote the *Peppermint Planes* script."

"Who did that?" asked Gary. "Was it Archie?"

"Someone wrote a script?" asked Quintrell. "How am I so uninformed?"

"I wrote it very late at night," said Archie.

"Put him on speakerphone," said Vanetta.

"But we're in the middle of revealing the murderer," said Detective Tedin, who at least had a respect for how these things were supposed to go.

"IT'S MORGAN FREEMAN," said Vanetta. "Put him on speakerphone. This could change everything. If he gets on board for this, it could save the project. Maybe DE wouldn't sell us. It could save the company!"

"Hello?" said the voice. Morgan Freeman's voice.

"Hello, Mr. Freeman," said Vanetta. "It's an honor to speak to you."

"Is this the person who wrote the *Peppermint Planes* script?"

"He's here," said Vanetta. "But it was kind of a group effort."

"Well," said Mr. Freeman. "I just wanted to say that in forty years of acting—in a storied career, mind you—I have never read a script as bad as the one you sent me."

"I see," said Vanetta.

"We're talking Henry Darger levels of unreadability here. It was bad. Really bad. The word is garbage, honestly."

"So," said Lawrence. "You're considering getting involved, or?"

"I've read scripts handed to me by cabbies, by people's weird emotionally damaged nephews, someone once handed me a script that was written in crayon, and I'm telling you, this is the worst thing I have ever—EVER—seen. What the hell is wrong with you? Are you on drugs? Did you write it in your sleep? Are you having massive problems in your personal life?" asked Morgan Freeman, quickly assessing the problems of Cahaba Apps. "It reads like a fever dream. A racist nonsensical fever dream."

"It could sell a lot of cereal," said Lawrence. "Look at Lucky Charms."

"I wrote it very late at night," said Archie. "So very late. And you fired the script doctor that was going to work with me."

"He was an ass," said Lawrence.

"I kept thinking that this was a joke—a practical joke. This couldn't be a real script. No one would write a script like this, much less send it anywhere for another human to consume."

"I'm sorry, Mr. Freeman," I said, "but the police are here and we're about to reveal who the murderer is. There was a poisoning here, you see."

"Oh, well, I'm sorry," said Mr. Freeman, who, having starred in a few police procedurals himself, appreciated how this was supposed to work. "I hope I didn't interrupt the narrative flow."

"No, I'm so sorry to interrupt your feedback regarding Archie's racist script," I said. "It's just that we're right at the penultimate moment here."

"I'll call back later," said Morgan Freeman. "Although I can just wait quietly on the phone, if you'd prefer."

"That would be very distracting," said Vanetta.

"Now I'm sort of curious to listen in," said Morgan Freeman.

Charice talked Morgan Freeman into hanging up, and after a moment we were ready to move back along. Or I was, anyway.

"Well, here's the thing. No one meant to kill Lawrence. Someone just meant to roofie him."

"That was extremely disappointing," said Quintrell, presumably about Morgan Freeman and not about no one meaning to kill Lawrence.

"It's true what they say," said Vanetta, also still, presumably, on Morgan Freeman. "Never meet your idols."

"Hooray," said Lawrence. "No one wanted me dead!"

"Oh no," said Gary.

"It was in your kefir," I said. "What was your tradition—kefir before a power meeting, bourbon after if it goes badly."

"Oh no," said Gary.

"That's the tradition," said Lawrence. "The truncated version, anyway. The full version is much more complicated. I have a flowchart."

"You had a power meeting," I said. "You were negotiating the control of the IP to DE."

"Yes," said Lawrence. "But I did that from home, you know, for the secrecy."

"But someone here thought they could scotch it, by drugging you."

"Ha," said Lawrence. "Well, that's ridiculous because I'm even better on drugs. Invincible, you might say."

"Oh no," said Gary.

"So we're all assuming it was Gary that did this, right?" said Vanetta. "Since he's said 'oh no' thirty times."

"Well, I never thought I could scotch the deal," said Gary.

"I fully realize that I'm just a tiny cog in a Lovecraftian enterprise for evil, but I thought I could at least humble you a little. Plus you roofied me first, for no reason, you jackass."

"It wasn't for no reason," said Lawrence. "Why do people keep saying that? I wanted to make sure they were safe."

"Oh my God," said Gary. "Let's just take his body and put it back in the Lemarchand's box and set it on fire."

"You got paid," said Lawrence. "You were on the clock the whole time and you spent the day sleeping. My God! I'm on it now, and it's great! I can't feel my feet!"

"Kill him with fire," said Vanetta.

"Joyce was in here picking up Cynthia's things," I said. "And for some reason she went into Lawrence's office. That's the part I can't quite work out—"

"She was looking for the Christmas tea," said Cynthia. "I had told her I thought Lawrence took it. She must have looked in your desk and found the kefir.

"Joyce loved kefir. She was always saying that it was her favorite fermented milk drink."

"That's it," I said, quite surprised. "It was the Christmas tea that led her in there."

"So, really, in a way," said Lawrence, "Cynthia is responsible for all this."

"Shut your dirty mouth," said Cynthia.

"But wait, the roofie just killed her because she was old?" asked Vanetta.

"Joyce had pancreatic cancer, and she was on a number of drugs to treat the pain. Such as methadone."

"That's not a good drug interaction. You have to be very careful mixing things with opioids," said Lawrence very solemnly, revealing a deep knowledge of drugs that, at this point, shouldn't have surprised me at all.

There was a stunned silence that affected everyone but Masako, who asked:

"So who was responsible for this death?"

"Gary, mostly," I said. "But Lawrence is really to blame, since he shouldn't have roofies to begin with."

"Oh no," said Gary.

"You have a private stash of roofies," said Tedin. "You tackled a detective. You're involved in a manslaughter. You're going to jail for a long time, son."

"I have lots of money," said Lawrence.

"Well," said Tedin, chastened. "Community service, then."

CHAPTER THIRTY-ONE

There is, traditionally in my stories, a chase about now, in which the murderer, after being unveiled, pursues me through an unlikely setting, such as a video game convention or a steamboat. It does not happen here, but in an effort to maintain tradition, I acknowledge it here. If you like, feel free to imagine such a chase, involving myself as well as Gary and Lawrence, and if you like, assists from Cynthia. Here are some keywords to encourage you on your own imaginative adventure:

- Lemarchand's box
- gateway to hell
- actual hell
- bumper cars
- Chris de Burgh concert
- confetti cannon

Please send your best chase stories to dahliamossrocks @gmail.com, where I will feature them in my delightful cavalcade of Things That Never Actually Happened.

The actual aftermath of the reveal was a little calmer than

you might have expected, although given the status of things, maybe calmer was the only direction left to go in. Tedin took Lawrence and Gary to the police station. There were no hand-cuffs, no more fights. Lawrence seemed to think it would be fun to ride in the cruiser, and who knows, maybe he was right.

But Gary was incredibly anxious, and he was the person I was worried about.

"Don't worry," said Quintrell. "The beds in there are amazing," he told his friend.

"Are they?" asked Gary.

"You'll think so," said Quintrell, who decided to also go along. There was no more room in the cruiser, so he followed along with Archie, who seemed happy that someone else's drama had eclipsed his own.

Cynthia, I gathered, also came along with Joanne. It must have been quite a time.

I had expected Vanetta to follow the party to the police station, given the earlier concern she had expressed for Quintrell, but she didn't. She instead looked at Daniel, of all people, and asked: "So are you still getting married today?"

"I can't imagine a reason why we wouldn't," said Daniel, despite pages and pages of reasons.

"There's an actual wedding?" asked Masako. "I thought this was some sort of theater thing."

With Charice in a wedding dress and Daniel in a tux, this could have been a ridiculous question, but given Charice's penchant for pageantry, it really wasn't.

"We are going to city hall," said Charice. "I am renewing my boat license."

"She's kidding," I said. "She's getting married."

"I see," said Masako.

"Although I am also renewing my boat license," explained Charice.

"You want to come along?" asked Daniel.

Masako looked to Tyler, who nodded.

Vanetta—who again, I'm not sure how, ended up in this party asked, "What are we going to do about him?" meaning Ignacio, on the floor.

"I can hear you," said Ignacio. "It's not like I can't hear you talking about me."

"Maybe we just leave him here?" wondered Tyler.

"Don't leave me," said Ignacio. "I want to go. It'll be good journalism."

And that's how we all showed up at city hall, for a wedding. There was a couple in front of us, two guys in their seventies, named Lloyd and Edgar, who somehow also wound up in our wedding party, and us in theirs.

The wedding itself was quick and un-notable, which is the way of the city hall wedding, and I think, for whatever reasons, that's how Charice wanted it. But the pictures were fabulous— Vanetta looking exhausted, Daniel looking romantic, Charice looking beautiful, Ignacio looking confused, and Edgar and Lloyd mooning at each other in a way that was very appealing.

I had, once upon a time, been anxious about Charice's wedding myself, and it was perhaps for the best that it came after such a climactic event because I did not have time to worry about it or make it about me, which is a thing that I am capable of doing.

I didn't have a date to the wedding, such as it was, but I found myself wanting Nathan there. I had solved a case and managed a little bit of heroism, admittedly a very little bit, and who else could I tell the story to? Okay, yes, reader, there's also *you*, but you and I can't really transition into making out on the sofa after.

After the wedding was over, Charice and Daniel went down the courthouse stairs and got into a goddamned horse and carriage that had been ripped straight out of *Cinderella*. That's Charice for you—it never looks like she's planning; but trust me, she's planning.

Charice persuaded everyone to throw rice (even though it's not good for the pigeons).

"Where are you going?" I asked as she was guided into her carriage by a straight-up, real-life footman.

"Reykjavik," said Charice.

"Iceland?" I asked. "Is it nice this time of year?"

"It's cheap this time of year," said Daniel. "And we can live like kings!"

"Thank you for all of this, Dahlia," said Charice. "This has been a big day for us."

"Yes," I said. "You got married."

"Well, yes," acknowledged Charice, "but I meant about becoming a mother."

"You're pregnant?" I gasped. No wonder she was in such a hurry about the wedding.

"No," said Charice. "Vanetta's baby. I'm going to adopt Vanetta's baby, assuming that it sticks. She didn't tell you about that?"

"That's what you were doing with Vanetta when I was—"

"—solving a crime? Yes, well, we can't all go around working out who committed accidental manslaughter, can we? Some of us are looking out for the children of tomorrow!"

This sounded awfully haughty, but then Charice winked at me.

"Are you sure?" I asked. "That's a really big life change. Really big. And probably a pretty complicated legal arrangement."

"I have never been scared of being big."

"Don't you want to be married to Daniel for a while without having kids?" I asked.

"Nope," said Charice, who at this point was being lifted into her carriage.

"When are you coming back?"

Charice looked me and smiled: "We'll be back; don't worry. But let's just say, don't wait up for us."

I threw rice at her, and she was gone.

When it was all done, I called Nathan.

"Listen," I said. "I'm sorry I've been weird lately."

"Lately?" said Nathan, although I could tell he was joking.

"Charice just got married. She's aboard a horse to Iceland even now."

"What?" said Nathan, sounding the most upset I've heard him to date. "She didn't invite me?"

"It was kind of a flash mob," I said.

Nathan considered this and said: "That sounds about right. So, what else did you do today?"

"I caught a whistle-blower, exposed an accidental death, lied to a reporter, and got yelled at by Morgan Freeman. What did you do today?"

"I gave a lecture on punctuated saltwater incursion events in the Southern Coastal Plain," said Nathan.

"That sounds amazing," I said, and I wasn't even lying.

I would love to tell you that I figured out who my mystery client was during my parade of deductive reasoning. It would make a better scene, but that's not how it happened. I did figure it out, but not until days later after I had emailed the stolen code to Emily and we were closing out the case.

I was nervous about talking to Emily. This is nearly always a sensible attitude to take, but I was worried that I had screwed the pooch. Yes, I had figured out who the whistle-blower was, and yes, I successfully managed to lift a little code, but I had also told everyone that I was a private detective.

Emily was surprisingly happy with me, though.

"It was great work, Dahlia. I'll pass along all that info to my mystery client. They'll be happy to know that the whistle-blower is out of the picture. And from what I hear, there's probably no saboteur—just lots of errors introduced by sleepy programmers."

"You don't have to keep calling them your 'mystery client,' Emily," I said. "I've figured out who I'm working for."

"Oh?" said Emily.

"Well, it's not DE, so the only other party that would make any sense would be the company that was looking to buy them up. The hidden object people—what was their name again? Dixon?"

"I can neither confirm nor deny that," said Emily.

"You can't confirm that they're the client, or you're not sure of their name?" I asked.

"Why is it," asked Emily, "that I feel I have to be so careful what I say around you?"

This was, as far as I was concerned, the highest possible praise I could receive.

"I suppose you think I'm clever?" I ventured.

"Yes," said Emily. "And loose lipped."

"Thanks for the job," I told her.

And there was a pause. I think if there's anyone who really has my back in these books, it's probably Emily Swenson, even if she is vaguely criminal.

"You know, Dahlia. You're really not bad at this. You could keep moonlighting on the side, but you ought to consider going into business for yourself."

"You know," I said, thinking of Shuler. "I've been having a conversation about that."

CODA

One Year Later

Cooper Black. That's the font we went with on the door. I hate it, honestly—if you're not familiar with that one, it's this bubbly-looking 1970s lettering that is totally at odds with the PI aesthetic. But these are concessions you make. In exchange for the weird-ass font, I got my name first.

Moss & Shuler Investigations. I thought it looked zippy, even with the dopey font, although most of the time I looked at it, it said "snoitagitsevnI reluhS & ssoM," which is not as inspiring as you might imagine.

I watched the door open now, hoping to see my first official client, but instead Charice walked in with Haile.

They were wearing matching clothes, Charice and Haile, despite looking nothing alike. Charice: white, skinny, pasty, late twenties. Haile: black, chubby, splotchy, three months old. It wasn't cloying—it's not like they were in matching sailor suits; they were just ladies in red. As the song goes.

"Oh my God," I said upon seeing Haile. "I haven't seen her

307

in weeks. And, Jesus, look at how much bigger she is in just this time. It doesn't make sense. It feels logistically impossible."

"She's smarter too," said Charice, suddenly careening into baby talk. "Why, isn't she the smartest little thing in the world? Yes she is!"

"She ought to be, considering her parents," I said. Haile cooed. "I gotta see her more, Charice. What kind of fake aunt am I going to be?"

"I'm sorry. I've been so distant lately," said Charice. "I've got a lot going on."

"Hey, you've been busy."

"Yeah. Somehow I got roped into painting Tyler and Masako's apartment," Charice said, then paused. "Oh, you meant with parenting."

I did mean parenting, but it was nice to know that Charice always had other projects going.

"Is Nathan coming to cut the ribbon?" asked Charice.

"He has to teach," I said. "We figure we'll let him clean up the first body instead."

Nathan and I, by the way, are still going solid and steady. But just steady and not anything more serious than that yet. We figure since all of our friends are getting married, there's no rush. Even Steven (remember that guy?) was getting married, and he was dating a druid.

Shuler, coming out of a larger side office—another part of my deal making, in getting my name first on the door—said:

"Hey, Haile! Hey, Charice!"

"The paint dry on this place yet?" asked Charice.

"Just barely," said Shuler. "I was thinking we should throw a guy through the door for good luck. Like, you know, a champagne bottle for a ship."

"There's a dentist office next door," observed Charice. "Throwing guys through doors probably wouldn't put the patients in the waiting room in a relaxed state."

"Yeah," I said. "But on the plus side, if the guy chips his tooth in the process, we'd be all set."

"And," said Shuler, "there's even a mortuary across the street. All of our bases are covered."

"All your base are belong to us," I said, quoting the Internet meme.

I laughed—at my own joke—but then Haile laughed at it too, and I was suddenly very happy, and oddly sad. In video games, there's such a thing as leveling up. You finish one chapter, one story, and things advance, and get harder, or better, or more interesting, before you take a turn again.

In real life, you never feel this. Not as it happens. You don't get the bling sound of the score raising, or rainbows shooting across the sky as "Ode to Joy" plays. It's a shame, really. We deserve it.

But even so, every so often, you can look around and see that it happened, even if you missed the interstitial movie. Things change. Life moves on. And here I was, in my own office, with my name on the door. I had a business partner who was smart and awesome and with whom I had not screwed things up. My best friend's baby was sitting on my desk—my desk!—laughing, maybe, at a dumb joke I had made.

I had leveled up.

And the next round was going to be awesome.

meet the author

Elizabeth Frantz

MAX WIRESTONE lives in Lawrence, Kansas, with his husband, his son, a very old dog, and more books than a reasonable person should own.

if you enjoyed
THE QUESTIONABLE BEHAVIOR OF DAHLIA MOSS

look out for

THE RULE OF LUCK
A Felicia Sevigny Novel: Book 1

by

Catherine Cerveny

Year 2950. Humanity has survived devastating climate shifts and four world wars, coming out stronger and smarter than ever. Incredible technology is available to all, and enhancements to appearance, intelligence, and physical ability are commonplace.

In this future, Felicia Sevigny has built her fame reading the futures of others.

Alexei Petriv, the most dangerous man in the tri-system, will trust only Felicia to read his cards. But the future she sees is darker than either of them could ever have imagined. A future that pits them against an all-knowing government, almost superhuman criminals, and something from Felicia's past that she could never have predicted, but that could be the key to saving—or destroying—them all.

1

I've always been a big fan of eyeliner. The darker, the better. Growing up, I'd heard the expression "Pretty is as pretty does" almost every day of my life—but I believe that sometimes pretty needs help. Since I've decided against tattooing my way to beauty or using gene modification, I do things the old-fashioned way. And as one of the only Tarot card readers in Nairobi, I've cultivated a certain look that is as much personal choice as mysterious mask. So the fact that I stood in the tiny bathroom of my card reading shop and scrubbed my face clean, opting for tasteful over flashy, made me feel like I'd sold out.

"All for the greater good," I mumbled, examining my nearly naked face. "I can look straitlaced and respectable for an hour. Two, tops."

A quick time check showed it was nearly seven in the morning. It made me glad I'd decided to close up shop early at two and catch some sleep on the reception room couch. At least I didn't look like complete garbage, even if my sleep was more tossing and turning than actual shut-eye.

I hightailed it to the front door. I needed to be on the other side of the city by nine sharp. To do that in an hour using the unreliable Y-Line would take all the prayers and karmic brownie points I had to spare. Maybe if I lit some incense sticks and offered a prayer for guidance...but no, no time for that.

Then I had to stop, my hand frozen in mid-reach on the way to the doorknob. Standing in the entranceway of my shop was the most beautiful man I'd ever seen. I know it's shallow to focus on looks since they are so easily bought and modified, and yet...

"I'd like a Tarot card reading, please," he said, his voice so deep, I was certain the windows rattled.

"I'm sorry, but we're closed. I can take your information and schedule an appointment for later this week." I infused my voice with as much formality as I could muster. Anything to prevent stammering like a drooling idiot in front of such a good-looking man. Even though "good-looking" barely covered it.

"This won't take long and I'm prepared to pay generously," he said, as if he'd already dropped gold notes into my account. Wonderful—arrogant enough to assume money buys everything and he thinks his time is more valuable than mine. Well, that was exactly the shot of ice water I needed to break the spell.

"I appreciate your offer, but I'm afraid you'll have to book an appointment." *Like everybody else.*

"Unfortunately, I'm leaving Nairobi today. This is my last stop before my flight. I've heard of your reputation as a card reader. My research says you're quite accurate."

And just like that, he pierced the proverbial chink in my armor. When people said they'd heard of me, I felt honor-bound to accept. If word got back to the source that I was ungracious or unobliging, I could lose business. Damn it, why had I let my receptionist, Natty, leave early? She could have dealt with this situation. Oh right, it was so I could sleep and get ready in private with no one the wiser. But why had I forgotten to lock up? I did not have time for this.

I studied him. He wore reflective sunshades that prevented me from getting the full picture, but there were still plenty of other clues to give me a sense of what I was dealing with. A well-cut carbon-gray suit and scuff-free shoes screamed gold notes and good taste. He was tall, very tall. His fashionably scruffy thick black hair brushed his suit collar and nearly met his very nicely broad shoulders. He was clean-shaven, with chiseled cheekbones and a slight tan that had to be Tru-Tan since no one exposed themselves to the sun anymore. Good tans cost a fortune. But his accent was the real giveaway. His deep voice carried a lilt that made it clear he was from the Russian Federation of Islands. In a word—money. Lots and lots of money.

But I wouldn't reschedule my appointment for all the money, contacts, or goodwill in the tri-system. I gestured toward the door, intending to walk him out. "I'm sorry, but perhaps next time you're in town."

He looked as if he hadn't the slightest intention of leaving. "If you're concerned about the time, my people can ensure you arrive at the fertility clinic before nine this morning."

I froze. "Excuse me, but that information is classified."

"And so it will remain. It would be a shame for One Gov to learn the true nature of your appointment, after all."

My eyes narrowed. "It's just a routine fertility consultation."

"Of course," he agreed. "I ask only for a brief reading. Surely you can spare a moment?"

I should have been both angry and terrified that he knew my plans. Hell, I hadn't even told my boyfriend, Roy! His words stopped just short of blackmail. And yet...I found myself intrigued, damn it. What would this Tarot reading show me? I had that odd feeling again—the one that hit deep in my gut and paid no attention to what I had lined up for the rest of the day, let alone my life. It demanded I follow through on whatever happened next. Over the years I'd learned never, and I mean *never*, to ignore that feeling no matter how pesky it might be.

He removed his sunshades and I was snared by blue eyes so intense I wondered if he had to hide them or risk turning people to stone—or women to mush. I peered closer, considering the whole package. The looks. The play of his muscles beneath his clothes when he moved. The symmetry. I wasn't sure why I hadn't caught it earlier: His MH Factor—Modified Human— was turned up high enough to scorch.

Out of my mouth came: "I can fit you in now with a short reading."

"Wonderful." He offered a smile that had no doubt removed numerous panties. Nice to know one of us was having a good time.

"I don't see many advanced-stage Modified Humans in my shop. Are you fifth generation?" My question was beyond rude. Asking about genetic modifications was worse than asking how much money someone made. But if he knew my business, I didn't see why I couldn't know his. "I heard it's less invasive to upgrade technological modifications later in life rather than opting for full pre-birth gene manipulation. The t-mods are supposed to be less expensive too."

"Perhaps it depends on how many gold notes exchange hands and how natural you want it to look," he said, noncommittally.

So there was some genetic manipulation involved. I knew it! But how much? Some people went overboard with their upgrades and the results weren't always as advertised.

315

I waited for more follow-up from him. Instead, the silence stretched. Okay, then. "Is there a particular aspect of your life you want to know about? Or an issue that's troubling you?"

"I'm concerned about a meeting and its success. Should I continue on my current path, or cut my losses and run? You no doubt receive many similar requests."

He was right; I'd built my business on less. I had a steady clientele including a few minor celebrities, but nothing had really launched my career. Not that I wanted to be a card reader to the stars, but I definitely wanted to ensure I never had to worry about money.

"Follow me," I said, and with those words went my last lick of common sense.

I removed the c-tex bracelet I'd put on—so that no one could accuse me of skimming the Cerebral Neural Net and faking a reading—then led him through the shop. Gentle lighting flicked on as we entered the back room. Soft music began, the automatic soundtrack set to a Mars chill funk vibe. The room was decorated with thick Venusian carpets, decadent pillows on velvet chaise lounges, and paintings of exotic Old Earth terrain and new-world Martian landscapes. Rich colors that begged to be touched—a tactile experience for the senses. Customers had certain expectations as to how a Tarot card shop on Night Alley, the most exclusive and decadent street in Nairobi, should appear. If my Russian stranger had been there the night before when business was in full swing, he would have seen my designer silk print dress and makeup just this side of too much, instead of the prim beige knee-length skirt and sky-blue blouse I now wore. I looked overdressed, conservative, and slightly out of style.

Oddly, the idea that he'd caught me this way made me feel vulnerable, like I'd allowed him to see the real me instead of the persona I wore when I cast a reading. That woman didn't care what her clients thought because she knew they were all in awe of her. In those silk dresses she was untouchable. She held their future in her hands. This stripped-down me was too exposed, too likely to get caught up in things that didn't concern her. Well, too bad. I wasn't letting a hot guy and an off-the-chart gut feeling get the best of me. What I wore now was just another disguise. After all, how could I convince the Shared Hope program's fertility Arbiter I should be allowed to have a baby if I didn't look like a respectable member of society?

"Have a seat." I directed him to one of the chaise lounges with an ornate gold-leaf table beside it. A chandelier that appeared to drip with gemstones, but were really artfully colored glass, hung overhead.

"Interesting décor," he said.

"Would you be as impressed with a rickety table and some collapsible benches?" I asked as I took the chaise across from him.

He laughed. "I suppose not. I understand the need for showmanship. At times, it can be as important as the act itself."

"Hence the décor." I gestured around us.

I smiled, so did he, and suddenly the table between us seemed ridiculously small. The feeling in my gut grew, paired now with a growing sense that this man, whoever the hell he was, held some significance for me. It hung in the air.

I took a breath to center myself and refocused on the box in the middle of the table. Whatever designs were once painted on its black lacquered wood surface had long since faded. What it contained was easily the most valuable thing I owned.

I opened the box and removed the Tarot cards. They'd been in my family for generations, dating back to a time before the Earth's axis shifted thanks to a series of massive global quakes, polar melts, and then the two wars of succession that followed. Family lore claimed they came from the Old World—an all but forgotten place that existed only in history books and on the bottom of the ocean floor.

"Since we're pressed for time, I'll do a five-card spread using only the Major Arcana," I explained. "They are the heart of the Tarot. Each card represents a different state of being. I'm forgoing a Significator since you're asking about yourself, but I want you to select five cards from the deck that represent what may or may not happen, what will prevent it from happening, why you're in this situation, what you can do to either encourage or change it, and finally, depending on the steps you take, what will happen."

As I shuffled, I fell into my usual banter where I reassured the client they were in capable hands. Its familiarity made me feel more secure. I could do this. No need to panic because I was looking into the bluest eyes I'd ever seen. Once done shuffling, I fanned out the cards, let him pick his five, then arranged and flipped them over.

I'd been doing this too long to gasp, but that was what I wanted to do. I had a bizarre affinity with this set of cards—more so than anyone in the family according to my dearly departed Granny G. In fact, the cards had bypassed two disgruntled and pissed off generations of Romani to come directly to me, per her wishes. So when I examined the cards, I never lost my smile, even though I'd cast this identical reading for myself only an hour earlier.

I've always believed that things happen for a reason, and when the universe taps you on the shoulder, you pay attention. This was the equivalent of the universe punching me in the face.

He leaned forward. "What does it mean?"

"This is the Emperor, reversed." I pointed to the first card. "You have goals, but waste energy on pointless things that get in the way. You have the will and strength to fight, but aren't using those gifts properly. Next, the Moon. You want to shape events, not be shaped by them. You need to learn to read what's happening around you and act accordingly. However, you also need caution. You have hidden enemies who've yet to reveal themselves. The third card is the Falling Tower. It's the destruction of everything you've built because of your own misunderstanding and lack of judgment. Your bad choices may have put you in a situation where you could lose everything."

The man laughed. It didn't sound forced nor did he look worried, but at the same time, I could tell something was going on in his head. "So far it appears I shouldn't have gotten out of bed this morning."

"It's not all bad," I said consolingly. "Fourth is the Lovers. It could mean attraction or love, but given the other cards, it appears to be a partnership and mutual commitment. This connection will help you overcome your difficulties and further your control of the events. Lastly, the Judgment. It represents the end of an old life, and the beginning of a new one. It's a radical change, but one you will need if you are to overcome your situation."

When I looked up, he was gazing at me with such an intent expression that I worried I'd offended him. Well, I didn't have time to couch the reading in the prettiest of terms; he got what he got. He had to smarten up or he'd lose everything. Sadly, the same applied to me as well. Quickly, I swept the cards back into their box.

"I hope you found it useful."

"Very. I appreciate you making the time to see me."

He was still looking at me. I mean, *really* looking. Looking at me the way a man did when he wondered how a woman

319

looked naked or was considering ways to get her naked. I wondered if he was thinking about the Lovers. Or maybe I was the one thinking that? My throat went dry. I hadn't been studied like that in a long time and it felt better than it should. Even if I didn't have an active MH Factor, I was no slouch. My almost-black hair reached mid-back, my olive skin held tones of Old World ancestry, and I could make my green eyes pop by dressing in shades of blue-green. My figure and height also fit One Gov's genetic specification guidelines, hence putting me in the Goldilocks zone: just right.

No, enough of this. What was I thinking? I had a boyfriend. I had plans for the future. In an hour, my whole world could change. And yet...

I stood. He stood with me. Even in my metal-clad high-heeled boots, my eyes were barely level with his shoulder. I felt feminine in ways I hadn't in years. The air felt charged with potential. My gut jerked again, reminding me to act before the moment disappeared. What the hell did it want me to do? Jump him? Rip his clothes off?

He held out his hand. I shook it. It swallowed mine. "Thank you, Felicia. I know how I need to conduct my future affairs now."

I froze when he said my name. Not that him knowing it was a surprise; it was how he'd said it. If I tried to describe it I'd sound crazy. He said it like he knew me. Or, had made it his business to know me. Or, planned on knowing me so well, I would someday learn what his body pressed against mine would actually feel like.

I flushed and released his hand as if it burned. "Feel free to leave your payment on the way out."

He laughed and a bolt of heat shot through me. "As I said earlier, my people can ensure you make your appointment at the clinic if you're concerned about time."

Again, I should have been terrified. If he contacted One Gov, getting arrested would be the least of my problems. Yet I had the oddest feeling that whatever this stranger knew, he'd keep it to himself. Still, I had to make some sort of a token protest, didn't I? "My private schedule is just that—private. I understand your investigating my flat-file avatar on the CN-net. Many clients do and access is always open. However, any personal information I've logged is off-limits. I would appreciate it if you left my shop now."

He seemed amused instead of angry. "My apologies. I'm glad to have made your acquaintance. Hopefully, we will have other dealings in the future."

Gut feeling be damned, I sincerely hoped not. However, I must not have managed to school my expression well enough since he added, "Despite what you may believe, the future isn't decided yet. There are always gray areas left to explore."

He turned on his heel to leave. Bemused, I followed. Outside, I found two personal bodyguards—all muscle and matching suits. They fell into step behind him as he continued down the sidewalk to the street. I saw four more musclemen at either end of the block, and a helicon hovering overhead in the dull gray sky. Street-side were two flight-limos ready for takeoff, one with its windows down. I could see the pilot in front while in back sat a gorgeous redhead. My mouth fell open. I know it did—just open and flapping in the breeze.

He paused before he climbed inside the first flight-limo. "Ms. Sevigny, you'll find my payment inside, as well as my halo should you need to get in touch. Your reputation is well deserved. Feel free to use me as a reference."

With that, he got into the flight-limo. I saw the redhead attempt to climb onto his lap and watched him push her away before the windows rolled up. The security detail ducked into the second flight-limo as the helicon zipped away. In a few seconds, the street was empty.

I ran back inside. On the reception desk was a blue chip wafer used to transfer funds between locked CN-net accounts. It was old tech, the kind used by people who didn't have direct CN-net t-mods. People like me. I tapped its face and the readout displayed an obscene amount of money. I charged seventy gold notes a reading. The readout said ten thousand—very near to the amount that had been in the savings account I'd recently decimated. I almost fainted. Beside the chip was the promised halo. Like the blue chip, it was also old tech. I touched it and watched the name unfurl in bold script.

So I'd been right about the accent. I knew the name. Who didn't? I'd just never seen his face. He rarely surfaced in public, and when he did, he came and went like smoke.

Alexei Petriv. Crown Prince of the Tsarist Consortium—though "crime lord" and "thug" would also be accurate descriptors. Robin Hood too, in some circles. Thorn in the side of One Gov. Pirate of the tri-system. In my office. Wanting a reading. The need to faint grew stronger. So did the feeling in my gut.

I had a terrible suspicion I was about to be made an offer I could not refuse.

if you enjoyed
THE QUESTIONABLE BEHAVIOR
OF DAHLIA MOSS

look out for

STRANGE PRACTICE

A Doctor Greta
Helsing Novel: Book 1

by

Vivian Shaw

Meet Greta Helsing, doctor to the undead.

Dr. Greta Helsing has inherited the family's highly specialized, and highly peculiar, medical practice. She treats the undead for a host of ills—vocal strain in banshees, arthritis in barrow-wights, and entropy in mummies.

It's a quiet, supernatural-adjacent life, until a sect of murderous monks emerges, killing human and undead Londoners alike. As terror takes hold of the city, Greta must use her unusual skills to stop the cult if she hopes to save her practice, and her life.

CHAPTER 1

The sky was fading to ultramarine in the east over the Victoria Embankment when a battered Mini pulled to the curb, not far from Blackfriars Bridge. Here and there in the maples lining the riverside walk, the morning's first sparrows had begun to sing.

A woman got out of the car and shut the door, swore, put down her bags, and shut the door again with more applied force; some fellow motorist had bashed into the panel at some time in the past and bent it sufficiently to make this a production every damn time. The Mini really needed to be replaced, but even with her inherited Harley Street consulting rooms Greta Helsing was not exactly drowning in cash.

She glowered at the car and then at the world in general, glancing around to make sure no one was watching her from the shadows. Satisfied, she picked up her black working bag and the shapeless oversize monster that was her current handbag and went to ring the doorbell. It was time to replace the handbag, too. The leather on this one was holding up but the lining was beginning to go, and Greta had limited patience regarding the retrieval of items from the mysterious dimension behind the lining itself.

The house to which she had been summoned was one of a

row of magnificent old buildings separating Temple Gardens from the Embankment, mostly taken over by lawyers and publishing firms these days. It was a testament to this particular homeowner's rather special powers of persuasion that nobody had succeeded in buying the house out from under him and turning it into offices for overpriced attorneys, she thought, and then had to smile at the idea of anybody dislodging Edmund Ruthven from the lair he'd inhabited these two hundred years or more. He was as much a fixture of London as Lord Nelson on his pillar, albeit less encrusted with birdlime.

"Greta," said the fixture, opening the door. "Thanks for coming out on a Sunday. I know it's late."

She was just about as tall as he was, five foot five and a bit, which made it easy to look right into his eyes and be struck every single time by the fact that they were very large, so pale a grey they looked silver-white except for the dark ring at the edge of the iris, and fringed with heavy soot-black lashes of the sort you saw in advertisements for mascara. He looked tired, she thought. Tired, and older than the fortyish he usually appeared. The extreme pallor was normal, vivid against the pure slicked-back black of his hair, but the worried line between his eyebrows was not.

"It's not Sunday night, it's Monday morning," she said. "No worries, Ruthven. Tell me everything; I know you didn't go into lots of detail on the phone."

"Of course." He offered to take her coat. "I'll make you some coffee."

The entryway of the Embankment house was floored in black-and-white-checkered marble, and a large bronze ibis stood on a little side table where the mail and car keys and shopping lists were to be found. The mirror behind this reflected Greta dimly and greenly, like a woman underwater; she peered into it, making a face at herself, and tucked back her hair. It was pale Scandinavian blonde and cut like Liszt's in an off-the-shoulder bob, fine enough to slither free of whatever she used to pull it back; today it was in the process of escaping from a thoroughly childish headband. She kept meaning to have it all chopped off and be done with it but never seemed to find the time.

Greta Helsing was thirty-four, unmarried, and had taken over her late father's specialized medical practice after a brief stint as an internist at King's College Hospital. For the past five years she had run a bare-bones clinic out of Wilfert Helsing's old rooms in Harley Street, treating a patient base that to the majority of the population did not, technically, when you got right down to it, exist. It was a family thing.

There had never been much doubt which subspecialty of medicine she would pursue, once she began her training: treating the differently alive was not only more interesting than catering to the ordinary human population, it was in many ways a great deal more rewarding. She took a lot of satisfaction in being able to provide help to particularly underserved clients.

Greta's patients could largely be classified under the heading of *monstrous*—in its descriptive, rather than pejorative, sense: vampires, were-creatures, mummies, banshees, ghouls, bogeymen, the occasional arthritic barrow-wight. She herself was solidly and entirely human, with no noticeable eldritch qualities or powers whatsoever, not even a flicker of metaphysical sensitivity. Some of her patients found it difficult to trust a human physician at first, but Greta had built up an extremely good reputation over the five years she had been practicing supernatural medicine, largely by word of mouth: *Go to Helsing, she's reliable.*

And *discreet*. That was the first and fundamental tenet, after all. Keeping her patients safe meant keeping them secret, and Greta was good with secrets. She made sure the magical wards around her doorway in Harley Street were kept up properly, protecting anyone who approached from prying eyes.

Ruthven appeared in the kitchen doorway, outlined by light spilling warm over the black-and-white marble. "Greta?" he said, and she straightened up, realizing she'd been staring into the mirror without really seeing it for several minutes now. It really *was* late. Fatigue lapped heavily at the pilings of her mind.

"Sorry," she said, coming to join him, and a little of that heaviness lifted as they passed through into the familiar warmth and brightness of the kitchen. It was all blue tile and blond wood, the cheerful rose-gold of polished copper pots and pans balancing the sleek chill of stainless steel, and right now it was also full of the scent of really *good* coffee. Ruthven's espresso machine was a La Cimbali, and it was serious business.

He handed her a large pottery mug. She recognized it as one of the set he generally used for blood, and had to smile a little, looking down at the contents—and then abruptly had to clamp down on a wave of thoroughly inconvenient emotion. There was no reason that Ruthven doing goddamn *latte art* for her at half-past four in the morning should make her want to cry.

He was *good* at it, too, which was a little infuriating; then again she supposed that with as much free time on her hands as he had on his, and as much disposable income, she might find herself learning and polishing new skills simply to stave off the encroaching spectre of boredom. Ruthven didn't go in for your standard-variety vampire angst, which was refreshing, but Greta knew very well he had bouts of something not unlike depression—especially in the winter—and he needed things to *do*.

She, however, *had* things to do, Greta reminded herself, taking a sip of the latte and closing her eyes for a moment. This was coffee that actually tasted as good as, if not better than, it smelled. *Focus,* she thought. This was not a social call. The lack of urgency in Ruthven's manner led her to believe that the situation was not immediately dire, but she was nonetheless here to do her job.

Greta licked coffee foam from her upper lip. "So," she said. "Tell me what happened."

"I was—" Ruthven sighed, leaning against the counter with his arms folded. "To be honest I was sitting around twiddling my thumbs and writing nasty letters to the *Times* about how much I loathe these execrable skyscrapers somebody keeps allowing vandals to build all over the city. I'd got to a particularly cutting phrase about the one that sets people's cars on fire, when somebody knocked on the door."

The passive-aggressive-letter stage tended to indicate that his levels of ennui were reaching critical intensity. Greta just nodded, watching him.

"I don't know if you've ever read an ancient penny-dreadful called *Varney the Vampyre, or The Feast of Blood,*" he went on.

"Ages ago," she said. She'd read practically all the horror classics, well-known and otherwise, for research purposes rather than to enjoy their literary merit. Most of them were to some extent entertainingly wrong about the individuals they claimed to depict. "It was quite a lot funnier than your unofficial biography, but I'm not sure it was *meant* to be."

Ruthven made a face. John Polidori's *The Vampyre* was, he insisted, mostly libel—the very mention of the book was sufficient to bring on indignant protestations that he and the Lord Ruthven featured in the narrative shared little more than a name. "At least the authors got the spelling right, unlike bloody Polidori," he said. "I think probably *Feast of Blood* is about as historically accurate as *The Vampyre,* which is to say *not very,* but it does have the taxonomy right. Varney, unlike me, *is* a vampyre with a *y*."

"A lunar sensitive? I haven't actually met one before," she said, clinical interest surfacing through the fatigue. The vampires she knew were all classic draculines, like Ruthven himself and the handful of others in London. Lunar sensitives were rarer than the draculine vampires for a couple of reasons, chief among which was the fact that they were violently—and inconveniently—allergic to the blood of anyone but virgins. They did have the handy characteristic of being resurrected by moonlight every time they got themselves killed, which presumably came as some small comfort in the process of succumbing to violent throes of gastric distress brought on by dietary indiscretion.

"Well," Ruthven said, "now's your chance. He showed up on my doorstep, completely unannounced, looking like thirty kinds of warmed-over hell, and collapsed in the hallway. He is at the moment sleeping on the drawing room sofa, and I want you to look at him for me. I don't *think* there's any real danger, but he's been hurt—some maniacs apparently attacked him with a knife—and I'd feel better if you had a look."

Ruthven had lit a fire, despite the relative mildness of the evening, and the creature lying on the sofa was covered with two blankets. Greta glanced from him to Ruthven, who shrugged a little, that line of worry between his eyebrows very visible.

According to him, Sir Francis Varney, title and all, had come out of his faint quite quickly and perked up after some first aid and the administration of a nice hot mug of suitable and brandy-laced blood. Ruthven kept a selection of the stuff in his expensive fridge and freezer, stocked by Greta via fairly illegal supply chain management—she knew someone who knew someone who worked in a blood bank and was not above rescuing rejected units from the biohazard incinerator.

Sir Francis had drunk the whole of the mug's contents with every evidence of satisfaction and promptly gone to sleep as soon as Ruthven let him, whereupon Ruthven had called Greta and requested a house call. "I don't really like the look of him," he said now, standing in the doorway with uncharacteristic awkwardness. "He was bleeding a little—the wound's in his left shoulder. I cleaned it up and put a dressing on, but it was still sort of oozing. Which isn't like us."

"No," Greta agreed, "it's not. It's possible that lunar sensitives and draculines respond differently to tissue trauma, but even so, I would have expected him to have mostly finished healing already. You were right to call me."

"Do you need anything?" he asked, still standing in the doorway as Greta pulled over a chair and sat down beside the sofa.

"Possibly more coffee. Go on, Ruthven. I've got this; go and finish your unkind letter to the editor."

When he had gone she tucked back her hair and leaned over to examine her patient. He took up the entire length of the sofa, head pillowed on one armrest and one narrow foot resting on the other, half-exposed where the blankets had fallen away. She did a bit of rough calculation and guessed he must be at least six inches taller than Ruthven, possibly more.

His hair was tangled, streaky-grey, worn dramatically long— that was aging-rock-frontman hair if Greta had ever seen it, but nothing *else* about him seemed to fit with the Jagger aesthetic. An old-fashioned face, almost Puritan: long, narrow nose, deeply hooded eyes under intense eyebrows, thin mouth bracketed with habitual lines of disapproval.

Or pain, she thought. *That could be pain.*

The shifting of a log in the fireplace behind Greta made her jump a little, and she regathered the wandering edges of her concentration. With a nasty little flicker of surprise she noticed that there was a faint sheen of sweat on Varney's visible skin. That *really* wasn't right.

"Sir Francis?" she said, gently, and leaned over to touch his shoulder through the blankets—and a moment later had retreated halfway across the room, heart racing: Varney had gone from uneasy sleep to *sitting up and snarling viciously* in less than a second.

It was not unheard-of for Greta's patients to threaten her, especially when they were in considerable pain, and on the whole she probably should have thought this out a little better. She'd only got a glimpse before her own instincts had kicked in and got her the hell out of range of those teeth, but it would be a while before she could forget that pattern of dentition, or those mad tin-colored eyes.

He covered his face with his hands, shoulders slumping, and instead of menace was now giving off an air of intense embarrassment.

Greta came back over to the sofa. "I'm sorry," she said, tentatively, "I didn't mean to startle you—"

"I most devoutly apologize," he said, without taking his hands away. "I do *try* not to do that, but I am not quite at my best just now—forgive me, I don't believe we have been introduced."

He was looking at her from behind his fingers, and the eyes really *were* metallic. Even partly hidden she could see the room's reflection in his irises. She wondered if that was a peculiarity of his species, or an individual phenomenon.

"It's all right," she said, and sat down on the edge of the sofa, judging that he wasn't actually about to tear her throat out just at the moment. "My name's Greta. I'm a doctor; Ruthven called me to come and take a look at you."

When Varney finally took his hands away from his face, pushing the damp silvering hair back, his color was frankly terrible. He *was* sweating. That was not something she'd ever seen in sanguivores under any circumstance.

"A doctor?" he asked, blinking at her. "Are you sure?"

She was spared having to answer that. A moment later he squeezed his eyes shut, very faint color coming and going high on each cheek. "I really am sorry," he said. "What a remarkably stupid question. It's just—I tend to think of doctors as looking rather different than you."

"I left my pinstripe trousers and pocket-watch at home," she said drily. "But I've got my black bag, if that helps. Ruthven said you'd been hurt—attacked by somebody with a knife. May I take a look?"

He glanced up at her and then away again, and nodded once, leaning back against the sofa cushions, and Greta reached into her bag for the exam gloves.

The wound was in his left shoulder, as Ruthven had said, about two and a half inches south of the collarbone. It wasn't large—she had seen much nastier injuries from street fights, although in rather different species—but it was undoubtedly the *strangest* wound she'd ever come across.

"What made this?" she asked, looking closer, her gloved fingers careful on his skin. Varney hissed and turned his face away, and she could feel a thrumming tension under her touch. "I've never seen anything like it. The wound is...*cross*-shaped."

It was. Instead of just the narrow entry mark of a knife, or the bruised puncture of something clumsier, Varney's wound appeared to have been made by something flanged. Not just two but four sharp edges, leaving a hole shaped like an X—or a cross.

"It was a spike," he said, between his teeth. "I didn't get a very good look at it. They had—broken into my flat, with garlic. Garlic was everywhere. Smeared on the walls, scattered all over the floor. I was—taken by surprise, and the fumes—I could hardly see or breathe."

"I'm not surprised," said Greta, sitting up. "It's extremely nasty stuff. Are you having any chest pain or trouble breathing now?"

A lot of the organic compounds in *Allium sativum* triggered a severe allergic response in vampires, varying in intensity based on amount and type of exposure. This wasn't garlic shock, or not *just* garlic shock, though. He was definitely running a fever, and the hole in his shoulder should have healed to a shiny pink memory within an hour or so after it happened. Right now it was purple-black and... oozing.

"No," Varney said, "just—the wound is, ah, really rather painful." He sounded apologetic. "As I said, I didn't get a close look at the spike, but it was short and pointed like a rondel dagger, with a round pommel. There were three people there, I don't know if they all had knives, but... well, as it turned out, all they needed was one."

This was so very much not her division. "Did—do you have any idea why they attacked you?" Or why they'd broken into his flat and poisoned it with garlic. That was a pretty specialized tactic, after all. Greta shivered in sudden unease.

"They were chanting, or... reciting something," he said, his odd eyes drifting shut. "I couldn't make out much of it, just that it sounded sort of ecclesiastical."

He had a remarkably beautiful voice, she noticed. The rest of him wasn't tremendously prepossessing, particularly those eyes, but his voice was *lovely*: sweet and warm and clear. It contrasted oddly with the actual content of what he was saying. "Something about...*unclean*," he continued, "*unclean* and wicked, *wickedness*, foulness, and...*demons*. Creatures of darkness."

He still had his eyes half-closed, and Greta frowned and bent over him again. "Sir Francis?"

"Hurts," he murmured, sounding very far away. "They were dressed...strangely."

She rested two fingers against the pulse in his throat: much too fast, and he couldn't have spiked *that* much in the minutes she had been with him, but he felt noticeably warmer to her touch. She reached into the bag for her thermometer and the BP cuff. "Strangely how?"

"Like...monks," he said, and blinked up at her, hazy and confused. "In...brown robes. With crosses round their necks. Like *monks*."

His eyes rolled back slightly, slipping closed, and he gave a little terrible sigh; when Greta took him by the shoulders and gave him a shake he did not rouse at all, head rolling limp against the cushions. *What the hell,* she thought, *what the actual hell is going on here, there's no way a wound like this should be affecting him so badly, this is—it looks like systemic inflammatory response but the garlic should have worn off by now, there's nothing to* cause *it, unless—*

Unless there had been something on the blade. Something *left behind.*

That flicker of visceral unease was much stronger now. She leaned closer, gently drawing apart the edges of the wound—the tissue was swollen, red, warmer than the surrounding skin—and was surprised to notice a faint but present smell. Not the characteristic smell of infection, but something sharper, almost metallic, with a sulfurous edge on it like silver tarnish. It was strangely familiar, but she couldn't seem to place it.

Greta was rather glad he was unconscious just at the moment, because what she was about to do would be quite remarkably painful. She stretched the wound open a little wider, wishing she had her penlight to get a better view, and he shifted a little, his breath catching; as he moved she caught a glimpse of something reflective half-obscured by dark blood. There *was* something still in there. Something that needed to come out right now.

"Ruthven," she called, sitting up. "Ruthven, I need you."

He emerged from the kitchen, looking anxious. "What is it?

"Get the green leather instrument case out of my bag," she said, "and put a pan of water on to boil. There's a foreign body in here I need to extract."

Without a word Ruthven took the instrument case and disappeared again. Greta turned her attention back to her patient, noticing for the first time that the pale skin of his chest was crisscrossed by old scarring—*very* old, she thought, looking at the silvery laddered marks of long-healed injuries. She had seen Ruthven without his shirt on, and he had a pretty good collection of scars from four centuries' worth of misadventure, but Varney put him to shame. *A lot of duels,* she thought. *A lot of...* lost *duels.*

Greta wondered how much of *Feast of Blood* was actually based on historical events. He had died at least once in the part of it that she remembered, and had spent a lot of time running away from various pitchfork-wielding mobs. None of *them* had been dressed up in monastic drag, as far as she knew, but they had certainly demonstrated the same intent as whoever had hurt Varney tonight.

A cold flicker of something close to fear slipped down her spine, and she turned abruptly to look over her shoulder at the empty room, pushing away a sudden and irrational sensation of being watched.

Don't be ridiculous, she told herself, *and do your damn job.* She was a little grateful for the business of wrapping the BP cuff around his arm, and less pleased by what it told her. Not critical, but certainly a long way from what she considered normal for sanguivores. She didn't know what was going on in there, but she didn't like it one bit.

When Ruthven returned carrying a tea tray, she felt irrationally relieved to see him—and then had to raise an eyebrow at the contents of the tray. Her probes and forceps and retractors lay on a metal dish Greta recognized after a moment as the one that normally went under the toast rack, dish and instruments steaming gently from the boiling water—and beside them was an empty basin with a clean tea towel draped over it. Everything was very, very neat, as if he had done it many times before. As if he'd had practice.

"Since when are *you* a scrub nurse?" she asked, nodding for him to set the tray down. "I mean—thank you, this is exactly what I need, I appreciate it, and if you could hold the light for me I'd appreciate that even more."

"*De rien,*" said Ruthven, and went to fetch her penlight.

A few minutes later, Greta held her breath as she carefully, carefully withdrew her forceps from Varney's shoulder. Held between the steel tips was a piece of something hard and angular, about the size of a pea. That metallic, sharp smell was much stronger now, much more noticeable.

She turned to the tray on the table beside her, dropped the thing into the china basin with a little *rat-tat* sound, and straightened up. The wound was bleeding again; she pressed a gauze pad over it. The blood looked *brighter* now, somehow, which made no sense at all.

Ruthven clicked off the penlight, swallowing hard, and

Greta looked up at him. "What *is* that thing?" he asked, nodding to the basin.

"I've no idea," she told him. "I'll have a look at it after I'm happier with him. He's pushing eighty-five degrees and his pulse rate is approaching low human baseline—"

Greta cut herself off and felt the vein in Varney's throat again. "That's strange," she said. "That's *very* strange. It's already coming down."

The beat was noticeably slower. She had another look at his blood pressure; this time the reading was much more reasonable. "I'll be damned. In a human I'd be seriously alarmed at that rapid a transient, but all bets are off with regard to hemodynamic stability in sanguivores. It's as if that thing, whatever it is, was directly responsible for the acute inflammatory reaction."

"And now that it's gone, he's starting to recover?"

"Something like that. *Don't* touch it," Greta said sharply, as Ruthven reached for the basin. "Don't even go near it. I have no idea what it would do to you, and I don't want to have two patients on my hands."

Ruthven backed away a few steps. "You're quite right," he said. "Greta, something about this smells peculiar."

"In more than one sense," she said, checking the gauze. The bleeding had almost stopped. "Did he tell you how it happened?"

"Not really. Just that he'd been jumped by several people armed with a strange kind of knife."

"Mm. A very strange kind of knife. I've never seen anything like this wound. He didn't mention that these people were dressed up like monks, or that they were reciting something about unclean creatures of darkness?"

"No," said Ruthven, flopping into a chair. "He neglected to share that tidbit with me. Monks?"

337

"So he said," Greta told him. "Robes and hoods, big crosses round their necks, the whole bit. Monks. And some kind of stabby weapon. Remind you of anything?"

"The Ripper," said Ruthven, slowly. "You think this has something to do with the murders?"

"I think it's one hell of a coincidence if it *doesn't*," Greta said. That feeling of unease hadn't gone away with Varney's physical improvement. It really was impossible to ignore. She'd been too busy with the immediate work at hand to consider the similarities before, but now she couldn't help thinking about it.

There had been a series of unsolved murders in London over the past month and a half. Eight people dead, all apparently the work of the same individual, all stabbed to death, all *found with a cheap plastic rosary stuffed into their mouths.* Six of the victims had been prostitutes. The killer had, inevitably, been nicknamed the Rosary Ripper.

The MO didn't exactly match how Varney had described his attack—multiple assailants, a strange-shaped knife—but it was way the hell too close for Greta's taste. "Unless whoever got Varney was a copycat," she said. "Or maybe there isn't just one Ripper. Maybe it's a group of people running around stabbing unsuspecting citizens."

"There was nothing on the news about the murders that mentioned weird-shaped wounds," Ruthven said. "Although I suppose the police might be keeping that to themselves."

The police had not apparently been able to do much of *anything* about the murders, and as one victim followed another with no end in sight the general confidence in Scotland Yard—never tremendously high—was plummeting. The entire city was both angry and frightened. Conspiracy theories abounded on the Internet, some less believable than others. This, however, was the first time Greta had heard anything about the

Ripper branching out into *supernatural* victims. The garlic on the walls of Varney's flat bothered her a great deal.

Varney shifted a little, with a faint moan, and Greta returned her attention to her patient. There was visible improvement; his vitals were stabilizing, much more satisfactory than they had been before the extraction.

"He's beginning to come around," she said. "We should get him into a proper bed, but I think he's over the worst of this."

Ruthven didn't reply at once, and she looked over to see him tapping his fingers on the arm of his chair with a thoughtful expression. "What?" she asked.

"Nothing. Well, *maybe* nothing. I think I'll call Cranswell at the Museum, see if he can look a few things up for me. I will, however, wait until the morning is a little further advanced, because I am a kind man."

"What time *is* it?" Greta asked, stripping off her gloves.

"Getting on for six, I'm afraid."

"Jesus. I need to call in—there's no way I'm going to be able to do clinic hours today. Hopefully Anna or Nadezhda can take an extra shift if I do a bit of groveling."

"I have faith in your ability to grovel convincingly," Ruthven said. "Shall I go and make some more coffee?"

"Yes," she said. Both of them knew this wasn't over. "Yes, do precisely that thing, and you will earn my everlasting fealty."

"I earned your everlasting fealty last time I drove you to the airport," Ruthven said. "Or was it when I made you tiramisu a few weeks ago? I can't keep track."

He smiled, despite the line of worry still between his eyebrows, and Greta found herself smiling wearily in return.